Salvation

Harriet Steel

Acknowledgments

I am grateful to Jonathan Wadman for his excellent editing and to Jane Dixon Smith for designing such a striking cover. My thanks also go to everyone who read and commented on the drafts of this novel, above all to my husband, Roger, whose patient advice and support has, as always, been invaluable.

**

Historical Note

In the 1580's, most London theatres were situated north of the Thames at Shoreditch. It was not until 1599 that the most famous of them all, The Globe, was built to the south at Bankside. This was also where London's bear pit was located but for the purposes of my story, I have changed its location to the north.

Chapter 1

A fox's bark disturbed the silence. Tom woke and tensed, then the raucous cry came again and, recognising it, he breathed easily. Dim moonlight filtered around the edges of the bedchamber's brocade curtains. He rolled over and propped himself on one elbow to look at Meg. Her glossy hair was a dark river against the lace-edged pillow. He reached out and caressed her shoulder. Startled awake, she turned.

'Tom? What is it? Did you hear something?'

'Only a fox.'

He drew her into his arms and she laid her head on his chest.

'What were you thinking about?' she whispered.

'How beautiful you are.'

'Flatterer.'

'It's true.'

She pinched his ear. 'Show me.'

He sighed. 'Again?'

She stroked his thigh and giggled. 'Too hot for you, am I, boy?'

His arms tightened around her. 'No, and don't you forget I'm older than you, madam.'

'Only a year.'

'And a hundred years wiser. Now stop talking.'

His lips traced a line of kisses from the hollow at the base of her throat to her belly. She closed her eyes. 'I love you,' she murmured.

'I love you too.' Later, she lay in the crook of his arm.

'Tom?'

'Mmn?'

'What are we to do?'

An ache tightened his chest. 'I wish I knew.'

'Edward will come back this afternoon and I don't know how long it will be before he sleeps away from home again. The days aren't safe with all the servants about.'

'Can't we meet somewhere else?'

'You'd have me up against a tavern door like a town drab, I suppose, or behind a tree in the woods?'

'I didn't mean that.'

Her expression softened. 'I know. But even if you did, it would be far, far better than doing it with Edward. He makes me feel like a cow serviced by a bull.'

'If he dares hurt you I'll—'

Meg put a hand over his mouth. 'Hush, not so loud. Someone will hear.'

She scrambled off the bed, went to the window and pushed one of the curtains aside. The sky was the colour of pearl.

'I shouldn't have let you stay so late. The maids will be up and about any minute.'

Quickly, she pulled on her nightgown while Tom rummaged through the discarded clothes on the floor. He fumbled to fasten his breeches and her fingers pushed his aside. 'Here, let me, you're too slow.'

'I'm going as fast as I can.' He tugged his cambric shirt over his head, put on his doublet and buckled his belt. As he reached for his boots, his hands were slippery with sweat and his fingers marked the tan leather.

6

'Your hose, you've forgotten your hose. For mercy's sake take them with you. Bess will know they'd never stretch around Edward's fat calves.'

He bundled the rough woollen hose down the front of his doublet then thrust his bare feet into his boots. 'I'm ready. Kiss me.'

His lips met hers. They were soft and warm, but he must not delay, even for a moment. He squeezed her shoulder. 'I'll think of something, I promise.'

He clambered over the window sill and jumped onto the roof of the side door porch below. His landing was clumsy and, brittle from last winter's frosts, a tile broke with a crack. To his ears, it sounded like a musket shot in the quiet of dawn. He froze and scanned the house. Was guilt making his imagination too lively, or did something move behind one of the windows? He must not risk staying so late again.

The drop to the grass was a longer one, eight feet perhaps. This time he stumbled and fell, his left foot buckling beneath his weight. He cursed under his breath. A moment wasted. If he was caught, it would mean disaster for them both. He hauled himself up then gasped as a stab of pain went through his ankle. A wave of nausea made him dizzy and he had to fight it down. Teeth gritted, he took the first step and hobbled away into the shadow of the trees.

*

A week later, Tom sat in the back room of Lawyer Kemp's house in New Street. He flexed his foot and winced. His ankle was still swollen and he had to force his boot on in the mornings, but it was nothing compared to the pain of missing Meg. He had gone to the oak tree at the edge of the Stuckton property where they left messages for each other, but there had been nothing. Perhaps after their narrow escape she was afraid to leave the house alone and arouse suspicion. The prospect of not seeing her, possibly for weeks, made his heart ache.

7

Gloomily, he studied the motes of dust floating in the sunshine that penetrated the high window. A couple of feet away, his fellow clerk, Ralph Fiddler, five years his senior, hunched over his work, his face half hidden by his black hair. Only the scratch of his quill on the parchment disturbed the silence.

With a sigh, Tom turned back to the document he was supposed to be preparing. It was an indenture for the sale of old John Barton's farm to Meg's husband, Edward Stuckton. Since Barton fell on hard times, the house and buildings had become derelict, but the land was fertile and well-watered.

Stuckton's face swam into Tom's mind. It wore the hard, self-confident expression of a successful man with a keen eye for a bargain. He had recognised old Barton was desperate enough to sell cheaply and this farm was ripe for adding to his already extensive holdings. Tom jabbed his quill into the inkhorn, remembering Stuckton's purchase of his own father's business. My poor father was no match for the rogue, he thought. Stuckton may not have been the author of Father's misfortunes, but he was swift to profit from them.

A sudden jog to his elbow took him unawares and the ink from the full quill splattered over the indenture. Ralph leant across. 'That'll have to be done again and Kemp'll leather you for the waste of ink.'

Tom scowled. Ralph never made any secret of his dislike. Even though he was Tom's senior, Lawyer Kemp paid him very little more. The fact that Kemp justified this by pointing out Tom was better educated did not help.

'Never mind,' Ralph went on with a sneer. 'I'm sure a certain mistress will kiss the weals better for you.'

Tom's heart missed a beat. Had the bastard found out about Meg? He shrugged. 'I don't know what you mean, but I'm sure no woman in possession of her wits would do as much for your sorry arse.'

His lip curling, Ralph jumped to his feet. Tom cursed himself for rising to the jibe. He dodged the first blow but was not fast enough to prevent Ralph's arm from encircling his neck. He gasped and lashed out with his foot, feeling his sore ankle burn as his boot struck bone. With a howl, Ralph slackened his grip for a moment. Tom seized his chance, broke free and landed a punch in Ralph's stomach.

Ralph doubled over, his face flushed and streaming with sweat. He licked his lips. 'Christ's blood, you'll pay for that,' he muttered.

Head down like a bull, he charged. The table shook as Tom's feet left the floor and he crashed backwards. Quills and documents scattered and the inkhorn toppled. The oily smell of the spilt ink filled his nostrils. He tried to shield his face as Ralph's fist smashed into it.

'Is this what I pay you for?' a voice rapped. William Kemp stood in the doorway, his beady eyes gleaming behind his horn-rimmed spectacles as he surveyed the pool of ink dripping onto the floor, the ruined indenture and the upended chairs.

'Master—'

Kemp raised his hand to cut Ralph short. 'I don't want to know who started this disgraceful affair. Goodluck, I'm taking two days from your pay. Two and a half from yours, Fiddler. As the elder of the pair of you, I expect you to set a good example. Look to it. Your work alone does not put you ahead of Tom.'

Ralph studied the floor as if in meek apology but Tom was close enough to see the glance of pure hatred he flashed in his direction: another nail in the coffin.

'I trust I'll hear no more of this,' Kemp said coldly. 'Now get back to your work.'

*

At his lodgings over the bakery in Oatmeal Row, Tom sat at the rickety table he used as a desk. His eyes smarted. It was nearly dawn and he had been trying to write for most of the night. With a grimace, he wished he didn't have to work this way. He was too tired to think properly. When he had first dreamt of making a living from writing plays, he hadn't expected to have to spend his days copying out dusty legal documents as well.

Carefully, he closed the book he had been writing in. It had been his father's commonplace book and the cracked spine was fragile and the leather cover faded. The auctioneer at the sale of his father's personal possessions had deemed it worth very little but to Tom it was precious. There should be enough blank pages left in it for him to write out his play.

His fingers explored the skin around his left eye. The place was still puffy and throbbing from Ralph's blow. Tom sighed. When he had chosen the story of Perseus and Andromeda as the theme for his play, it had seemed so fitting. The predicament of the mythical Perseus, deprived of his inheritance and cast out to live by his wits, was not so very different from his own. But yesterday's fight with Ralph brought home one very important difference: Perseus was a demi-god who won his battles.

He pushed a lock of his light-brown hair out of his eyes. The play was almost finished, but did it have any merit? Was he a fool to dream anyone would perform it? If he was, months of work had been wasted. It would never make him the fortune he needed if he was to rescue Meg. Even then, escaping together would not be easy. Stuckton was an influential man in the city.

With a yawn, he stretched his long legs. Self-pity would not help him. He had promised Meg he would think of a way out and he mustn't fail her. His father had sometimes returned from his business travels with tales of men who had crossed oceans and discovered new lands. If such stories were true, there must be some far corner of the world where Edward Stuckton could not follow them.

He blew out his candle and went to the window; there were streaks of red in the eastern sky. He was about to turn away when he noticed a small colony of ladybirds in the crevice between the window frame and the wall. He poked

10

them with his forefinger and they scurried about in alarm. Did they have thoughts, as people did, he wondered, or did they simply eat, breed and then die? Perhaps he seemed like a god to them, destroying their little world for sport.

The voices of early customers floated up from the baker's shop below. Tom's mouth watered at the aroma of fresh bread. He picked up his cap and went downstairs, ducking to avoid the low beam at the bottom.

In the kitchen, the baker's wife looked up from stirring the big, iron pot hung over the fire. Her face was red and shiny. She raised her eyebrows. 'You're supposed to open doors before you walk through them, y'know.'

'I'll remember next time.'

'Who hit you then? That eye has more red in it than a shepherd's warning.'

'Ralph.'

The baker's wife shook her head. 'You don't learn, do you? He sounds like a nasty brute. Better to keep out of his way.'

'It's hard when we share a room the size of a privy.'

'A good-looking lad like you should find a nice girl and settle down, not spend your time brawling.'

'I would, but you won't have me.'

She laughed. 'Keep your pretty compliments for your sweetheart when you find her. Here, you can have some of this porridge if you want. Bring me a bowl and spoon.' She gestured in the direction of the oak dresser. Tom held out the bowl while she ladled in a dollop, then he sat down to eat on the stool near the hearth.

'The food of the gods,' he said, in between mouthfuls. 'No one makes porridge like you, Mary.'

She put down her wooden spoon and poured him a cup of small beer from a glazed earthenware jug. 'What are you after then?'

'Kemp stopped some of my wages.'

'Mean old bugger. So you're short for the rent, I suppose?'

11

He nodded reluctantly. 'I can pay almost three-quarters.'

'And you want me to talk His Highness into waiting for the rest?'

'I'll get up an hour earlier and chop wood for the ovens if he wants.'

She pursed her lips. 'Maybe I'll ask him.'

He put an arm around her waist and planted a kiss on her moist cheek. 'You're an angel.'

'I only said maybe,' she chuckled. 'Now be off with you, I've work to do.'

Chapter 2

The following week, May Day dawned bright and clear. By the time the sun reached its zenith, the Salisbury guildsmen and their wives sweated in their fur-trimmed robes and silk and velvet gowns.

The young men and girls of the city had spent all morning winding the maypole with coloured ribbons and fixing on bunches of spring flowers and herbs. A great roar went up when the pole arrived at the water meadows on the city's edge, carried on a cart belonging to Edward Stuckton. It was drawn by ten oxen, the tips of their horns decorated with nosegays of clove-scented pinks, buttercups and daisies.

The girls stood back and shouted encouragement while the men eased the pole off the cart and hauled it up into position, securing it with long ropes. Before long it towered over everyone, flags and ribbons fluttering from its top and the men's faces were flushed and streaming.

Tom joined the group herding the oxen back to their fields. He had no heart for jollity and the smiles of the girls he passed were wasted on him. He flicked the rump of the reluctant beast he walked behind with a birch switch to keep it moving and glanced sideways at the canopied dais where Meg sat with her husband and the other guildsmen and their wives. His heart lurched at the sight of her. Dressed in a green silk gown, with her dark hair coiled up in a net of gold thread, she was surely the loveliest woman there.

Her father, Henry Bailey, was deep in conversation with Edward Stuckton, while her mother, Anne, gossiped with the other wives. Tom grimaced. In the old days, his parents would have taken their place alongside the Baileys on the dais, his father a respected guildsman, his mother as finely dressed as any of the other ladies.

He remembered how his father had liked to joke about Henry Bailey, who was a grumpy, pompous little man. His mother had been kinder about Anne Bailey. 'It's no wonder she often looks cross,' she would say, wagging an admonishing finger at Tom's father. 'If you found fault with everything as Henry Bailey does, I would be cross too. Poor Anne holds her tongue and studies her rings, but I don't know how she finds the patience.'

Tom smiled at the memory of his mother's innocent sympathy. According to Meg, her mother's patience soon vanished when the Baileys had no company.

'Am I worth it?' Meg once asked. 'Do you really want to marry into such a family for my sake? Our house is like a bear pit sometimes.'

But she already knew the answer. For her he would have joyfully embraced even Nero and Messalina as in-laws.

He looked again at Anne Bailey. Above her pristine ruff, her face was coated with too much white lead and rouge and her eyes were sharp. It was hard to feel sorry for her, particularly when she had made it abundantly clear he was no longer welcome in her house.

By the time the oxen were peacefully grazing and he returned to the fair, the feast was about to begin. A small band of musicians played on trumpets and sackbuts as a roasted suckling pig was carried to the top table, apples stuffed between its gaping jaws and its crisp, brown skin shining from a basting of honey and butter. The smell of rich meat made Tom's stomach groan with hunger. He had not been able to afford any extra food all week and seven days of living on Mary's porridge and William Kemp's meagre midday allowance of bread and cheese certainly sharpened the appetite. He found a place beside Kemp's groom, Adam, and helped himself to a large piece of pie filled with mutton, garlic and leeks. It tasted like heaven.

14

There was no shade at the table and the sun beat down on his head. He drank a cup of ale and then another. Adam grinned tipsily at him and threw an arm around his neck.

'Yurr a goo' fellow, Tom,' he mumbled through a mouthful of pickled herring. His breath could have felled a horse but Tom returned a smile.

'How do, Adam.'

Adam swallowed his herring, wiped his greasy lips with his sleeve, and belched up a gust of vinegar and fish that made Tom gag.

'Bad.'

'Why's that?'

'You gotta woman, Tom? I ain't gotta woman.' He stopped and blinked then belched again, his mouth wide, showing raw gums and brown, uneven teeth.

'Maybe you should clean those teeth of yours for a start.'

'Doan 'old with all that poking about with twigs, 'gainst nature.'

'Only trying to help.'

'E'en tha' turd can get one.' Adam scowled towards where Ralph sat with a buxom fair-haired girl on his knee. Around them, people whooped with laughter as he poured ale into her open mouth, spilling some of it down her neck then licking it off while she squealed with delight. With a stab of alarm, Tom recognised Bess, Meg's maid. He'd never noticed her and Ralph together before.

'How long's that been going on?'

Adam shrugged and winked. 'Long enough for him to get wha' 'e's after, I'd say.'

The eating and drinking lasted for several hours before the trumpets rang out once more. The party of notables on the dais stood up. Tom saw Meg put her hand on Edward Stuckton's arm before he led her down the staircase. He bent to murmur something in her ear and she smiled. As she touched the pearls at her throat, Tom felt a violent stab of jealousy. He could not afford expensive trinkets for her.

15

What were they talking of? Was she really so unhappy with Stuckton?

Adam blundered to his feet. 'Need a piss,' he hiccupped.

Guilt overcame Tom. How could he doubt Meg? He had so little to offer and she so much to lose, yet she risked it all to snatch their precious hours together.

Wearily, he pointed Adam towards the trees. As he watched the groom go, he wondered whether it would be better to be like him and have no one rather than always be halfway between happiness and despair. A fog of misery engulfed him. Nothing had turned out as it should. He was meant to have been Meg's husband, son to a prosperous guildsman, not a paltry clerk snatching hole-in-the-corner kisses.

A small band of carpenters was already dismantling the dais. They soon had the wooden struts and planks repositioned to create a low, makeshift stage. Around two-thirds of its perimeter, they hammered long poles into the ground and hung lanterns from them, ready to be lit at dusk.

Tom's hands were clammy. Ever since he had heard that a visit from some London players was expected, he had been awaiting this moment. He had often taken part in the local theatricals, even written some of the speeches for them, but a performance by a company from one of the London theatres was altogether different. His hand went to the book tucked into the pouch at his belt. The leather felt dry to his touch. He rehearsed the words of introduction he had wrestled with all week and wished he felt more confident. If he did manage to speak to the man in charge of the company, he might only have a few moments to make a good impression.

Adam had returned from the trees and now his face was resting on the table amid the dirty trenchers and cups. When Tom shook him, he lifted his head. His skin had a greenish pallor and there were scraps of food entangled in his beard.

'No more ale for you, my friend,' Tom said. 'And you're lucky old Kemp isn't here to see you. He'd duck your head in the horse trough if he was, and no mistake. Still, you've time to sober up. Come on, let's go and watch the play.'

The shadows were lengthening across the meadow and the air had cooled. A tent stood at the back of the stage, the flap pinned back where the players would make their entrances and exits. First on was a wiry man in a jester's yellow-and-red costume. He carried a staff tipped with silver bells. A few people had remained at the tables, guzzling the last of the food and drinking the dregs of the ale, but most of them crowded around the stage to see the fun. Tom saw Ralph Fiddler near the front, Bess hoisted on his back for a better view. Her skirts had ridden up, showing a glimpse of scarlet stockings. Tom recognised the stockings; he was sure they belonged to Meg. He wondered if she had noticed them too.

When the jester's jokes and capers were over, the play, *Pyramus and Thisbe*, commenced. Tom found himself as interested in the reactions of the onlookers as he was in the story, even though the play far exceeded anything Salisbury had to offer. How much he wanted to have this power to move people from laughter to tears, to hold them, even if only for an hour or two, in the palm of his hand.

The play ended in tragedy – voices around Tom murmured that a tragic end was often best – and the crowd cheered as the hero and his beloved returned miraculously to life and took their bows. Tom's pulse raced. This was his chance, there might not be another.

'Where you going?' Adam grasped his arm.

'I need to talk to someone.'

'Doan' leave me.'

Tom looked at his bloodshot eyes and swaying body. 'I'll walk back with you later. We'll get you as far as that tree for now and you can wait for me there.'

He half-dragged the protesting groom through the press of people and propped him up against an alder near the players' tent. Adam's head sagged on his chest and he started to snore. Tom took a deep breath then walked the last few yards to where one of the players stood.

'Your friend has had a good day, I see,' the player remarked in an accent unfamiliar to Tom. He still wore the lion's costume he had sported on stage but he had rubbed off half of the yellow greasepaint on his face, revealing an olive complexion. His wiry, dark hair was plastered to his skull in damp strands and there was a strong smell of sweat and alum about him. He wiped his forehead. 'I sweat like a pig in this,' he muttered.

Tom stood clutching the commonplace book. His mind had suddenly emptied. The player shot him a quizzical look.

'Is there something I can do for you?' he asked.

'I was hoping to speak to the manager,' Tom stammered, finding his voice.

With a mock flourish, the player bowed. 'You behold him: Alexandre Lamotte – proprietor and manager of The Unicorn.'

A flush crept up Tom's neck. 'I'm sorry, I didn't mean to offend—'

'It's all right,' Lamotte interrupted him with a chuckle. Then, seeing what was in Tom's hand, he asked, 'So, you have something to show me?'

Awkwardly, Tom proffered the book. Lamotte took it, but as he scanned the opening pages, a frown came over his face. 'Notes for a journey to buy cloth in Antwerp?'

Tom wished the earth would swallow him. 'Those are my father's. My work comes after them.'

Lamotte flipped over a few pages. 'Ah, I see.'

'It's a play, but I'm afraid it may not be much good,' Tom ploughed on. His cheeks smarted.

'Then we'll say farewell and you can take it home with you.' Lamotte shut the book and held it out.

Tom's spirits sank then he noticed the twinkle in the player's eyes.

'You won't have to be so serious if you want to get on in the theatre, lad, that's the first lesson. By the way, do you have a name?'

'Tom Goodluck, sir.'

'And how old are you, Tom Goodluck?'

'Nineteen, sir.'

'Ah, to be so young again, the world yours for the taking.' Lamotte shook his head and sighed. 'But you haven't come to listen to my meanderings. Give me a moment while I glance at your play.'

He opened the book once more. Tom waited, watching his face intently, not daring to speak. His pulse raced. Perhaps this man was not going to dismiss him out of hand.

'*Perseus and Andromeda*, eh?' Lamotte said when he reached the bottom of the first page. 'Well, no one's tried it yet, at least as far as I can recall, and it's a good tale. There'd be a fair bit of skill and trickery needed though, have you thought of that? Your gentlemen writers can poetise to their ladies for pages on end, but if you want to pull in the audiences, you need to show them the action. I've been fifteen years in this business and I know what I'm talking about.' He laughed. 'If you're to succeed, give audiences what they want, even if they don't know at the time what that might be. A storm when Perseus sets off on his quest to destroy the Gorgon would be a better beginning than you've got here. A storm always pleases the groundlings – cannon and fireworks for the thunder and lightning – costly, but worth it.'

He stroked his greasepaint-streaked beard. 'I'd need to read more, of course, and I'd want to see plenty of drama – drama and horror,' he rolled the words off his tongue with relish.

He nodded to another player passing nearby. 'There'd need to be some ugly mugs for the hags who show Perseus the way to the Gorgon's lair, but that will not be hard in our company, we've plenty will suit.' The other player grinned.

'They could burst up from Hell in a flash of lightning,' Lamotte went on. 'That usually raises a gasp from the pit.'

'From Hell?' Tom asked, puzzled.

'Through the trapdoor in the stage. You do have a lot to learn, don't you? And Perseus will need his winged sandals to fly across Asia to rescue Andromeda. Do you intend to knit those?'

Tom's flush deepened. He should never have come after all.

'Only a little pleasantry, you mustn't take everything so to heart,' Lamotte said more kindly. 'Well, I'll make you an offer. We stay here a few more days to play for the Countess of Pembroke. I'll read the rest of your play and tell you what I think before we leave. Will that please you?'

A surge of delight went through Tom. 'More than I can say. Thank you a thousand times.'

Lamotte grinned. 'I've not given you my opinion yet. Save your thanks until I have. Come and see me the day after tomorrow. We lodge at the Blue Boar.'

As Tom left the tent, his blood tingled. He found Adam still snoring under the alder tree and shook him. 'Home now, if you can stand, that is. I'm not carrying you.'

Adam coughed and spat out a gobbet of phlegm. 'Awright, doan shout.'

Tom sighed. It was going to be a long walk.

They stumbled through the dark streets, Adam weighing down Tom's shoulder. Long before they reached William Kemp's house in New Street, his back ached. He dragged Adam the last few steps along the cobbled passage leading to the stables. In the stable yard, they disturbed the household's chickens, making them cluck and fuss about. The cockerel puffed up its wattle and made a run at them, but Tom aimed a kick in its direction and carried on to the outhouse behind the stables. There, with relief, he unloaded Adam onto his straw bed where he settled down to sleep at once.

Tom rubbed his throbbing shoulder. Suddenly tiredness overwhelmed him. He thought of the night watchmen. Most of the revellers would have returned to their homes by now; he would be an object of suspicion and he did not care to be fined or beaten.

He rolled Adam onto his side with his face pressed to the roughcast wall, and lay down beside him. Outside, the chickens were still agitated. Maybe a fox was about. With luck it would carry a few off and serve Kemp right. His nose wrinkled. Christ, Adam stank. In spite of that, he was soon asleep and dreaming of Meg.

*

At cockcrow, he woke with a start and sat up. Dry-mouthed and stiff, even the dim light in the outhouse made his eyes smart.

Adam stirred. 'Carn' a man sleep in peace?' he grumbled.

'You can if you want but I've work to go to and I need something to eat first.'

Outside, chilly tentacles of mist enveloped him. He had almost reached the shed where Kemp kept his pig for fattening when he heard something move. It didn't sound like the pig shifting in its straw. Was it a fox, perhaps? No, foxes moved more stealthily than that. Disorientated by the mist, he froze when the sound came again, much closer this time. Too fast for him to resist, something coarse, scratchy and smelling of dung dropped over his head. Chaff filled his throat, choking him. With a bruising thud, he hit the ground; his lungs felt as if they would burst and pinpricks of scarlet light danced before his eyes. Pain seared his wrists and ankles as someone roped them.

'That'll hold you for a while,' a familiar voice said.

Tom struggled as he was dragged across the yard. Sharp flints ripped his shirt and cut into his flesh, but before long, the ground softened and something crackled beneath him. He must be on straw. The sack came off and he gulped air, starting off another fit of choking. Through streaming eyes, he saw the sloe-black, button eyes of Kemp's pig close by him. It squealed and backed away, then braced its legs and let out a stinking stream of piss. With difficulty, Tom jerked his head sideways to avoid it.

'So, Tom Goodluck, how do you like your new bedfellow?'

Ralph Fiddler.

'Something in your throat, Tom?' he asked silkily.

'A drink, give me a drink,' Tom wheezed.

'You're in luck. I know Adam's secret.' Ralph rifled through a pile of straw in a corner and produced a dusty bottle. He pulled out the cork and sniffed the contents.

'Even Adam might not want this, but it won't kill you.'

He put the rim of the bottle to Tom's lips. Tom spluttered as most of the liquid ran down his chin, but his coughing gradually subsided and he started to struggle again.

Ralph tossed the bottle back into the straw. 'I'd stop that if I were you. Waste of time fighting. I tie good knots.' He bent down and grinned into Tom's face. 'Now what shall we talk about?'

'Let me go, you bastard. I've nothing to say to you.'

Ralph gave a nasty laugh. 'Oh, I think you'll find we have plenty to say to each other. I have your best interests at heart. You should listen if you care for your own hide,' he lowered his voice, 'and for sweet Mistress Stuckton's.'

Tom froze. Had Meg's maid, Bess, suspected something and gossiped? He should have known there might be more than one reason why Ralph dallied with her.

Ralph raised an eyebrow. 'I see we understand each other.'

'What do you want, Fiddler? If it's money, you must know I don't have any.'

'No, not money.'

'What then? If it's sport you're after, untie me and we can fight fair and square.'

'And give up the advantage I've won? Do you take me for a fool?'

22

'A fool would have more honour, you bastard.'

'Curse me all you like, it will do you no good, but a civil tongue might.'

'Ask for what you want. If it's in my power, I'll give it to you, then let there be an end to this.'

'Yes, it's in your power.' Ralph paused, smiling. 'I want you gone.'

Tom's heart plummeted.

Ralph squatted down and began to trace a pattern in the dust with his forefinger, then glancing at the cautiously advancing pig, picked up a stone and shied it at its glistening, pink snout. With an angry grunt, the animal retreated to the corner of the shed.

'Forgive the interruption. The brute is fascinated by the misfortunes of others. Much like our own species, don't you agree?'

'What if I refuse?'

'You'd be making a foolish mistake. What use would you be to Mistress Meg after Stuckton finished with you? Then there's her fate. I wonder what he would do to her. Beat her? Lock her up? That's if he was merciful.'

'Why are you doing this?'

'I'm offering you the chance of a lifetime,' Ralph sneered. 'You can take your grammar school learning with you and go to London to seek your fortune.'

Tom groaned. There was no denying he had often dreamt of London, but always with the hazy idea that somehow he would take Meg with him. Then a flicker of hope stirred. If he pretended to agree, Ralph might lower his guard.

'If you're thinking of playing tricks,' Ralph said, 'I warn you there's someone else who knows the same as I do about you and Mistress Stuckton. Even if you rid yourself of me, it will make no difference to your fates.'

Tom watched Ralph's eyes. Did he mean Bess, or was he bluffing? It was impossible to be sure.

'Very well, I'll go. But you must swear you'll do her no harm afterwards.'

Ralph gave a wolfish grin. 'I'll be gentle as a lamb.'

'Touch her and I promise you, one day, I'll be back to break every bone in your body.'

'Only a jest. Edward Stuckton is too big a man for me.' He looked out at the mist drifting across the yard. 'The sun'll be up soon. Time we were away. I have your word you'll go quietly?'

Tom nodded, but it was a struggle to resist the urge to attack Ralph as he untied his bonds. Freed, he staggered up and they walked out into the dawn. Beyond New Street, the reek of the town ditch greeted them as they passed by. They skirted the deserted market place and went on towards the Winchester gate. A night watchman, yawning home to bed, gave them an incurious glance.

At the gate, the porter had already opened the massive oak doors and gone back inside his lodge to warm himself by his fire. Ahead, the road snaked upwards to the sheep-scattered plain.

Ralph stopped. 'You can go on alone from here.' He tossed a small purse at Tom and it fell to the ground. Tom stooped to pick it up. Inside he found a handful of coins – enough for a few days' food.

'I suppose you expect thanks?'

'As you wish.'

Tom gave a curt nod then swallowed hard. 'Swear to me again you won't harm her.'

Ralph shrugged. 'I've already told you that.'

With a swift movement, Tom seized him by the collar of his shirt. 'Swear it,' he hissed.

Ralph's eyes narrowed. 'Don't be a fool.'

For a moment, they held each other's gaze then Tom's shoulders slumped and he let Ralph go.

'That's better,' Ralph said coolly. 'Now be on your way.'

Without another word, Tom set off. It was a steep climb out of the valley and in spite of the morning chill he was warm by the time he reached the ridge. There, he stopped to rest. He wrapped his threadbare cloak around him and gazed at the city below. Its walls glowed in the morning sunshine and the mist had rolled away to reveal the silver ribbon of the Avon threading through the green fields. The spire of the great cathedral soared into the pale blue sky. The image of Meg rose in his mind. She was probably sleeping, unaware they would never see each other again.

Rage seized him. He had to go back; he would kill Ralph if it was the only way.

Then a chill entered his veins. If Ralph had spoken the truth, the risk of exposure was too great. He might destroy Meg's life as well as his own. His heart's battle with his head was soon over. It was a chance he dared not take.

Wretched, he turned and walked away.

Chapter 3

'Is there something you're not telling me, child?'

Sat with her mother in the parlour at Stuckton Court later that day, Meg's head swam. It was a question she had dreaded ever since Tom had stayed so late on their last morning together. With a great effort, she steadied her voice.

'What do you mean, Mother?'

'By the time I was your age, I had given birth to both your brothers. Edward wants an heir and your task is to give him one.' She tapped a be-ringed finger on the arm of her chair, 'It is a year since you married.'

Meg's head cleared. They were still safe. It was only her mother's usual reproach - the subject she fastened on with increasing frequency, like a terrier shaking a rat. She could not bear to listen to it yet again.

'Perhaps it is not God's will that I should have a child,' she said, lowering her eyes.

'God's will? God's will? What nonsense you talk, child. Why should the Lord concern himself with you?' Anne Bailey's eyes narrowed. 'Edward does come to your bed? You do not deny him? It is a wife's duty to submit to her husband, let no one say I haven't taught you that.'

Meg's knuckles blanched. 'I never wanted to marry Edward, you knew that.'

'Your father and I did what was best for you.'

'Marrying me to a man I could never love? Was that what was best for me?' Meg bit her lip as tears sprang to her eyes.

'It is not your place to question our judgement.'

'I'm not a child, Mother.'

'No, and by now you should have learnt to accept the way the world works and be grateful. Most women would be proud to be mistress of such a house as this.'

With a frown, Anne Bailey rose from her chair and shook out her silk skirts. 'This floor is dusty. You must be harsher with the servants. The house was without a mistress for far too long after poor Jane Stuckton died. They have become slack.' She glanced around the room. 'That silver jug is tarnished and the fire irons are black with soot.'

Meg coloured, but she did not want to prolong the argument or the visit by retaliating so she remained silent.

'Well, I must return home,' her mother sniffed. 'Your father has visitors coming to do business this afternoon. They will want refreshments and I must make sure the new cook prepares them properly.' She pursed her lips. 'Think on what I've said. It surprises me you don't seem to share my concern. Even if Edward doesn't chide you now, the time will come, I assure you.'

Meg didn't trust herself to speak.

At the door, her mother turned. 'I know these things don't always run smoothly,' she said. 'Perhaps we should consult a physician. There are herbs. Cupping to correct the humours.'

'Please, Mother, not yet. Something will happen. I'm sure it will.'

'Very well, we shall wait, but for all our sakes, I hope you're right.'

She swept out, leaving a lingering scent of expensive sandalwood in her wake. Meg buried her face in her hands. A child was only the half of it. If Mother ever found out about Tom, imagine how ferocious her reaction would be. With a shudder, Meg pushed the thought to the back of her mind. She must compose herself. At least she had a few hours alone before Edward returned from inspecting his farms.

She picked up the embroidery she had neglected for days and sat down on the scarlet-cushioned window seat, but after a few stitches, the canvas slipped to the floor. Was this all life held for her? Married to a man she could not love; trapped in a gloomy house that surrounded her like an ugly cloak she didn't want to wear? She leant her cheek against the stone mullion and felt the warmth it had absorbed from the morning's sun. Its smooth texture reminded her of Tom's lean, hard body. All at once, such a strong rush of longing and sorrow went through her that she almost cried out.

She still sat by the window when, close to dusk, she heard the clatter of hooves on the cobbles outside. There was a hammering on the front door and a voice she did not recognise spoke briefly with Stephen, the steward. Through the window, she saw a man vault onto his horse and ride away. It was late for a messenger to come to the house. She wondered what news he had brought.

A few moments later, there were hurrying footsteps on the stairs and an urgent knock at the door. Wide-eyed and flustered, Bess rushed in.

'Whatever's the matter?' Meg frowned.

'The master sent to say he isn't coming home, madam.'

Meg repressed a guilty surge of relief. 'Oh? Is that all? Did he say why?'

Bess drew a deep breath. 'Something terrible's happened, madam.'

Meg felt a stirring of irritation. 'Well?' she asked sharply.

'He's gone to New Street, madam. Lawyer Kemp's been found dead in his bed, dead as a doornail, an' Stephen says Tom Goodluck killed him.'

*

'It can't be true, Mother!'

'The law will be the judge of that when he is caught, but your father and Edward have little doubt in their minds. Why would he run off if he was not guilty? In any case, when Ralph Fiddler went to tell him of Master Kemp's death, he found a good deal of money at the wretch's lodgings, far too much for a poor clerk to have come by honestly. The baker's wife wept and said he must be innocent, but these common women are always fools for a sweet-tongued villain.' She scrutinised Meg. 'In any case, what is Tom Goodluck to you now?'

'Nothing ... I just never thought ... He was such a gentle boy when we were young.'

'You are easily swayed, child. Ralph Fiddler told your father and Edward that Tom Goodluck had a violent temper if he was crossed. Fiddler said he was even afraid for himself at times. Master Kemp often had reason to chastise Tom for idleness and bad work, but instead of accepting the rebukes humbly and learning from them, he often boasted he would be revenged on his master one day. Mark me, his father came to no good and bad blood will always out.'

Meg stiffened. Her sweet Tom was not a murderer, she was sure of it. She wanted to cry out against the injustice of it all but she knew she must resist. She steadied her voice, determined not to let her feelings show.

'Does anyone know where he's gone?' she asked.

'Ralph Fiddler says he often heard him boast he would go and fight in the Low Countries and make his fortune, but I doubt that a coward who kills an old man in his sleep to steal his money would make much of a soldier.' She smoothed her skirt. 'Edward thinks Ralph Fiddler is a very able fellow, and the sorrow he showed over his master's death did him great credit. I shouldn't wonder if Edward won't do something for him, now Kemp is gone.'

That was not the Ralph Fiddler Meg recognised from Tom's description of him. She would be surprised if he felt any grief for Lawyer Kemp's fate.

'Fiddler lodges in the house,' her mother was saying. 'It was he who found his master. When he returned from the May Day celebration, he was alarmed to see the side door unlocked, but nothing seemed out of place so he decided it must be an oversight. He went up the attic stairs to make

29

sure Kemp's servant had returned, and heard him snoring in his bed. Master Kemp had not gone to the celebrations and Fiddler knew he always retired early, so Fiddler was reassured and went to bed as well. In the morning, he began work at his usual time. There was no sign of Tom Goodluck but that did not surprise him. He was concerned, though, that his master hadn't appeared. Kemp's servant said he hadn't seen him so Fiddler went to enquire if he was ill, and that's when he found the body.'

Anne Bailey stopped and peered at Meg. 'You're very quiet, child. Are you quite well?'

'Only a headache,' Meg said hastily. 'It will soon pass, I'm sure.'

'Well then, I'll leave you to rest.' She planted a cool kiss on Meg's cheek. 'You must come and visit us soon.'

'Thank you, Mother.'

The moment the door closed, the tears Meg had been restraining brimmed over. Her mind was full of jumbled thoughts. If Tom was innocent, and how could it be otherwise, who had killed William Kemp? She racked her brains and tried to think who might speak up for Tom. Adam, Kemp's groom, had been at the May Day celebrations. She had seen Tom lead him away, but he had been so drunk it was unlikely he would remember anything that had happened afterwards.

Her stomach churned at the memory of Edward's descriptions of the cases he presided over as Justice of the Peace. His readiness to believe that any defendant must be guilty, particularly if they were poor and lacked influential friends, had always seemed to her far from any notion of a fair trial. If he was already against Tom, the situation was desperate.

It was some time before she dried her eyes and resolved what she should do. Perhaps all was not lost; this might be the spur they had needed. If Tom hadn't left Salisbury yet and was hiding somewhere, she must try to find him so they could escape together.

Edward had left the house early that morning. He would not return until it was time for supper. Her heart pounding, she crept to his study and found paper and ink. Hastily, she scrawled a note then dusted it with sand. It seemed an eternity before it was dry enough to shake off, and all the while, her ears strained for any sounds from the rest of the house, but none came. In the passageway, she closed the door as quietly as she could then hurried back to the parlour. This afternoon, she would slip away to the oak tree where she and Tom left messages for each other. She prayed there would be something from him that would explain everything.

*

The path led through the garden Edward's first wife had laid out, bushes of lavender and roses set in knots of neatly clipped box, but Meg was oblivious to the heady perfume the flowers gave off. Her heavy silk dress seemed to drag her down and her hair felt damp under her gabled hood. By the time she reached the lime walk and the shade it afforded, her head throbbed.

The ancient oak at the far end was well hidden from prying eyes, but she still glanced over her shoulder to be sure she had not been followed before kneeling at the base of the tree. With a sharp flint, she scraped away at the earth. Her throat was dry. At the first glimpse of the rough, rag paper Tom used, she snatched the letter up and tore it open, scanning the words anxiously, but the letter was several days old. It made no mention of Kemp's murder.

Dismay overwhelmed her. She pressed her forehead against the hard ridges of the oak tree's bark. If Tom had left Salisbury as her mother claimed, he had gone without a word of explanation.

A scarlet-and-black butterfly settled on a patch of sunlit grass nearby, fanning its wings. Tomorrow its life would be over; how she envied it. She bowed her head and several minutes passed before she regained her composure and vowed not to give up hope. Tom would never abandon her in such a cruel way. She had to believe it or she would go mad. She read the letter once more. As it was a few days old, it proved nothing. She would come tomorrow, and the next day, and the one after that if she had to. Tom would not fail her.

She planted a kiss on the letter she had brought with her, tucked it among the tree's roots and refilled the hollow with earth. A handful of moss scattered on top satisfied her that no one but Tom would ever guess the ground had been disturbed.

When she returned to the house, one of the grooms was leading Edward's mare towards the stable yard. Meg's head reeled. Oh why did Edward have to come home earlier than expected? Today of all days, she could not face one of his ill-tempered lectures. She bit her lip. There was nothing to be done about it. She must endure his moods as best as she could. Ignoring the groom's curious glance, she picked up her skirts and hurried on across the cobbles.

Indoors, the lofty, oak-panelled hall was cooler than the garden. Roundels of stained glass brightened the high windows, and the late afternoon sun, streaming through them, cast patches of gold, green and crimson on the stone-flagged floor. Edward sat in his chair by the fireplace, still in his riding clothes.

'I'm sorry I was not here to greet you, husband,' she stammered, not meeting his eye.

'Where have you been?'

'Reading in the park.' She held up the book she had taken the precaution of carrying to hide her letter.

He glanced at it then stretched his legs.

'Idle nonsense. It's been a hard day and I'm weary. Pull off my boots. This business with old Kemp has the whole city in an uproar, seeing murderers everywhere. Some fools would be afraid of their own shadows. All the same, the sooner Tom Goodluck hangs the better.'

Knelt at his feet, Meg felt her heart give such a violent jolt that she was surprised Edward did not notice anything. If Tom was found, he would have no hope. She struggled to keep her hands from trembling. The leather creaked as she pulled off the first boot.

Edward gave a satisfied grunt. 'Ah, that's better. What a pretty thing you are.' He tilted her chin and bent to cover her lips with his, pushing his tongue into her mouth. His hand moved to fondle her breasts. Meg forced herself not to recoil. When he let her go, she looked down to hide her burning cheeks and busied herself in pulling off his other boot.

'Tell the servants to serve our meal early,' he said.

At dinner, Meg sat at the far end of the long table, watching him eat copiously and with relish but the smell and sight of the roasted meats sickened her. She toyed with some bread and took a few sips of wine, wishing she was alone.

'You're very quiet, wife,' Edward observed, when he had gnawed the last of the flesh from a capon leg and wiped the grease from his lips.

'Forgive me, husband, my head aches and the heat has tired me.'

'And the reading, no doubt,' he grunted. 'It's time you had other occupations. Too much time spent with books does women no good. Their brains are weak and should not be overtaxed.'

He tossed back the last of his wine. Meg winced as he stood up and his chair grated over the stone floor. 'Steward!' he shouted. 'I have no appetite for more. Clear all this away.'

Stephen, the steward, hurried forward.

Meg waited for Edward to help her up from the table. He put his arm around her waist and drew her to him. His breath was laden with garlic and wine. 'But I have an appetite for something else,' he murmured. 'Tell your maid to make you ready for bed. I have some accounts I must look over, but it will not take long.'

Upstairs, Bess helped her out of her clothes and into her nightgown.

'Shall I unpin your hair, my lady?'

'No, I'll do it myself. You may leave me now.'

Bess bobbed a curtsey and went to the door; it clicked shut behind her.

Left alone, Meg opened a drawer and took out the letter from Tom she had found that afternoon. She knew she should burn it. Tom always insisted they should not keep each other's letters once they had read them, but she was tempted to disobey. She could hide it somewhere. Even if Bess or one of the maids came across it, it would not matter. None of them could read. She looked around the room but then changed her mind. Tom was right. Even if it was unlikely the letter would be discovered, it was a risk she need not take.

Reluctantly, she carried it to the hearth and placed it gently on the stone. She took a candle from the mantelshelf and touched its flame to the paper then watched the letter flare up. Slowly it twisted and shrivelled until nothing but ashes remained. It seemed to her that her heart had turned to ashes too. Suppose the letter was the last she ever received from Tom? What would she do then?

A breeze from the garden made the candle flame flicker and stirred the tapestry on the wall beside the open window. The bright, silken huntsmen and baying dogs it depicted moved in endless, fruitless pursuit across the imaginary greenwood. If nothing changes, she thought, and what hope is there of that, my life will be as empty as theirs.

She put down the candle and sat on the side of the bed. If only disaster had not visited Tom's family, everything would have been so different. She and Tom might have been husband and wife by now, but as it had fallen out, it had been impossible to oppose her parents' wishes. She wrapped her arms around herself for comfort. In the corridor, Edward's familiar footsteps approached.

34

*

When she woke, the sun was up and the air in the room was stifling. Beside her, a deep indent remained in the crumpled sheets. She shuddered as she remembered Edward's shoulders heaving above her and the sweat glistening on his forehead.

With a great effort, she banished the image and got up to look out at the day. In the courtyard below, a horse she did not recognise was tethered to the post by the porch. Fear overwhelmed her. Had the rider brought news of Tom?

'Good morning, madam.'

Startled, she turned but it was only Bess setting down a basin of water on the dressing table.

'Do you know who our visitor is?' Meg asked, trying to make her voice sound casual.

'I don't, I'm sure, madam.'

Bess dipped a cloth in the basin, pinned up Meg's hair and sponged her neck and arms in silence. Rose petals scented the water and usually it was a pleasant and refreshing morning ritual but today nothing eased Meg's mind. Was Bess telling the truth? There was something furtive in her voice and it was unlike her to be so quiet.

'Are you certain, Bess?'

Bess flushed. 'I am, madam. Will you breakfast up here today, madam?'

Meg hesitated, torn between the longing to find out who the early visitor was and fear that she might betray her emotion in front of Edward. At last she nodded.

'I'll go and tell Cook straight away, shall I?' Bess asked, scooping up the unused pins and clips and dropping them back into the jewelled box on the dressing table.

'And come back and tell me who has called. My mother was unwell yesterday. Perhaps it's a message to tell me how she is.'

Meg paced the floor as she waited. Her hand was on the door latch to go downstairs when she heard voices outside the window. Hurrying to look out, she saw Bess talking to the horse's rider. His broad-brimmed hat shadowed his face, but Bess's plump, pretty one was clearly visible. She seemed to be pleading with him, clinging to one of the stirrups as if she did not want him to go. Meg frowned. So Bess did know who he was after all. Why had she told a lie?

All of a sudden, the rider brushed Bess aside and jumped into the saddle. Meg caught a brief glimpse of his face, handsome in an arrogant way and framed with black hair. He looked a few years older than Tom.

Her heart raced. The rider fitted Tom's description of his fellow clerk, Ralph Fiddler. Now she thought of it, she had noticed him with Bess at the May Day celebrations. Mother had said she should reprimand Bess for allowing him to be too free.

A strong feeling of foreboding that she could not fully explain came over Meg. Afraid she might be noticed, she shrank back into the room. A few moments later, the clatter of the horse's hooves faded into the distance.

Chapter 4

All day Tom walked and by evening he had reached Winchester. Footsore and weary, he found an inn just inside the city walls. As he passed an open window looking into a steamy kitchen, the smell of rabbit pie drifted towards him. He tipped out the coins in the pouch and counted them. Ralph had not been generous but there was enough for a pie and a jug of ale. After that he would have to hope he was lucky enough to beg a piece of bread here and there to sustain him.

He found a quiet corner and settled down with his food and drink. The inn was warm and after he had filled his stomach, his eyelids drooped. He woke from a dream of Meg to find a burly man with a florid, pock-marked face shaking him.

'Wake up, lad. You can't stay here unless you've money for a room.'

'Wha'?'

The landlord scowled. 'Go on, out with you. The cold might sober you up.'

Tom struggled to his feet. 'I'm going.'

Outside, the moon dangled over the gabled roofs and countless stars burned fiercely in the clear sky. As Tom passed the row of loose boxes where the inn's customers stabled their horses for the night, a bay mare craned her head over her stall door and whinnied. He rubbed her nose and she nuzzled his hand, her ears twitching.

'I'd share my food with you if I had any, old lady, but I haven't.'

As if she understood, the mare lost interest and started to pull hay from the net hanging on the wall. A little further on, a wooden ladder led to an upper storey. Tom climbed it and found himself, as he had expected, in a hayloft, clean and dry with plenty of hay for bedding. The sweet meadow scent reminded him of how he and Meg had played in the fields together when they were children. What was she thinking now? He couldn't blame her if she hated him. His only hope was that she would not believe he had abandoned her of his own free will. The words of the last poem he had written for her repeated in his head and he groaned. If only he had been able to give it to her. Unworthy as it was, it would have been a token of his love and might have pleased her. But it was too late now.

A chill came over him. The baker back in Salisbury would surely go through the possessions he had left behind to see if there was anything worth selling to cover the unpaid rent. Suppose he found it? But no, the poem didn't name Meg. It might have been addressed to anyone. The baker would suspect nothing. Scooping a pile of hay together, he lay down and pulled some more of it over him. He closed his eyes and soon he drifted into sleep. His last thoughts were of Meg.

*

When he woke the next morning, he stared at the beamed ceiling for a long moment before, with a heavy heart, he remembered where he was. He scraped wisps of hay from his hair and coughed up the chaff that had settled in his throat overnight. If only he had something to drink.

He slid down the ladder and peered out cautiously. Two travellers wearing crimson and green doublets and black cloaks trotted into the yard and a groom ran forward to take their horses. Tom waited until the men had swaggered off into the inn before he emerged. He was starving but he dared not follow them in case the landlord recognised him.

38

He thought wistfully of last night's rabbit pie as he made his way past the back entrance of the kitchens towards the street. A tantalising smell of fresh baking wafted from the open door. Just inside it, he noticed a tray of loaves cooling on a shelf. Surely no one would miss one? His heart thudding, he grabbed the nearest. It was so hot he almost dropped it at first then, quickly tucking it under his arm, he hurried away into the street.

That night and the next, he slept under hedges by the roadside, and woke in the morning with his clothes and hair damp with dew. By afternoon, clouds the colour of pewter scudded in from the west, bringing hours of heavy rain that soaked him to the bone and turned the rutted roads to a sea of mud.

Most of the time in his days of walking, his thoughts were of Meg, but sometimes they turned to Ralph and anger flooded through him. A wild desire to return to Salisbury and confront Ralph seized him. It was only the thought of the likely consequence that stopped him from yielding.

There was fear too. Was it really only a wish to rid himself of Tom that drove Ralph? Could he be trusted to keep his word to leave Meg alone now? In Tom's darkest moments, the thought of her at Ralph's mercy tormented him. At other times, he held onto the belief that Ralph's self-confessed wariness of Edward Stuckton would keep her safe. It was, however, a bitter pill to swallow that it might be Stuckton's wealth and position alone that protected her; the realisation made Tom all the more wretched about his own helplessness.

By the fourth day, the blisters on his feet throbbed with every step and he had to stop to pack leaves inside his boots in the hope of easing the discomfort. Halfway through the morning, he came to a bustling town huddled beneath the ruins of what must once have been a great castle.

'Guildford,' a stallholder answered when he stopped in the marketplace to ask the name of the town.

'How much further is it to London from here?'

The man scratched his chin with a calloused finger and considered for a while.

'Two days, maybe, if you walk fast.'

He turned to serve a customer and Tom looked hungrily at the truckles of cheese set out on the stall. A small piece remaining from one of them was very close. After glancing around to see if anyone was watching and then again at the stallholder, who was still talking to his customer, Tom whisked it away and hurried off. For a few minutes, he felt breathless, expecting a hand on his shoulder, but none came. He was not sure whether to be ashamed or gleeful at his success.

As the day wore on, other roads joined the one he was on and the way became much busier. Carts and wagons trundled along piled high with bales of hay, sacks of flour and heaps of vegetables. Shire horses strained to pull great drays creaking under their loads of timber and bricks. Tinkers' carts rattled past laden with pots and pans and pedlars humped sacks of trinkets, lace and ribbons on their backs. Once he came up behind a team of drovers herding four hundred head or more of cattle and had to squeeze his way past, his nose wrinkling at the smell of dung and warm, cuddy breath. It seemed as if London was a huge maw sucking in the produce of the land for miles around.

Eventually, the meadows and market gardens on either side gave way to sparsely wooded lanes, where decaying hovels sheltered between the trees. Soon the buildings stood close together and the trees disappeared entirely. Ragged children with wary eyes and dirty faces scampered in and out of doorways and skinny dogs and cats scavenged in piles of rubbish. Here and there, towers of rickety wooden scaffolding swarmed with workmen building larger houses than the hovels around them, but many appeared to be no sturdier than the scaffolding.

All at once, there seemed to be more people than ever, all going in the same direction with an air of excitement.

'Over here, sweetheart!' The stout woman who had called out slipped her tattered dress off one shoulder exposing a pendulous breast. She winked. 'What's your hurry, my lovely? Plenty of time to see the fun.'

Tom frowned. He had no idea what she meant.

With a hoot of laughter, she got up and waddled towards him and he realised she was drunk. 'I'll be on m'back all night when it's over,' she slurred, 'but stay awhile and you can have first pick at the lock.'

He flushed; that at least was clear. Before he had time to get away, she grabbed his hand and clamped it over her puckered nipple. 'Don't be shy.'

He dodged around her and hurried on.

'Not good enough for you, am I?' she yelled at his retreating back. 'Fuck yourself then, country boy.'

Tom winced. Did he look such a bumpkin? A feeling of despair came over him. He had not only lost Meg, but he had also been a fool to think he could make his way in London. Sweat beaded his forehead and, like malevolent giants, the houses on either side of the lane towered over him, narrowing the sky to a slit of blue.

The crowd was enormous now, driving him forward as if he were a piece of flotsam on a powerful wave. It was hard to keep his feet from slipping on the slimy ground and his ears rang with the din around him. A girl emptied a chamber pot from an upper window and he jumped out of the way to avoid the stinking contents.

'Watch where you're going,' a thickset, heavily bearded man growled. 'Or I'll black your eye for you.' Muttering an apology, Tom wove round him and hurried on. Then, just as he thought he could go no further, a burst of light dazzled him.

The sight before him took his breath away. A huge expanse of water, far broader than any he had ever seen, glittered in the sunshine. He had heard of the Thames but had never imagined it would be so wide or so filled with boats. A great tide of people poured out of the surrounding lanes, all heading east along the muddy strand. He had no choice but to join them. Swept along, he marvelled at the wonders on the opposite bank: the vast silhouette of a cathedral that outdid even Salisbury's; magnificent houses and palaces with gardens running down to the river and landing stages festive with bright flags. Amid the general commotion, street vendors shouted out offers of ale and hot pies. The aroma of freshly baked pastry rekindled Tom's hunger with a vengeance.

Up ahead, a huge stone bridge, supporting a jumble of tottering buildings, spanned the river. People hung from the windows, calling out to the boatmen below. Above the rooftops wheeled hundreds of large, black birds that from time to time swooped down to rest on poles set up along the bridge's parapet. As Tom came closer, he peered at them curiously then wished he had not. The poles were crowned with human skulls. The eye sockets were empty but in places flesh was still attached to the bone. The crowds swept him onto the bridge as he averted his eyes from the ghoulish sight. The cobbles were slippery with mud and waste; he felt his feet slide and he struggled to stay upright, terrified that if he fell he would be trampled. Suddenly, he felt a slight tug at his belt. Looking down, he saw a small brown hand, its ragged nails rimmed with dirt.

'No you don't!' He snatched the boy's wrist.

'Lemme go, I didn't take nothing.' The boy's grubby face screwed up in a scowl of defiance. He was skinny with lank ginger hair and dressed in filthy clothes. Ten or eleven perhaps, though it was hard to be sure. He must be desperate to risk a beating, or worse.

'If I had any money, I'd share it with you,' Tom said, feeling a surge of pity.

The boy stared at him for a moment then broke away. Soon, he was lost in the crowd.

On the north bank of the river, a huge, square building made of stone gleamed in the sunshine, pennants fluttering from its corner turrets. From its martial appearance, Tom guessed it must be the famous Tower of London. As he drew close, he felt awed by its forbidding, lofty walls. They dominated the open expanse of sloping ground in front of its massive gates.

On the left-hand side of this open space, a long stand draped with scarlet and black banners had been set up. In the middle, on a smaller platform, a broad-shouldered man wearing a black jerkin and black breeches waited. Tom could not see his face for it was covered by a black hood, but from his stillness it seemed he was unmoved by the hubbub around him. His right hand rested on the shaft of an axe.

Tom shivered. Now he understood the reason for the throng. There was to be an execution. He had never witnessed one before today.

Excited people were trying to push closer to the platform but a crescent of guardsmen battled to keep them back. Against the duns and greys of the crowd, the guardsmen's scarlet coats made a startling splash of colour.

A drum roll silenced the crowd and all eyes turned to the gates. A party of three richly dressed men walked slowly out into the yard and took their places on the long stand. Moments later, another drum roll sounded but this time, the men who came out from the Tower were shabby and jostled along by guards. The younger of the two held his head high but the cries and protestations of the other man were pitiful to hear.

The group climbed the steps onto the platform. The terrified man redoubled his struggles as two guards dragged him to a tall post but his screams were inaudible now, drowned by catcalls and whistles from the crowd. The captain of the guard conferred with the executioner for a few moments then barked an order to his men. They hauled one of their victim's arms above his head and tied his hand to the post. His body went limp and his head lolled. Tom's blood froze as the executioner advanced. Something in his hand glinted in the sunlight. When he raised it, the shape was clear. It was a heavy hammer, like the ones Tom had often seen farriers use at home. In his other hand, he held a large, iron nail.

'What have those men done?' Tom asked a man standing beside him.

'Don't you know?'

Tom shook his head.

'Treason. Now shut your trap and let me watch. Topcliffe's the best there is. You don't often get the chance to see him at work.'

The noise from the crowd died away and, in the silence, a wail broke from the prisoner: a high, thin, eerie sound like the howling of the north wind. With a single blow, the executioner, Topcliffe, drove the nail into his victim's hand, skewering it to the post. The prisoner writhed and screamed.

Topcliffe turned to his audience and pulled a long knife from his belt. He drew the blade slowly through his fingers then tested it against his thumb.

Tom saw flushed, eager faces around him. His neighbour licked his moist, red lips. Tom closed his eyes as a gasp like a wave ebbing over shingle swept through the crowd. When he opened them, the prisoner lay limp at the base of the post, blood pumping from the frayed stump where his hand should have been. Blood also dripped from the severed hand still nailed to the post. With the edge of his knife, Topcliffe levered out the nail and brandished the hand in front of his victim's eyes before holding it up to show the onlookers.

Tom fought down nausea. He was sweating but the scene had an awful fascination that he could not resist.

A sharp nudge threw him off balance. 'Watch yourself, lad,' his neighbour scowled. 'If you're going to spew up, do it somewhere else.'

The younger prisoner was silent as he was led forward. A lump rose in Tom's throat. The man looked only a few years older than he was and seemed so dignified. He bowed his head to allow the executioner to place the noose around his neck. The other end of the rope was thrown over the blood-streaked post's crossbeam.

Topcliffe adjusted the noose with deft hands then stood back and gave the signal. With a crash, a trap door opened beneath the man's feet and the rope went taut. As his body thrashed convulsively, Tom willed his agony to be over.

'Old Topcliffe'll do it now,' Tom's neighbour muttered.

Topcliffe stepped forward and pulled the prisoner clear of the trapdoor then sliced through the rope. The man slumped to the ground, his arms and legs jerking as the guards heaved him across the platform and lifted him onto a low table. There, four guards held his arms and legs while one by one, Topcliffe picked up the instruments lying at the foot of the table and studied them. At last he selected a cleaver and, taking a pace backwards, lifted it above his head. It came down with such force on the man's ribcage, Tom was sure he heard the bones splinter. Pity and horror overwhelmed him.

Topcliffe took up a short, broad knife and set to work again. He might have been one of the butchers at the Salisbury shambles, ripping the guts from a pig. Soon his arms were scarlet to the elbows and the smell of blood and excrement filled the air. Tom's head reeled. Through a haze, he saw Topcliffe hurl the entrails into a glowing brazier nearby and go back to work on the groaning man. Blood was everywhere, pooled on the table and dripping onto the floor. How could there be so much blood in one man?

Ignoring curses and blows, Tom turned and blundered through the crowd. He just managed to get clear of it before he doubled over.

As the haze cleared, he heard a wheezing voice nearby. 'All right, lad?' the question came from an old man sitting on a wooden bench. The wrinkles on his face deepened as he gave a gummy smile. 'Your first, is it?'

Tom swallowed the bile in his mouth and nodded.

'You'd better sit a bit.'

His legs shaking, Tom tottered to the bench. 'What did they do?' he asked after a while.

'The first one was a printer up Cheapside way. Swore he only printed Catholic pamphlets to stop his wife and thirteen children from starving. The other one wrote and paid for them, so no mercy for him.' He lapsed into silence for a few moments then cleared his throat and spat out a gobbet of phlegm. 'Always a pleasure to watch Topcliffe work,' he remarked. 'Artist he is. I'd have been up there at the front if my legs were up to it.'

A crafty look came into his eyes. 'Occurs to me you might like to buy an old man a jug of ale for helping you?'

'Helping me?'

The old man scowled. 'Well, get off my bench then – puking like a green girl – no gratitude.'

'This one giving you trouble, granddad?' A broad-shouldered fellow tapping a cudgel against his meaty hand loomed into Tom's vision. Tom didn't wait for the reply. He stumbled off into the crowd praying he would not be followed.

He took the first turning he came to and found himself in an alley bounded by high walls. It seemed to lead nowhere except to a crumbling tenement at the far end, but as he retraced his steps, he noticed an archway to his right. Through it he saw another tenement on the far side of a dingy, rubbish-strewn courtyard. He was about to turn away when he heard a yell and saw a flash of movement. It was the scrawny boy with the ginger hair. One man had him pinioned by the arms and another wearing a green cap stood watching with a knife in his hand.

Tom took a few steps into the yard. 'Let him go,' he shouted. It was a shock to realise that the words came from his own lips.

'What's it to you?' Green Cap sneered. The knife glinted in his hand. Already Tom was regretting the impulse that had driven him to become involved.

'We don't need any bloody Samaritans getting in the way,' Green Cap went on.

A low-pitched moan came from the boy; his eyes rolled in his chalky face. On one side of his head, his hair was already dark with blood.

With a wolfish grin, Green Cap tapped his knife against his palm. 'Now, shall it be the ears or the nose?' he asked. 'Do you want to watch?'

Tom stood his ground. 'I said let him go.' Surreptitiously, he measured the distance between them. 'There are constables about. If I call out, you'll be taken,' he said, trying not to betray fear in his voice.

All at once, there were voices in the alley and he offered up a silent prayer of thanks. The man holding the boy shuffled nervously. 'Maybe we should let him go, Jeb?'

Green Cap leered at Tom. 'Why don't you come and get him?' He stood aside.

Tom shook his head. He had learnt enough from fighting with Ralph to know not to let an opponent get between him and his escape route. The voices grew louder.

'All right,' Green Cap said sourly, 'let him go.' He aimed his boot at the boy's backside as he broke free and started to run. 'But don't you forget I'll have you next time when your friend's not about,' he shouted.

'Quick,' Tom muttered as the boy reached him, 'before they change their minds.'

In the street, they ran until they reached the place of execution once again. The crowds were already melting away and no one gave them a second glance. Tom took the boy over to a horse trough and, scooping up some water in his palms, splashed it on the place where his hair was bloodied. The boy yelped. 'It hurts.'

Tom peered at the exposed gash. 'It doesn't look too deep. You'll live.'

The boy pushed his wet hair out of his eyes, 'Thank you,' he mumbled.

*

47

After the brightness outside, it took Tom a few minutes to accustom himself to the dingy basement tavern. Smoke from the damp logs in the fireplace rasped his throat. The boy pushed him over to an empty table and sat him down.

'Stay there, I'll be back.'

He returned with a hunk of bread and an onion. Producing a pocket knife, he sliced the onion into thin rings, put some of them on a piece of bread then offered it to Tom. 'For helping me,' he said.

Tom took the food and started to eat. The bread was no staler than he was used to and the onion was sweet and crunchy. 'Thank you, that was good,' he said when he had finished. 'My name's Tom. Are you going to tell me yours?'

The boy hesitated for a moment before he spoke. 'Jack, my name's Jack.'

'You don't sound very sure.'

'People call me lots of things, but I like Jack best.'

'All right, Jack it is.' Tom smiled ruefully. 'To tell you the truth, Jack, I think I may need your help more than you do mine. London's a lot bigger than I expected. I've nowhere to sleep and no money.'

'I got money.' Jack dug down into one of his battered boots and, with a chinking sound, brought out a small black velvet purse. 'They didn't think of looking there,' he said with a grin.

Tom frowned. No doubt it wasn't come by honestly, but now he had stolen himself, he had no business telling the boy off. In any case he had had enough punishment for one day.

'I didn't steal it,' Jack said defiantly. 'The old codger was asking for someone to take it off him.'

Tom raised an eyebrow at this piece of logic.

'You ate the food,' said Jack with a scowl.

'I know, and I'm grateful, really I am.'

Jack grinned. 'There's enough to pay for a proper bed tonight and more food tomorrow.'

'Don't you have anyone who looks after you?' Tom asked and, seeing the grin leave Jack's face, immediately regretted it.

'I will,' Jack said, recovering, 'just as soon as my dad comes for me. My dad's a general. He's fighting the Spanish in the Low Countries. He's the most important man in the whole army and my ma, she's a great lady,' his voice faltered, 'but she had to go away.' He glowered. 'It's true, it is. Don't you look at me so queer.'

'Sorry.'

Jack's face brightened. 'So you'll come?'

'Yes.'

Out in the street, night was drawing in. A swaying man relieved himself against the wall of the tavern then tottered away into the gloom. Smoke curled from every chimney, filling the air with particles of soot and making it hard for Tom to see where Jack was leading him. But trusting the boy seemed the best choice he had, so he followed.

Chapter 5

On Whit Sunday, Salisbury's market square rang with the sound of Morris bells. Birch boughs decked the cathedral and the city churches, but Meg's heart was heavy. There was no news of Tom and she missed him sorely.

She noticed that Bess too seemed wretched and, remembering how she had seen them together in the courtyard, she suspected Ralph Fiddler was the cause of her distress. In the weeks after William Kemp's death, he was often at Stuckton Court but there was little doubt in Meg's mind that it was not to seize any opportunity to meet Bess. He seemed to spend every hour there talking in private with Edward. Once, when she and Bess met Fiddler leaving the house as they returned from a visit to market, the way Bess hunched her shoulders and turned away like a whipped dog told its own story.

In June, the weather turned dull and wet. Edward left for the market at Dorchester and Meg was alone with only the servants for company. When two days of foul weather confined her to the house, her spirits sank to their lowest ebb.

Sat in her small parlour, she listened to the steady drumbeat of the rain on the windowpanes and thought of Tom. It couldn't be true that he was a murderer. He would never commit such a terrible crime. But then why had he left Salisbury? Was it because he knew he would be charged or was there some other reason? And what was he doing now? If he still loved her, couldn't he have found some way of sending a message to tell her where he was? Surely if he had been arrested, Edward would have mentioned it? Perhaps he was already forgetting her and making a new life.

Tears filled her eyes and she felt ashamed of her angry resentment. If they could not be together, was it not far better that he was happy without her? But it was so hard to give up her dreams.

A mud-caked messenger came from Edward to tell her he would be delayed a week. A flooded river had prevented him visiting some land he planned to buy and he intended to wait until the difficulty was past. Wryly, Meg reflected that even her mother's company might have been better than this loneliness, but Anne Bailey claimed to suffer from a weakness of the chest and never ventured abroad unless the sun shone.

On the third day, to Meg's relief, strong winds drove the rain away to the west. The morning was blustery, but by afternoon, soft breezes and azure skies returned. Filled with longing for fresh air, she changed her pretty slippers for riding boots and fastened a cloak over her dress. Bess had gone to help in the kitchens for the afternoon and she left her there. What harm could there be in riding out alone? She would not go far, and besides, uncharitable as she felt for thinking it, Bess's glum face would do nothing to lift her spirits.

'Shall I come with you, m'lady?' the groom asked when she ordered him to saddle her chestnut mare, Spirit.

'No, I prefer to ride alone today.'

His brow furrowed. 'Master Stuckton would not like it, m'lady.'

'Master Stuckton is not here, and he would like it even less if you disobeyed me,' she snapped. Grumbling, the man disappeared to fetch the mare.

Confined too by the rain, Spirit backed and skittered as the groom tacked her up, her eyes rolling.

Meg caught the bridle and stroked the mare's velvety muzzle. 'Hush, you want to be off but be patient; we will be soon.' The groom tightened the girth and led the mare to the mounting block. Sat side-saddle, Meg gathered up the reins then waited while he adjusted the stirrups and handed her the whip.

'Don't look so anxious, Gabriel. I shall be perfectly safe. I've ridden since I was a child, you know.'

'But the ground is treacherous after so much rain, my lady.'

'Then I promise I shan't go far.' She smiled and, touching the whip to Spirit's flank, she trotted away.

It was glorious to be free of the house. She rode towards the city, admiring how the mellow stone of the cathedral glowed in the sunshine. In New Street, she cast a wistful glance at Kemp's house as she passed by, then urged Spirit on again to cross the river at Crane Street Bridge. The water gurgled along under the arches, its swift-flowing current smoothing out long, emerald skeins of waterweed.

The road became a track that led out into open meadows. As she urged Spirit into a gallop, the wind smacked colour into Meg's cheeks. In the old days, she and Tom had ridden together like this without a care in the world, sure of what the future held for them. For a few moments, exhilarated by speed, she forgot everything that had happened since, but then cold reality returned and tears misted her eyes. Shivering, she pulled the horse up near a stand of silver birch and Spirit bent her head to crop the grass. Meg fought down the lump in her throat. She must not give up. Whatever Tom's reasons for leaving Salisbury, she had to keep faith that one day, all would be well.

The stable yard was quiet when she returned and Gabriel was nowhere to be seen. She leant forward and patted Spirit's neck. 'He can't have gone far, old lady. He's probably dozing in the hayloft, the idle good-for-nothing.' She dismounted and led the mare along the row of stalls to the barn, but there was still no sign of the groom, only the old cob no one rode any more who whinnied when she saw

Meg and Spirit then went back to pulling hay out of the net hanging on her stable wall.

Spirit whinnied in return and pawed the ground.

'You're hungry, are you?' Meg smiled. 'Never mind, you'll have your hay soon. We won't wait for Gabriel, but I'll have sharp words with him when I do find him.'

She led Spirit to her stall and took her in. The mare tossed her head and her bit jangled. Meg made a low, soothing noise as she steadied Spirit's head and lifted off the bridle. In the tack room, she hung it on a peg then found a net and stuffed it with hay.

When she returned, Spirit pricked up her ears and started to munch happily. Meg looked at the saddle. It was heavy but she did not want to leave it on until Gabriel reappeared, for Spirit needed a rub down.

'Lucky I know how to do it,' she muttered crossly, unbuckling the girth. She heaved the saddle off and with difficulty carried it to the tack room. On the way back, she heard a noise as she passed the barn.

'Gabriel? Is that you?'

Inside the doorway, she peered through the gloom. Had something moved in the shadows or had she imagined it? No one answered her. Perhaps it was only a rat or a mouse, but as she turned to walk away, she heard another rustle, closer this time. She gasped as a strong hand gripped her elbow and spun her round. The next moment, she was looking into the eyes of Ralph Fiddler.

She wrenched her arm out of his grasp and backed away.

'Forgive me, Mistress Stuckton. I didn't mean to alarm you.'

Meg's nostrils flared. 'I was not alarmed, sir. I'm looking for Gabriel, our groom. Have you seen anyone about?'

Ralph shook his head. 'Can I be of assistance?'

'No, thank you. Gabriel can deal with Spirit.'

He gave a low laugh. 'If he was here, but as he's not, why not let me help you?'

'No.'

She tried to pass him but he matched her step. Her heart hammered so loudly she was afraid he must hear it. She took a deep breath to steady her voice. 'Master Fiddler, let me pass.'

His arm snaked around her waist and his free hand covered her mouth.

Meg's legs turned to water. Her cloak slid to the floor as he pushed her up against the barn wall. She felt rough stone against her back.

He stooped, his lips brushing her neck. 'Your bed must be cold without Tom Goodluck. I could warm it for you.'

She jerked her head to one side and sank her teeth into his ear. With a curse, he recoiled, but before she had time to run, he grabbed her again.

'So you have a temper. Be careful, madam. If you cross me, you'll be sorry.'

'You're mad. How dare you insult me like this. My husband will have you flogged.'

'I doubt it. Not when he sees what I have to show him. I've had my suspicions for a long time and now I have proof. Tom has an aptitude for poetry, I'll grant him that – his protestations of love are very touching – but since you are the subject of them, your husband may take a different view. I imagine most men don't like to read of the pleasures enjoyed by others in their wives' beds.'

'You wouldn't dare—' Meg stopped, furious she had allowed herself to be so easily trapped. She wanted to strike him and wipe the smile from his face but she knew antagonising him was likely to do more harm than good. He might be trying to trick her but if he had really found a poem to her in Tom's lodgings, he was a dangerous enemy. Oh, how could Tom be such a fool when he had always been so adamant she must be careful?

'That's better,' Ralph murmured, loosening his grip a little. 'I don't want to hurt you, and believe me you are well rid of that scoundrel.'

With a struggle, she recovered her composure. 'I have no idea what you mean. Tom Goodluck is a stranger to me. I cannot be blamed for a young man's foolish fancies, and there are many women with the name Meg.'

'A stranger, my lady? You surprise me. I believe you were once far from strangers. Indeed, wasn't there some expectation you would be married? Tom's description of you is admirably exact as well as passionate. When your husband reads the poem, I think he will find it hard to credit your feelings for each other have changed. There was a letter too. I imagine Tom's carelessness in leaving such private things for anyone to find was due to his anxiety to avoid arrest.'

Meg's heart pounded.

'Some men would take you now,' Ralph said softly, bringing his face close to hers. 'But I'm not a brute and you will learn to love me.' He caressed her throat. 'You've only known an old man and a boy. A beautiful woman deserves more.' He grinned. 'I bear a passing resemblance to your husband. When you are with child, he will never know he has me to thank for doing his duty for him. After he's in his grave, I'll make you my wife, and we can enjoy his estates together.'

He took her chin in his hand and tilted her face up to his. 'Think on it, madam. Accept my proposal and you look forward to a continued life of riches and ease. Turn it down and be assured, I shall bring about your ruin.' He smiled. 'Such a lovely face – go now, I'll come to you tonight.'

*

In her room, Meg flung herself on the bed, shaking. She was lost. One part of her hated Tom for abandoning her. Even if he had been forced to leave Salisbury, why had he not taken her with him?

A face came into her mind: Bess. Ralph had mentioned suspicions. Had Bess guessed something was going on and blabbed to him? Was it the poem and the letter that had

55

given her away? Whatever the case, she was powerless to save herself now. Challenging him was too great a risk to take. Edward's reaction was all too easy to imagine and she could not be sure her family would protect her.

A soft sound made her raise her tear-streaked face from the pillow. Bess stood beside the bed.

'Madam, are you ill?'

Meg was past dissembling. 'What is Ralph Fiddler to you, Bess?' she blurted out. 'Have you helped him? If you have, you are a fool. He doesn't care for you; he only wanted to use you.'

A look of horror and dismay came over Bess's face and she began to cry. Hardly able to make out her words, Meg jumped off the bed and shook her.

'Tell me!'

'I didn't mean to do any harm...' Bess's voice disappeared in sobs.

'Stop that! I want to know what you told him.'

Bess hung her head and heaved a shaky breath. 'I said I thought I'd seen Tom Goodluck in the orchard near your window early one morning.'

'Did Ralph promise you money?'

Weakly, Bess shook her head. 'He said he loved me and lovers didn't have secrets from each other. He laughed about how you and Master Tom were lovers just like him and me.' A catch in her throat stopped her and she dragged a hand across her eyes.

Meg tottered and sank back onto the bed. Her stomach felt hollow.

'Oh madam, I'm so sorry. I should never have believed him,' Bess said, her voice cracking, 'I should have known he never really cared for me. I wasn't good enough for him.'

A flicker of pity kindled in Meg; she reached for Bess's cold hand. 'You are far too good for him, Bess. Ralph Fiddler's a scoundrel.'

'What shall we do, madam?'

'There's only one thing to be done. We must escape before it's too late.'

Meg's words surprised even herself and Bess's jaw dropped. 'Escape, madam? But where would we go?'

'Anywhere, as long as it is far enough away for no one to follow us. Perhaps we could find Tom. If it's true he's gone to join the army, where would he go? We may not be too late to catch up with him.'

A look of concentration came over Bess's face and a few moments passed before she spoke. 'Steward Stephen said if he wanted to do that, he'd go to Plymouth. That's where the soldiers set out for the Low Countries from.'

'Do you know where Plymouth is, Bess?'

Bess's expression clouded. 'No, madam, but Stephen said you went by the Exeter road, and if the constables had been quicker to keep a watch on it, Master Tom might be caught and hanged by now.' She stopped, confused. 'I'm sorry, madam.'

Meg took a deep breath. She would not think of that. 'So we must go west.' The germ of a plan swelled in her mind. 'Help me cut off my hair then find me some old clothes like the footmen wear and a strip of linen to bind me. If anyone asks us, we are brother and sister, orphaned and looking for work. We shall have to walk. If we take Spirit, we might look too prosperous and draw attention to ourselves.'

She went to her embroidery basket and took out a pair of scissors. 'Here, use these.'

Bess hung back.

'Oh, stop looking like that, girl.' Meg grabbed a hank of hair and hacked through it. 'There, I've started, now finish it. And hurry – the gates close at sundown.'

Chapter 6

London
June–July, 1586

Tom woke to the peal of church bells. For a few moments, he forgot he was no longer in Salisbury but then the events of the last few days flooded back.

Jack's 'proper bed' had been a pile of straw in a gentleman's stables, where the ostler had let them sleep in return for the price of a quart of ale. The straw crackled as he reached over and shook Jack by the shoulder. In an instant, the boy was on his feet, fists raised.

'Easy! It's me: Tom.'

Jack rubbed his eyes, sneezed, and wiped his nose with the back of his grubby hand. 'We'd better get out of here 'fore he wants more money for not turning us in to the constables for trespass.'

'But you gave him money last night.'

Jack shrugged. 'Won't make no diff'rence.'

He would never get used to this place, Tom thought. Outside in the street, he found it impossible to walk more than a few steps without someone barging into him. Londoners must have some kind of dislike for their fellow men that they felt the need to walk straight through them. The noise too made his ears throb. In Salisbury, there were plenty of street sellers but here they were a thousand times more numerous, and all of them competing with each other to shout the loudest.

'Come on, do you want him after us?' Jack grabbed Tom's hand and tugged him into a warren of twisty, narrow alleys. Just as Tom's brain started to reel with confusion,

Jack stopped halfway along one of them. He rapped at a door then put his ear to the rough wood.

'It's all right,' he whispered, standing on tiptoe so his face was in front of the spyhole above the door knocker, 'she'll let us in soon.' Tom heard the sound of heavy bolts drawing back and the door opened.

'Where did you get to all night then? ' A frowsy woman with grey hair straggling from a soiled white cap blinked at the morning sunshine. 'If you want breakfast, you'd better have the money to pay for it.'

Jack grinned. 'Let us in, Janey. I got lots of money.'

She sighed. 'Don't tell me how you got it and watch what you say – him upstairs couldn't hold his drink last night. He'll have a sore head this morning and a nasty temper to go with it.'

They followed her into a room where the remains of a fire smouldered in the hearth. The ceiling was low and smoke had blackened the walls. On the earthen floor, a frayed rag rug provided the only hint of cheerfulness. Tom thought of the cosy kitchen at Oatmeal Lane and the baker's wife's gleaming pots and pans. From the top of the stairs that led out of this room came a stream of curses then a thud.

Janey scowled. 'I won't let him in again if that's his game.'

As heavy footsteps thumped on the stairs, she scuttled with surprising agility to the corner by the hearth and snatched up a broom. The corpulent, red-faced man who appeared shook his fist.

'I'm going and good riddance to the lot of you.' He pulled back his sleeve and stuck out a brawny arm marked with scarlet bumps. 'Your mattress was full of bed bugs and that little whore crawls with lice.'

The door slammed behind him and the tin mugs and plates on the table jumped.

A frightened girl crept down the stairs. A rapidly darkening bruise disfigured one side of her face, and her mouth oozed blood.

'Let me see.' In spite of the girl's protests, Janey prised open her mouth and looked inside. On the upper row of teeth, one was lopsided and the gum bled profusely. Janey wiggled it and the girl screamed and pushed her away.

'Jack, run to the tavern and get a tot of brandy. It'll have to come out.' Janey searched her garments for a penny and gave it to him with a tin mug. 'And don't you touch a drop on the way back.'

The girl huddled by the dying fire, weeping quietly. Tom felt sorry for her. Janey stroked her hair. 'Never mind, girl. I don't expect he'll be coming back and if he does, I'll make him wish he hadn't.'

She straightened up and looked over at Tom. 'So who are you?'

'Tom Goodluck.'

'I suppose if Jack brought you, you can stay.'

'Thank you.'

'You're not from round here by the sound of you.'

'I'm from Salisbury.'

'Where's that?' She frowned.

'In the west.'

'What do you want to be in London for?'

Tom hesitated: best not to tell the whole truth. 'I came to make my living in the theatre.'

'You young lads think there's a crock of gold there,' Janey said, shaking her head. 'Most of you end up running errands and holding the horses for the gentry while they go in and amuse themselves.' She shrugged. 'Don't look so miserable now. Perhaps you'll be one of the lucky ones. But summer's not the best time to try it, mind. If the sweating sickness breaks out like last year, all the theatres'll close.'

When Jack returned with the brandy, Janey wiped her hands on her apron.

'Now then, Bel, enough mizzling.' She held the tin mug to Bel's lips and forced her to drink. Bel squirmed when Janey reached into her mouth for the loose tooth, but the brandy had helped, the tooth came out easily and she only

60

gave a little yelp. Janey put the mug to her lips once more. 'Swill the rest round and spit it back in the mug,' she ordered. Bel did as she was told.

A wail rose from near the hearth. Janey shook Bel's shoulder. 'No dozing for you, you'd better see to the little 'un. I can't be doing everything.'

Reluctantly, Bel stood up and walked over to a wooden box. She lifted out a bundle swathed in shawls. Tom could just see a fuzz of yellowish-white hair and two small, wrinkled hands that seemed to want to claw their way out of their prison. Bel went back to her place by the fire and opened the front of her dress. Mewling like a kitten, the baby latched on to her nipple and began to suck.

'What're you staring at?' she asked, glowering. 'Don't they have babies where you come from?'

Tom felt his face warm. 'I'm sorry. I just wasn't expecting it.'

'Food's ready.' Janey tapped her wooden ladle against the side of the pot. It was only a thin mess of oats, but to Tom's hungry stomach, it was very welcome. With apparent relish, Jack shovelled his helping down and when Bel had finished feeding the baby, she ate hers cautiously, snuffling all the while. When the last morsel had been scraped from the pot and eaten, Jack handed over a penny. Janey slipped it into the pocket of her apron.

'You can come back and sleep by the fire tonight if you want. I can't promise any more to eat, though.'

Jack shrugged. 'We'll see.'

'Where d'you want to go?' he asked when he and Tom were back in the street.

'Some players came to Salisbury before I left and I spoke to their chief man. I think he might help me. I don't know if they're back in London yet but could we go and find out? The theatre's called The Unicorn.'

'I know it.'

As he followed Jack through the maze of streets and out of the city towards Shoreditch, Tom's pulse quickened with excitement, but when at last they reached The Unicorn, they found the round wooden building deserted. The limp flags depicting the mythical horned beast flapped listlessly against the poles on top of its four turrets. Tom's spirits sank.

'Maybe they'll be back in a few days,' Jack said cheerfully. 'You'll know when they are, 'cause they always blow the trumpets to show the play's about to start.'

On the way back to the city, Tom noticed a large, wooden building. The noise coming from behind its gates stopped him in his tracks. 'What's that?' he asked.

'Sackerson and Harry Hunks. Come on, let's go and watch.'

'Ha'penny each,' said the man at the gate. Jack pulled out a penny and the man tested it with his teeth before letting them in.

In a ring strewn with sawdust and surrounded by a paling fence, two black bears prowled around each other. Tom had seen dancing bears when the fairs came to Salisbury but compared with them, these were Goliaths. Both had scarred muzzles and one had a badly torn ear. Jack nudged Tom. 'That one's Harry Hunks. He won last time.'

Letting out a roar that made Tom jump, Harry Hunks reared up on his hind legs and crashed down on the other bear. Sackerson flung up his great head and with a snarl, sank his teeth into his attacker's throat. Soon all Tom could see was a whirling mass of black fur and slashing claws. The excited yells and cheers from the crowd grew louder as deep crimson patches darkened the ground.

At last, the fight slackened. Sackerson broke away and loped to the fence near where Tom and Jack stood. The bear's eyes were bloodshot and blood streamed from a great gash in his shoulder. He skulked against the fence as Harry Hunks prepared to charge.

Tom's gorge rose. He had always hated seeing any creature tormented and it was obvious this one was too weakened to fight any longer. Then to his relief, just as it seemed the bear's fate was sealed, a group of men rushed into the ring carrying a strong net. They threw it over Harry Hunks and in spite of the bear's struggles, managed to drag him over to a wheeled cage. The iron door clanged shut after him and they turned their attention to the cowed Sackerson. Collapsed on his belly in the dust, he was easily trapped with the net. When the men dragged him from the ring, the crowd hooted and clapped. Tom noticed for the first time that his shirt was soaked with cold sweat. He was glad of the animal warmth of the crowd as he followed Jack out into the street and on to a tavern nearby.

*

Days turned into weeks and Tom grew more accustomed to life in London. He earned a little money where he could and, at Janey's suggestion, came to live at the house in Angel Lane. To supplement the small income she made from taking in clothes to mend, he gave her a share of his earnings in return for his bed and board. There was still no sign of The Unicorn resuming business but he didn't give up hope.

One hot afternoon, Tom was in the yard at the tavern where he did a few hours' work each week, chopping wood for the ovens. The smell of resin was strong in the heat, it made his eyes water. He straightened his back and rested his axe against the woodpile, running his fingers under the damp collar that chafed his neck. The logs he had done should be enough to satisfy the landlord: time to collect his wages. If he was lucky, the landlord might throw in a free drink.

He went over to the stone horse trough and splashed his face then walked into the tavern. As he pushed his way through to the counter, a man turned to him. 'Watch where you're going, lad,' he said abruptly.

Tom opened his mouth to apologise then his heart missed a beat. 'Master Lamotte!'

'Yes, and you are—?'

'Tom Goodluck, sir – from Salisbury.'

63

'Ah yes, I remember. You're fortunate to find me. We should still be down in the country but the audiences are poor this year. People are tight for money. But I'm surprised to see you so far from home. Why didn't you come back for your play?'

'I wanted to,' Tom stammered. 'Please don't think I wasn't grateful.'

'So what brought you to London then?'

Desperately, Tom searched for a reply. He wasn't sure whether to admit to the truth.

'Never mind, I suppose it's none of my business. Your play wasn't bad, by the way. It needs some mending but I've read worse. Don't go getting your hopes up too high, but I may be able to do something for you, unless you've changed your mind, that is.'

A rush of joy overcame Tom; for a few moments, he was unable to speak.

'I see you haven't,' Lamotte grinned. 'Come, let's find a table where we can sit down. I'll buy you a drink and then we can talk.'

The tables in the front room were all taken. 'Go to the back,' Lamotte shouted in Tom's ear, 'there's usually room there.'

When they had found an empty table and sat down, Lamotte waved to one of the serving girls to bring them a jug of ale. Tom drained his cup in one go and wiped his lips. It was wonderful to ease his parched throat.

Lamotte refilled his cup. 'Well, are you going to tell me after all why you left home?'

On reflection, Tom decided he didn't look the kind of man to disapprove too strongly of a love affair. Perhaps it was the easiest thing to tell him. Haltingly, he began but he had not got far before Lamotte interrupted him.

'I can see you won't believe me yet,' he said, 'but you're better out of it, lad. A married woman's more trouble than she's worth, even if she is a beauty.' He grinned. 'Don't look so sorry for yourself. There are plenty of pretty girls in this city to help you forget her.'

Tom opened his mouth to protest but already Lamotte was not listening. His eyes roved around the tavern. 'There's a couple of men over there you'll soon know of if you get into the theatre. That one's James Burbage, who owns one of the playhouses, and the great mound of putrid flesh talking with him is Robert Greene. Very fond of Rhenish wine, pickled herrings and his own opinion which is that he's the finest writer of plays in London, nay, in the world. University man with no time for the rest of us.'

He broke off as a young man with a mild expression and prematurely receding hair that accentuated a high forehead approached the table where the two men sat. 'Now there'll be a bit of fun,' Lamotte muttered. 'That young fellow's new up to London like you and wants to make his way in the theatre. I hear he shows great promise. Goes by the name of William Choxper. Greene can't abide him, which is enough of a recommendation to most people.'

Tom felt numb. In Salisbury, it had been possible to believe his dreams might come true, but now he was here, it came home to him he was just one of many. How simple he had been not to realise there would be other men with the same ambitions as his, but probably more talent to achieve them.

'Are you going to give me an answer then?' Lamotte's voice cut through his dejection. 'You'd better make up your mind before I change mine. I've no room in the company for a mooncalf.'

Dismayed, Tom looked at Lamotte's stern face then saw that his black eyes twinkled. Throwing back his head, Lamotte guffawed. 'You've a face for tragedy, lad. I'll say that for you.'

'I'm sorry,' Tom stammered.

'You need to be a player to learn how to write plays properly. I'll give you two months' trial. What do you say to that?'

It was all Tom could do to stutter his thanks.

'You'll start with the small parts to see how you get on. If things go well, and you polish up your play to my satisfaction, I might give it a run for a night or two. Drink up. I should be getting over to the theatre now. You may as well come with me and start to make yourself useful. There's always plenty of work to do around the place.'

Chapter 7

Tom lifted the latch and called out a greeting. Janey looked up from her darning and nodded as he came in. 'I didn't expect you home yet.'

'I had to go down to the quays with some of the others to fetch the timber Lamotte ordered for the new seats. It was heavy work hauling it back so he gave us a couple of hours off before the performance tonight. Baltic oak it was, Lamotte says there's no English to be had at a good price since most of it went for building houses.'

He went over to the makeshift crib by the hearth and stroked the baby's head. It was marvellous to him how much little Hal had grown, even in the space of a few weeks. He lay on his back, chubby fists stretched above his head. His pink, dewy cheeks and blond curls reminded Tom of the angels in a painting he had once seen in Salisbury Cathedral.

'I've sent Bel and Jack out to try and buy some cloth to make a shift for him,' Janey remarked. 'The only time he stays still is when he's asleep. I shan't be surprised if he isn't crawling about soon. I've told Bel those rags she wraps him in won't be no good then.'

'Maybe Lamotte will let me play some of the bigger parts soon and I'll make more money.'

She smiled. 'You've helped us already, Tom, and we're very grateful, but you mustn't spend all your money on us.'

Tom went over to the table and took an apple from a bowl. 'What else should I spend it on?' he asked through a mouthful. 'You and Bel and Jack are the closest thing I have to family.'

A lusty bellow came from the crib and Janey frowned. 'Pick him up for me while I find something for him to eat.'

Hal butted Tom's chest with his head. 'That won't do you any good.' Tom took the bowl of gruel from Janey and tried to spoon some between Hal's lips. Most of it dribbled down his chin but what went in seemed to satisfy him and he squirmed to be let down. Tom put him on the floor and he crowed and kicked his feet in the air.

'He won't be a quiet one like my granddaughter,' said Janey. 'All for keeping herself to herself, she is.' She glanced at him. 'Bel's a good girl, you know, just a bit of an innocent, believing the promises some men make her.'

'Like the one who was here the first time I came?'

'And the soldier who got her with Hal, God rot him. But then she wouldn't be the first girl to make that mistake.'

She heaved herself out of her chair and grabbed Hal before he rolled into the embers of the fire. His face purpled and he squalled. Tom scooped him up and jiggled him on his knee until the crying turned to laughter.

'You're good with him,' Janey said with a smile. 'Just like Jack, but then he's always been on Bel's side. They could be brother and sister, those two. I remember when his ma died and I brought him here, how Bel used to cuddle and comfort him. That was eight summers ago and look at him now. He'll be taller than her in a year or two.'

'Who was his mother?'

'One of the girls at Henslowe's place.' Tom recognised the name of one of Lamotte's rival theatre managers who also owned several brothels. 'Jack can't have been much above three years old when she died.'

'When I first met him, he told me his mother was a great lady and his father a general.'

'And I'm the Queen of Arabia.'

Tom finished his apple and took another.

'There's some bread and a bit of cheese in the crock. You have that as well or you'll be starved afore you finish tonight.'

'It's all right. I'll get something at the theatre. You keep it for the three of you.'

He stood up. 'I'd better be off. See you later, Janey.' He rumpled Hal's curls. 'And you, little fellow, be good for Janey while I'm away.'

On the way to the theatre, Tom turned Janey's words over. From her remarks over the last few weeks, he knew what she was hoping. He sighed: Bel was not for him, but was he a fool not to look for another girl? Clearly Master Lamotte thought so.

Meg's face hovered in his mind. He wondered what she was doing now. Had she already forgotten him? Remembering the day of the May Fair and the smiles she gave her husband, Tom kicked at a stone in his path. Perhaps she was perfectly happy with her life after all and his leaving troubled her no more. After all, there were plenty more necklaces and fine clothes for Stuckton to give her. A rising tide of bitterness almost unmanned him then it ebbed, leaving him hollow with shame. It was too easy to blame her and unfair to wish her a wretched life because they had to be apart.

At The Unicorn, an actor was perched on the edge of the stage with his head bent over a sheaf of papers. He looked up. 'Lamotte'll skin me if I don't know these lines by tonight,' he groaned. 'He wants to see you, by the way. You'll probably find him backstage.'

Lamotte was supervising two men who were preparing the stage cannon.

'Ah, Tom, just the fellow. Will Pooley fell down drunk last night and cracked his head open.' Lamotte bundled a yellow wig and a midnight blue robe, spangled with golden stars, into Tom's arms. 'You're playing Juno,' he added, dumping a small stack of paper on top of the dress. 'These are your lines. You'd best be getting on with them. Don't look so worried; just speak clearly and try not to bump into anyone. Oh and here,' he fished a penny out of his pocket. 'Get a shave or the groundlings will hiss you off the stage.'

In the queue for the barber's chair, Tom scanned the lines. Fortunately, there weren't too many of them but it was a bigger part than the walk-ons he had done so far. The evidence of Lamotte's confidence in him made him happy. He mustn't let him down. Whatever else has gone wrong for me, Tom thought, I was lucky to fall in with him.

The barber took the penny, soaped Tom's face and scraped away expertly at the light-brown beard which had grown since he left Salisbury. Rinsed and dried, he got up to leave, glancing in the small mirror hanging by the door as he passed. He looked his old self once more. Before the shave, even Meg might not have recognised him at first sight. He had been rather proud of the beard though, perhaps he would grow another one someday.

A nearby church clock struck the hour. He quickened his pace. He didn't have long to learn his lines and work out how to put on the wig and dress.

*

Later that evening, when the performance had ended, Tom walked out with Lamotte into the courtyard separating the theatre from Shoreditch Street. Most of the food vendors had packed up their stalls and gone home but a cockle woman was sweeping up the shells her customers had discarded and stuffing them into a sack. Close by, the remains of a spit-roasted hog turned slowly over a fire, tended by a burly man. An apron spattered with cinders and grease covered his capacious belly.

Lamotte stopped. 'Evening, Ned.'

'Evening, Master Lamotte. Will you have some of this fine hog? The best meat in London, even though I say it myself.'

'Then I'll take some,' Lamotte said with a grin. 'And you'd better give my friend some too. He's had a hard night of it.'

Tom's mouth watered as the man carved thick slices of the succulent meat, slapped them between doorsteps of bread and handed them across the trestle. 'No charge,' he said.

'That's very good of you.'

'My pleasure.'

'How was business tonight?'

'Could be better, but no use complaining.'

Lamotte shrugged. 'It's the same everywhere. People feel the pinch and we suffer.'

'You never said a truer word, Master Lamotte. A merchant up from the West Country told me there's riots there over the price of food. A farmer who supplies him lost a dozen head of sheep to rustlers a few weeks back. It's a disgrace. Mark my words - times will get worse before they get better.'

'You're right about that. Well, good evening to you.'

'And to you, master.'

Out in the street they walked along munching in companionable silence.

'You did well with your speeches tonight,' Lamotte remarked when he had finished the last mouthful. 'But you'll have to practise walking in a dress. You gave a better impression of a calf with the staggers than the Queen of Olympus.'

Tom flushed. 'It was harder than I thought it would be.'

'Never mind, it raised a laugh, even if that wasn't quite what the author intended. Will Pooley's head will mend soon, you needn't do it for long.'

They turned in at the Dolphin. Lamotte led the way to his usual table in one corner and sat down. He took a tobacco pouch out of his pocket, crumbled a few dried leaves and packed them into the bowl of his clay pipe. Lighting a taper from the flame of the table candle, he puckered his lips around the pipe stem and drew a long breath. The tobacco

71

began to smoulder and glow. He leant back with a sigh of satisfaction.

'So, when shall I put on this play of yours?'

Tom's heart skipped a beat. 'You mean you think it good enough now? I don't know how to thank—'

'Most people want to know the price I'll pay before they thank me,' Lamotte chuckled.

'The price doesn't matter.'

Lamotte tapped the bowl of his pipe and an oaky smell drifted across the table. 'The price always matters, lad. Never sell yourself short, it gives the wrong impression. Shall we settle on a sovereign? We'll put it on in a few weeks' time and if it goes down well, I might be able to stretch to a bit more.'

It would have taken Tom many weeks to earn as much from William Kemp. A haze of delight warmed him.

'It's a good piece, but it remains to be seen whether audiences like it – you can never tell in advance. Your audience is an unpredictable beast, ready to lick your hand one minute and savage it the next.'

For a few moments, Lamotte directed his attention to his pipe. Tom took the opportunity to revel in silent glee.

'I expect your family will be glad for you,' Lamotte observed when at last the pipe drew to his satisfaction.

'They'll never know, I fear.'

Lamotte gave him an enquiring look.

Tom's brow furrowed. He didn't fully understand why he felt such an urge to confide in Lamotte. Perhaps because he had been kind about the play, but perhaps also because it was a long time since an older man had shown some sympathy for him.

'My mother died of the sweating sickness when I was fourteen.'

'Go on,' Lamotte prompted gently.

'After that, my father cared for nothing and neglected his business. He stopped going to Antwerp to strike his own bargains with the cloth merchants there and trusted all his negotiations to agents, who cheated him. I've heard people say he held on too long to the old ways of trading as well. By the time he died, everything had gone.'

Lamotte nodded. 'My father dealt in cloth too, but I was the youngest son of four and I wanted to make my own way, so I trained in the law and went into government service. I understand something of how the cloth business works, though. Life grew hard for the men in the provinces when the London Staple became so powerful.' He shrugged. 'The world changes and we must all change with it. Were your parents all the family you had?'

'I had a sister, six years older than me. She was already married to a Dorchester physician. He agreed to pay for me to be apprenticed to a local lawyer, but then he wanted nothing more to do with me.'

'And your sister obeyed him?'

'Yes.'

A serving girl came past with a jug of ale and Lamotte motioned her to refill their pewter mugs. 'Let us drink to better days, and the destruction of all Spaniards.' He drained his mug and banged it down on the table.

'I had a family once,' he said after a pause. 'A wife and a young son. I lived in Paris then. The city where I was born.'

He fell silent once more as if he had forgotten Tom was there. Tom waited for him to speak.

'You're too young to have heard of the St Bartholomew's massacre,' Lamotte said at last, 'but even though it happened fourteen years ago, the horror of it will be etched on my memory for ever. It started with a marriage, which should be a time of joy: the celebration of the union of the King of France's sister and the Huguenot prince, Henry of Navarre. Most of the Huguenot nobility were in Paris for the occasion.'

'Huguenot?'

'Forgive me, the Huguenots are what you call Protestants in England. In France, though, their situation is

73

not the same as it is here. They are less powerful than the Catholics and the king only pretends to champion them while really he's terrified of offending the Catholics.'

Tom frowned. He felt very ignorant. In Salisbury no one talked of France except to complain that the French were taking away trade in good English cloth with their silks and satins. He listened as Lamotte went on.

'The leader of the Huguenots, a man called de Coligny, was invited to attend a meeting with the king and his council at the Palais du Louvre. Even though it was high summer, the roads in Paris were deep in mud and rutted by carriage wheels. When de Coligny made the journey to the Louvre, he wore overshoes to protect his fine footwear. Those overshoes saved his life. At the very moment when he bent down to adjust the straps on them, a shot was fired at him from the window of a house nearby. The bullet shattered his left elbow but did no further damage. His men carried him home bleeding.'

Lamotte paused again. His pipe lay smouldering and forgotten on the table. Tom had never seen him so serious before. His usual jocular tone was quite gone.

'Two days later, at midnight, the bells of St Germain rang out. It was the signal the Catholics were waiting for to begin the killing. De Coligny was one of the first to die, stabbed as he lay convalescing in his own bed. The killers flung his body out of the window into the street where men waited to hack off his head and drag his body away. They hung it in chains on the public gibbet at Montfaucon.'

Tom remembered the cruel scene he had witnessed at Tower Hill and shuddered. 'But didn't you say that the king's sister was to marry a Huguenot prince?' he asked. 'Did the king do nothing?'

Lamotte grimaced. 'As I said, he was terrified of the Catholics. Royal guards were supposed to protect de Coligny but they stood aside and watched him die. After that, the Catholic mob was mad for blood. Henry of Navarre escaped, but many of the other leaders lost their lives.

'Then the mob turned its attention to lesser folk like my family. White crosses were daubed on the doors of Huguenot houses to make sure the mob knew where to go. The bloodshed went on for three days and by the end of it, more than three thousand lay dead in the streets: men and women, young and old, slaughtered without mercy. Even children were not spared. The Catholic butchers laughed and joked as they went about their work, stopping to refresh themselves at taverns when they tired. The streets were crimson with blood. It was as if the rivers of Hell ran through them and their banks were heaps of corpses, blackened by flies. The stench of death was unbearable.'

'Were your wife and son spared?' Tom asked quietly, fearful of the answer.

'On that first morning, we didn't expect the horrors to come, so I went as usual to my work at the Palais de Justice, but by midday, everyone left and hurried home. I ran to mine. There was a man I believed would help us if we could just reach him, but our door was kicked in and the house had been ransacked. My wife and son were nowhere to be seen.' Tears gleamed in Lamotte's eyes. 'I searched for hours, hiding from the soldiers when I had to, sickened when I witnessed them cutting down their victims, and sickened too by my own powerlessness to help those tormented souls.'

Tom waited for him to go on.

'When it was over, I clung to the hope I might still find Amélie and Jean, but I never did.' His head drooped. 'Once I loved Paris, she seemed to me the greatest city on earth, but after that night, I hated her for taking away the family I loved.'

For a few moments, they sat in silence. Tom tried without success to think of words of comfort then Lamotte picked up his pipe and reached for another taper. Suddenly, he was brisk as if he wished he had not said so much.

'So I came to England,' he said, in between drawing on his pipe. 'And she is my country now.' He shrugged. 'I started a new life in the theatre. People say lawyers and actors are not so far apart. It was hard at first, I won't deny it. The English don't always welcome foreigners. But I have tried to make myself into an Englishman to pacify them. Forgive me, it's better not to dwell on the past, we can't change it although perhaps we can learn from it.'

He caught the elbow of the serving girl who passed. 'Bring us more ale.'

She nodded.

He leant back in his chair and blew out a puff of smoke. 'After that we should be on our way. I want to be up early tomorrow to make sure those lazy carpenters hurry up with the new seating. I'm losing money every day it's not ready.'

They parted outside the tavern and Lamotte walked home to Throgmorton Street. A sleepy servant unbolted the heavy oak door. 'A message came for you, master,' he said.

Lamotte took off his cloak and hat. 'Where is it?'

'In your study, master.'

As he mounted the creaking stairs, Lamotte noticed the dust at the back of the treads. For the second time that day, he thought sadly of his wife. Amélie had never allowed anything to remain dusty or unpolished. The house in Paris had smelt of beeswax and lavender. This house was a bachelor's abode, the furniture dulled by neglect, the rugs frayed and the walls scuffed. Was it a wonder when the place had no mistress?

He shook his head with a sigh. Occasionally he had come across a woman who might have changed that, but nothing ever came of it – perhaps he had not really wanted it to.

In his study, he sat down at his desk. This room at least was cosy, with its dark oak panelling, its shelves crammed with papers and books and a chair that welcomed his weary bones like an old friend.

The message was from Sir Francis Walsingham. Folding the paper, Lamotte leant back in his chair and stroked his chin. The spymaster rarely summoned him at short notice unless it was urgent but it was too late to set out for Barn

Elms tonight. There would be no boats going upriver. He would leave at daybreak.

Chapter 8

The tide had just turned as the ferry slipped from its moorings and set off upriver. The air was humid and oppressive and the stench of the murky, rubbish-strewn water was strong. Lamotte pulled his cloak over his nose to shut it out. He hoped this visit would be worth leaving his bed for.

As he always did when The Unicorn's company travelled into the country, he had kept his ears open for any information Walsingham might find useful, but he had made his report weeks ago and there had been nothing the old spymaster seemed to find important, although it was always hard to read his mind. Presumably something new had arisen. He hoped it would not involve too much work. With business flagging, he needed to devote as much time as possible to the theatre.

He sighed. In truth, he had no right to resent Walsingham's demands. Where would he be now if Walsingham had not helped him to get out of Paris after St Bartholomew's Day and given him money to set up a new life? Nothing came without a price.

Of course by that time, he had already been in thrall to Walsingham for several years. He remembered the first approach from one of the spymaster's agents: an affable fellow who had struck up an acquaintance with him in a tavern one hot July evening over a bottle of good burgundy. He had been smarting at the insults one of the local gangs of Catholic youths had hurled at him. The agent had stopped him doing anything foolish – there were five of them and only one of him.

Lamotte remembered how subtly matters had progressed from there. First the exploration of his loyalties, then the discreet questions about what work he did at the Palais de Justice; what knowledge his job made him privy to and what else he might be able to ascertain by stealth. Like a moth to the flame, he went a little further and a little further until the information he was passing on would have hanged him if it had come to light.

He had to admit, his motives were not entirely pure. Yes, he was serving the Huguenot cause, but he also enjoyed the spice of danger and excitement. Now, he thought, in my soberer years, spying seems a grubbier trade than it did when I was young.

The river was already busy with other craft and noisy with the shouts of boatmen. Frequently, the rowers were forced to slow in order to avoid ramming or being rammed. Soon, the massive bulk of St Paul's came into view, towering over the spires of the city churches at its feet. Further on, the grand houses of the rich and powerful sprawled along the north bank, imposing edifices with many courtyards and fine gardens running down to the river.

At the bend by the village of Wandsworth, the rowers veered towards the north bank to avoid the mud flats thrown up by the annual floods. The stench of river mud was even worse here but when they drew level with the wharves at Putney the air sweetened. On the bank, lighter men jostled to load boxes and bales of goods onto the boats going down to the city. The boat docked and Lamotte scrambled out onto the quayside. The last part of the journey to Barn Elms provided a pleasant walk and he would be glad to stretch his legs.

When he reached the gates, he paused for a moment to look at the house before him. It was an old-fashioned, modest one compared with the palatial residences of men like Lord Treasurer Burghley, and Sir Christopher Hatton, the Lord Chancellor. Lamotte suspected Walsingham had made less money out of his office than most of his peers, but his tastes were also more frugal. On occasion too, he had hinted that Queen Elizabeth's notorious parsimony often forced him to spend his own money on maintaining his network of spies.

Lamotte skirted the sheep-cropped lawn, taking advantage of the cover of a narrow belt of trees to reach a side entrance. In his study, Walsingham sat at a desk piled high with papers.

Bowing, Lamotte doffed his black velvet cap. 'Forgive me, Sir Francis, I didn't receive your message yesterday until it was too late to set off.'

'It's no matter, sit down. May I offer you refreshment?'

Lamotte shook his head. He noticed the slight tremor in Walsingham's right hand and the shadows around his eyes. Clearly, something was amiss.

'Very well, to business. I wish to talk to you about Antony Babington.'

Lamotte nodded. A few years ago Walsingham had asked him to befriend the young aristocrat and report on his movements. Babington had been an attractive, intelligent young man whose personable qualities had recommended him to Mary, Queen of Scots, when he was a page in a house where she was imprisoned. Walsingham had suspected him of carrying secret letters for her. Not long afterwards, Queen Mary was removed to Chartley, a manor house in Staffordshire, where security was better enforced.

'Do you have reason to suspect him again?'

'Yes. I have my doubts he is particularly dangerous acting alone, but he may be part of a group that poses a serious threat. Five years ago, a priest named John Ballard landed in England. He was swiftly discovered and arrested but after a few months in prison, he escaped with another priest and fled the country. Nothing was heard of him for a while then in March this year he was seen supping with Babington at an inn near Temple Bar. In May, they left England together and I have since learnt that they visited Mendoza, the Spanish ambassador, in Paris. When they returned to England, Ballard was overheard boasting he had persuaded Spain to provide sixty thousand troops to support an uprising.'

'A formidable threat.'

'As I say, it may well not be true, but a lie can be as dangerous as the truth if it has the effect of attracting more men to Mary's cause.'

'So Queen Elizabeth would be in greater danger than before?'

'Indubitably.'

'Did you have Babington and Ballard arrested?'

'I wanted to know more first. Since Mary has been in the charge of Sir Amyas Paulet at Chartley, everyone who comes and goes there is searched, even the laundresses, although initially Paulet's scruples made him loath to order it. It was a necessary precaution but it meant that the flow of correspondence between Mary and her supporters dried up and their suspicions were aroused. I wanted that to change so there would be letters we could intercept.'

'Was that possible?'

'By a stroke of good fortune, it was. A young Catholic called Gifford, who is an agent for Mary's supporters in France, was apprehended at Rye and brought to me. I perceived him to be a weak, irresolute character. It was not hard to alter his loyalties.'

Lamotte felt a chill go through him. It was only too easy to imagine the effect a few meetings with the grim-faced spymaster might have on a frightened young man.

'I arranged for Gifford to tell Mary and her friends that he could deliver their letters safely. Before taking them to Chartley, Gifford brings them to me. They are deciphered and resealed to look as if they have never been tampered with. Gifford then takes them to the brewer who supplies Chartley. He encloses them in waterproof canisters and hides them in the barrels. Mary's replies are brought out in the same way.'

'You are sure the brewer can be trusted?'

Walsingham raised an eyebrow. 'He has put his prices up, knowing Paulet won't obtain supplies from anyone else. I think money will ensure his support.'

'And the letters?'

'At first, the volume was considerable but most of them were old and of no great importance. Then we intercepted a letter from Babington. In the clearest terms, he set out a plan to rescue Mary and rally her supporters. At the same time, some of the conspirators were to go to Court and murder the queen.'

'But how would they get near her?'

'You know as well as I do that the queen has never been sufficiently concerned for her own safety. She refuses to be properly guarded. Provided the conspirators were appropriately dressed and appeared confident, it would not be hard.'

'But surely the plot changed her mind?'

Walsingham shook his head. 'I had good reasons for keeping it from her.'

Lamotte started. 'But the danger to Her Majesty - would it not be wiser to arrest Babington?'

'Hear me out,' Walsingham snapped. 'I needed to hold back for Mary's reply. It was everything I could have hoped for. She embraced the plan and analysed it with remarkable perspicacity. If I had not known otherwise, I would have thought a seasoned military commander had written the letter. Where Babington had been imprecise and optimistic, she was exact, recognising every flaw and danger. After all the years I had waited, I knew her fate was sealed.'

For a moment, Lamotte felt a twinge of pity. A man had to be hard of heart not to feel sorry for the tragic queen, her health and beauty fading as she endured interminable years of lonely imprisonment in a succession of damp, draughty castles.

'Do not grieve for her, Alexandre. Mary is not the heroine of one of your plays. She's a scheming vixen who would drag England back to the old religion and into the arms of Spain. Both of us know what that means.'

'Forgive me. You're right, of course. So what is my part in all this?'

'I want you to stay close to Babington and try to find out who, other than Ballard, is involved in the plot.'

'But is further secrecy not unwise?'

Walsingham's eyes narrowed. 'It is not for you to question my decisions. Will you accept the charge, or not?'

The back of Lamotte's neck prickled. He should have known when to keep his mouth shut. 'I shall do as you command, Sir Francis.'

'Good.'

As he walked back to the river, Lamotte contemplated this unexpected interruption, potentially a dangerous one, to his peaceful life. The bald fact had to be faced too that whatever Walsingham said, in the last resort he would put country above everything else. If it was necessary to achieve his ends, Lamotte thought, he would drive the dagger between my ribs himself.

Back at the Putney quay, a boat waited by the landing stage. Lamotte gave a coin to the ferryman and sat down in the bow. The rhythmic creak of the oars and the slap of water on the hull helped to compose his thoughts. From the height of the sun, he guessed it was past twelve. There was no time to begin his search for Babington before he needed to be at the theatre, but after the day's performance he would start with some of the old haunts. Sadness clouded his mind, for Babington had been an engaging companion. However mistaken the lad's beliefs, he wished he did not have to contribute to his downfall.

*

'Babington!'

When the young man swung round, Lamotte saw with relief that he had identified him correctly. The search had not

83

taken as long as he'd feared it would. He glimpsed the apprehension in Babington's eyes before his expression turned to one of recognition.

'Lamotte! Well met.'

'I thought you must have left London.'

'I did for a while, but as you see, I have returned.' Babington smiled apologetically. 'Forgive me for keeping myself apart for so long. Family business has occupied me a great deal.'

Lamotte waved a hand. 'We're all too busy these days. Your wife and daughter are in good health, I hope?'

'They've gone to Margaret's family in the country.'

'I'm surprised you didn't join them. I would avoid London in this heat if I could.'

Babington stared at the ground and mumbled something indistinct.

'Well, at least take a drink with me for old times' sake.'

For a moment, Lamotte thought Babington would demur but then he nodded. As they walked to a nearby tavern, however, conversation was stilted. It was clearly too soon to extract any confidences from him. Perhaps wine would loosen his tongue a little.

Sat at a small table in the hot, noisy room, Lamotte pulled out his pipe and filled it. 'You've not adopted the new habit yet?'

'What? Oh, no.'

'You should try it, very soothing. All one's troubles seem to dissolve in the smoke.'

A startled look flitted across Babington's face. Had he touched a nerve?

'So are you busy at the theatre?' Babington asked abstractedly.

'Trade's brisk enough, although it could be better. You should come and visit us.'

Covertly, Lamotte noticed how Babington's hand shook as he raised his wine to his lips. Draining it in one gulp, he suddenly jumped to his feet, bumping the table and making the wine bottle and glasses rattle.

'I'm sorry,' he said. 'I can't stay.'

Lamotte knocked out his pipe. 'I'll come with you.' But Babington was already halfway across the crowded, smoky room. Lamotte followed, keeping far enough back to be out of sight.

After half an hour of walking through the darkening streets, he saw his quarry stop and look back. Quickly, Lamotte merged into the shadows but it was likely Babington had not noticed him for, seemingly reassured, he dived into a nearby alley bordered with terraces of tall, narrow houses. Lamotte was just in time to see him enter one of them. It was not where he remembered him living. Had he come to meet someone? After a few moments, restless shapes moved backwards and forwards in the yellow light of a first-floor window.

Lamotte settled down to watch and wait. Time dragged and he shifted his weight from foot to foot. His back ached and he had not had time to eat since morning. The air had cooled a little but the reek of the open drain running along one side of the alley was powerful. Once, a noise made his hand fly to the hilt of his sword, but it was only a rat that scuttled away squeaking. At last, the light in the window went out. Lamotte waited another half hour then returned home. He would have to take the chance Babington was going nowhere until tomorrow.

When he slept, he dreamt of St Bartholomew's Day and woke shaking. Moonlight illuminated the room and, naked, he sat on the edge of the bed. He was stocky in build with muscular arms and legs, but there was a slackening of the belly that had not been there a few years ago. He grimaced and sucked in his stomach. At least he had kept plenty of thatch on his head.

He rubbed his thighs and got up to fetch his old night wrap. His knees cracked and he scowled; he felt more like sixty than forty-five. Pulling the night wrap around him, he returned to his bed. He wished Amélie were there to warm it for him. It was because of Catholics like Babington she was dead. No matter how personally charming he was, the sooner he and his kind were destroyed, the better.

He woke again at dawn but before he had the chance to leave the house, a message came from Walsingham. Lamotte read it then struck a spark from his tinder box, set the paper alight and dropped it in the fireplace. He watched the paper's crimson glow fade to grey.

Sometimes it was impossible to fathom how Walsingham's mind worked. One minute he wanted you to fasten onto Babington like a tick on a dog's belly, the next to stay away from him. With a sigh, Lamotte went to his study. Well, at least he was free to devote his attention to business now, and there was plenty of work to be done before he was due at The Unicorn.

*

Three days passed before another summons came, this time to attend Walsingham at Richmond where he was engaged on Court business. Once again, Lamotte made the journey upriver. The stench of the water seemed even more noxious than before. Passing Putney, Mortlake and Kew, he disembarked at the landing stage for the vast royal palace. It reared up before him, its awe-inspiring bulk bristling with forbidding battlements and towers.

The Royal Standard was not among the pennants fluttering from the flagpoles. He was glad of that. It meant the guards would let him through without too many officious questions if the queen was not in residence. It looked as if she soon would be, though. On the road to the gatehouse, packhorses, mules and carts jostled in the hot sun, their drivers cursing and grumbling. Their loads included sides of venison and beef, squawking crates of poultry, braces of game birds, exotic fruits, French wines and barrels of beer.

Lamotte slipped unnoticed past the guards at the gatehouse as they held up a belligerent carter and demanded to see his permit. With a confident stride, he then made his way through the throng in the main courtyard and found the staircase Walsingham had told him to use. A few minutes later, he was in his presence.

'I appreciate I owe you an explanation, Alexandre.' Walsingham motioned him to sit down. 'When I ordered you to stop following Babington, it was because I had decided to arrange a meeting with him. It was my intention to explore how malleable he was and whether an appeal to his love of his country and his sovereign, matched of course with a promise of pardon for any treasonable acts he has committed, would persuade him to change his allegiance.' Walsingham leant back in his chair and placed the tips of his fingers together. 'He stubbornly refused to understand me.'

'So he has been arrested?'

'No, I don't want him seized yet.'

Lamotte frowned. He would not risk questioning Walsingham's judgement again, but the old spymaster did seem alarmingly willing to let the plot come close to fruition. Was he really so determined to frighten Elizabeth into dealing once and for all with Queen Mary? It was a very dangerous course to take.

'On my orders, Richard Young, the London Magistrate, has sent his men to arrest John Ballard, but I want you, Alexandre, to find Babington again and stay with him until you hear from me. Give him this letter. In it I have assured him Ballard's arrest is nothing to do with him and told him to keep close to you to avoid being taken by Young's men. You look dismayed, but I promise you, I know what I'm doing. I return to London in the morning. If you have a message for me, I shall be at home in Seething Lane.'

*

The house where Lamotte had seen Babington go that night was shut up. As he searched the areas and taverns the young man used to frequent, Lamotte felt his irritation rise. The task might take days and Babington might not even be in the city now. The whole business began to resemble a bungling comedy rather than a treasonable plot. He found his part in it increasingly frustrating and obscure. Eventually he recalled that in the old days, Babington had often spent time at St Paul's. The nave of the great cathedral was a popular place for picking up gossip and exchanging news.

Pamphleteers and beggars jostled for his attention as he crossed St Paul's Churchyard and hurried into the cool interior of the cathedral. He pushed through the crowds, his pulse quickening. Tall enough to be seen over the sea of heads, Babington stood to one side of the nave with a rough-looking, bearded man. He talked volubly, his hands chopping the air, while the bearded man stared at the ground, his shoulders hunched.

All at once, Babington took a ring from his finger and a purse off his belt and tossed them at the bearded man, who let them fall to the floor before turning on his heel and walking away. Staring after him, Babington stood with his hands hanging limp at his sides; to Lamotte he looked like a lost child.

Babington gave a start when Lamotte put a hand on his shoulder. 'What are you doing here?' he exclaimed.

'I've come to help you.'

Lamotte took his arm and steered him to a side chapel. Wearily, Babington allowed himself to be guided and collapsed onto one of the front pews, gazing distractedly at the bare walls. 'How can you do that?' he mumbled.

'I have a letter for you from Sir Francis Walsingham.' At the name, Babington's face went from pale to red and back again. He shrank away, his eyes wide. If fear has a scent, Lamotte thought, I can smell it now.

'You are Walsingham's man?'

'It's not what you think. He wants me to tell you he knows you have no part in the conspiracy to take the queen's life. Here,' he put the letter in Babington's hand, 'read for yourself.'

Babington fumbled with the letter then handed it back unopened. 'I can't do it.'

Lamotte unsealed the paper and gave it to him. He waited while Babington scanned the words.

'If Ballard is taken,' he said at last, 'why should I be spared?'

'Because Walsingham understands you were led astray and, in your heart, you are the queen's loyal subject.'

Wordlessly, Babington turned his face away.

'Come along,' Lamotte said briskly. 'You must eat and regain your strength then we'll decide what to do.'

'I don't want to go where anyone knows me.' Babington shot him a wary glance.

'Don't be afraid. I'll find somewhere we won't be disturbed.'

Outside, they left the churchyard, eventually stopping at a tavern in one of the alleys off Eastcheap. Babington ducked his head under the lintel of the low door and Lamotte followed him in.

The place was deserted except for half a dozen drinkers and a group of old men playing cards at the table in the window. Lamotte left Babington to sit down and went to the counter.

'Send one of your potboys to Seething Lane, by St Olave's Church,' he said in an undertone. He slipped a shilling into the landlord's hand. 'Tell him to take a message to Sir Francis Walsingham's house.'

'What message?'

'Just say Alexandre waits here with the goods he asked for.' He raised his voice. 'If you say your beef is good then bring us some of it, and a flagon of wine.'

When the food arrived, Babington spurned it but swiftly drained a glass of wine and poured another. Apart from the low murmur of conversation from the other drinkers and the shuffle of cards, the tavern was quiet and sounds from the alley drifted distinctly through the open windows. Whenever footsteps approached, Babington's eyes swivelled to the door, fixing on it until the sound died away.

The candle holder in the centre of the table held a stump surrounded by a heap of dead flies. A few live ones buzzed over the plate of discarded bones. Lamotte swatted them away and took out his pipe. 'The beef was tolerable,' he remarked. 'A pity you wouldn't try it.'

Babington was not listening to him. He was staring at a man who had just come into the tavern. At the counter, the man spoke briefly to the landlord then approached their table.

'Master Lamotte? I have a message for you.'

Lamotte took the note and scanned it. It was from Walsingham. The arrests had begun.

Babington's fingers beat an agitated tattoo on the table top. He jumped to his feet. 'I'll pay our shot,' he said abruptly. Leaving his cloak and sword on the settle, he hurried off in the direction of the counter.

'You fool,' Lamotte hissed at the waiting messenger.

The man bridled. 'I've only done as I was bid.'

'I'm sure you were not told to speak to me directly. Tell your master I'll send word again when I am able to, now go away.'

His eyes turned to the counter. The card players had finished their game and were arguing about the reckoning. With a jolt, he realised Babington had gone. He leapt up, pushed past the startled messenger and rushed out to the privy in the backyard but there was no sign of his quarry. Back in the tavern, the landlord stood in his way. 'Your friend's already left. Don't think you can too without paying the bill.'

Lamotte dug out a handful of coins and tossed them at him. Outside, the alley was deserted. With a sinking heart, Lamotte checked the adjoining streets but Babington was nowhere to be seen. If he wanted to elude pursuit, it would be hard to find him. Unless I have some luck soon, Lamotte thought, I shall have to face Walsingham and admit I have failed him.

*

Lamotte's mouth was dry as he finished his tale. Across the desk, Walsingham's face remained impassive.

'I'll continue my search, of course,' Lamotte concluded lamely. To his surprise, Walsingham gave a dismissive wave of the hand. 'You may leave that to others. Ballard has given me all the information I need to secure a conviction. The man you saw at St Paul's was probably John Savage. He was the man eventually chosen to carry out the vile murder of Her Majesty. He has failed but at last the queen understands that her cousin Mary must die.' He gave a chilly smile. 'You are at liberty to go, Alexandre.'

Uncertain whether to be relieved or not, Lamotte got to his feet. 'Thank you, my lord.'

In the days that followed, the humid weather continued. In the city streets, rotting piles of discarded fruit and vegetables crawled with flies. The Fleet and the Tyburn shrank, exposing clayey mud littered with rubbish and the bloated carcasses of cats and dogs. No longer sluiced by the rivers, the city's ditches became tepid, brown puddles, reeking of excrement. In the shambles, meat crawled with maggots and flies; milk curdled in the dairies.

The rich went about with clove-studded oranges clamped to their noses to keep out the gamut of stenches. Fearing the spread of the sweating sickness, the Lord Chamberlain closed the theatres and Lamotte occupied the sweltering days working on his accounts and future plans. Included in these was the first performance of Tom's play.

Ten days after Babington's flight from the tavern, a summons came from Barn Elms. Walsingham was in an

91

affable mood as his servant poured them goblets of yellow-green Rhenish wine then left the room. 'Babington and his friends were sighted in Westminster,' he said. 'They eluded Richard Young's men but later some huntsmen out after wild boar and deer in St John's Wood reported a suspicious group of men wandering there. They had no hounds with them and were not dressed for hunting.'

He paused and drank some of his wine. 'After that, men of their description, recognisable even though their faces had been blackened by walnut juice, were sighted in the village of Harrow. Young's men finally tracked them to the nearby home of a recusant family we have had our eye on for some time.'

'What will happen to them?'

'They have all been arraigned on a charge of high treason. The trials are set for the first week of September.'

Lamotte shut his mind to the thought of how they would be faring in their captivity.

A few weeks later, when the verdicts of guilty were brought in, in every case, the sentence was death. Lamotte did not join the thousands who flocked to the scaffold at St Giles in the Fields to see justice carried out. On the first day, Babington, Ballard and five others were executed. Afterwards, hearing that the butchery had been performed with far more savagery than usual, Lamotte was glad he had not witnessed it. Even the London crowd, hardened to cruelty, was shocked by the way Richard Topcliffe and his henchmen employed all their skills in inflicting agony on their helpless victims.

When the turn of the remaining conspirators came the following day, they were allowed to hang until they were dead. It was put about in the streets that the queen had so detested the previous day's cruelty that she had ordered clemency. But Lamotte was more inclined to believe that Walsingham had advised her to show it to keep her people's love.

Chapter 9

West of Salisbury
July, 1586

'Wait for me, madam,' wailed Bess.

Meg tried to hide her irritation. It was unkind to snap. The journey had been her idea, and even she was beginning to think it had been a great mistake. They were both exhausted and, in truth, she was not sure if they were going in the right direction, let alone with any chance of finding Tom at the end.

'Try to remember to call me Matthew, Bess,' she restrained herself to saying.

'Yes, mad— Matthew,' Bess replied in a dubious tone.

Meg managed a smile. 'It can't be much further to Plymouth. Soon all this will be over.'

'Yes, M - Matthew.'

As they trudged on, Meg looked up at the louring sky. She hoped the rain would hold off until they found shelter. They would need food soon as well and she had no idea where they would find it. She squared her shoulders; she must not let Bess see her doubts. The thought of finding Tom kept her own flagging spirits up but it was more difficult for Bess.

The second day was harder, and the one after that worse still. Both she and Bess were hungry and thirsty. In the villages and hamlets they passed through, people greeted them with suspicion and sometimes even downright hostility, overcharging for what little food and drink they were prepared to sell. The small store of money they had managed to bring with them diminished at an alarming rate.

Men's clothes might be easier to walk in but the leather of the old shoes Bess had found for Meg to wear was hard and cracked. Her feet blistered until every step was a penance. Bess drooped and it was a struggle to make her keep on walking.

That evening, as they breasted a hill, a cottage surrounded by tumbledown outbuildings came into view. A plume of smoke rose from the chimney. When they came closer, Meg saw two scraggy brown cows in a pen and a grey cob tethered to a pump by a water trough. She wondered if they should walk on past. These people might be as unfriendly as most of the others they had encountered and it was a lonely spot, but Bess pulled at her arm.

'Those cows look like milkers, madam. Perhaps the farmer will let us have a drink.'

'I don't think we should, Bess. It will be safer to go on.'

Bess's lower lip jutted and she started to cry. Meg felt a stab of guilt. Poor Bess! She had pushed her very hard today. The long-threatened rain had finally fallen, leaving their clothes damp. She had to admit, the prospect of cool, fresh milk to drink and somewhere to dry off was irresistible.

'All right, but you must promise to be careful. No calling me madam, understand?'

'I promise,' Bess said meekly.

A surly man answered Meg's knock.

'What d'you think you're about, disturbing honest folk at this hour?'

'We only want to buy some milk, and any other food you can spare,' Meg answered, trying to put on a gruff voice. 'My sister and I have travelled all day and we're hungry and thirsty.'

The man looked them up and down for a moment. 'You'd best come in then,' he said grudgingly.

What must have been years of smoke had blackened the low ceiling of the windowless room into which they stepped. The only light came from the small fire burning in the hearth. In its glow, patches of damp glistened on the wattle

94

and daub walls. Two three-legged stools, a table made from rough planks of wood and two wooden buckets comprised the furniture. The rushes strewn on the floor looked as if they had not been changed for months. Next to the grimy hearth were a poker, a few chipped earthenware bowls and two battered iron pans.

A lanky, tow-haired youth Meg had not at first noticed shambled out from the alcove by the fireplace, rubbing his eyes. Behind him was a stained mattress with wisps of straw poking through the holes in its ticking. He goggled at the sight of Meg and Bess.

'My son,' the man grunted.

'Pretty.' The youth sidled up to Bess and stroked her fair hair. Her blue eyes widened and she flushed.

'Fetch some milk, you halfwit,' the man snapped. The youth hung his head. He slouched over to the hearth and picked up an earthenware bowl then dunked it in one of the buckets. As he lifted it out and carried it to Bess, milk dripped from his calloused hand.

His father scowled. 'You're wasting it, you idiot. D'you think I'm made of money?' He snatched the cup and handed it to Bess. 'Here, share that with your brother.'

Eagerly, Bess gulped half the milk. Creamy froth smeared her lips as she gave the rest of it to Meg to finish.

'Thank you, that was good,' Meg sighed when she had drunk the last drop. Her eyes alighted on a hock of ham hanging from a beam. The man followed her glance. 'Where's your manners, Jeb?' he barked at the youth. 'Get some bread from the crock and cut the lady and gentleman a good slice of ham.' He grinned at Bess. 'Can't have you and your brother going hungry, can we?'

Blushing once more, Bess lowered her eyes. He laughed. 'Your sister's a shy little thing, ain't she?' Meg didn't answer.

'Where're you travelling to?'

'Plymouth. We have an uncle and aunt there who will take us in. Our parents are dead.'

'Land stops at Plymouth, I heard.'

'Yes. Our uncle works in the shipyard there.'

The talk carried on in a desultory fashion. Relieved, Meg congratulated herself. They had passed their first real test. Neither the man nor his son seemed to think there was anything out of the ordinary about her and Bess, and although he had seemed so unwelcoming when they arrived, he was now quite friendly. She felt sorry for his son. It was not his fault he was simple but clearly his father had very little patience with him.

As soon as they finished their meal, she stood up. 'We haven't much money but we'd like to pay you for your kindness. Will tuppence be enough?'

'Nay, lad, I won't take your money and it's almost nightfall. The roads won't be safe. You can stay here and go on tomorrow. Gentlefolk like you shall have the bed. Jeb and I'll sleep in the barn.'

Meg hesitated.

'I'm so tired, Matthew,' Bess pleaded. 'It would be wonderful to sleep in a warm bed.'

'But we can't take their bed.'

'We doan' mind, do we, Jeb?'

Jeb sniggered and his father shot him an angry look.

'Please,' Bess whispered.

'All right. And we're very grateful,' Meg added quickly.

The man yawned. 'There's cows to milk in the morning and candles cost money. It's time we were turning in. Jeb'll fetch you some more wood to keep the fire in until you go to sleep, won't you, lad?'

Muttering, Jeb went outside and came back with an armful of brushwood which he stacked by the hearth. He straightened up and stared at Bess again until his father's boot landed on his backside, making him yelp.

'Get to the barn with you,' he growled then turned to Meg and Bess and nodded. 'We'll be off then. Goodnight.'

The door closed behind them and Meg let out a long breath.

Bess sank onto one of the stools. 'Oh madam, they've gone, thank goodness.'

'Sssh,' Meg whispered with a frown. 'They might be listening outside the door. I'm sure I can hear something.'

There was a grating sound, then footsteps and after that silence. Motionless, Meg waited a few minutes then went to the door and pressed her ear to the wood. 'I think they've really gone now,' she whispered at last. Cautiously, she lifted the latch on the door and tried to open it a fraction. It didn't move. She tried again but it was stuck fast.

Bess's hand flew to her mouth. 'They've locked it, we can't get out.'

Meg felt her heart thud against her ribs but for Bess's sake she tried to stay calm. 'I'm sure it's nothing to worry about. I expect they usually lock their door at night. This cottage is in such a lonely place they might be afraid of being robbed. I expect they did it out of habit.'

Bess's eyes filled with tears. 'Oh madam, I'm frightened.'

Something in Meg snapped. 'Stop it, Bess! You were the one who wanted to sleep in a warm bed.'

Tears streaked Bess's pink cheeks and contrition replaced Meg's anger. She went to her and squeezed her arm.

'I'm sorry I shouted at you. Look, if we pull the table across to the door, no one can come in.'

Bess took a deep, shuddering breath and wiped her face with the back of her hand. Together, they dragged the table over the layer of mouldering rushes and wedged it against the door.

'Now for pity's sake, let's get some sleep,' Meg muttered. 'We may not have another chance like this for days.' She pulled off her painful shoes and groaned. 'At last, that's better.'

She climbed onto the mattress and pulled the sheepskin up to her chin. It was none too clean and smelt of animal grease but at least it was warm.

Doubtfully, Bess examined the skirt of her dress and the petticoats underneath. 'They're dry now but they're still all caked with mud. I shouldn't lie in the bed in them.'

'I hardly think it'll make much difference to it,' Meg said with a grimace. 'Anyway, you'll have to unless you want to sleep naked.'

Bess shook her head.

They lay side by side in the dark listening to the small sounds of the night.

'What do you think that scuffling is?' Bess asked in a frightened whisper.

'Mice probably. I expect this cottage is full of them.'

'Or rats,' Bess said, a tremor in her voice. 'I hate rats. Suppose they come on the bed and bite us?'

'I'll hit them with these horrible shoes you found me.' Meg reached out and fumbled for them. 'Now stop fretting and go to sleep.'

'There's someone outside, I know there is,' Bess said after a few more minutes. Meg felt a stab of alarm; she heard something too. If it was an animal, it was a large one. With a shiver, she wondered if there were still bears in these parts. Suddenly, a man's voice cursed and the door shook.

Bess screamed as it scraped open a few inches then a few more until the table crashed onto its side. In the firelight, Meg saw Jeb and his father clamber over it. Reaching Meg first, the older man seized her by the throat and hauled her up from the mattress.

He licked his lips. 'Take this one, Jeb. When you've tied him up, you can watch while you wait your turn with the sister. It's time you learnt what a woman's for.'

Bess's screams jangled in Meg's ears as Jeb grabbed her under the arms and dragged her across the floor. One of the outstretched table legs smashed into her shoulder and she cried out. Through the pain, she heard a slap and Bess's screams turned to a whimper.

Suddenly, rage rushed through her. Jeb had dragged her as far as the hearth now. He pinned her down with his heavy

98

boot and reached for the rope hanging from a large hook on the wall. She fastened onto his ankle and pulled with all her might, throwing him off balance. As he tottered, she scrambled to her feet, seized the poker from the hearth and swung it at him. The blow caught him on the face. He yelled and clasped his bleeding nose. Without stopping to think, Meg raised the poker again and landed another blow on the top of his head. Terrified, she jumped out of his way as he staggered and fell. The poker flew from her hand and clattered across the floor.

On the mattress, her skirts bunched around her waist, Bess struggled under the weight of Jeb's father. Before Meg could retrieve the poker, he saw she was free. With an oath, he rolled off Bess, leapt up and lunged. Wildly, Meg scrabbled for the poker but it was too far away. Afterwards, she could not remember the sequence of events clearly but suddenly, she had a branch of smouldering brushwood in her hand. The heat seared her skin but she clung on and brandished it at him, fanning the flames.

'Let us alone or I'll set fire to you,' she shouted.

He came at her roaring and tried to snatch the branch but recoiled with a howl as the flames scorched him. The pain in Meg's hand was unbearable. She flung the branch back into the hearth. Panic almost blinding her she dodged around the small room. Jeb's father was much stronger than she was; it would not take him long to catch her. She couldn't save Bess or herself.

Suddenly, a crash made her heart miss a beat. In the dim, orange light cast by the remains of the fire, Jeb's father lay sprawled and winded beside his son. A surge of hope renewed Meg's energy. She dashed to the bed and seized Bess by the hand. 'Hurry,' she urged.

Bess only stared at her with the eyes of a frightened rabbit and would not move. With strength she had not known she possessed, Meg yanked her off the bed and hauled her to the door. Pushing her through, she slammed it behind them. Dizzy with relief, she saw the big iron key sticking out of the

99

lock. It turned with a clunk that sounded like music. She felt the reassuring hardness of the wood against her back before she slumped to the ground and retched.

Huddled on the muddy ground, Bess rocked to and fro, weeping noisily. After a few moments, Meg crawled over and tried to comfort her. In the moonlight, her face was wraithlike. They clung together for what seemed like an eternity then there was a thud and Meg looked up in horror. The door bowed and a chunk of rotten wood broke off its bottom. Meg glimpsed the toe of a heavy boot. Another blow, this time near the lock, almost wrenched the door from the jamb.

'They'll kill us,' Bess wailed, her face contorted with terror.

'We won't let them.' Meg gritted her teeth and looked around the yard. Roused by the commotion, the grey cob tossed his head and whinnied.

'Good fellow.' Meg stroked his soft muzzle. 'You'll save us, won't you?'

She ran back to Bess and pulled her to her feet. 'You must help me, we need to find a saddle and bridle. Come on, let's search the sheds.'

As they rummaged in piles of rubbish that must have taken years to accumulate, she prayed the cob's tack was not in the cottage. If it was, they would have to ride bareback and it would not be easy. Her head throbbed, then just as she had almost given up hope, she saw the edge of an old saddle poking out from under a piece of sacking. Triumphantly, she hauled it out and found the bridle. 'Bring the sacking too,' she said to Bess. 'We might need it.'

Back in the yard, another blow shook the splintering door. Soon it would be off its hinges. Together they heaved the saddle onto the cob's back. Meg fumbled to buckle the girth and stuff the sack in the saddle bag. She lifted the bridle over the cob's ears and slid the bit into his mouth. 'It's a mercy you're so placid,' she murmured.

With a shriek, Bess grabbed her arm. 'The door! It's breaking!'

Meg swung round and saw that the lower hinge was already loose. Scrambling up the side of the water trough, she launched herself onto the cob's back and reached a hand down for Bess. 'Climb up as I did and I'll help you on.'

Bess didn't need to be told twice. Once she was perched behind Meg, she flung her arms around her waist.

With a final crash, the door gave way. As it did so, Meg dug her heels into the cob's flanks. She felt a hand grasp her ankle and she kicked out with all her strength. There was a string of curses and the cob threw up his head and bolted.

'Hold on, Bess,' Meg shouted. She wound her fingers into the cob's coarse mane and clung on as they galloped out of the yard.

*

The cob's hooves squelched as he picked his way across the boggy ground. A low mist made both girls shiver and left a taste of wet earth in Meg's mouth. Behind her, she felt Bess's chest heave as she coughed.

'Must we go this way?' she asked.

'Yes, it will be safer than going on the road, we agreed that.'

'I'm freezing,' Bess said plaintively.

Meg sighed. It was probably as much the terror they had felt as the weather. Her own hands were so numb she could hardly hold the reins. 'We'll stop when we get to dry ground and you can walk around to warm yourself.'

Bess fell silent and after a while, feeling the girl's weight slumped against her back, Meg realised she was dozing. She was afraid to wake her in case a sudden movement made her fall off but she made a heavy burden; Meg's shoulders soon ached unbearably. When she could endure it no more, she pulled the cob up and prodded Bess. The girl woke with a start.

101

'Stay there,' Meg ordered, sliding off the cob. She winced as pins and needles pricked her legs then reached up for Bess and helped her off the cob's back. 'We shall have to walk for a while. I'm so stiff, I can hardly move.'

Neither of them spoke much as they stumbled along. Fitfully emerging from behind ragged clouds, only the moon lit their way. The hours seemed endless to Meg and constant doubts assailed her. She was even more afraid than before that she had been wrong to bring Bess on this dangerous journey. She should have come alone. Beside her, Bess started at every crack of a twig. Once when they disturbed some night creature that scuttled noisily away into the bushes, she seized Meg's arm with such violence Meg nearly lost her balance.

'It might be a witch.' Bess's voice trembled. 'Mother used to say we must never go out at night or the witches would snatch us and we'd never be seen again.'

Meg felt a chill creep up the back of her neck, but she fought her fear. 'Don't be foolish,' she said sharply. 'It's probably just a badger or a fox.' But Bess's continuing whimpers told her Bess was not reassured.

Meg's relief when a faint light appeared on the eastern horizon was unbounded. Slowly, it warmed to streaks of crimson and she saw they had left the low ground behind and stood on a grassy plateau strewn with huge boulders. Before them, an undulating plain stretched away into the distance. Pulsing like a ball of fire, the sun struggled above the horizon, its rays turning the boulders from dull grey to rose and gold. Meg held her breath and smelt the sweet scent of dewy grass. She felt as if she witnessed the secret ritual of some alien religion whose origins were buried deep in the folds of time. Even Bess was silent.

Then a bird sang; others answered and soon the bushes were alive with song and the beat of wings. The enchantment was over. Meg's eyes filled with tears. If only Tom had been there to share it with her.

She felt Bess's hand on her arm. 'Madam? There's no need to cry. We're safe, aren't we? Shouldn't we go on?'

Meg sniffed and wiped her cheek. 'You're quite right, Bess, we should.' Her back to the sun, she pointed ahead. 'I think west is that way. Come on.'

*

A week later, Meg gazed sadly at the peacefully grazing cob. In the short time they had been together, she had grown fond of him and christened him Samson for his strength and his gentle ways, but they could not keep him.

'He's all we have to sell,' she said, 'and we must have money.'

'Where could we sell him?' Bess looked alarmed. 'What if someone recognises him?'

'I think we should be far enough from the farm to take the chance that no one will.'

The next day, they saw a town in the distance. Meg left Bess in a small wood and went with Samson to find the market place. It bustled with merchants and buyers and it felt strange to her to be among crowds of people again. As she wandered around the stalls, the smell of hot bread and pies made her mouth water but she had no money to buy anything yet. On her way past a stall selling nuts and apples, however, she noticed an apple that had fallen on the ground. When she ducked to retrieve it, she saw it was already bruised, but the first bite tasted like nectar. She promised herself she would buy a whole basketful when she sold Samson.

She licked the last of the juice from her lips and went to the front of the stall to ask if anyone was buying horses.

'Horse fair's a sennight and forty miles away.'

Meg's heart sank.

'You could try Ned Skelly. His mare dropped dead in the shafts last week. He might make you an offer.' With a jerk of his head, the stallholder indicated a thick-set man inspecting the goods on an ironmonger's stall nearby.

'Ned?' he shouted out. 'Lad here's got a nag to sell.'

The man's puffy cheeks and sagging upper eyelids almost obscured his watery blue eyes and a large boil erupted from one side of his sharp, pointed nose.

He came over to where Meg stood, grabbed Samson's bridle and peeled back the cob's lips. He looked askance at the animal's teeth before spitting on the ground. 'Not worth much. Give you a shilling and that's only 'cause I'm a charitable man.' The words came out of the side of his mouth as if he begrudged every one of them.

The stallholder guffawed. 'That you are, Ned. That you are.'

Meg hesitated. It didn't sound nearly enough and Skelly didn't look a kind man either. The thought of Samson being overworked and cruelly treated made her heart lurch.

'No thank you,' she answered and, snatching back Samson's bridle, hurried past.

'Please yourself,' Skelly shouted after her.

An hour went by and she grew tired of walking round the market. She was even hungrier than ever with the sight of so much food and no one was interested in Samson.

Disconsolate, she led him back through the market towards the high road. I've let Bess down, she thought miserably. We shall starve and it will be my fault.

Samson jibbed and she glanced up to see the puffy-cheeked man blocking their way. She smelt beer on his breath.

'No takers, eh?' he sneered. 'Want to change your mind? Like I said, not worth much, but I've had a good afternoon, so the offer's still open.'

Anger bubbled in Meg chest. 'Don't waste your breath,' she snapped. 'I wouldn't sell him to you at any price.' She barged him aside and strode off, Samson trotting at her side. A stream of abuse followed them but no footsteps.

By the wall of a noisy tavern, she paused and leant against the rough-cast wall to wait until her cheeks cooled and her heart stopped thumping. It was then an idea came to

104

her. Through an open window, she saw that the smoky interior was packed with impatient customers roaring for their beer and food as harassed serving girls flew around the tables trying to keep up. Perhaps the landlord would welcome another pair of hands on such a busy market day.

At the back of the building, she found the door to the kitchens and knocked. After a long wait, a stout woman with a clean white apron over her green wool dress bustled out. Her face was ruddy under her muslin cap.

'Work, you say?' she grumbled after Meg had said her piece. 'I should think I've got work when my husband's a lazy good-for-nothing who spends all his time drinking and playing dice.' Her eyes narrowed. 'Your hands are very soft for a kitchen lad. What can you do?'

Taken aback, Meg cast about for an answer. No one had asked her that question before. She doubted the woman had embroidery or madrigals in mind.

'Perhaps I could clear tables,' she faltered.

'You can wash pots.' The woman glanced at the toes poking out of Meg's left shoe. 'I've some old boots I'll give you in return. Tie your nag up by the pump and you can keep an eye on him while you work.'

'I'd like some food as well,' Meg replied.

The landlady put her hands on her hips. 'I'll see if you're a good worker first.'

It was as much as Meg could do to carry the huge iron pots to the pump. There she scrubbed them with handfuls of coarse sand as the landlady showed her until her hands were raw, then she sluiced away the loosened lumps of charred gruel and stew with water from the pump. Puddles of greasy water spread over the cobbles. Inside her broken shoes, her feet were so wet and cold she might as well be barefoot.

'They'll do,' the landlady said briskly when she came to inspect Meg's work. 'There's sacks of swedes and onions in the store. You can peel them and cut them up for me. Keep the peel thin, mind. I can't afford to waste good food.'

By the time Meg had finished, her eyes smarted from the fumes of the onions and she had cut her finger more than once. If this was cooking, she hoped she never had to do any more of it, but at least the landlady gave a grudging nod of approval when she came out.

'Here, put the peelings in this,' she said, holding out a tin bucket. 'You can take them up to the pigs.'

The pigs lumbered from their wallow and raced squealing to the fence when they saw her. She tipped the scraps over into the mud and watched them squabble and jostle for them. They couldn't be hungrier than she was, she thought ruefully. The empty bucket clanking at her side, she hurried back to the tavern, her stomach aching for food.

When she went to untie Samson from the pump later that day, Meg glimpsed her reflection on the dark surface of the water in the trough and grimaced. What a scarecrow she looked with her spiky hair and grimy face. Still, the visit to town had been worthwhile. The landlady had given her the boots and parted grudgingly with half a loaf of bread. When the market traders packed up for the night, she had also managed to beat the local urchins to a fair amount of the fruit and vegetables discarded in the square. She and Bess would have a veritable feast tonight.

Cresting the hill, she reached the place where she had left Bess and groaned. Where had the silly girl gone to? She had been looking forward to showing off her trophies. Then her irritation turned to fear. Bess had sworn not to wander off. Suppose someone had taken her? She shaded her eyes from the low sun. It would be dark soon and she would have no hope of finding her.

A twig cracked and she tensed. Fearfully, she looked round then breathed again. 'Bess! You scared me, where have you been?'

'It's you.' Bess seemed close to tears.

'Who else would it be?'

'There were voices,' Bess stammered. 'They might have been goblins or giants.'

106

Meg laughed. 'Oh Bess, I'm sure other people walk through these woods too. It was probably just some travellers. Anyway you're safe and that's what matters. Now come and see what I've brought back. There's enough food to last us for days, and look,' – she stuck out one foot – 'I have new boots.'

At a place where lichen-covered boulders strewed the ground, they found a dry, shallow cave almost hidden by the branches of a large beech tree. 'We'll spend the night here,' Meg decided. 'Tomorrow we can pick up the road again.'

Free from hunger for the first time in days, it was not long before they were both asleep. When Meg woke, it was dark as pitch outside. She lay still for a moment, wondering what it was that had disturbed her. A light breeze stirred the beech tree and somewhere a hunting owl hooted but the sound had been different: an insistent rustling noise, close at hand. Very carefully, she edged to the opening of the cave and peered out. She was sure she heard something breathe – or was it someone?

Motionless, she waited until the moon sailed into a cloudless patch of sky. A figure a few feet away from her jumped up, the sack containing the remains of the food in its hand. Meg lunged and missed as it darted away. She scrambled to her feet and followed, but the thief was already yards ahead and running fast. Meg's anger flared. Even though it was unlikely she could catch up, she must try. Hampered by her ill-fitting boots, she crashed and stumbled through the undergrowth, brambles scratching her face and arms. As the thief leapt over a tree trunk straddling the path, Meg's lungs felt as if they would explode but she steeled herself for a last burst of speed.

All at once, the thief let out a surprisingly high-pitched shriek and fell, one foot trapped under an exposed root snaking across the path. It seemed the thief was a girl. Before she could recover, Meg threw herself at her, pinioning her to the ground. 'That food's ours, you shan't have it,' Meg hissed.

107

The thief went limp. Dragging the sack out of her unresisting hand, Meg let the bundle drop and rolled her over to see her face.

Then something cold and sharp pressed against her neck and she froze.

'If you move,' a voice said softly, 'I'll kill you.'

Chapter 10

A makeshift hut of branches and animal skins stood in a clearing in a wood. Close by, a small fire smouldered, sending a braid of blue smoke into the afternoon air. Meg watched the young man beside her shape a small piece of wood with his knife. The sight of the blade still gave her an uncomfortable feeling. To banish it, she asked, 'What are you making?'

'A doll for Agnes.'

'You're very kind to your sister, Andrew.'

He shrugged. 'I thought it might cheer her up.'

'I'm sorry if she was scared, but she frightened me as well. And she shouldn't have tried to steal our food.'

'Then I'll make a doll for you too if you like,' Andrew said and grinned. He stopped as a shrill sound came from a nearby clump of gorse.

Meg shuddered. 'What a horrible noise. What was it?'

'Wait and I'll show you.'

A few moments later, he was back. 'Hare,' he said triumphantly. 'I've been waiting for that trap to work for a week. Hare's Mother's and Agnes's favourite.' He sat down and picked up his knife again. With an expert hand he slit the hare's belly and gutted it then tossed the innards towards the bushes. In a flurry of black and white, three magpies swooped to peck at them.

Meg's stomach churned. With a chuckle, Andrew handed her a wooden bucket. 'You're green as the grass. Why don't you go and fetch some water from the spring? I'll have him skinned and ready for the pot before you come back and you needn't watch.'

As she walked away, Meg felt angry with herself. Would a man flinch at the sight of a gutted hare? She wondered what Andrew was thinking and how long it might be before her disguise was uncovered. Before now, people had only seen her briefly and apparently not for long enough to arouse their suspicions. Now it would be harder to keep up the pretence.

But, she reflected, discovery might not be such a disaster. Increasingly, it seemed to her that Andrew's family was no stranger to secrets either. In the few days she and Bess had been with them, she had gleaned very little of their story for usually they were skilful at avoiding questions, but from the way they spoke, she felt sure they were gentlefolk. Andrew was about Tom's age, Agnes, his sister, still a child. Their mother, Sarah, was friendly but quiet with an air of sorrow about her. They had no father with them.

Meg returned with the water and handed Andrew the bucket. He held up the glossy, brindle pelt.

'Agnes will have a fine pair of gloves for the winter. But I'll have to clean and prepare this first.' He dunked the pelt into the water and weighted it down with a heavy stone. 'When it's soaked for a bit, I'll scrape away the blood and fat, then you keep changing the water until it runs clear.' He looked at her with a grin. 'Too much for you?'

Meg scowled. She didn't like him teasing her. 'Of course not,' she said stoutly. 'What will you do with it then?'

'Cut out the pieces with my knife and then sew them up to fit Agnes's hands.'

'How did you learn to do that?'

He glanced at the entrance to the hut then back to the fire. 'My father taught me. He was a glove maker, the best in the town.'

'What happened to him?' Meg asked.

'He died.'

He turned his attention back to the fire. 'Mother will be cross if I let this go out,' he muttered.

A twig cracked and Meg saw Sarah coming to sit with them.

'Bess is telling Agnes a story,' she said. 'I thought I would come out and join you.'

How weary she looked, Meg thought, even more so than yesterday. Her eyes were unnaturally bright in her pale face. For a few moments, they talked of the hare and the gloves Andrew planned to make for Agnes.

'Andrew told me your husband was a glove maker,' Meg said. 'My father always said it was a good trade. Maybe if Andrew could find someone to have him as an apprentice, you wouldn't need to live in the woods any longer.' She stopped, dismayed by Andrew's expression. What a fool she was. She had gone too far and caused offence.

'What else did he say to you?' Sarah asked quietly.

'I didn't mean to tell her anything, Mother,' Andrew said sulkily.

Sarah put her hand on his arm. 'I'm not angry. Matthew may as well hear the truth. We haven't known each other for long, have we, Matthew? But my heart tells me we can trust you, as I hope you trust us.'

Meg flushed but Sarah did not seem to notice.

'Our tale is not a happy one,' she said. 'Our family was Catholic but, God forgive me, when our religion was outlawed, I was willing, for the children's sake, to give it up. My husband was not, even though many people in our town shunned us. I begged him to make peace with his conscience and worship secretly while observing the laws requiring attendance at the queen's church – as many did – but he wouldn't listen.'

She paused. 'Have you heard of recusancy fines?'

Meg shook her head.

'They are levied on people who do not attend church. No matter how much it cost us, my husband still refused to go. In the end, we couldn't pay and he was arrested.' Her voice sank so low, Meg strained to hear the words. 'I was forbidden to visit him. A year later, he died in prison.'

111

Sarah's voice caught in her throat and it was a moment before she was able to continue. 'My husband was a stubborn man, but I loved him. I pray he has been rewarded for his faith. As for me, I am punished and the children with me. Almost everything we owned was confiscated. That is why the woods are our home now.'

Dismayed, Meg put a hand on her arm. 'But is there nothing you can do? Surely someone will help you?'

Sarah shook her head. 'Help us? Who would help us?' she asked sadly. 'Do you have any idea what it's like to try and scratch a living when you are poor? I've heard that in the days before the old king tore down the monasteries and convents, the monks and nuns sometimes offered succour to the homeless, but now there's nothing except to throw yourself on the mercy of the parish.' She grimaced. 'I think I'd prefer to starve with dignity.'

Meg bit her lip and traced a line in the dust with her forefinger.

'I'm sorry,' Sarah said quickly. 'I'm sure life has been hard for you too. You would not be here otherwise.'

Meg hesitated. They were bound to find out in the end, and they had been so kind, it seemed wrong to try and keep the secret from them any longer. 'I have something I'd like you to know too,' she said quietly. 'My name isn't Matthew.'

'I'm not surprised to hear it,' said Sarah with her gentle smile. 'I've never met a woman called by that name.'

Meg stared at her. 'How long have you known?'

Sarah's cool fingers touched Meg's chin. 'Your skin is too soft and smooth. If you were a young man, a beard should have come by now. Andrew is as hairy as a haystack.'

Her son glowered at her.

'Your hands and feet are too small for a man's and sometimes you forget to walk as a man would.'

Meg hung her head. 'I'm sorry I tried to deceive you.'

'Don't be. When we met, we gave you little enough reason to trust us, although I hope we have put that right now.'

A surge of relief overwhelmed Meg. 'Of course you have, and I'm so glad I don't need to pretend anymore.' Tears welled up in her eyes.

'Shall we walk for a while?' Sarah asked.

Nodding, Meg got to her feet.

'I'll get on with cooking the hare,' said Andrew. He paused. 'So what is your name then?'

'Meg.'

He cocked his head, rubbed his sunburnt hand over his fair beard then nodded. 'It suits you better than Matthew.'

'Now we can talk in peace,' Sarah said as they walked off into the trees.

Slowly, under her sympathetic questioning Meg told her story. 'I don't know what you must think of me,' she ended. 'I've sinned, I know, but I was so unhappy and afraid.'

Sarah kissed her cheek. 'Your parents were harsh to make you marry where you did not love, and I don't blame you for running away from a man like Ralph Fiddler. I hope you find your Tom.'

It seemed to Meg a great burden had been lifted from her. Fresh tears filled her eyes. 'Thank you.'

'You say he may have gone to join the army in the Low Countries.'

'It was what Ralph claimed he planned to do. I didn't know where to begin looking for him but then I heard he might start out from Plymouth, so we decided to look for him there. Do you think that was foolish?'

'Not foolish, but it will be a hard task. Plymouth is a bigger place than Salisbury and because it is a port, people come and go a great deal more.'

Meg stopped and pulled a leaf off an oak branch. 'You think he won't be there, don't you? You think our journey is a waste of time.'

'I never said that, Meg. The fact that something is not certain to succeed is no reason not to try.' She held out her hand. 'I'll talk to Andrew if you like. Perhaps he could go with you and help you search. Bess, Agnes and I will be perfectly safe here.'

Meg's heart leapt. 'Do you really think Andrew would do that for me?'

'I think Samson could carry both of you then it will only be a few days' ride. Come on, let's go back. Andrew will have the hare ready soon.'

She squeezed Meg's shoulder. 'One thing you need to learn is the importance of enjoying what you have, however little it might be.'

When they returned, Andrew was stirring the pot with a peeled stick. The pungent scents of sorrel and wild thyme wafted through the air.

'It will be the tastiest hare anyone ever ate,' said Sarah. 'Fit for a king.'

Chapter 11

London
October, 1586

'Time you started copying out the parts for your play, Tom,' Lamotte said as they drank at the Dolphin one blustery afternoon, shortly after the Lord Chamberlain had given permission for the theatres to reopen. 'We should start rehearsals soon,' he went on. 'I'd like something new to reel in the fishes.'

'If I have them ready the day after tomorrow, might it be worth a few more shillings?'

Lamotte raised an eyebrow. 'I suppose since you've remembered my advice, I've no business to complain. Half a crown if you deliver on time then.'

The first performance was a success and, brim full of excitement, Tom couldn't wait to get home to Janey's house with the news.

'Can we have mutton pies? Shall I go and get them now?' Jack tugged at his sleeve, grinning and ignoring Janey's disapproving clucks.

'Mutton pies, roast beef, strong ale – anything you like. And buy more candles and firewood while you're about it.'

'Go with him, Bel,' Janey said. 'He'll never carry all that on his own.'

'You're very generous, Tom,' she said after they had gone. 'But don't forget what I said about saving some of your money. You might need it one day.'

'I know.'

They waited for Bel and Jack to return, Hal dozing in Tom's lap. An hour had passed when the baby woke and grizzled. Tom looked at him apprehensively. 'Is he hungry?'

'Not much I can do about it if he is. Rub his back and see if he'll settle again.'

'All right.'

'There,' she said after a few moments. 'You're always good with him. He's usually afraid of men.'

'He's not afraid of me,' Jack said, coming in with his arms full of firewood and candles.

Bel laughed. 'Of course not. You're a boy, not a man.'

To Tom's surprise, Jack flushed. 'I'll be a man soon,' he grumbled. 'And you're not much older than me anyway.'

She tossed her hair and stuck out her tongue.

'That's enough. Stop it, the pair of you,' Janey snapped. 'Anyone'd think you were brother and sister the way you squabble. Don't sulk, Jack, leave a few of those logs for the fire and stack the rest out the back.'

She rolled her eyes after he had gone. 'You shouldn't tease him, you know, Bel.'

'I didn't mean any harm.'

Hal stirred and woke again. Bel stretched out her arms and he slithered off Tom's lap and staggered over to her with wobbly steps. She caught him and pulled him onto her lap, unfastening her bodice. He latched on and sucked hungrily.

'And the boy's getting too old for that,' Janey added. 'Time he was weaned.'

Bel shrugged. She glanced at Tom and gave him a shy smile. He looked away quickly, feeling his cheeks glow.

'Have it your own way,' Janey sniffed. 'I don't know what's got into you these days.'

The beef from the cook shop was rare and delicious and the mutton pies sizzling with rich, fatty meat. When he could eat no more, Tom sank back in his chair, warm and contented.

His face flushed by the strong ale he was not used to drinking, Jack suddenly sprang onto his hands and walked

116

around the room upside down before righting himself nimbly.

'Who taught you to do that?' asked Tom.

Jack's chin tilted. 'Taught myself, didn't I?'

He picked up three of the apples he and Bel had bought and started to juggle with them, but soon dropped one which exploded in a mush as it hit the ground.

'That's wasted,' Janey said crossly.

'Teach you to show off.'

Jack glowered.

'Leave him alone, Bel,' Tom said easily. 'We can afford to lose one apple.'

Flashing him a look of gratitude, Jack put the remaining apples back on the table. 'One day I'll earn lots of money then I can buy anything I like.'

In bed that night, Tom's head was too full to allow him to sleep. He had seen his characters come to life on The Unicorn's stage and it had been everything he had dreamt of. The head of writhing snakes the costume maker had concocted for the Gorgon, Medusa, won a round of applause from the audience. The entrance from Hell of the three hags who helped Perseus to find her received another.

The legend said the hags had only one eye which they shared between them. Lamotte had been right to insist the actors played that scene for laughs. The mixture of horror and hilarity had won the groundlings over from the start. The way they all fell silent in Perseus's big speech was, Lamotte told him, a great compliment. They weren't always so attentive. Best of all was Lamotte's agreement to put on three more performances before Christmas.

Yet in the midst of his happiness, Tom felt a rush of sorrow. If only Meg was here to share all this with him. He wondered what she was doing now. Lying in Edward Stuckton's bed, he supposed. The thought twisted in his gut like a butcher's hook. Had she forgotten him yet? He could not blame her if she had, but he wished he could have seen

117

her one last time to explain he hadn't wanted to leave. He had done it for her.

*

When the time came for the next performance, Jack and Bel came to watch and Lamotte let them in for free. Janey stayed at home with Hal. 'The theatre's not for me anymore,' she said. 'I'm too old to walk so far, or to do all that standing. But I'm proud of you, Tom, you know I am.'

After the visit, Jack began to haunt the theatre, fascinated by the jester's jokes and acrobatics. Soon he was badgering Tom to ask Lamotte if there was any work for him.

'Would I be right in thinking it'll be the first time he's earned an honest penny?' Lamotte asked shrewdly.

'It's not his fault.'

'No?' Lamotte hooked his thumbs in his belt and smiled. 'Well, if you vouch for him, I suppose I can find ways for him to be useful.'

'Thank you.'

'So how's the next play coming on?'

The question took Tom aback. He had not even thought about it.

Lamotte shook his head. 'Robert Greene would probably have finished two more by now, not that any of his are much good and I'd encourage you to do better, but they boil the pot. If you want to find out how to pen a mighty line, it's Kit Marlowe you should study. Go and see *Tamburlaine*. Burbage puts it on next week.' He chuckled. 'Marlowe's a dangerous young man. Mercurial, quarrelsome and, as for the subject of religion, it's best to keep away, but he's a magician with words.'

*

118

The following week, Tom left the city by Bishopsgate and went north up Shoreditch, past the Bethlehem Hospital and the bowling alleys and pleasure gardens of Fisher's Folly to St Mary Spital. There he skirted the wall of the artillery yard where the Tower gunners came to practise each week and turned west until he came to The Unicorn.

It was one of those late autumn afternoons when the ghost of summer briefly appears. There was no performance at the theatre for a few days and Lamotte had instructed that the time be used to catch up with running repairs, but the small band of workmen had downed tools to doze in the sunshine. Lamotte would have given them the rough edge of his tongue had he been there, thought Tom.

Above the thatched circular roof, the flags drooped. The only sound was the tap of their lanyards on the poles and the gentle whump of canvas when a breeze stirred. In Tom's imagination, though, the scene was not so peaceful. Fanfares of trumpets announced one of the many plays he would undoubtedly write and a thousand feet clumped up the wooden steps to the auditorium.

'What are you staring at?'

The vision disappeared and Tom saw one of the workmen awake and scowling at him.

'Nothing.'

'Then go and look at it somewhere else.'

With a shrug, Tom walked away. It would take more than a surly workman to spoil the afternoon.

Further along at The Theatre it was a very different scene. Early arrivals swarmed outside, eating food from the stalls set up against the building's wooden walls. Tom noticed a pickpocket or two prowling the crowd and clamped his hand over his purse. When the trumpet blared, he paid his penny and crammed into the yard with the rest of the groundlings. He felt a mixture of excitement and apprehension at the prospect of Marlowe's play. On one hand he might learn from it, but he might also come away

119

afraid he would never match, let alone better, Marlowe's work.

The play commenced and as the tyrant Tamburlaine pursued his relentless ambitions, Marlowe's verse swooped and soared. Bodies soaked in chicken's blood piled up on the stage; like mules, the kings of Asia dragged Tamburlaine's victorious chariot and Zenocrate pleaded for her father's life. In the audience, the smell of blood-lust and excitement was palpable. It swept Tom along with it. When the play ended, he felt at the same time elated and wrung out. To his relief, far from discouraging him, the experience had filled him with determination.

Outside, the weather was changing. Over towards Limehouse, a bank of storm clouds loured. Tom turned up his collar and struck out across the fields in the direction of Bishopsgate. The sails of a windmill he passed creaked in the rising wind. Soon a sheet of rain swept in. It quickly turned to hail, stinging his face and bouncing off the grass. A herd of cattle stood close together under an oak tree, steam rising from their flanks.

By the time he reached Angel Lane, he was soaked through and the sun had almost set. To his surprise, the windows on the ground floor of the tenement were dark but the door was not locked. He frowned. Janey and Bel would have lit a candle by now if they were in. Perhaps Jack was on his own and sleeping. If Janey found out, he'd get a clip round the ear. Peering into the gloom, he went in; suddenly a light flared. Huddled by the fireplace, he saw Janey, Bel and Jack looking at him with frightened eyes. There were three strangers in the room too. It was a moment before Tom realised they all carried muskets.

Bewildered, he stared at them. The one who seemed older than the rest spoke first.

'Tom Goodluck?'

'Yes.'

Before Tom had time to move, the other two men had his arms pinioned. 'What's happening?' he gasped. 'I've done nothing wrong.'

The eldest man gave a bark of laughter. 'That's what they all say.' A portentous note crept into his voice. 'Tom Goodluck, in the name of Her Majesty Queen Elizabeth, I arrest you for the murder of William Kemp of Salisbury.'

The blood roared in Tom's ears. 'William Kemp murdered? But I know nothing of it. I didn't kill him.'

'The court will decide that. Until then, you'll lodge in Newgate.' He nodded to his companions. 'Bring him along.'

'Go and find Master Lamotte, Jack,' Tom shouted as he was dragged struggling to the door. His heels bumped over the threshold. 'Tell him what's happened.'

*

Within Newgate's forbidding walls, Tom soon lost count of the iron gates they went through. Manhandled up and down dark stairways and along narrow corridors, he felt as if he were being sucked into the entrails of some monstrous beast.

At last they reached a small, bare room illuminated by a single candle. A burly gaoler with the long, lugubrious face of a bloodhound sat at a table slicing the raw onion on a plate in front of him. The pungent smell assailed Tom's nostrils, mingling with the reek of wet wool he and his captors had brought with them. His stomach churned and there was an acid taste in his mouth.

The gaoler speared a slice of onion with his knife and surveyed Tom.

'Well, lads, what have you brought me?'

'Thomas Goodluck – charge of robbery and murder.'

The gaoler slid the onion slice into his mouth and chewed it slowly. He jerked his thumb at the purse hanging from Tom's belt. One of the guards unfastened it and dropped it on the table. The gaoler loosened the drawstring and tipped out the coins.

'Won't buy much in here,' he remarked, scooping the coins into a drawer.

'Maybe he'll swing 'fore too long and save himself some money,' one of the guards sniggered.

The gaoler pared another slice from his onion. 'Fifth cell along: solitary.'

As they went along the corridor, Tom's ears rang with the commotion. Men of all ages with ravaged faces and haunted eyes jostled to be first at the bars of their cells, cursing and pleading, shaking the bars with grimy hands. A greybeard spat at the guards and one of them smacked his stick over the old man's bony knuckles. He recoiled, howling.

The cell they stopped at was smaller than the others with space only for one man. The guards pushed Tom in and the door clanged shut behind them. The echo of their footsteps faded and with it, the brightness of the lanterns they carried. It was some time before Tom's eyes adjusted to the dim light coming from a slit in the wall above his head.

The cell was just deep enough for him to lie straight. Its walls glistened with damp and the air was rank with the smell of stale urine and excrement. Dazed, he sat down on the hard ground. The heavy irons around his wrists and ankles cut into him and his jaw ached where one of the guards had hit him. His mind raced. William Kemp murdered? Who would have wanted him dead? He had been alive the day before Tom left Salisbury. When had it happened?

Desolation swamped him. He understood enough about the law to know how hard it was for a poor man to prove his innocence. Suppose he could not do so? What then? Remembering the guard's grim jest, a chill crept over him. The cold seemed to invade his bones and his feet and hands were numb.

The sound of heavy footsteps in the corridor roused him from his lethargy. Half blinded by lantern light, he saw a shadowy face on the other side of the bars. A leathery hand with grimy nails pushed a metal pan through the small gap at the bottom of them.

'Gruel, and be thankful, you're lucky to get it at this hour,' a rheumy voice muttered.

'How am I to eat it? Will you take these irons off?' Tom held up his chained wrists.

The guard gave a wheeze of laughter that dissolved in coughs. 'You'll find a way when you're hungry enough. The irons don't come off until the guvnor gives the nod, and that costs money.'

'But you've taken my money.'

'Entry fee and the gruel.'

Tom struggled to get up but then stumbled and, unable to put out a hand to save himself, fell down again hitting his head on the wall.

'You can't hold me here,' he gasped. 'I'm innocent.'

'Of course you are, just like everyone else in this hole. Well, you'd better hope some friend of yours finds a way to prove it.' The guard slouched away, taking the light with him.

Tom jerked himself away from the wall and edged across the floor to the gruel. Eventually he managed to get the bowl to his mouth. The sloppy mess was bland and cold but he ate it up to the last scrap. Afterwards, a sudden urge to piss seized him. He doubted he would be allowed out of the cell for that either without paying.

He tottered to his feet, shuffled to a corner and fumbled with the strings of his breeches. When he had finished, he went back to the bars and huddled up against them. Closing his eyes, he fell into an exhausted sleep.

*

The toll of a bell woke him from a fitful doze. He blinked at the misty grey light in the narrow window. It must be dawn.

'What did the bell mean?' he asked the guards who arrived later with a cauldron of some evil-smelling brew.

'Death knell,' answered one of them. 'It's always rung at dawn 'fore a prisoner goes to Tyburn. This one slit his old lady's throat.' He jerked a thumb at his mate. 'Walt here knew her. Says she was a shrew, but murder's murder.'

He sniffed the air. 'You better learn to keep your water for the yard unless you want to live in your own filth.'

'The yard?'

'Twenty minutes you get. You're a lucky one too,' he went on. 'Someone's paid for easement of irons for you.' He opened the door. 'Walt stays out here so don't try anything clever.'

The guard unlocked the irons and removed them. Tom rubbed his sore wrists. Red weals encircled them and in places the skin had broken. He put one to his mouth and tasted the mineral tang of blood.

The guard stepped out smartly and the door clanged shut once more. 'Now push out your tin,' he said.

The broth he ladled into it was thin with soggy lumps of turnip and a few grains of barley floating under its scummy surface. Ravenous, Tom wolfed it down in spite of its rancid smell. As he wiped his lips he wondered if it was Lamotte who had paid the money. He doubted the family at Angel Lane could have found enough to satisfy the gaoler. Perhaps that meant Lamotte would come soon. A glimmer of hope entered Tom's heart.

'When are we let out?' he shouted after the guards but there was no answer. There was nothing for it but to wait.

Not long afterwards, he was taken from his cell and roped in a line with six other prisoners. At an awkward trot, he stumbled along the corridors behind an old man with ragged hair and shrivelled arms and legs protruding from tattered clothes.

The yard was bounded by a high wall and measured about twenty feet square. Tom reckoned there were thirty men and a handful of women penned up there. A cold drizzle fell from the leaden sky and he wrapped his arms around his body for warmth. Some of the other prisoners gave him

124

curious looks but most ignored him, furtively relieving themselves against the nearest wall or simply staring blankly, apparently oblivious to their surroundings.

On the side opposite the door back to the cells was a kind of cage. Some of the prisoners were crowding around it noisily. When Tom moved closer, he saw it was full of people but, from the way they were dressed, they were not inmates.

Lamotte pushed his way through the crowd and grasped the bars.

'Tom! Thank Heaven I've found you.'

A violent trembling seized Tom. He fought to hold back tears. 'Master Lamotte!'

'Jack told me everything,' Lamotte said. 'I've paid for you to be moved to a better part of the prison. Tonight you should be given blankets, more food, soap and candles. I want to know about it if you're not. It's all I can do at the moment.'

'I didn't kill him.'

'I believe you. Do you have any idea who the guilty man might be?'

Tom shook his head.

'Was there anyone in Salisbury who wished you ill?'

'Only the other clerk who worked with me at Lawyer Kemp's.' Quickly, he explained about Ralph. When he had finished, Lamotte looked grave.

'I understood you left Salisbury because you feared exposure from some quarter was coming, but not because this fellow had actually threatened you with it. Why didn't you tell me?'

Tom flushed. 'I was ashamed that I let him beat me.'

'You shouldn't be. There was nothing you could have done. All the same, it doesn't make Ralph Fiddler a murderer.'

'No,' Tom said unhappily. 'It doesn't.'

A bell rang and guards moved in from their posts around the yard, sticks and halberds at the ready.

125

'We'll talk more of this,' Lamotte called out as Tom was roped back into line with some of the other prisoners. 'There'll be a way to get you out of here. Until then, I'll make sure you're as comfortable as possible.'

*

In the hope of obtaining an audience with Walsingham, Lamotte left Newgate and hurried to Seething Lane. He was not as confident as he had pretended to Tom. Walsingham was not long returned from Fotheringay, where he had sat as one of the commissioners appointed to try the Queen of Scots for treason. He was likely to be angry that a verdict of guilty against his bitter enemy had not been reached and the proceedings had been adjourned. The evidence was to be reviewed at a later date in the Star Chamber at Westminster.

'Sir Francis is out at Barn Elms,' the servant who came to the door told him. Lamotte hurried home and called for his horse. It would be faster to ride than go by river. Hatless and throwing on the first cloak that came to hand, he rode to Mortlake.

'The master is hawking in the park,' said the footman who answered the door. Lamotte jumped back in the saddle and cantered away. Soon, the sight of a bird of prey soaring above a spinney then diving earthwards directed him to where Walsingham and his falconer stood.

'Alexandre!' Walsingham's expression was surprisingly affable. 'Come and see Artemis, she has killed four times today.'

Lamotte offered up a silent prayer of thanks. The old spymaster was far more jovial than he had expected. It seemed the crisp autumn weather and his pleasure in hawking had put him in a good mood.

The goshawk's fierce, ochre eyes were trained on the bloody gobbet of flesh the falconer held out to it. It dropped the dead rabbit dangling from its razor-sharp beak and snatched the meat. With a deft movement, the falconer

126

slipped the hood over its head and fastened the jesses to his gauntleted wrist.

'Excellent work.' Walsingham stroked the goshawk's dappled plumage. 'Enough for today,' he said to the falconer. 'You may take her back to the mews.' The man nodded.

'Do you have some information for me?' Walsingham asked as the man walked away. The tone of his voice was sharper now they were alone. Once more, Lamotte felt uneasy, reminded that by coming uninvited without any intelligence Walsingham might want, he had put himself on uncertain ground. Still, Tom needed his help: he must press on. He swallowed hard.

'I regret I've brought no information, Sir Francis, and I hope you will forgive me for coming unbidden, but a young man of my acquaintance has been wrongly arrested.'

The shrewd, dark eyes scrutinised him. 'Wrongly arrested?'

Lamotte held to his resolve. 'Yes.'

'On what charge?'

'Murder.'

'No light matter. What is he to you, this young man?'

'A friend - his name is Tom Goodluck.'

'Your reasons for being so sure of his innocence?'

'Only my instinct, but I believe I can claim to be a good judge of men.'

'And you seek my help? Why should I give that?'

Lamotte looked down. He had been a fool to come. He had presumed too much.

'Do you know where he is held?' Walsingham asked more kindly.

Lamotte's spirits revived a little. 'Newgate, Sir Francis.'

Walsingham pondered for a few moments. 'I must not be seen to interfere in the process of the law but I'll endeavour to make a few enquiries,' he said at last.

'A thousand thanks, my lord.'

'I make no promises, you understand? Now I have business to attend to. I must return to the house. Farewell, Alexandre.'

On the ride back to his house in Throgmorton Street, Lamotte rehearsed what he would say to Tom. It was important to keep the lad's spirits up, even if it was impossible to banish his own anxiety. He was not confident they could count too much on Walsingham's help.

The strength of his distress surprised him. He had met many young hopefuls in his years in the theatre, what was so different about Tom? He shook his head. Who could say why they felt a stronger attachment to some people than others?

Except for a sleepy night watchman, the servants had gone to bed and the house was cold and desolate. Lamotte wished Amélie were there with her warm smile and wise advice. She had always known how to comfort him.

Chapter 12

By early November, Meg and Bess had moved to a different part of the woods with Sarah and her children.

The ruins of a small chapel stood at the centre of the clearing in which they camped. It must have been beautiful once, a graceful arch, ornamented with delicate carvings of leaves and flowers, still remained although most of the walls had vanished. Andrew said the stones must have been stolen over the years since it had been abandoned. He mined the scattered heaps of blocks that remained to build shelters for them all.

'It's a strange place to have built something so fine,' Meg remarked as she and Sarah sat together one morning by their camp fire. Tethered nearby, Samson cropped the grass.

Sarah held out her hands to the flames. 'I remember my father telling me that sometimes monks from the great abbeys would go into the forest to live simply. Perhaps that's why it's here. When King Henry closed down the abbeys, they might have lived on for years without knowing it, but as they died, no one would have come to take their places.'

'How sad.'

Sarah shrugged. 'So many sad things happen. Our parents and grandparents saw a lot of changes in their lives. You and I have too, haven't we?'

'That's true. In the old days, I often spent whole days doing nothing but sitting and sewing or gazing out of the window, but here we are always busy.'

Sarah rubbed her red-rimmed eyes and coughed. 'I'm not as busy as I should be.'

'Oh, Sarah.' Meg's knife paused over the rabbit she was skinning. 'You can't help it if you're not well. Why don't you go and lie down? You were awake half the night. I can cook our meal.'

'Are you sure?' Sarah asked hesitantly. 'I admit I'd be glad of a rest.'

'Then have one.'

After Sarah had gone into the hut, Meg stripped the last of the pelt from the rabbit and jointed the carcass. And that's another change, she thought, wiping her blood-smeared hands on a rag. In my old life, I would never have done this.

She sighed. Her journey to Plymouth with Andrew had been fruitless. They had enquired at the docks but Tom's name was not on any of the ship registers and after a week of asking at every inn and tavern, she had despaired of finding him. If he had ever been at Plymouth, it seemed that he was not there now. Reluctantly, she returned with Andrew to Sarah and the others. Since then, it had been a strange existence, part of her distracted by the demands of her new life, part of her regretting the comforts she had lost, but the greatest part yearning for Tom. Waking or sleeping, his face was never far from her mind. Did he still carry her in his thoughts?

Samson lifted his head and whinnied. Meg glanced up and saw Andrew walking across the clearing.

'Did you catch anything?' she called out.

'A perch and two bream.' He held out a basket of woven green willow.

'Good. I'll gut them for you. We can eat the bream tonight and put the perch in the salt barrel.'

'Where are the others?'

'Bess has taken Agnes for a walk. I asked them to bring back some wild thyme if they can find it. I want to burn some bunches in the hut to sweeten the air. Perhaps it will help Sarah's cough.'

'Is she sleeping?'

130

Meg saw his troubled expression and felt a pang of sorrow. She wished she could comfort him but they both knew Sarah was rapidly worsening.

At harvest time, they had left the woods and found work helping a local farmer bring in his crops. The money they earned had paid for necessities they could not make or catch themselves – cloth, thread, needles, yeast and salt – but Sarah had been too weak to come with them. Bitterly, Meg often regretted she had not profited more from her mother's knowledge of herbs and how they could be used to make healing poultices and infusions. If only she had done, she might have been able to lessen Sarah's suffering, but it was too late now. Every day, she grew frailer.

With a sniff, Andrew scrambled to his feet. 'I'll go and check my traps,' he said.

Sadly, Meg watched him disappear into the trees. She tossed the jointed rabbit into the pot and wiped the knife before making a slit along one side of the perch and scraping out its guts. For Andrew's sake, she had tried to seem cheerful. No doubt he did the same for her, but underneath it, they both knew a long winter loomed ahead. With a shiver, Meg wondered what was in store for them all.

*

December came and the nights grew colder. In the mornings, the grass was stiff with frost. One day, when even by noon the watery sun had not burnt it all off, Andrew put more wood on the fire and sat staring into the flames. Coming out of the hut where she had been tending to Sarah, Meg smelt the comforting scent of wood smoke and went to join him. Her heart lurched when she saw his haggard expression.

'I heard Mother coughing all night,' he said dully. 'She's getting much worse, isn't she?'

'I fear so.'

There was a scurrying of feet and she put her finger to her lips. 'Hush, Agnes is coming.' But it was too late.

Barefoot and huddled in a patched woollen cloak, Agnes ran to them and buried her head in Meg's lap. 'I don't want Mother to be ill,' she mumbled. 'Make her better.'

Gently, Meg lifted her chin and smoothed the hair from her tear-stained face. 'We all want her to be better, dearest, but it won't help if you catch a chill running about with no boots on. Go back to Bess and she will help you dress properly.'

She sighed as she watched Agnes trail off. 'Poor child, it's so hard for her.' She rubbed her hand over her forehead. 'Andrew, I don't think we should stay in the woods this winter. It's getting colder every day. Soon we shan't be able to keep the hut warm. I don't know how we'll manage with Sarah then.'

'But where else can we go?'

'We need to find work somewhere so we can make her comfortable.'

Andrew shook his head. 'Getting work at harvest time was one thing but in the winter? We tried before and it was no use.'

Meg squared her shoulders. 'We must try again.'

The next day Andrew busied himself splitting lengths of wood and lashing the pieces together with strips of hide from the animal skins they had collected over the summer months to form a makeshift sledge. 'As soon as the snow comes,' he said, 'we'll harness Samson and he can pull it.'

The first fall was a week later. With their few possessions in sacks slung like panniers over Samson's broad back, the five of them set off. Before the little camp disappeared from sight, Meg turned for one last look. She hoped she had done the right thing persuading the others to leave it.

They walked all day before coming to a road. Although fresh snow filled the troughs of rutted mud, it was still difficult for Samson to drag the sledge over such rough ground so Andrew led him across the deeper drifts along the side. By dusk, they reached a hamlet where lights glowed in the windows of the cottages, but Meg hesitated to knock on doors. People might be suspicious of travellers arriving so late in the day. Instead, they found a deserted barn and stayed there for the night.

Two more days passed before they came to some cottages scattered along the road then they were in the centre of a village. Most of its houses looked prosperous. A church built of stone, surrounded by a graveyard, stood on a hill a little way off. A thatched inn with whitewashed, rough-cast walls had an inviting air, a plume of smoke rising from its chimney.

Bess shivered. 'I'm so cold. Do you think they will let us in?'

'It looks like the only place we might find work,' Andrew said gloomily.

'We don't want any beggars here,' the woman who answered the door snapped. A gust of warm air and the smell of baking billowed out from the room behind her. She was dumpy with a crisply starched coif and a voluminous linen apron covering most of her brown, homespun dress.

'We're not beggars, we'll work.'

'I've no work for the likes of you,' the woman said flatly.

She noticed Sarah and suddenly pulled her apron up over her face, backing away. 'Thomas!' she shouted. A moment later, a hefty, florid man emerged. His hands were as big as hams and he held a thick, knobbed stick. Behind him, a large black dog bared its teeth. Agnes shrank closer to Bess.

'Be off with you,' he snarled. 'And don't come back.'

Meg's stomach tightened. 'There's no need to talk to us like that, we're going.'

The man stepped back inside and slammed the door in their faces. The inn sign creaked on its rusty chains like a mocking laugh.

'Now what do we do?' Bess asked miserably.

'We keep on walking. Somewhere there must be someone who will help us,' said Meg.

133

She hoped she sounded more confident than she felt. It was three days since they had left their encampment and almost all their store of food was gone. So far at night, they had been lucky in finding remote farm buildings to sleep in but they might not always be so fortunate. Sarah's listless demeanour alarmed her, and the others, even Andrew, were close to exhaustion. If they didn't find help soon, she feared the worst.

That afternoon, the wind veered to the east, driving sleet in their faces. Samson's breath turned to steam in the frosty air, settling again in tiny shards of ice on the long lashes fringing his mournful eyes.

Meg's fingers and toes throbbed. Earlier in the day, she and Bess had tried to keep Agnes's spirits up by singing songs but now Agnes dozed on Andrew's back as he struggled grimly through the snow, leading Samson. Meg scanned the white waste ahead: nothing but bare trees and hedgerows as far as the eye could see. They would hardly provide adequate shelter for the night that was fast approaching.

In the gathering gloom, the road was slippery as glass. All at once, Bess's feet shot from under her and she fell on her back. Meg reached for her and saw that the colour had drained from her face.

'I can't get up,' she sobbed. 'My leg hurts. I think it might be broken.'

'You have to,' Meg shouted over the wind. 'If you don't, you'll freeze to death.'

'I don't care.'

Another gust buffeted Meg. She blinked back tears. 'Bess, this is hard for all of us, please be sensible. The others are already ahead now. We must catch them up.'

'You go then. Leave me here.'

'No, but I'll run on and get Andrew. If I take Agnes for a while, he'll come back for you. Samson isn't carrying so much now that most of our food is gone. Maybe you could ride on his back.'

134

Meg stifled her anger as she hurried ahead. Bess probably hadn't broken her leg but it was unfair to blame her for giving up. I am close to it myself, she thought.

Suddenly, beneath the howl of the wind, she heard a different sound. She turned and saw a sight that chilled her blood. On the road behind Bess, a bulky shape lumbered towards them, its outline growing gradually clearer until Meg realised it was a wagon. She broke into a run and reached Bess. She seized her by the shoulder.

'Bess! Get up, you can't stay there.' Bess shook her head. She didn't seem to have noticed the wagon.

Frantic, Meg stood up and flailed her arms, screaming at the top of her voice, but the wind only flung her words back at her. The rumble of wheels filled her ears then the wagon was upon them. As the muddy ground seemed to rear up to meet her, Meg was dimly aware of voices shouting and the alarmed whinnies of horses, then there was darkness.

When she recovered her wits, she hadn't the strength to raise her head. She felt cold slush beneath her but she didn't care. All she wanted was to lie down forever. Slowly, though, the dizziness receded and she became aware of someone beside her. With difficulty, she turned her head to see who it was but all she could discern were shadowy figures. She closed her eyes and rested her head on the ground once more.

'Oh Richard, is she badly hurt?' The voice was a woman's.

'I can't tell in this light,' a deeper one answered. 'Martin! Fetch another lantern.'

Meg blinked and tried to shield her eyes as the light grew brighter.

'She moved.' Relief flooded the woman's voice. Meg smelt a faint perfume of lavender and felt warm breath on her cheek.

'Can you stand?' the woman asked.

'I think so,' Meg said shakily then all at once, she remembered the wagon. 'Bess! Where's Bess?' she cried.

A hand stroked her shoulder. 'It's all right, she's safe. Now let's get you up off this cold ground. Richard! Martin! Help her to her feet.'

Meg felt strong arms lift her. Tentatively, she shuffled forwards and stumbled.

'You're still too weak to walk,' the woman said. 'Martin, our groom, and my brother, Richard, will help you to the wagon. Martin can drive you to our house. It isn't far away.'

'My friends…'

'Of course. Richard will look after them. We have another conveyance. When you are safe, Martin will come back to help.' She caught her hood as the wind tried to whip it back from her hair. 'No one should be out of doors on a terrible night like this.'

Still trembling with shock, Meg let herself be led to the back of the wagon. She was overjoyed to see Bess already there tucked between the trunks and boxes. The woman disappeared into the darkness and a few moments later, the wagon started to jolt along. Its progress was slow and Meg winced at every bump but eventually it lurched to the left and passed through a wide stone gateway. Bess, who had been very quiet, clutched Meg's hand. 'Oh madam, wherever are we going?'

'I don't much care,' Meg replied, 'as long as it is somewhere dry and warm.'

As Martin, the groom, helped them down from the wagon, a cloaked rider passed them and halted close by. By the light of the lanterns on either side of a great oak door, Meg had a dim impression of an imposing stone house with gabled roofs that boasted a forest of elaborate chimneys. They were in a walled courtyard and the wind had dropped a little.

Martin hurried to help the rider dismount and as the hood of the cloak fell back, Meg saw it was a woman. Meg guessed she must be the same one who had helped them on the road. She was tall and moved very gracefully.

136

'Martin, find Alice and tell her to unlock the door, then take my horse back and help Master Richard,' she said.

But their arrival had already been noticed for the door creaked and a wedge of orange light spilt out. A plump woman stood there, her hands thrown up as if she were polishing the air.

'Mistress Beatrice! We were not expecting you. The fires are not all lit. When I think you've travelled on such a terrible night as this! The coach might have been overturned or struck by falling trees.'

'But it wasn't. Dear Alice, as you see, I am safe, and Master Richard is not far behind.' She pointed to Meg and Bess. 'We found these travellers in difficulties on the road.'

Alice looked Meg and Bess up and down with an expression that made Meg very uncomfortable.

'They'll need dry clothes,' Beatrice went on. 'And so will their companions, a lady, a young man and a little girl. Please look out something ready for them too.'

Alice's disapproving expression deepened. 'I don't know we have anything suitable.'

'What about in the old nursery? Surely you can find something for them there?'

Alice's grey dress strained over her ample bosom. 'If you say so, Mistress Beatrice.'

'After that they will all need some food. Is the fire in the kitchen still alight?'

Alice nodded.

'Excellent. Then it will be warm in there at least.'

She turned to Bess and Meg. 'Forgive me, I've not told you my name: it's Beatrice Lacey. 'May I know yours?'

Meg's mouth was dry. Bess shot her a worried look. She still wore her boy's clothes, but the likelihood of keeping her sex a secret for long was slim. She thought of the shame of being found out by Beatrice Lacey's brother or one of the menservants.

Beatrice looked puzzled. 'Is something the matter?'

137

Resolutely, Meg drew a breath. 'This is Bess, and my name is Meg.'

A long silence ensued. Alice was first to break it. 'Wickedness,' she muttered. 'That such wickedness should come under this roof.'

Beatrice gave her a reproving glance. 'There will be time for explanations later, Alice. Please take both of them upstairs and find some clothes.'

When they came downstairs again, after a tight-lipped Alice had produced dry clothes for them to wear, Beatrice was in the hall with Sarah and Agnes. Sarah was on her feet but her face was grey with fatigue. There was no sign of Andrew.

'Here you are.' Beatrice gave them an encouraging smile. 'Is there a room ready where this lady, Sarah, may rest?' she asked Alice.

Alice nodded stiffly.

'Good.'

Agnes ran to Bess.

'May I help Sarah?' Meg asked. 'Bess will look after Agnes.'

'Of course.'

Exuding disapproval, Alice led Meg and Sarah up a narrow flight of stairs to a small but pleasant room. She lit the candles on the mantelpiece and glanced at the grate.

'Will you be wanting a fire?' she asked in a curt tone.

'We don't want to be any trouble,' Meg said meekly.

'Then I won't light it.'

She went to the door then paused. 'I'll fetch some nightclothes for you. I suppose you have none of your own.'

'Thank you,' Sarah stammered.

'You mustn't mind her,' Meg whispered, when Alice had left. 'We have shelter for the night. That's all that matters.'

Sarah sank down on the bed. 'What must they all think of us?'

138

Meg shrugged. 'At least Beatrice Lacey is kind, even if her servant is not.' She put her arm around Sarah's heaving shoulders. 'Don't cry,' she begged. 'Tomorrow when you've slept everything will seem better.'

They sat there quietly until there was a peremptory knock at the door and Alice came in with an armful of linen. She put it down on the floor with the covered cup she also carried. 'These nightclothes are the best we can offer, and Mistress Beatrice says you're to have this posset to help you sleep,' she said shortly. Without waiting to be thanked, she left the room.

Meg helped Sarah to change and get into bed. Sarah leant back against the pillows with a deep sigh. 'I don't care so much what that woman thinks of me now.'

'I'm glad to hear it.' Meg crossed the room, brought back the covered cup and removed the lid. A sweet, spicy aroma rose from the contents.

'I've never seen you in a dress,' Sarah remarked when she had drunk a few sips. 'It's very becoming.'

Meg laughed. 'It feels strange. These skirts seem determined to trip me up at every opportunity.'

'You'll soon be used to them again.'

Meg smoothed a finger down one of the side seams. There were tiny needle marks in the sage-green cloth. 'I think the seams have been let out many times. Do you think Alice wore it in her slimmer days?'

Sarah managed a weak chuckle. 'I can't imagine Alice being slim.'

She held out the cup. 'Will you have some too?'

Meg shook her head. 'No, you drink it all. I'm sure they will give me something later. Could you eat if I ask to bring some food up?'

Sarah shook her head. 'This is enough.' She drained the cup. 'I feel as if I'm in a dream,' she said sleepily. 'I never thought a stranger would do so much for us.'

'Most of them won't,' Meg said dryly. 'Beatrice Lacey is unusual.'

'I wonder why.'

Meg took the empty cup. 'Perhaps we shall find out tomorrow. Now sleep. I'll ask if I can have a room nearby so I'll hear you if you call in the night.'

Sarah's eyelids drooped. 'Bless you, Meg,' she murmured.

Downstairs, the smell of food made Meg realise how hungry she was. She followed the sound of voices to the kitchen where she found Bess and Agnes. A tabby cat was curled up in the inglenook. 'Her name's Clover,' Agnes said. 'She's very fat. The lady says she's going to have kittens soon. I hope we're here to see them,' she added wistfully.

Bess pointed to the food set out on a table nearby. 'Mistress Beatrice says we can have what we like.'

Meg sat down and ate. She had forgotten how good fresh cheese and white bread tasted. There were apples and a jug of ale as well.

She had just finished when Beatrice came into the room. Meg and Bess rose quickly to their feet but she motioned them to sit again.

'Andrew has already gone to the menservants' quarters and Alice has made a room ready for you near to where your friend Sarah is sleeping. I hope she is more comfortable now.'

Meg nodded. 'Yes, and I don't know how to thank you. Your kindness is far more than we deserve. We must not impose on it for long. We'll travel on tomorrow.'

Beatrice frowned. 'I fear the bad weather may be set in for some time and it may be unwise, but let's discuss it in the morning. If you have had enough to eat, Alice will show you to your room. I hope you will excuse me if I say goodnight. It was a tiring journey today.'

'Of course, and thank you again.'

*

140

Meg was too tired to stay awake that night but she woke early, her mind full of anxiety. In the cold light of morning, last night seemed like a dream. Unquestioningly kind as Beatrice and her brother had been, they were bound to be curious and want answers soon. She did not know what to tell them.

After a while, there were faint sounds from the next room, where Sarah lay. Slipping out of bed, Meg crept out into the passageway and knocked on her door. 'Sarah?' she whispered. 'It's me, Meg.'

Sarah lay in bed looking brighter than she had for many days. 'You must tell them the truth about our family,' she said firmly when Meg had confided her fears. 'But I'm afraid only you can decide what to say on your own behalf. One thing I do feel sure of, though, is that Beatrice and her brother would not want to do you harm.'

'I hope you're right,' Meg said gloomily.

When Meg dressed and came downstairs, Beatrice was nowhere to be seen. As Meg ate her breakfast with Bess and Agnes in the kitchen and then took some up to Sarah, her fears mounted. The storm had blown over but from the upstairs window, she saw that it had ripped whole branches from some of the trees in the park. The sky was still a leaden grey. A journey today would not be easy.

Several hours passed before Beatrice asked her to come to the Great Hall. Clearly it had once been a magnificent room but Meg noticed signs of decay in the shabby furniture and the worn brocade curtains that hung at the tall, narrow windows. An enormous fireplace of carved stone dominated the long wall opposite the windows and a cheerful fire blazed in the grate.

'Did you sleep well?' Beatrice asked. 'I'm sorry Richard isn't here. He is occupied with other matters this morning.'

Meg felt a surge of relief. It would be easier talking to Beatrice by herself.

'I hope you will forgive Alice's behaviour last night,' Beatrice continued. 'She's not always so uncharitable but

141

she brought Richard and me up after our mother died. Sometimes I think she forgets we are no longer children and quite capable of making choices for ourselves.'

'Even if your choice is to bring strangers into the house? I doubt many people would have done so.'

'You needed help. I hope no Christian would have left you on the road.'

'I fear not everyone thinks as you do.'

There was a pause. Meg felt her heartbeat quicken. 'I expect you wonder why we were there,' she ventured.

'I confess I do. Are you prepared to tell me? I don't wish to pry, but as you are in my house, I would like to know.'

Meg lowered her eyes. 'Your generosity gives you every right to. I only hope that when you do, you will not regret you ever helped us. Sarah and her family have fallen on hard times through no fault of their own. My case is different. However you judge me, I hope you will pity them.'

She looked up at Beatrice's face; the kindness in her dark eyes was reassuring. Suddenly, Meg felt as if a great weight had slid from her shoulders. She began to tell her story.

Chapter 13

February, 1587

A raw east wind made Lamotte's eyes water as he rode out of London on the road to Fotheringay. His breath hung in miniature clouds on the icy air. It was evil weather for travelling, but Walsingham required him to witness Queen Mary's execution and he must obey. Walsingham had refused to attend himself. He was suffering from one of his frequent bouts of ill health, but even if that were not the case, Lamotte suspected he would have stayed away. In the face of tremendous odds, he had done what was necessary to protect his queen and country. He was not a man to gloat in victory.

Over three months had passed since Mary had been found guilty of treason and a less cautious monarch than Queen Elizabeth would probably have long ago signed the death warrant. Characteristically, however, Elizabeth had prevaricated, giving impenetrable answers to her ministers' pleas. Lamotte knew he was not alone in suspecting she would have preferred her cousin, Mary, to be assassinated, to avoid having the Scottish queen's blood on her hands. But what man in his right mind would do that? Almost certainly, the queen would preserve her honour by denouncing and executing him afterwards.

The snow blanketing the road had already been churned up by other travellers. In places it had hardened into treacherous sheets of ice. Often, Lamotte had to slow his horse and ride with great caution to avoid a fall. 'Seventy-five miles on this God-forsaken road,' he muttered, 'seventy-five miles with nowhere but flea-ridden wayside inns to lay my head.'

It was with relief that a few days later he trotted over the drawbridge into Fotheringay Castle. A cart piled high with barrels of beer and tuns of wine rumbled into the outer bailey after him. Over by the kitchens servants unloaded sides of beef and mutton from another cart; boxes of onions and roots were stacked nearby. More servants bustled in and out of doorways with bedding and chamber pots, no doubt preparing visitors' lodgings.

Leaving his horse at the stables, Lamotte walked through to the inner bailey and entered the keep. Mary's gaoler, Amyas Paulet, met him at the head of the stairs and took him to his private quarters.

'She will be told tonight that the execution is due to take place at eight o'clock in the morning,' Paulet said grimly. 'The business is best done with as little ceremony as possible. I don't want Mary to have the opportunity to make trouble.'

Lamotte wondered what trouble a frail, middle-aged woman, already condemned to death and surrounded by guards, could make, but he let the remark pass.

'You have a letter for me from Sir Francis?' Paulet asked.

With a nod, Lamotte handed it over and watched Paulet scan it. He found him an unprepossessing man with his pinched, sour face and drooping moustache.

After a few minutes, Paulet folded the letter, placed it in the box at his elbow and turned the key. 'As always,' he remarked, 'Sir Francis is most exact in his instructions. You may tell him the queen's body and her worldly goods will be disposed of as he commands. Does he wish you to remain here until the proceedings are over so you may report to him?'

'Yes.'

'Then I advise you to see John Hobbey, our steward, without delay. He will find you lodgings.'

Lamotte withdrew and went to find Hobbey.

*

When he entered the Great Hall early the next morning, Lamotte was glad to see a good blaze roaring in the big fireplace. The room was empty of furniture except for a low dais, looking uncannily like the kind of stage a company of travelling players would use, set up at one end. Black velvet covered the whole construction and a high-backed chair with a footstool, also draped in black, stood in one corner. Opposite it was the block.

Yet in spite of its lack of furniture, the room was far from deserted. In defiance of Paulet's wishes, it buzzed with onlookers. Lamotte guessed there were at least two hundred people gathered there.

'Local knights and gentry eager to have something to tell their grandchildren,' the man walking in beside him chuckled. 'A thousand more by my reckoning in the outer bailey, but they are common folk.'

As the hour of the execution approached, the crowd grew restive. Lamotte had not attempted to talk with anyone; he thought it best to draw as little attention to himself as possible, but he had picked up plenty of snippets of the chatter around him. He would be able to assure Walsingham that, in Fotheringay at least, Mary's death would cause little sorrow.

He shifted his weight and rolled his shoulders to ease his aching back. The straw mattress last night had been lumpy and thin. Breakfast had not been much better. The sooner this was over and he was on the way home the happier he would feel.

Three hours passed and still there was no sign of Mary. At last, the sheriff's men arrived and took up their stations by the stage, their halberds planted in front of them and their eyes staring blankly ahead. The noise stilled to a hum and then silence as the Earls of Shrewsbury and Kent entered the hall. Amyas Paulet came next, walking ahead of Mary herself. Four guards and two of her women brought up the rear. Both of the women wept.

Apparently oblivious to the officer on whose arm she leant, Mary led the forlorn little party to the dais and, with the quiet air of one going to her prayers, slowly ascended the three steps. As she took her place on the high-backed chair, the audience remained very still. Her small figure, dressed also in black, was almost lost against the black velvet drapes and the feeble light dulled the gleam of her white veil and ruff. The only colour it could not suppress was the vivid auburn of her hair.

A murmur rose from the onlookers. Lamotte studied her closely. The outlines of her beauty were still visible in her melancholy, dark eyes and wistful mouth, but her heart-shaped face was lined and careworn. So this was the woman for whom so many men had died: Babington, Rizzio, Darnley, Norfolk and the thousands who had lost their lives on northern moors and scaffolds in the Great Rebellion; the woman whose legend had hung over England like the sword of Damocles for twenty years; the granddaughter of Henry VIII's elder sister, Margaret; the woman who, in the view of staunch Catholics, had a better claim to the throne of England than her cousin, Elizabeth.

The clerk to the Privy Council stood to read the execution warrant. As his words died away, a shout of 'God save Queen Elizabeth!' rang out. Lamotte marvelled at Mary's calm expression in the face of death.

The clerk sat down and, rising stiffly, Richard Fletcher, the Dean of Peterborough, prepared to speak. Clad in black with hunched shoulders and a scrawny neck, he had the air of a vulture.

'Madam,' he began in his braying, nasal voice, 'the Queen's Most Excellent Majesty, notwithstanding this just preparation for the execution of justice to be done upon you – ahem – for your many trespasses against her sacred person, offers you the comfortable promises of Almighty God to all penitent believing Christians.'

Lamotte winced at the mangling of language. Mary raised her hand in an imperious gesture.

'Master Dean! Do not trouble yourself or me, for I am settled in the ancient Catholic and Roman religion, and in its defence, with God's help, I mean to spend my blood. I am not afraid to die, and I pray for my cousin's soul.' Her voice was clear and musical, and Lamotte felt himself respond to its seductive timbre. Around him, men craned forward.

The dean bridled. 'Madam, I did not come here to dispute with you.' He flushed as a ripple of laughter rose from the audience.

'Forgive me.' Mary lowered her eyes. 'I thought you wished to discuss religion.'

'This is unseemly, madam.'

Her chin lifted. 'Do you not think what you do today is "unseemly", sir?'

For a moment, their eyes locked. If it were possible, Mary's face had grown even paler in contrast to the dean's choleric flush, but her bravado, Lamotte saw, was paper thin; already tears streamed down her cheeks.

The dean abandoned his lecture and started to pray. Mary stumbled from the chair and fell to her knees. In a voice choked with sobs, she prayed for the Catholic Church and for her own deliverance. She prayed too for her son, James, to whom she had, many years ago, been forced to surrender the Scottish throne. Finally, she prayed for the salvation of Elizabeth's soul. Her ladies-in-waiting joined in, drowning the dean's words, as the audience watched aghast.

The Earl of Kent lumbered to his feet. 'Madam, I beseech you, settle Christ in your heart. Leave aside these popish trumperies.'

Mary ignored him.

Sweat pricked Lamotte's forehead. How much longer would Paulet let this farce continue? As the scene teetered on the edge of disaster, Bull, the executioner, stepped to

147

Mary's side and spoke quietly in her ear. With a shuddering sob, she ceased her prayers. He helped her to her feet and led her to the block. She waited calmly for him and his assistant to disrobe her, her face transformed by the ghost of a smile.

'I have never had such grooms attend me before, nor put off my garments in such company,' she remarked. Once more, her voice was clear as water.

The black dress slipped from her shoulders to pool at her feet. With the rest of the onlookers, Lamotte gasped. Underneath, she wore a scarlet shift: the scarlet of the Catholic martyrs. Walsingham would be enraged.

She gave Bull her blessing and forgiveness then one of her ladies stepped forward to tie a white kerchief over her eyes. She knelt and put her neck on the block, stretching her arms out on either side.

With a shudder, Lamotte watched Bull's muscular biceps swell and ripple. The tension in the hall was palpable.

'Into your hands, Lord—' Mary cried out, but before she could finish, the axe fell. The audience gasped as the blade struck the knot of the blindfold and rebounded. A barely audible moan broke from Mary's lips.

Bull hefted the axe again. This time his aim was true. Blood spurted from Mary's severed neck as her head toppled to the floor. Laying down the axe, Bull grasped a handful of her luxuriant, auburn hair to lift her head for all to see. A gasp erupted from the crowd as the head, covered only with grey stubble, fell and rolled away, leaving Mary's wig dangling in Bull's hand.

Lamotte felt a surge of pity. A final, pathetic secret had been revealed for all to see.

*

'The witch made fools of us.' Amyas Paulet's ugly face twisted in a scowl. 'The insolence - praying for Her Majesty's soul. And didn't I say none of her people should be allowed to attend her?'

148

'Enough, Paulet,' the Earl of Shrewsbury said sharply. 'A man would have to be inhuman to have denied her the comfort of her people at the end. How could Kent and I refuse her entreaties?'

Kent muttered his assent.

'Certainly, when she was in your charge, you had difficulty resisting her,' Paulet rasped.

Shrewsbury's hand shot to the hilt of his sword then he turned his back on Paulet and stalked to the far end of the room. Kent gave Paulet an uneasy look.

'Well, there's nothing to be done about it now,' Paulet snapped. 'Lamotte, tell your master all the clothes and drapes will be burnt as he commanded. The heart and other organs will be removed and buried secretly. The plate and other valuables have already been secured and her servants are confined to their quarters until arrangements can be made to send them away. You may leave for London at your earliest convenience.'

Lamotte left the room, glad to escape the poison in the air. Outside, the acrid smell of smoke drifted in from the outer bailey. He picked his way over the icy cobbles and found the bonfire had been lit. Flames sputtered around the freshly sawn wood of the dismantled dais but as servants threw on the blood-spattered drapes, the fire picked up heat. By the time the scarlet reminder of Mary's pitiful defiance joined them, it roared. Lamotte watched the fabric writhe and blacken, then it was gone.

Later, as he snatched a meal from the kitchens and collected his horse, he wondered whether Mary's memory would be so easily eradicated.

When after many hours he rode wearily into London, Lamotte found swifter messengers had outpaced him and the city was already rejoicing. Bells rang from church towers and bonfires were being built in the streets. He stopped to watch a procession go by accompanied by a deafening chorus of pipes, tambours and musket salvos.

149

Only his steward, Brocket, was at home in Throgmorton Street. 'I'm sorry, Master Lamotte,' he said anxiously. 'There's such a stir in the city. It's as if a black cloud's been lifted and no mistake. I let the rest go and see the fun. I hope I did right.'

'It's all right, Brocket,' Lamotte yawned. He flopped into his favourite chair and stretched out his legs. 'Pull these boots off, will you, and find me some clean clothes? I seem to have brought most of Northamptonshire home on me. Is there any food in the house?'

'I'll go to the kitchens and find out, Master Lamotte. If needs be I'll prepare something myself, just as soon as I've fetched the clean clothes. Shall I light the fire before I go?'

'Thank you, Brocket. Were there any messages for me while I was away?'

'No messages, master.'

Left alone, Lamotte went to the fire in his stockinged feet and spread his hands out to the flames. His toes throbbed as the blood coursed back. With a sigh, he looked forward to his comfortable bed. He only hoped Cook had left something tasty in the kitchen. He had little faith in Brocket's efforts.

*

When he woke the following morning, his first thought was of Tom, but before he went to Newgate, he must make his report to Walsingham at Seething Lane.

The door opened and Brocket appeared with his breakfast.

'Is James sick?' Lamotte asked. It was usually the manservant's duty to attend him in the mornings.

Brocket flushed. 'The celebrations went on rather late last night, master.'

'I see.' Lamotte broke off a piece of bread and smeared it with damson jam. At least jam was a food the English

150

knew how to cook. 'I'll be out all day. Have dinner ready at five.'

'Yes, master.'

The simplicity of ordinary folk was touching, Lamotte thought as he ate his breakfast. They seemed to believe all England's problems could be solved at a stroke by the death of one frail woman.

Restored by his night's sleep, he set out an hour later for Seething Lane, but when Walsingham's secretary opened the secluded door at the back of the house, he was brisk and dismissive.

'Sir Francis is not receiving anyone today.'

'I think he will see me.'

'My orders are clear, master: no visitors. Sir Francis is unwell.'

A worm of irritation stirred in Lamotte but he decided to retreat gracefully. If Sir Francis was in no hurry to hear his report, so be it.

Up at The Unicorn he satisfied himself nothing had gone amiss in his absence then set out for Newgate. He must do whatever he could to keep Tom's spirits up. Walsingham had intervened to delay his being taken back to Salisbury to stand trial, but it was only a reprieve. The shadow of the scaffold still loomed.

*

Tom woke drenched with sweat. A few moments passed before he noticed that the square of sky in his tiny window had turned from black to grey. It was morning and the bells that had pursued him through his dreams had ceased. They had not rung to herald his death.

He rolled off the bed and winced as his joints cracked. Master Lamotte had paid for him to be removed to a higher floor where the cells were cleaner and drier but the plank he had to sleep on was still like iron.

Immediately, he felt ashamed for his ingratitude. Thanks to Master Lamotte, he had better food and warm blankets. He had soap and candles too and even a bucket so that it was possible to keep his cell clean. Lamotte had also paid for him to have paper, quills and ink so he could write. He had made several attempts to start on a new play but eventually discarded them. It was some time before he found the theme he wanted: the story of a man suffering a punishment like his own, shut away for a sin he did not commit.

Lamotte had been doubtful about the idea, but when Tom discussed it further with him, he became more enthusiastic. 'Your hero could be cast away on a far-off island,' he had suggested. 'An island peopled with monsters and magical spirits would catch the attention of audiences. Think of the spectacle, the devices we could use. Such a setting would chime with the spirit of the times too. Since Drake's voyage, people are interested in the idea of new worlds to be discovered.'

Yet looking around his cell in the bleak morning light, Tom's spirits drooped. What was the use of writing? He might never be free to see the play performed. His thoughts turned to Meg. She was the reason he had so wanted success. If he had lost her it ceased to matter. He remembered their last night together and put his knuckles to his mouth, biting down hard to dull the pain.

There were footsteps in the corridor. A face like a pale, round moon appeared on the other side of the iron wicket.

'Morning, Barwis.'

The old turnkey grunted a greeting.

Tom preferred him to the others. He was not such a brute as most. Going to the bars to take his food, he noticed the tremor in Barwis's hand and his glistening forehead.

'Are you sick, Barwis?'

Barwis belched up a beery gust. His eyes were bloodshot.

'Nah, had a good night and never went t' bed.'

Tom frowned. 'What's happened?'

'They chopped off the Scottish devil's head. Eat up, you've got extra.' With another belch, he shuffled away.

So it was done. Poor Mary Stuart was dead. Now he knew why the church bells had rung last night. A surge of hope went through him. Walsingham had sent Lamotte to witness the execution. If it was over, he should return soon. Now Walsingham had achieved his aim, perhaps he would listen favourably to Lamotte's pleas on his behalf.

He finished his porridge and lay back on the bed, watching motes of dust drift in the rays of light coming from the high window. Soon it would be time for the yard.

*

'On your feet.' Barwis hawked up a gobbet of phlegm and spat it out on the floor as he selected the key from the heavy iron ring and unlocked the wicket. 'Hope your friend comes today. Guvnor doesn't take kindly to anyone falling behind with the money.'

In the yard, the winter sun almost blinded Tom as he tried to make out faces in the crowd of visitors in the cage. His heart sank. There was no sign of Lamotte. Then he noticed a boy waving; the spiky red hair was unmistakeable. Shouldering his way to the cage, Tom stood grinning. 'Jack!'

Lamotte pushed through the crowd to join them. 'I thought you'd like to see this rogue today.'

'I would. How are you, Jack?'

Jack looked down. 'Wish you were home,' he mumbled.

'He will be, you'll see.' Lamotte ruffled his hair.

'I'm very glad to see you safely returned, sir,' said Tom.

Lamotte smiled. 'I assure you it's a great relief to me too.'

He put a finger to his lips. 'Keep your voice down. I don't want anyone hearing his name, but I'm afraid Walsingham's people say he's sick and won't see anyone. You have to be patient. I'll go again tomorrow and I'm not giving up until we have you out of here.'

153

Tom stifled his disappointment and smiled down at Jack. 'Tell me what's happening at home. Is everyone all right?'

'Janey's always complaining the cold gets into her bones, and Bel has the ague.' He grinned, 'I told her that red nose'd do to guide ships home and she tried to clock me but she's slower 'n me.'

'Is Hal walking properly yet?'

'Five steps on Monday before he fell over and bawled.'

As Jack chattered on, a pang of sorrow went through Tom. How much he missed the house at Angel Lane and its inhabitants.

'I'll go to Seething Lane in the morning,' Lamotte said quietly as the twenty minutes drew to an end.

A hand descended on Tom's shoulder. 'Time,' Barwis grunted. Reluctantly, Tom said his goodbyes and let himself be led away.

Chapter 14

London
March, 1587

'Good morning, Master Lamotte.' The printer wiped his inky hands on a soiled rag as he came out from the back of his Cheapside shop. Behind him, his workmen laid out type on the bed of the big printing press. Stacks of paper and pails of ink filled every available space in the workroom.

'And to you, master. Is there any news to be had today?'

The printer rubbed one hand over his chin. 'William Davison, who brought word of the Scottish queen's death to Her Majesty, has been thrown in the Tower. People say Elizabeth denies she wanted her dead and blames anyone else she can think of for it. She gave her ministers a good tongue lashing for sending the warrant to Fotheringay and she's still in a rage.'

'Then why did she sign it?'

The printer shrugged. 'She's a woman, isn't she? Who knows? Here,' he took a broadsheet off the stack on his table, 'take a copy and read about it.' He looked over his shoulder and shouted into the workroom. 'Have we got those handbills ready for Master Lamotte?'

Over the clatter of the press, one of the workmen shouted back something that was inaudible to Lamotte.

'Be ready tomorrow,' the printer said, turning back.

Lamotte nodded. 'I'll send someone down for them.'

He walked on scanning the broadsheet. It contained all the details of Mary's execution, down to the breed of her little dog – a Skye terrier – which had hidden under her petticoats and had to be dragged away from his mistress's lifeless body.

So, as people had suspected, Elizabeth wanted to deny she was to blame for her cousin's death. Lamotte wondered how long it would be before she let the matter drop. It might be true that Walsingham was sick; his health had deteriorated alarmingly in the last few years, but clearly it was an opportune moment to be away from Court. And if Walsingham was staying at home, away from Court affairs, he might have more time to listen to Tom's case. Perhaps it was a good moment to press it again. On the other hand, he would probably be preoccupied with finding out how much damage Mary's death had done to the English cause abroad, so an appeal might only irritate him.

Lamotte's brow furrowed. It was more than four months since Tom had been taken to Newgate. He was young and healthy but life was precarious within those noxious walls. More hardened men than Tom had also succumbed to despair and lost their wits. At least this new play he was writing distracted him a little.

It was a strange piece, Lamotte mused, with neither the heroic battles nor the rib-cracking comedy that were needed to keep an audience of restless groundlings quiet. This play dealt with the inward life of a man: the deep recesses of the soul where few chose to venture. Somehow, Lamotte doubted it would come to anything but perhaps if he could spice it up with some good effects there might be a play worth showing.

Near the stalls of the fishmongers and butchers at the Stocks Market, Lamotte bought a pamphlet from a man claiming a personal acquaintance with the famous astrologer Doctor John Dee. At home in Throgmorton Street, he read it as he ate. It propounded the well-worn prophecy of doom based on the Book of Revelations, the belief that all of history since the first year of Our Lord was divided into a series of cycles, totalling fifteen hundred years. Applying to these the multiple of the mystical numbers ten and seven –

the length of time the Israelites were slaves in Babylon – each cycle was terminated by some gigantic event.

The last completed cycle had ended when Martin Luther defied the Pope and nailed his colours to the door of the church at Wittenberg. From that event, there only remained one final cycle before the Seventh Seal was opened and the Last Judgment was at hand, and as that day approached, portent would pile on portent until there was a mountain of divine anger to sweep down and crush mankind.

Lamotte finished the pamphlet and tossed it into the fire. Nothing he had not heard before and a penny wasted. Yet were all these prophecies untrue? He liked to think he was a rational man, but there were more things in Heaven and Earth than mere mortals could understand. Of one thing he was certain, though: England was not out of danger just because Mary Stuart was dead.

Chapter 15

Meg, Bess, Sarah and her family spent the winter months at Lacey Hall and Meg never ceased to marvel at Beatrice's kindness. Whenever the question of their leaving arose, she always insisted they wait a little longer. It was a great relief to them all. Sarah was still very weak and not in any condition to withstand a journey.

They lived quietly, for the Lacey family did not seem to mix with their neighbours. Meg often wondered why. She wondered too whether some of Beatrice's desire for them to stay stemmed from loneliness. Richard Lacey spent a great deal of his time shut away in his own rooms. When he emerged, it was more likely it would be to go for long walks with his wolfhound, Hector, than to keep the rest of the family company. Good-hearted as Meg discovered Alice was, her conversation was not of the kind to banish winter boredom.

The snow was heavy that year. Much of the family's exercise had to be taken in the Long Gallery, which ran the whole length of the top floor of the house. From its panelled walls, the Lacey ancestors looked down on them with forbidding eyes.

When the weather was fine enough, however, Meg accompanied Beatrice on walks out of doors. It was on one of these walks that they went as far as the peaceful graveyard surrounding the little family church. Carpets of snowdrops gleamed beneath the snow-capped yew trees and near the lychgate the translucent blossoms of a winter cherry spangled its dark branches. Beatrice brushed the snow from a gravestone.

'I was ten when Mother died,' she said. 'Richard was eight.' Meg read the inscription: *Caterina Lacey, Beloved wife of Godfrey Lacey, born 1510 and departed this life 1557 Requiescat in pace.*

Beatrice pointed to a gravestone a few yards off. 'Father is buried there.'

'You said your mother was Italian. How did she and your father meet?'

'My father was a diplomat in King Henry's service. He was on a mission to Rome. Mother was fifteen and he was twenty-five. They fell in love and married and he brought her home to England. Mother was a devout Catholic but it was not a problem in those days, England was still a Catholic country and Catherine of Aragon was Henry's queen. When he married Anne Boleyn and closed the monasteries, things became more difficult for Mother but it was even worse when Edward became king. He was driven by the determination to root out every trace of the old religion in a way his father never was.'

'How did your parents manage?'

'Father was a practical man. He always said the safety of the family and its estates was more important than anything else. It was different with Mother. Her nature was more passionate and her devotion to the old faith ran deep.' A troubled look clouded Beatrice's face. 'I fear for Richard,' she said softly. 'His nature is like hers.'

Meg waited for her to continue. She had to admit, she found Richard hard to fathom. His remote manner was so different from Beatrice's warmth and informality. Often, she feared he was deeply unhappy. He spent hours shut up alone in his study and when he came out, apart from a few courteous words, he had little to say.

'Alice looked after us,' Beatrice went on, 'and Mother rarely left her chamber. Even though Alice tried to keep us

159

from hearing them, I remember how Mother and Father quarrelled.'

Meg thought of the cold silences and violent outbursts in her own home. She reached out and put her hand on Beatrice's arm.

'Thank you,' Beatrice said with a smile. 'I'm afraid what happened in my family may not have been uncommon. It was little better when Queen Mary brought back the old religion. So many cruel things happened in God's name. Mother must have hated that.'

She gave Meg a quizzical look. 'I imagine you're wondering if their unhappiness is the reason I never took a husband.'

Meg inclined her head slightly.

'I never planned it that way. My father didn't press me to marry, although if I had found a man I could love, I would have been glad to. But I never did, and now who would choose a woman in her fortieth year? She shivered. 'I've kept you standing here for too long. You must be frozen. Let's go into the church. I'll show you the family monument.'

Snow crunching beneath their overshoes, they walked along the path to the church porch. Icicles hung from the eaves and inside the building there was a strong smell of damp. The wooden pews were dull from lack of polish and cobwebs festooned the windows.

'The church is never used now,' Beatrice said. 'Not since we started to go to the one at King's Barton to make sure we were seen to attend.'

Her wooden heels clicked on the uneven stone flags as she went down the aisle to the altar table. Fingering the delicate lace embellishing the cloth that covered it, she sighed. 'Mother had this made in Honiton. She wanted candles and silver plate too, but Father forbade it.'

In a side chapel, two life-sized effigies lay on a low tomb. The man was dressed in full armour but the visor of his helmet was pushed up to reveal a stern, clean-shaven

160

face. Curled up asleep at his mailed feet, a stone dog showed he had died in peace. Beside him reposed a woman with calm, smooth features, her tiny hands clasped in prayer on the stone folds of her flowing dress. On the wall above, a plaque listed the names of all the Laceys who had come after them.

'My ancestors, Godfroi and Mathilda de Lacey. Godfroi came from Normandy with King William.'

'He looks very stern,' Meg said.

'I expect he was.'

Back in the churchyard, the sun was out and its warmth gladdened Meg.

'It will be lambing time in a month or so,' Beatrice remarked. 'John has promised he'll teach Andrew everything he can. He says Andrew is very quick to learn and has been a great help to him these past months.'

Meg had noticed how much time Andrew spent with John the steward and she had been pleased. It was not too soon to think of how he would earn his living. The office of steward was respected and well paid, he could do far worse.

'I'm sure Andrew will be very grateful, and Sarah too. I know she worries about how her children will make their way in the world. Everyone here has been so good to us, Beatrice. I still shudder when I think of what might have happened if you hadn't taken us in on that awful night.'

'It is you who do us a kindness with your company. We'd miss you if you went away. Even Alice.'

Meg chuckled. 'She does seem to have thawed a little.'

'I doubt she would admit it, but I think she loves having a child in the house again, and Bess to order about of course. I remember how she used to terrify the nursery servants when we were young. It's lucky Bess is so good-natured.'

Leaving the churchyard, they followed the rough path back to the house. As they came into the hall, they found Bess carrying a steaming bowl of posset from the kitchen. The comforting smell of hot milk and brandy wafted towards them.

161

'Alice told me to take this up to Sarah. She's resting in the solar. Alice says it will ease her cough. She was awake half the night.'

Meg frowned. Sarah's health had improved a little in the early days at Lacey Hall but it still left a great deal to be desired. When the doctor came from King's Barton he prescribed numerous expensive tonics and remedies but none of them seemed to bring lasting benefit. At least if the need arose, he had promised to vouch for the fact she was not fit enough to attend church.

'I'll take it to her, Bess. I've not seen her today. Will you come with me, Beatrice?'

Beatrice shook her head. 'I promised Richard I would look over some papers with him as soon as I came home. I should let him know I'm back.'

Meg took the bowl and napkin and climbed the creaking oak staircase. At intervals, carved figures of dragons and eagles surmounted the handrail. On the first landing, a ray of sunshine shone through a round, stained-glass window throwing pools of crimson, blue and gold light on the polished floor. For a moment, Meg paused, admiring the rich colours. Over the months since she had come to Lacey Hall she had grown very fond of the old house. With its dusty nooks and corners and old-fashioned furniture and fittings, it was so different from her home with Edward but she did not miss the newness and modern conveniences of Stuckton Court in the slightest.

She set off down the passage leading to the solar. Her hand was on the latch when she heard voices within. Abruptly, the door opened and Richard Lacey almost collided with her. Clutching the bowl, she steadied herself.

'I was looking for Beatrice,' he mumbled, his eyes avoiding hers.

Before Meg had a chance to speak, he passed her and hurried away down the corridor. She frowned. Surely he knew Beatrice had gone out walking?

'I didn't expect to find Richard here,' she said putting the bowl down beside Sarah.

'He wanted Beatrice.'

Meg noticed a flush on Sarah's cheeks and let the remark pass. Whatever was between Sarah and Richard, it would be wrong to distress her by prying. 'Alice has made this posset for you and you must drink every drop. If you don't, she will scold me.'

'Then I'll try.' Sarah smiled. 'Everyone is so good to me and I'm such a nuisance.'

'Nonsense. Now shall I help you to sit up more so you can drink comfortably?'

'Thank you.'

Meg put her arm around Sarah's thin shoulders, tilted her forward and rearranged the cushions at her back. She feels as fragile as a bird, Meg thought sadly. If only her appetite was better, she might have more strength to fight what ails her.

A fit of coughing seized Sarah and took some time to subside.

Meg's brow furrowed. 'I'm sorry I was so clumsy.'

Gasping for breath, Sarah shook her head. 'You're not to blame. This stupid cough starts so easily.'

Meg fetched a footstool and sat down opposite her. She placed the napkin in Sarah's lap and handed her the bowl. Sarah took a sip and blinked. 'Alice makes posset very strong.'

'She never does anything by halves,' Meg chuckled.

'That's true.'

Cautiously, Sarah took another sip. 'Tell me what you've done today.'

'I went with Beatrice to the church. It's a lovely old place, far nicer than the one at King's Barton.' While she recounted the conversation with Beatrice, Meg saw Sarah's expression fill with sadness at the mention of the quarrels between Beatrice and Richard's parents. Meg broke off. 'Forgive me, I didn't mean to remind you.'

'It's not your fault,' Sarah said with a sigh. 'The memory is often with me.' A pulse throbbed at her temple. 'If I could go back, there are many things I'd do differently. Richard says I ought not to. . .' She stopped.

'Yes?'

'Oh, nothing. Go on, please.'

The news about Andrew brought a smile to Sarah's worn face. 'It's a great chance for him and I'm sure he'll welcome it,' she said. Then her expression clouded.

'What's wrong?'

'Agnes is still so young, though. You will look after her, won't you, Meg?'

'Of course I will, but you'll be here to see her grow up. We'll find her a kind husband. She'll have a family and you will have grandchildren to dote on.'

Sarah's brown eyes regarded her steadily. 'Dearest Meg, I think we both know that will never be.'

A lump rose in Meg's throat. 'Don't say that.'

'I have to face it, and as long as the children are safe, I'm not afraid.'

On her way to the kitchens with the empty bowl, Meg turned Sarah's words over in her mind. If there was something between her and Richard, it seemed strange she should contemplate death with such equanimity.

Alice was sewing by the kitchen fire. 'It's better than naught, I suppose,' she grunted. 'But a bit of posset won't put flesh on her bones. She hardly ate a mouthful this morning, or yesterday for that matter. Not even that lovely cut of beef John brought up from the farm or Cook's preserved plums tempted her, poor lady.'

She snapped off her thread and shook out the smock she had been mending. 'If I've told Agnes once,' she tutted, 'I've told her a hundred times she's not to climb trees and tear her clothes. She'll be a grown woman before we know it and then where will she be?'

*

On a fine Sunday in March, as a blustery wind swept rags of cloud across the azure sky, a small party set out from Lacey Hall to attend church at King's Barton.

Meg and Beatrice travelled in Beatrice's carriage while Richard rode alongside. The last traces of snow had melted from the ruts in the road and mud squelched under the wheels and the horses' hooves. On the trees the acid-green knuckles of budding leaves softened the sharp lines of the branches and birds darted in and out of the undergrowth.

'Alice promised to keep an eye on Sarah,' Beatrice said. 'With the roads as slow as this, I doubt we shall be back until late afternoon.' She looked out at the sky. 'I think the weather will hold but Alice says we shall have a storm later.' She smiled. 'She says her big toe aches and of course that is always a sure sign.'

The church at King's Barton was much larger than the one at King's Lacey. As the carriage reached the village, they heard the bells ringing and saw people hurrying along the road. By the time they went in, many of the pews were already full. A few people nodded to Beatrice but there was no warmth in their greetings. As always, Meg wondered why their neighbours were so cool towards the Laceys, but in spite of their friendship, it was not a question she liked to ask Beatrice.

Settled in a pew halfway down the nave, she looked around her. Candle smoke darkened the walls but in places rectangles of paler stone showed where devotional pictures had been removed. There were no statues in the niches and at the tops of the arches and columns, forlorn stumps of stone carvings were a reminder of what had been hacked away. Meg wondered what they had represented and whether the ghosts of long-dead masons still bewailed the destruction of their painstaking handiwork. Was God really better served by it? A sea of bowed heads offered no answer to her question.

The parson fussed about at the plain, wooden lectern marking places in his bible. With a sigh, Meg hoped his sermon would not be as dull as it had been last month. He had a reedy voice she found very irritating. The impious thought made her feel guilty and she sank to her knees to pray. As she always did, she prayed for Sarah's return to health.

When she sat back in her seat, Richard had come in from making arrangements for the horses and the carriage. He leant towards Beatrice, whispering agitatedly in her ear. She looked startled, but hard as Meg tried to hear what they were saying, the noise of the congregation rising for the first hymn drowned the words.

Richard knelt to pray. The knuckles of his clasped hands were the colour of bone.

'What is it?' she asked Beatrice in an undertone.

'Queen Mary has been executed. Richard heard someone talking about it in the churchyard.' She put her finger to her lips. 'I'll have to tell you more after the service.'

When the service came to its end, Richard stood up abruptly. Beatrice caught his sleeve as he left the pew but he didn't seem to notice her.

'The execution was carried out a month ago,' she muttered as she and Meg followed him out of the church. 'With the roads so bad, the news has taken this long to reach us. Richard says Mary's kinsmen in France will not allow such villainy to go unpunished, neither will Philip of Spain.' She craned her neck to see where Richard had gone. 'I hope he will be careful on the way home,' she said anxiously. 'He's so angry I'm afraid he'll ride too fast, and the road is still very treacherous.'

A draught of cold air met them at the doors. Wrapping her cloak around her, Meg stepped outside. Knots of people stood on the path and between the gravestones. From the animated way they were conversing, she was sure they were talking about the execution. She was about to answer Beatrice when suddenly she froze. Over by a large tomb

166

surrounded by iron railings, two men stood talking. Her head swam. Surely she must be mistaken? But a moment later, she knew she was not. The younger man's face was unmistakeable. He was Ralph Fiddler.

*

The groom was already leading Richard's bay mare to the stables when they reached home. Beatrice was in too much of a hurry to go to her brother to notice Meg's agitation.

In her room, Meg fumbled with the pins securing her green velvet hat. She let out a cry of pain and exasperation as one of them jabbed her finger and drew blood.

'Whatever's the matter, madam?' Bess's blue eyes widened.

'He was at church. I saw him.'

'Who, madam?'

'Ralph Fiddler.'

The colour drained from Bess's cheeks and her hand flew to her mouth. 'Oh madam, do you think he saw you too?'

'I don't know, Bess.'

'Have you told Mistress Beatrice?'

'No, she has enough to worry about.'

'Is he looking for us, do you think?'

Perplexed, Meg shook her head. 'I don't know, Bess. It might be some other reason entirely that brings him here, but until I'm sure he's gone, I shall never feel safe.'

'But how shall we know, madam?'

'John often sends Andrew to Barton on errands. Perhaps he can find something out. But he must be careful who he talks to. I don't want anyone suspecting we are asking questions about Ralph Fiddler.'

There was the sound of running feet and the door flew open. Agnes rushed in and buried her face in Meg's skirts. 'Uncle Richard is cross with me,' she sobbed, 'but I promise I haven't been naughty.'

167

Meg lifted Agnes's chin and looked at her tearful face. 'Are you sure?'

'It's nothing Agnes has done.' With a rustle of silk, Beatrice appeared in the room. Gently, she disentangled Agnes from Meg's skirt. 'Bess, please take Agnes downstairs. Agnes, I'm sure Bess will play a game of spillikins with you, won't you, Bess?'

Bess nodded and, taking Agnes by the hand, led her away.

'Richard did not mean to be harsh,' Beatrice said when the door closed behind them. 'He's usually perfectly willing to listen to Agnes's chatter when he sits with us. It's just that this news has distressed him so much.'

At any other time, Meg would have responded with sympathy but her mind was too full of her own fears to do so. The image of Ralph's salacious eyes and sly smile would not leave her. She had thought she would never see him again. She felt as if an iron band had tightened around her chest.

'Meg?'

She jumped as Beatrice put a hand on her arm.

'You're not listening to me, are you? Is something wrong? Are you unwell?'

With an effort, Meg recovered her composure. 'It's just a headache. If you don't mind, I'd like to lie down for a while.'

'Of course. Shall I bring you something to ease it?'

Meg shook her head. 'Thank you, but you mustn't trouble yourself on my account. An hour or two's rest is all I need. I'm sorry about Richard,' she added hastily. 'You go back to him. There's no need to worry about me.'

After Beatrice had gone, Meg drew a deep breath to steady her racing heart. She went to the window and opened the casement to let in some fresh air. One part of her wished she had confided in Beatrice, as her advice was always so wise, but the other part was glad she had not. This was a problem she must resolve on her own. It would be wrong to involve the Laceys in her troubles. They had already done enough.

Over in the west, dark clouds obscured the horizon. Alice was right about a storm. In the hearth, a half-consumed log burnt through and fell with a hiss. She shuddered. Ralph Fiddler here in King's Barton; if only she knew what he was after.

Chapter 16

April came and drifts of daffodils brightened the countryside. The trees were in full leaf and the hedgerows frothed with hawthorn blossom.

Alice turned the house upside down with spring cleaning. Rugs and tapestries were hauled outdoors for the dust to be beaten out of them; the floors and wainscoting were polished with lavender-scented beeswax. Window leads were scoured to a shine with sharp sand and the panes polished until they sparkled.

To Meg's relief, Ralph seemed to have left the area. Perhaps there was no more need to hide. She began to wonder whether she should resume her search for Tom, but she did not know where to begin and Sarah and the rest of her companions were safe and happy at Lacey Hall. It was unfair to expect them to come with her and the prospect of going alone was a daunting one. Sometimes she even wished she did not still feel so much for Tom. It would make her life so much simpler. But it was no use pretending. She still loved him.

As spring went on, the weather cooled. Mist often covered the gardens and fields when the household awoke in the mornings. The early promise of a fine summer receded but on the rare warm days, Beatrice and Meg encouraged Sarah to sit in the garden while they tended the herb beds and sowed the seeds Beatrice had collected and stored in the autumn. At first, it had surprised Meg that Beatrice did such lowly work, but she had long ago realised that Lacey Hall did not have as many servants as might be expected in such a large house. Her mother had had almost as many with a much smaller establishment.

In any case, Meg was glad to be out of doors. She enjoyed the simple, repetitive tasks gardening demanded and she relished the sweetness of the air and the earthy tang of the rich, red loam. She was proud of her improved knowledge too. She might never match Beatrice's skill, but she understood the properties of many herbs now. Agrimony staunched and healed wounds; thyme treated sore throats. Lemon balm cured melancholy and indigestion.

'Here is a new test for you.' Beatrice pointed to a burgeoning plant with fleshy green leaves. She broke off a piece to show its hollow stem. 'What's this?'

Meg's forehead puckered. 'Lovage?'

'Excellent, we shall make a proper housewife of you yet. How should it be used?'

'*Lyte's Herbal* says it will cure colic, fever and other pestilential disorders.' She giggled. 'The ancients used it to induce lust.'

'Meg! I'm sure *Lyte's* doesn't mention that.'

'No, I found it in Pliny's *Natural History* in Richard's library.'

'And he would chide me for letting you choose what to read unsupervised.'

'If Pliny is the greatest danger I encounter in life, Beatrice, I shall be a lucky woman.'

'That's true, but all the same, don't let Richard find out.'

She raked down the last ridge of soil to cover the sweet basil seed she had sown, straightened up and sighed. 'I hope these seeds germinate properly. The weather is not as I'd like it to be for the time of year, the earth is colder than usual. It needs to warm if we are to have a good crop.' She glanced up at the sky. 'Enough for today, we must take Sarah indoors before the sun goes behind the house.'

The lilac trusses of a venerable wisteria cascaded over the arbour at the end of the herb garden. Beneath it, Sarah dozed in her chair, with a warm, woollen coverlet over her

171

knees. At their approach, she opened her eyes. 'The scent is like honey,' she said and smiled. 'It makes me so drowsy, I could stay here forever.'

'And catch cold when the sun goes down and the dew falls,' Meg scolded. She helped Sarah to her feet.

The path back to the house lay through the rose garden where the neatly pruned stems swelled with bronzy leaves and plump buds that gave off a sweet, spicy scent.

Beatrice brushed one with a fingertip. 'When the time comes to gather the flowers, I'll show you how to distil rosewater from them, Meg.'

'I was famous for my rosewater,' Sarah said wistfully. 'No matter how much I made, it was never enough for everyone who wanted it.'

'Then you must show me how to improve my skill.' Beatrice squeezed her hand.

Sarah sighed. 'I doubt there's anything I could teach you, Beatrice. In truth, I fear my days of housewifery are behind me.'

*

'Cook's chill is worse,' Alice grumbled. 'I warned her it would be if she didn't rub her chest with bergamot oil, but she never heeds my advice. I shall have to prepare dinner myself if there's to be any today.'

'Oh dear,' Beatrice sighed. 'I would help you but I promised this afternoon to Richard.'

'Then let me,' said Meg.

'That's very kind.'

In the scullery, Meg cleaned her hands with water from the pump and put on the apron Alice found for her. A shoulder of mutton was to be the main dish and when it was seasoned and roasting in the oven, Alice took out a deep pie dish from one of the cupboards.

'Those cupboards aren't as tidy as they might be,' she sniffed, going over to inspect the large, wooden chopping block on the table in the middle of the room. 'This will do. Fetch me the two chickens hanging in the pantry then I'll need onions and sage.'

Meg returned to find Alice kneading pastry. When she had scooped it into a ball, she laid a clean cloth over it and wiped her floury hands on her apron.

'Put it to rest there by the oven, then you can slice the onions, but mind, I want them very fine.'

With a private smile, Meg decided that being Alice's kitchen maid might prove a considerable test of a person's patience.

While Alice cut up the chickens, Meg peeled the onions and sliced them into thin, translucent rounds. Glancing up from her work, Alice gave her a grudging nod of approval. 'You've done that before,' she remarked. 'Did your mother show you how?'

Perhaps it was better not to say that although Mother had exacted high standards from others, she never did any of the work herself.

'She was very particular.' Meg smiled.

'That's a good thing in a housewife, when I had a husband and a home of my own nothing left my kitchen until it was just so.'

'I didn't know you were married, Alice.'

'It was long ago, but I can still remember what it's like to live with a man who treats you cruelly.' She gave Meg a shrewd glance and Meg felt uneasy.

'My husband was a brute,' Alice went on. 'And I was a fool to be taken in, but then after he left me, for a while I was afraid I'd be worse off than ever. I thank the Lord every day that Master Godfrey and Mistress Caterina took me in to look after Master Richard and Mistress Beatrice when they were babies. I've been here ever since.'

She fetched the pastry from beside the oven, slapped it down on the floured table and attacked it with her rolling pin. 'I don't want you thinking I don't understand why you ran away from your husband,' she said.

Meg's pulse slowed. She should have known she could trust Beatrice to keep her promise not to divulge the whole story.

'Thank you for saying that, Alice,' she said quietly.

'That's all right.'

All briskness again, Alice lifted the pastry into the dish, filled it with the cut-up chicken, onions and sage then sprinkled cinnamon and a dash of nutmeg on top. 'We must be getting on with this pie or dinner will be late. It will have to be apples and custard afterwards. We haven't time for jellies or tarts. I don't know where Bess has got to with my eggs. She knows I need them and I sent her to the farm an hour ago.'

Meg went to the kitchen door and looked out. There was no sign of Bess. 'Shall I go and find her?' she asked.

'Yes, and tell her she can expect a piece of my mind when she gets here.'

'Don't be too cross with her. It's such a lovely day and she does work hard most of the time.'

Alice made a harrumphing noise.

Taking the route through the kitchen garden, Meg had not gone far before she saw Bess with the basket of eggs over her arm. At the sight of Meg, she broke into a trot.

'Alice is after you, Bess. Where have you been?'

Bess lowered her head. 'Nowhere, madam, just to the farm as she told me.' And without another word, she hurried on in the direction of the kitchen.

Chapter 17

Hooves thudded on the turf and the ground beneath Meg's feet shook. Some instinct told her the rider was Ralph Fiddler. Her heart hammering against her ribs; she ran into the woods to escape but he pursued her. Sharp brambles snaked around her bare legs and pulled her down into the mud, which filled her mouth and half-blinded her. Struggling up, she stumbled on and reached a deep pool. She stepped in and the coldness of the water made her gasp. It swirled around her, pricking her skin like shards of glass. Then something moved and a face rose slowly to the surface. Its skin was the colour of pewter, and where the eyes should have been, eels swam in and out of empty sockets. The creature reached out for her with skeletal arms. Filled with horror, she knew it was Ralph. She felt hot breath on her neck and the smell of tallow invaded her nostrils.

'Wake up, Meg!'

She struggled to sit up.

'Is he here?' she gasped.

'What are you talking about? It's me – Beatrice.' Candlelight flickered over Beatrice's anxious face.

Meg was suddenly wide awake. 'What's the matter?'

'It's Sarah, please come.'

The bitter, cleansing aromas of wormwood and rue pervaded the room. Sarah's breathing was laboured, her face grey as a November morning. She looked no bigger than a child in her cocoon of quilts and coverlets.

Meg knelt by the bed and saw flecks of blood on her lips. She reached out and stroked the damp hair away from her forehead but Sarah seemed oblivious to everything around her.

'I've seen this before with one of our old servants,' Beatrice whispered. 'Poor Margery suffered for months then we thought she had rallied, but we were mistaken.'

'What happened to her?'

Beatrice bowed her head. 'We did everything we could, but it was hopeless.'

Sorrow rolled over Meg like a stone. 'Have you woken Richard?' she asked.

For a few moments, Beatrice seemed reluctant to answer. When she did, her voice was hesitant. 'Richard has ridden to Exeter.'

'But doesn't he want to be with her, now of all times? And anyway, why can't we call the doctor from King's Barton?'

Beatrice's voice was very quiet. 'Richard hasn't gone for a doctor, Meg. He's gone to fetch a priest. He promised Sarah.'

Meg stared at her.

Beatrice frowned. 'Meg, I know it's dangerous, but Richard cannot break his promise.'

'No, it's not that. They were so often together, I thought—'

'You thought they cared for each other?' Beatrice asked quietly. 'I suppose in a way they do, but it is not love as you mean it. The bond between Sarah and Richard is their faith.'

'But Sarah has no use for priests. She's told me many times how she begged her husband to give up the old beliefs. They were the ruin of her family and she always said she wanted nothing more to do with Catholics.'

'Her feelings altered as the illness took hold. Richard has helped and guided her over the past few months. They've talked a great deal about death and he says she begged him many times not to let her die unshriven.'

A dry cough racked Sarah and her eyes opened; they were full of pain but the ghost of a smile quivered on her

176

lips. Meg stroked her hand and leant forward to try and hear what she was saying but it was impossible and she drifted away from them once more.

'Did none of you trust me, Beatrice?' Meg asked bitterly. 'I feel such a fool.'

'It wasn't that. We didn't think it fair to burden you with knowledge that might put you in danger.'

'But you and Richard attend church.' She stopped seeing the distress in Beatrice's eyes.

'Richard does so for my sake even though it is against his conscience. Our family has lived at Lacey Hall for hundreds of years. I couldn't bear the prospect of losing everything. If we were not seen to attend, the recusant fines would ruin us as they did Sarah's husband. She shivered and lowered her voice. 'Fines might not be the worst fate we suffered.'

'How does Richard know where to get a priest?'

'You remember the night we found you on the road?'

'Yes.'

'We were coming from a house where the family was hiding one. Richard wanted to speak with him and I thought we should travel together. It might arouse less suspicion. Richard believes that priest is with a family close to Exeter now. It's a day's ride from here. If he's right and the priest agrees, they should be back in time.'

'In time?' Meg's throat filled.

Another bout of coughing turned their attention to Sarah. She was paler than ever and the blue-grey tinge around her lips spread like a fresh bruise. Her breathing was quick and shallow.

Panic seized Meg. 'We must do something! How can we help her?'

'I have some medicine in the stillroom. It can be dangerous and I didn't want to use it, but I fear there's no choice. Will you stay here while I fetch it?'

Left alone, Meg clung to Sarah's hand as she tossed and moaned. Tears pricked her eyes. How little she really knew

177

Sarah, or Beatrice and Richard for that matter. Why could they not have trusted her?

'Meg?'

Unnoticed, Beatrice had come back into the room. Meg wiped her eyes. 'I'm sorry,' she snuffled.

Beatrice put an arm around her. 'Don't be, I understand. We all love her, but we must be glad for her if she can find peace.'

The door creaked and Alice hurried in, a shawl thrown over her nightclothes and her grey hair straggling to her shoulders. 'Oh, the poor lady,' she gasped. 'Yesterday morning she seemed so bright and cheerful.'

'I fear an illness like this worsens very suddenly.'

Sarah groaned and Beatrice bent close to her ear. 'Sarah? Can you hear me? Try to drink this. It will help with the pain.'

She held the cup to Sarah's lips. Its contents gave off an unpleasant, mousey smell. Sarah managed to take a small amount but then turned her head aside. With a piece of linen, Beatrice dabbed a trace of the dark liquid from her chin and tried again but it was no use.

'What is it?' Meg asked.

'The Italians call it 'beautiful lady', belladonna. It is very powerful so you should only use a little.'

'Will she sleep?'

'Yes.'

Gradually, Sarah quietened; her pale features settled into repose and her breathing slowed. Meg suffered a pang of dread. Sarah's stillness reminded her of the effigy of Mathilda de Lacey in the church. She wanted to rouse her, to see the old Sarah's gentle smile and hear her laughter.

Alice's voice broke the silence. 'Both of you must rest. Let me watch over her now.'

'You promise you'll call us if she wakes?' Beatrice asked.

'Of course I shall.'

178

Alice did not call her and Meg slept until the sun was high in the sky. That day, she and Beatrice took turns to sit with Sarah. After the restless night, she was quiet, so quiet that at times Meg feared she might slip away before Richard returned.

Towards evening, dark clouds gathered in the west. Soon rain swept in and a strong wind rattled the windows. Richard arrived after dark with the priest. He was a head shorter than Richard, pock marked, with prominent grey eyes that reminded Meg of a startled hare. As soon as dry clothes had been found for him, Beatrice and Richard took him to Sarah's room. Beatrice came back alone, her expression full of sorrow.

'I hope she knows he's there and can take comfort from it, but it's hard to be sure.'

'Do you think Andrew and Agnes should see her?'

'Yes. When Father Weston comes out. Poor children - I shall never forget the night my mother died. I was not much older than Agnes.' A look of disquiet crossed her face. 'Richard says he had a hard job persuading Father Weston to come. He thinks there are priest hunters in the area and he didn't want to leave the house where he was hiding.'

Meg remembered Edward talking about a priest who had been caught in Winchester. She shuddered at the image of the horrible fate he had suffered. It was no wonder Father Weston looked frightened. When he left Sarah's bedroom, he asked to rest for a while. Alice had prepared a room and she showed him to it. Meg could tell from her tight-lipped expression that she did not approve of the man.

'Shall I find Andrew and Agnes now?' she asked Beatrice. 'I'm sure the sight of them will do more good for Mistress Sarah than anything.'

'Thank you, Alice.'

When Alice had left the room, Beatrice turned to Meg with a sigh. 'I confess, Father Weston is not all I had hoped

179

for, but we had to respect Sarah's wish to see a priest.' Her brow furrowed. 'I only hope we shan't regret it.'

Alice returned with Andrew and Agnes and Meg's heart went out to them both. From their stricken faces, it was clear they understood their mother was rapidly sinking. After a while, Beatrice gently told them to say their goodbyes and Alice led them away.

A few times in the night, Sarah stirred, confused and in pain. On each occasion, Beatrice administered careful doses of the medicine to soothe her again. Watching helpless, Meg blessed Beatrice's calm presence. It horrified her to think that if matters had fallen out differently, they might still have been wanderers.

Just before dawn, Sarah's breath became more laboured and her chest heaved. There was a rattling sound in her throat then silence.

'What is it?' Meg asked anxiously. 'What's happened?'

Beatrice took Sarah's wrist between her thumb and forefinger and waited a few moments. Deep furrows creased her brow.

'I'm so sorry, Meg,' she whispered. 'It is over.'

Tears coursed down Meg's cheeks. Beatrice took her hand.

'We must pray for her.'

*

Two days later, John the steward, Father Weston, Richard and Andrew carried the coffin to the old family church and Father Weston conducted the service in accordance with the Catholic rites. Afterwards, they all went to the churchyard where the open grave waited. Andrew had studded the sides with Sarah's favourite violets.

The four men lowered the coffin into the ground, making the sign of the cross, and Father Weston pronounced a last blessing. John came forward and threw the first shovel of earth onto the coffin. It fell like a shower of hail on the wooden lid.

When the task was done, Andrew placed the small wooden cross he had made at the head of the plot then stood up. He wiped his eyes. John put a hand on his shoulder. 'We'll find a good piece of stone and see she gets a proper marker, won't we, lad?'

Andrew mumbled something and nodded.

For a few moments, no one spoke, lost in their own memories. Silently, Bess helped Agnes lay a bunch of wild flowers at the foot of the cross.

'We should go back to the house,' Richard said at last. 'There is nothing more we can do here.'

*

'Father Weston has decided to return to France,' Beatrice announced a few days later as she and Meg picked flowers to take to Sarah's grave. 'There are still rumours of priest hunters in the area. Richard is sending Andrew to Exeter to see when there's a ship sailing.'

'But will it be safe to travel?' Meg added another flower to her bunch.

'Remaining here is very little safer if the rumours are to be believed.'

Meg felt sorry for Father Weston. Even the crack of a log in the fire made him start. He rarely spoke and then only when he was spoken to. She found it hard to understand how such a nervous creature had ever contemplated the dangerous life he had set himself to lead. Perhaps his faith explained it.

The household's usual routines helped the sad days to pass. As was his custom, Richard spent them in his study. Alice and Bess took turns to be with Agnes and see to it she was consoled.

'I wish Andrew was back from Exeter,' Beatrice sighed as she and Meg worked in the stillroom late one afternoon. The citric tang of bergamot oil hung in the air. Outside, long shadows lay on the grass and feathers of cloud dappled the sky. 'I don't understand why he hasn't come home yet. I hope nothing is amiss.'

'I'm sure no harm has befallen him,' Meg said soothingly. She paused, listening, her pestle resting on the cloves she was crushing to make a poultice for Alice's toothache. 'That can't be Alice coming in such a hurry. If it is, her toothache must be much better.'

But it was John the steward who rushed in, his weather-beaten face flushed and his hat crumpled in his big, farmer's hands.

Beatrice dropped the glass stopper of the bottle of oil she was holding. It rolled off the table and smashed on the stone floor. Her hand flew to her mouth.

'M'lady, Jed and Abel have just come from Forty Acre Wood. I'd sent them down there with the wagon – the trees we felled last week needed fetching in.'

'Never mind the trees, John, tell me what's happened.'

'Horsemen, m'lady: seven of them. They came upon Jed and Abel all of a sudden in the part of the wood closest to the house. Didn't look too pleased to see them, Abel said. The one who seemed to be in charge – youngish fellow, but ordering the rest about as if he was born to it – told Abel they were travelling to Exeter and had lost their way, but Abel didn't like the look of him, so when he'd sent them back off to the high road, he came straight up to tell me.'

Meg's heart gave a jolt.

Beatrice looked grave. 'Find Master Richard, John. Tell him what's happened and ask him to join us in the Hall.'

As she and Beatrice hurried through the screens passage to the Great Hall, Meg's head hammered. 'Who do you think they are?' she asked Beatrice as they waited for Richard.

'I'm not sure but I don't like the sound of this.'

When Richard came in, she ran to him. A few paces behind, Father Weston's spare form seemed even more swamped than usual by his black garments.

182

Gently, Richard put his hands on Beatrice's shoulders. 'You mustn't be afraid.'

'Oh Richard, how can you say that? These men - suppose they mean us harm?'

'We were always aware this might happen. If they are priest hunters, we shall be ready for them. God is with us.' He touched Beatrice's cheek and regarded her solemnly. 'You mustn't betray the smallest hint of fear. Do you promise me you won't?' He turned to Meg. 'And I need the same promise from you.'

Meg nodded. This was a Richard she had not seen before, no longer reserved and scholarly but decisive and commanding.

'Come, Weston, we must eat,' Richard went on. 'If we have to hide, it may be some time before we have the opportunity to fill our stomachs again. John, send two of the farm workers to the top field so that they can keep a lookout on the road. Tell them to watch for riders cutting across country towards the Hall as well.'

John bowed and hurried away.

Father Weston seemed rooted where he stood. When Richard shook his arm, he blinked owlishly.

'What? Yes, yes, you're right.'

At the hastily assembled meal of cheese and bread, Richard ate swiftly and in silence but Meg noticed Father Weston barely managed to swallow more than a few mouthfuls.

Richard put down his knife. 'The maids should be sent to the village,' he announced. 'Will you see to it, Beatrice? I don't want them questioned. They're young and fear is likely to make them indiscreet.'

He pushed his plate aside. 'Weston? Shall we go to the chapel? When my sister has dealt with the maids, she can bring your belongings to be hidden as well. Beatrice, you know what to do with my books.'

There was a commotion in the screens passage and John the steward burst in.

183

'They're already at the farm! They must have come over the heath from the Barton road.'

Father Weston gave a low moan and his legs crumpled. Richard grasped him by the elbow. 'Help me with him, John; we need to make haste.'

Dragging the priest like a sack of flour, they hauled him in the direction of the chapel, his boots scraping over the stone-flagged floor.

'It's too late to send the maids away,' Beatrice said urgently. 'Find Alice, Meg. She must make all the servants understand it's of the utmost importance they don't tell these men that Richard and Father Weston are in the house. If they are asked, they are to say that Richard is in Exeter on business. Tell Alice everyone should carry on with their duties as if nothing has happened. When you have done that, come to Father Weston's room and help me.'

'I knew he'd bring bad luck,' Alice said grimly when Meg found her in the dairy. 'If it weren't for poor Mistress Sarah, God rest her' – she crossed herself – 'I'd have sent him packing, but there's no help for it now. I'll see to everything here, don't you worry. You go and help Mistress Beatrice.'

Upstairs, Meg found that Beatrice had already gathered Father Weston's few possessions into a heap on the bed. She was staring at them with a perplexed expression.

'Alice is speaking to the servants, Beatrice. Beatrice?' She saw that Beatrice was crying.

'I'm sorry,' she gulped. 'I tried not to, but I couldn't stop myself. I'm so afraid. Oh Meg, suppose they are discovered?'

'We won't let it happen.' She snatched up Father Weston's black cloak, bundled everything onto it and tied the opposing corners together. 'Where does Richard want these?'

'In the chapel.'

'I'll help you.'

184

As they lifted the bundle, Meg froze. 'I think I heard someone outside.' She dropped her end of the bundle, ran to the window and stared into the dusk.

Beatrice's voice trembled. 'What is it? Is someone there?

Meg strained her eyes, but nothing moved. Her heartbeat slowed a little. 'Perhaps it was a fox or the wind in the trees.' She went back to the bed. 'Let's hurry.'

Together, they dragged the bundle onto the landing. Father Weston's silver cross and communion instruments clattered against each other as it bumped down the stairs.

At the bottom, Beatrice stopped. 'Richard's devotional books... his missal, *The Lives of the Saints* and Loyola's *Spiritual Exercises*.'

'Where are they?'

'In his room.'

Up in Richard's room, Meg soon found the books on the table in front of an internal window looking directly into the chapel below. In the chapel, the tall chest that had once been used to store vestments had been moved to one side. She was just in time to see Richard and Father Weston slip through a small door in the oak panelling behind it.

As she hurried out, Meg heard a distant sound like the breaking of glass. She raced downstairs and found Beatrice. Her face was bloodless as she pointed in the direction of the Great Hall. 'Oh Meg,' she gasped. 'They are already in the house.'

'Then we can't go that way to the chapel.' Meg tried to sound calm. 'We'll have to hide this somewhere else.'

Footsteps made them both swing round in alarm but it was only Alice coming from the kitchen. 'You go in and keep them talking, Mistress Beatrice. Meg and I will deal with everything.'

In the kitchen, Cook stood astonished as Alice wrenched open the iron door at the base of the big range and recoiled from the heat that billowed out. 'What are you doing?' she remonstrated.

'There are priest hunters in the house,' Alice replied.

185

'Merciful Lord!' Cook's knife clattered to the floor.

Alice untied the bundle. 'We shall have to burn all this.' She snatched up a poker and started to push Father Weston's bands into the flames.

'But what about the silver?' Meg asked. 'It won't burn.'

Cook recovered her wits. 'The dairy. The milk churns were full this morning. Hide it there.'

'I suppose it might work,' Alice said grudgingly, her face flushed with heat.

Cook scowled. 'Do you have a better idea?'

'This is no time for arguments,' Meg snapped. 'Take them please, Cook, and I'll help Alice.'

Father Weston's threadbare vestments did not take long to reduce to ashes. Alice looked woefully at Richard's books. 'They were Mistress Caterina's,' she said.

Meg touched her shoulder. 'If she were here, she would not want them to put Richard in danger.'

With an expression of renewed determination on her face, Alice jabbed the first volume into the flames and soon the others followed. The iron door clanged shut and she wiped her streaming forehead with the hem of her apron.

Meg brushed a strand of hair out of her eyes. 'We should go to the Great Hall. Beatrice will need us.' She started for the door but never reached it. Into the kitchen came six men dressed in rough, soldiers' clothes. They stood to one side, muskets at the ready. Then a seventh man entered and ice filled Meg's veins. It was Ralph Fiddler.

*

At dawn, Meg sat in the Great Hall waiting for him to return. Five of his men had gone with him, while the sixth stood guard, his musket at the ready if she or Beatrice tried to move. She felt sick with apprehension. Hours had passed since the servants had been taken away for questioning. Alice would have the strength to resist, but the rest? It was little consolation that they probably did not know exactly where Richard and Father Weston's hiding place was.

There was the sound of a scuffle in the screens passage and Ralph appeared, propelling a spitting Alice before him. Twisting her arm, he forced her down onto the settle by the fireplace. 'Keep her here,' he barked at the guard. 'If she gives you trouble, shoot her.'

Beatrice jumped up. 'This is an outrage. You have no right to abuse my people, or to hold us against our will.'

'I have the queen's warrant, madam; that is all the right I need. If you, or your servants, try to obstruct my exercise of its powers, I may do with you as I wish.' He scowled at Alice. 'This harpy would do well to take heed.'

Alice lurched from the settle but the guard was too quick for her. The butt of his musket caught her across the throat and she sank back with a gasp.

Ralph's lip curled as he offered Beatrice his arm. 'I have no objection to your accompanying me on my search, madam. Or Mistress Stuckton if she so wishes.'

In the entrance hall, a heavy-set guard met them. His black hair and beard were silvered with plaster dust and he held a thick iron bar in his hand.

'We've opened every chest and wardrobe, master, and broke into the wall where you said, but there's nothing.'

A line deepened between Ralph's eyebrows. 'Then get back to work with the measuring rods and go over the house again, inch by inch if you have to. Call me when you find anything that does not tally. Are the others still in the kitchen quarters?'

'Yes, master.'

The stench of beer greeted them and a dull tapping sound. Swaying a little, one of the guards was working his way across the flagstones, tamping a metal rod on each one as he went.

'Nothing yet, master,' he slurred.

Ralph grabbed him by the throat. 'Did I say you could drink?'

'No, master.'

'Borresbie! Shore!'

Two more guards appeared.

'Take him outside, find a pump and sober him up.'

As the tipsy guard was manhandled away, Ralph glanced around the large kitchen. 'Borresbie and Shore can continue in here when they come back.'

He raised an eyebrow when Borresbie returned. 'Apart from the cellars, where have you searched?'

'The dry pantry, master.'

'Show me.'

In the pantry, Meg stared in dismay at the ripped sacks and smashed jars. A tide of flour, sugar, oats and salt covered the floor, dark and sticky where preserves had mixed with it. Months of stores were unusable. Beatrice's eyes flashed. 'Just what did you think to find here, sir?'

'There are many types of evidence, madam. Be assured I shall uncover them all, however long it takes.' He turned to Borresbie. 'Where now?'

'No one has been in the dairy or the outhouses yet, master.'

Meg's heart missed a beat. The dairy was separate from the house; she had hoped it might be overlooked. She didn't dare glance at Beatrice as Borresbie led them there.

In the cool, shadowy room, the air had a milky, sweet scent to it. Neat rows of muslin-wrapped cheeses were ranged on the shelves alongside the earthenware crocks containing fresh curds and butter. Meg winced as Borresbie removed their covers, plunged in a ladle and emptied them out, scowling when he found nothing. Silently, Ralph pointed to the churns in one corner. Meg saw Beatrice grip the folds of her skirt.

The first churn hit the floor with a thump. The lid flew off and milk streamed across the floor. Ralph stepped back with a grimace as it spattered his well-polished boots and black hose. At least, Meg thought, it was a small punishment, but in a few moments, it would be nothing.

When the second churn went over, something metallic glinted in the white liquid. Borresbie picked it up and Meg knew at once they were lost. Ralph took the chalice and rotated it slowly so that the silver caught the light.

'You seem to have taken some pains to keep this hidden. Do you still expect me to believe you are not harbouring a priest?'

When Beatrice did not answer, he brought his face very close to hers but she remained impassive.

'Make no mistake,' he said silkily, 'I shall dismantle this house stone by stone until I find what I'm looking for. Why not tell me now where the priest is and make things easier for yourself?'

'I have nothing to say to you, sir.'

'Take her upstairs, Borresbie, and lock her in her room. I'll deal with her later.'

A chill came over Meg as she remembered Ralph's ways.

Beatrice shook the guard off. 'I have no need of your assistance.'

Ralph waved a dismissive hand. 'Tell the others what we have found, Borresbie, and tell them to keep searching.'

Alone, Meg and Ralph stood facing each other. His eyes glittered and she smelt the sharp tang of his sweat.

'Not many people surprise me, Mistress Stuckton, but I must admit you have. I did not expect to find you in such company. I imagine I don't need to tell you that your departure caused your husband considerable distress. Naturally, he was unable to believe a woman in her right mind would reject what he had to offer.' He pulled her close. 'You scorned me once. I do not advise doing so again, unless you want me to inform your husband of your whereabouts.'

Meg tensed, half-knowing what was to come. Suddenly, his expression was sombre. 'I hope we understand each other,' he murmured. 'The priest and Richard Lacey are here. Sooner or later I shall find them. Unless…'

Meg's mind raced. 'Unless?'

189

'Don't pretend to misunderstand me. I still want you. I think it is a fair exchange for two men's lives, don't you?'

Meg felt her stomach lurch. 'Why should I trust you?' The moment the words were out of her mouth, she regretted them.

'So they are here.' He smiled grimly. 'Well, what is your answer?'

She bowed her head. 'What will you tell your men?'

'That you have confessed that Lacey and the priest were here but they left before we arrived.'

'And then?'

'Borresbie and Shore will escort you to London while I and the rest follow the "trail". Of course we shall find nothing.'

'You swear to leave here without harming my friends?'

'I swear by everything that is holy.'

'Then I will come.'

Chapter 18

The hallway of the London house was narrow with dark, battered wainscoting and shabby walls. As Meg followed the manservant into a small parlour, the rushes on the floor crackled under her feet, giving off a musty smell. In the parlour, an uncurtained window looked onto a blank brick wall. So this was Ralph's house – as ugly and unappealing as he was.

The journey to London had left her weary and desolate; the memory of her departure from Lacey Hall still twisted in her gut like a knife. She had saved Richard and Father Weston, but the confusion and hurt in Beatrice's eyes at what must have seemed like a desertion would not be easy to forget.

The days of waiting for Ralph began. Anticipation of the consequences of their bargain only deepened her distress. More than once, she dreamt of escape – what did it matter if Ralph carried out his threat and Edward found her? Only the fear of endangering the family at Lacey Hall held her back.

Her sole companion was William, Ralph's manservant, who had been left in charge of the house in his absence. William brought in meals from a nearby cook shop and attended to what little work he deemed necessary in the house. Meg wondered wryly what her mother would have said about such a lax regime.

Ralph arrived a week later. It was evening and they sat in the parlour as he recounted the events after she had left Lacey Hall. On his orders, his men had abandoned the search there, but for several days he had made them scour every other house, cottage and barn in the locality.

191

'I thought that would do to convince my masters that if the birds had ever been in the area in the first place, they had long ago flown.' He reached for the bottle of wine at his elbow and refilled his glass.

'Did Mistress Beatrice give you any message for me?' Meg asked.

'No. Are you sure you won't join me in a glass of wine?' He held up the bottle. 'It's a good vintage.'

'No thank you.'

He drained his glass and poured another. 'Meg, I have kept my side of the bargain. Now you must keep yours. Surely it's not impossible for us to live together amicably?'

Meg coloured. 'I'm sorry.'

He filled a second glass and held it out to her. After a moment's hesitation, she took it. What was the use of antagonising him? She was in his power now and whatever he had promised, quarrelling with him might still endanger Richard and Father Weston.

'No doubt you are wondering why my circumstances have changed so much since the days we enjoyed together in Salisbury.' Ralph lounged in his chair.

Meg bit back the urge to offer a scornful reply. 'Enjoyed' was not a word she would have used.

'I have you to thank for it,' he went on.

'Me?'

'I had been dissatisfied for a long time with my life there. The work of a clerk is often tedious and there was little prospect of advancement. After your sudden departure, it occurred to me it was time to turn the situation to my advantage. I already had your husband's confidence. A certain piece of information put him in my debt. After all, what man would want it known he was a cuckold, particularly a man of his pride and standing?'

Meg felt sick. 'You told him about Tom?'

'At first he flew into a rage but then wiser counsels prevailed. On my advice, he let it be known you had miscarried and the tragic loss had driven you out of your

192

wits. For your own safety, you had been removed to an asylum some distance from Salisbury. The physician there insisted on complete seclusion.'

Meg stared at him. 'He told people I was mad?'

Ralph laughed. 'In your husband's mind, you were, in truth, not far removed from that condition.'

'But my family? Did he tell them the same thing? Surely they would not have let me be taken away.'

With a shrug, he fetched a new bottle of wine, opened it and replenished his glass. 'As far as I could tell, their main concern seemed to be the avoidance of a scandal. My departure from Salisbury suited everyone,' he went on. 'Thanks to your husband's generosity, I arrived furnished with a goodly sum of money to make a fresh start. I never looked back - London is a city full of opportunity for those who know how to make use of it. The work I am engaged on is only the beginning.'

He tossed off his wine, stood up and took an unsteady step towards her. 'Enough of this talking. Shall we to bed, madam?'

It was the moment Meg dreaded, but she was painfully aware she had no choice. She took his proffered hand and let him raise her to her feet. The room swam. The wine had been stronger than she realised.

Upstairs, in his sparsely furnished room, she shivered. Ralph put the wine bottle on the table and scowled at the empty grate. 'I told that lazy fool of a servant to light a fire.'

'It doesn't matter,' Meg said quickly. The banal exchange heightened the strange awkwardness of the situation. Ralph's inability to meet her eye made her think he felt it too.

With difficulty, she suppressed a shudder as he unhooked her gown then clumsily unlaced the ties of her bodice and petticoats. Naked but for her shift, she clasped her arms over her breasts and watched him strip off his breeches and hose.

He came towards her and uncrossed her arms then pulled down the loose neckline of her shift. His mouth explored the curve of her breasts, his tongue running hungrily over her skin. Beads of sweat matted his hair and his breath smelt of wine. 'Lie down,' he muttered.

The mattress sagged as he clambered onto the bed beside her. His legs straddled hers and his hand reached for his manhood. Meg tensed, waiting for him to enter her. She felt his probing fingers and a wet, slippery pressure, but after a few moments of fumbling, he started to curse. All at once, the grotesque comedy of the situation overtook her and an involuntary gurgle of hysterical laughter rose from her throat.

The sinews stood out on Ralph's reddened neck and his eyes narrowed. 'You cold bitch,' he snarled, 'this is your fault.'

The first blow split her lip and she cried out at the stinging pain. The second smashed into her left cheekbone.

'I'll teach you to mock me,' he hissed. 'I'll give you a lesson you won't forget.'

Twisting towards the foot of the bed, he pinned her by the chest with his knee and seized the wine bottle. He wrenched her shift up to her waist. The remains of the wine spattered her as Ralph rammed the bottle's cold rim between her thighs. Desperate, she jerked up her head and with all her force sank her teeth into his bare buttock. He yelled and in the brief moment that he relaxed his grip, she shoved him away and jumped from the bed. In the corridor, she raced towards her room. If she could lock herself in, she would be safe, at least for a while.

At the head of the stairs, Ralph's servant, William, loomed out of the shadow, the light of a candle illuminating his astonished face.

'Get back to your quarters, man,' Ralph bellowed. 'This is no business of yours.'

Meg almost fell into her room and slammed and bolted the door. Outside, there was the sound of a scuffle then a

194

series of thuds and a cry. The door latch rattled and a fist hammered on the wood. She sank to the floor and covered her face.

At last the hammering stopped and there was silence for a few moments. Meg waited with her heart in her mouth then Ralph's voice came through the door. 'Hiding in there will do you no good. You'll have to come out in the end, and when you do, I'll be waiting.'

In the silence that replaced the sound of his fading footsteps, she crawled onto the bed and pulled the covers around her. She was too exhausted to think about what she would do when she had to face the morning.

*

Grey light bathed the room when she awoke from the last of a series of fitful sleeps. No sound disturbed the silence. She was not sure how much time passed before she heard shuffling sounds in the corridor and a tentative knock at the door. She stiffened and did not answer; the knock came again.

'Mistress? It's me, William. Are you awake?

Meg crept to the door and put her head to the wood. 'Are you alone?' she whispered.

'Yes.'

She hesitated. What if he was lying and Ralph was waiting beside him? She pressed her ear to the door once more and listened intently.

'A message came for him just before dawn,' William said. 'He went out and didn't leave word when he'd be back. It's the truth, as God's my witness.'

Meg pulled a blanket from the bed and wrapped it around her then opened the door a fraction. William really was alone. She let him into the room.

'I'm not staying in this house,' he said. 'Not after last night.' He rubbed his shoulder. 'He could have killed me, knocking me down the stairs like that. As it was I thought

195

he'd broken my arm. I only took this job because he offered me good pay but he's got the Devil's own temper and half the time I don't get the pay he promised anyway.' He reached out to touch her swollen cheek and she flinched. 'You can come with me, if you like.'

'I don't know. . .'

'You don't want any more bruises on that pretty face of yours, do you?'

Numbly, Meg shook her head.

'We'd better be getting ready then. I'll bring you your clothes from his room. Put whatever else you want to keep on the bed. I'll bundle it up to take with my stuff. Not too much, mind, I'll have to carry it.'

Dressed, Meg came downstairs. She found William rifling through the drawers in Ralph's study. He looked up with a frown. 'They're all empty - no money, no papers. I thought at least I'd find the wages he owes me. I'm going to have a look upstairs. You can go through in here again, in case I've missed something, but I don't think I have.'

Meg hesitated.

'It wouldn't be stealing if that's what you're afraid of. He owes me, I tell you.'

Unwillingly, Meg started to search, but as William predicted, she found nothing. Then at the back of a dusty cupboard, she noticed a small, tarnished, brass box. Inside was a block of sealing wax and a ring. The ring was engraved with two letters: *WK*. From the traces of wax lodged in the letters' grooves, it had been used as a seal. *WK* for William Kemp?

William's footsteps thumped down the stairs. Quickly, Meg slipped the ring into her bodice and hid the box in the cupboard again before he appeared in the doorway.

'Nothing there either,' he said crossly. 'We may as well be off.'

'Where are we going?'

'My sister's place, it'll have to do for now.'

They left the city by a gate guarded by a forbidding, high-walled building. William told her it was Newgate prison. Further on they crossed a stone bridge over a sluggish, stinking river. The roads were slick with mud after the morning's rain. Acutely conscious of her bruised, swollen face, Meg tried to hide it with the hood of her cloak.

'That's Lincoln's Inn,' William remarked as they passed a large group of buildings set in open fields. 'My sister gets most of her customers from there. She's a laundress. Lawyers need their linen washed like everyone else.'

Soon they came to Holborn, where William's sister lived. Her cottage, with its rough, lime-washed walls, was one of the larger ones in the village. It had several windows under its deeply overhanging thatched roof. 'Peg's done well for herself,' William remarked as they approached.

A young woman with chestnut hair came out of the door carrying a willow basket piled high with linen. 'Hello William,' she said cheerfully. 'You've picked a fine day to come. Your sister's done nothing but grouse all morning.'

'What are you dawdling for, Susan?' a voice shouted from inside the cottage.

'It's William,' the girl called back.

A short, stout woman appeared in the doorway. Grey haired with a grumpy expression, she looked much older than her brother. An apron covered her brown fustian dress and her sleeves were rolled up to her elbows, revealing forearms like ninepins. She elbowed Susan aside.

'So it's you, is it,' she scowled. 'Keeping this ninny talking when she's work to do? Be off with you, Susan.'

'All right – I'm going.'

Peggoty looked Meg up and down. 'Who might you be?'

'This is a nice welcome and no mistake,' William muttered.

She swung round on him. 'Who mashed up her face like that? You?'

197

'Of course not, she fell,' William replied testily.

'Did she now? Well you'd better be telling the truth. If it was her husband, don't think I'll lie for you if he comes looking.'

Meg winced.

'So that fine master of yours gave you the sack, did he?' Peggoty went on.

'No, I sacked him.' William rubbed his hands together and blew on them. 'Now let us in, won't you, Peg? It's nippy out here.'

Meg followed William inside, blinking at the haze of steam filling the room. When her eyes grew accustomed to the dim light, she saw the steam came from several large copper pans heating over a fire. Sheets, pillowcases, shirts, shifts and stockings hung from lines strung around the room and there was a strong smell of soap and lye.

'Well, I haven't time to be bothering with you,' Peggoty grumbled. 'Look at all this work to be done. Too cold and wet these days to dry anything outside and the cottage gets damp as damp. I can't bring in the wood for the fire fast enough and it takes twice as long to get the clean linen back to my customers. They kick up a right fuss, I can tell you.'

'We only want to stay a few days, Peg,' William broke in. 'I'll chop wood for you and Meg can help with the washing.'

Peggoty snatched Meg's hands and inspected them. 'These haven't seen much work, I'll be bound.'

Meg lifted her chin. She was weary and despondent but Peggoty's bad-tempered reception aroused some irritation in her. 'More than you think,' she replied.

'I suppose you don't look as if you eat much,' Peggoty said grudgingly. 'As long as it's only for a few days, you can sleep with Susan. There's straw and sacks in the outhouse, William. Make yourself a bed out there. And don't you forget, when you find another job, I expect every penny you've cost me back.'

William raised an eyebrow. 'I'd have laid money on that.'

She shook her fist at him. 'And don't think I'll put up with any of your nonsense either. I've a living to earn just like anyone else.'

Chapter 19

London
July, 1587

The muffled sounds of carriages rumbling by and hawkers crying their wares drifted up to Lamotte as he sat opposite Walsingham in his study at Seething Lane. Walsingham took out a purse from his drawer and put it on the desk.

'Husband it well. I hear Paris is an expensive city these days.'

Lamotte took the purse with a feeling of reluctance. Many years had passed since he had last been in the city that was once his home. It had been a troubling experience, unearthing memories he preferred not to disturb.

'When do you want me to leave?'

'By the end of the week.'

This was a complication Lamotte had not expected, and he did not welcome it. This mission might last some time and he was due to take the company on a summer tour of the West Country soon. The country business had taken years to establish and he did not want to cancel the engagements. All the same, it was unwise to refuse Walsingham, particularly as Lamotte still hoped for his help with Tom. He would just have to get back as soon as he could and, if necessary, send the others on ahead. He nodded.

'The man you are to meet is a Genoese banker by the name of Riccardo Manfredi,' Walsingham went on. 'I have used his services for some time now but as always, take care.'

'Of course.'

'His business takes him to Spain as well as France and I understand he was in Cadiz in April when Drake struck. He should be able to give you an account of the tonnage and cargoes of enemy shipping sunk. I also want any information he has on the effect the losses have had on Spain's plans. See to it you pay him well.'

Ah, Lamotte thought, the purse was not only for him.

Walsingham shuffled through his papers and Lamotte noticed the tremor in his gnarled, blue-veined hands. In spite of a blazing fire that made the room oppressively hot, he wore a robe of thick, black velvet. Above his crisply starched ruff his skin had a greyish hue. Finding the piece of paper he wanted, he passed it across the desk. It was a map of southern England, annotated in a spidery hand.

'Details of some of our costal defences: I want you to memorise them. At some point in your conversations with Manfredi, when you think it will not arouse suspicion, mention them to him. The information is false. For example here,' he pointed to a promontory, 'and here,' his finger moved on, 'none of the guns listed actually exist, but I should like to set a little test for the *signore*. It is always interesting to find out where information comes to rest.' He leant his elbows on his desk and pressed the tips of his fingers together. 'Have you any questions?'

Lamotte shook his head.

'Good.'

Lamotte stood up and bowed. He was used to Walsingham's habit of eschewing the pleasantries most people dealt in. In truth, it would be a relief to escape the stifling heat of the room.

On the walk home to Throgmorton Street, he wondered whether in the early days of their acquaintance Walsingham had set traps for him too. Perhaps, he thought wryly, he still did. It was uncanny how, in spite of all the years he had served him, the workings of Walsingham's mind remained unfathomable. Indeed, did anyone truly understand or come close to him? His wife, people said, was a severe, haughty woman and he did not have a courtier's skills to make him a favourite at Court with the queen even though, if she was as wise as she was reputed to be, she must recognise the value of his loyalty and dedication.

Lamotte sighed. Was his situation so very different? He could not think of a single person he was able to confide in completely. Increasingly, he found himself dwelling on how his life might have turned out if Amélie and the boy had not died. Jean would have been the same age as Tom. He hoped he would have had the same passion for the theatre as Tom did. When all was said and done, what was the use of building up a business if you had no one to leave it to?

He turned a corner and a gust of wind buffeted him, nearly dislodging his hat. With a frown, he clapped it more firmly on his head. What a summer: it didn't deserve the name. Already the theatre's audiences showed signs of dwindling and who could blame them? If the bad weather went on much longer, profits were bound to suffer. It was another reason for keeping to the tour. Country folk had less entertainment available to them and tended to appreciate it more. Audiences were likely to be better there in spite of the weather.

He turned his mind to what had to be done before his departure. It was not unknown for him to be absent from The Unicorn and the players would not be surprised if he claimed urgent business took him away for a while. If he prepared them for it, the seasoned players were capable of leading the tour without him for a short while if need be. More importantly, he must see Tom before he left and make sure he was provided for.

*

At Newgate the following day, he went to see the chief warder and paid the money he demanded for providing Tom's food for the next few weeks. The fellow knew how to strike a hard bargain, Lamotte thought irritably as he left the

202

lodge, but no doubt he was not the only one of his kind to profit from his position.

By the time he reached the yard, a crowd of other visitors was already jostling for the places closest to the bars. It was drizzling and the smell of damp wool mingled with the odour of stale sweat. Elbowing his way to the front, he scanned the prisoners on the other side. Eventually, he sighted Tom and shouted out his name but, at first, the hubbub was too loud for him to hear. With disquiet, Lamotte observed how dejected and worn down he seemed, alone and gazing dully at the activity around him. It was hardly surprising. After almost a year of imprisonment, Newgate's grim confines would test the strongest resolve.

He cupped his hands around his mouth and shouted louder than before. This time Tom's head went up. As he pushed his way to the bars, Lamotte braced himself for the disappointment that would inevitably show in Tom's eyes when he had to tell him there was no news of a release. How he wished he had something more to offer him than the usual empty promises.

He mustered a jovial smile. 'Tom! Did you think I wasn't coming?' He grasped Tom's hand through the bars. It felt like ice. 'I gave the warders money for a warmer blanket for you last time I was here,' he said. 'Did you get it?'

'Yes, I'm very grateful.'

'And your food? They haven't tried to skimp on that?'

'No. It's just so damp and cold inside, even though it's summer, but there's nothing to be done about it.' He looked crestfallen. 'I suppose there's no news?'

'I regret not but we mustn't give up hope.'

'I know.'

'Tom, I have to go away for a while. After that I need to take the company to the country for the summer tour, but I shall visit you before I leave. For now, I've left money for your food and I'll make sure you never go short.'

'Will you go to Salisbury on the tour?' Tom asked.

'Yes.' Lamotte saw the pain in Tom's eyes. 'Do you want me to see what I can find out about Meg?'

'I know it's no use,' Tom said awkwardly, 'but I would like to know if she's well. She's probably forgotten me by now,' he added bitterly. 'Better for her if she has.' His head drooped and his next words seemed to be said half to himself, 'But I think of her all the time.'

A bell tolled and the warders on duty started to herd the prisoners towards the tunnel leading back to their cells. Not far from Tom and Lamotte, a young woman screamed as the man she had been talking to was roughly dragged into the line. Lamotte felt a stab of pity for her and for the grubby, bewildered little girl clinging to her skirts.

'I have to go,' Tom said as a warder approached them.

'Have courage. I promise I'll do what I can to find out about Meg.'

Sadly, he watched Tom swallowed up in the mass of prisoners then he turned to leave.

Chapter 20

Two days later, Lamotte spurred his horse over London Bridge and set out for the coast. The mist lifted by the time he reached Blackheath and the road was busy. As always, hundreds of wagons and carts lumbered up to London from the countryside, laden with the timber, bricks and foodstuffs that the great city needed.

There were wattle cages crammed with hens and ducks, herds of cattle and sheep and once a great white sea of honking, hissing geese that made his horse shy and nearly collide with a passing cart. His horse almost unseated him again when a sudden hailstorm threw everything into confusion. It was a relief when evening came and he stopped at a wayside inn. There he ate supper and drank a quart of ale then retired to bed.

The following day, orchards and market gardens gave way to rolling downs grazed by vast flocks of sheep. He had not slept well and the crack of whips and the curses and shouts of wagon drivers struggling to move their loads over the rough road made his head ache; dust caked his boots and irritated his eyes and throat.

At Folkestone, he found a room at an inn near the port and sent his servant, James, who had ridden from London with him, to enquire when the next ship sailed for Calais. He ordered beef and beer then settled down to wait for him to return.

As far as he could tell, most of the other customers were travellers. Out of force of habit, he watched them and picked up snippets of their conversation but none of them seemed to pay him any attention.

Eventually, his servant returned with news that the *Maid of Kent* sailed at eight o'clock the next morning.

'Good,' Lamotte yawned. 'Make sure you wake me at six. After I've left, take the horses back to Throgmorton Street. Here's some money for the journey. Mind they're properly fed and stabled at night.'

He settled his account and went upstairs. In his room, the shutters were closed and barred. He opened them and looked out onto the street. It was the main thoroughfare to the sea, but compared with what he was used to, it was very quiet. Above the rooftops of the houses opposite, a full moon sailed between rags of cloud. With his elbows propped on the sill, he mused on what the next few days would bring. He was reasonably sure he would not be recognised in Paris – many years had passed since he had lived there – but it was hard not to feel apprehensive. However cautious one was, ventures into Walsingham's murky world often involved danger.

It began to rain. Lamotte closed the shutters, undressed and lay down on the bed. A plague on this journey! He was not looking forward to the crossing. There was always the risk of storms in the Narrow Sea.

And Paris: there were so many memories waiting for him there. Sadly, he thought of Amélie. She was irreplaceable of course but fifteen years was a long time to come home to a solitary hearth and a cold bed. There was no getting away from it, a wife made a man's life more comfortable. Maybe he should try to find one. True, he would not see forty again and his love of good food was becoming evident. His hair and beard were greying too but his limbs were still well muscled and his face unmarked by the pox. He was not, he hoped, an entirely repulsive sight. Then again, with the secrets he had to keep, it might not always be easy having someone else in his life. She would need to be worth it.

*

Contrary to his expectations, the crossing was a calm one. From the deck of the *Maid of Kent* he watched the grey-green water slap and froth against the hull and felt the breeze ruffle his hair. The ship was reassuringly sturdy, built of good Kentish timber. Under sail she lumbered along like a stout laundress pegging out sheets to dry.

When he disembarked at Calais, the language of his birth enfolded him as he wandered through the maze of canals and small harbours. Occasionally, he had been allowed to accompany his father when business brought him to the city. Calais had belonged to England then and the cross of St George had streamed from the mastheads of the ships riding at anchor. They had watched sailors toiling to unload vast quantities of English iron, wool and lace. English was spoken in the taverns and markets and English merchants swaggered through the streets. All that had changed now. Calais was French again and the English merchants had to hustle for trade with the rest.

In one of the markets he bought bread and a piece of oozing, pungent cheese. Eating as he strolled around the stalls, his mouth rejoiced. The English might be less likely to plunge a knife into his Protestant belly but the French understood food. After years of instruction, his cook at Throgmorton Street served up a near-edible meal but his sauces would never match Amélie's rich, delicious concoctions of wine, cream and herbs.

The diligence set out early the next morning from the main square near the old watch tower. Crammed in between the side of the coach and a stout, Parisian merchant who smelt strongly of garlic, Lamotte was glad to escape during the stops to change horses and allow the passengers to eat and rest.

Three days after they set out, the Calais road plunged into the outskirts of Paris. It had rained the previous night and the streets were still a quagmire, slowing their progress. Lamotte cleared a circle in the steamed-up window with his finger. The narrow wooden houses with their steeply gabled roofs and upper stories jutting out over the street were as he remembered. Many were decorated with little shrines to the Virgin Mary or one of the saints, embellished with bunches of flowers and candles. Black cloth draped numerous windows. Paris mourned the Scottish queen.

The diligence creaked around a corner and bumped over a particularly large rut. The merchant's head jerked up. He peered out of the window. 'Does the wretch want to shake us all to pieces? He'll get no pourboire from me.'

'Not far to the river now,' another passenger remarked. 'It'll be better when the paved roads begin.'

'Even then there are so many holes a coach can easily break its axle,' complained a gaunt man with a sallow complexion. 'Only last week, my cousin was thrown from his horse and badly injured when the animal stumbled into one the size of a cannonball.'

The coach rumbled on past the massive walls and towers of the Palais du Louvre and soon reached the river. Lamotte stepped down and surveyed the city's great artery. Unlike the Thames, for most of its course it flowed between banks of solid rock and its beauty was not marred by a muddy strand, strewn with rotting sewage and carcasses. Among the hundreds of boats on the gleaming water, he recognised the great Burgundian barges come up from the south, loaded with wheat, timber and wine. On the far bank, the soaring towers of the Abbey of St Germain des Prés dominated the skyline.

He shouldered his luggage and set out to find lodgings; there, he called for something to eat. Two hours later, refreshed, he headed for the nearest of the wooden bridges leading onto the Île de la Cité.

Dilapidated houses lined the rickety walkway and in places, through broken planks, he saw the river racing along thirty feet below. The bridge was a death trap. Clearly it had been neglected for years but no doubt neglect was a malaise he would find all over the city. It was common knowledge that Henri of France was a weak, dissolute monarch. With his resources eaten up by the need to appease and control the powerful religious factions threatening to unseat him, not much was left for poor Paris.

Relieved to be on the far bank, he strode past the Palais de Justice, glancing at the hordes of black-clad functionaries hurrying in and out. Busy with being busy, he thought wryly. It was hard to believe he had once been among them. If he had never been approached by one of Walsingham's agents for the information to which his work made him privy, he might still have been there.

He found the goldsmith's shop to which Walsingham had directed him, rang the bell and waited. A few moments passed before the wooden cover of the small spyhole in the door shot back. An elderly, bald man with a beaky nose and a prominent chin squinted at him. Lamotte showed the gold ring he wore on the fourth finger of his left hand. After a pause in which he heard the rasp of several bolts being undone, the door opened.

In the dimly lit shop, he studied the gold plate and jewellery gleaming in the barred cabinets behind the counter while the goldsmith examined the ring through an eyeglass. At last he seemed satisfied and handed it back.

'It's a nice piece, but not worth much.'

'Are you certain? When I purchased it in Genoa, I paid fifty ducats. It must be worth more now. Surely you know someone who would give me that at least?'

A flicker of interest disturbed the goldsmith's impassive expression. 'I suppose I could make enquiries.'

'There will be a generous commission in it for you.'

The goldsmith lowered his voice. 'Come tomorrow at five. Signor Manfredi will meet you. I have a room where you can talk without being overheard.'

Outside, Lamotte scanned the street for anyone loitering to watch him leave but the passers-by all seemed intent on their own business. He was not ready to return to his lodgings so he turned towards the eastern end of the island and walked until he reached Notre Dame.

Set off by the wide expanse Parisians called the Parvis, the cathedral's magnificent Gothic façade reared up into the sky. The hundreds of statues decorating it were black with the dirt and smoke of generations but impressive nevertheless. Looking around him, Lamotte wondered why the authorities did not sweep away the ugly shanty town of wooden hovels that clustered like rotting fungi at its feet. Many of the hovels had washing lines strung between them displaying an assortment of tattered clothes. Gangs of shrieking urchins ran around or squabbled over each other's finds in the heaps of refuse that were everywhere. Alongside this chaos of poverty-stricken lives were stalls selling fruit, vegetables, flowers, books, pamphlets and cheap trinkets. On the heels of a small party of Benedictine monks, Lamotte threaded his way through the hubbub to the cathedral and went in.

After the noise of the Parvis, the silence was like cool water. He had forgotten how beautiful the rainbows of light falling from the tall windows were. They seemed to dissolve the walls into shimmering veils. The arcades and columns supporting the great vault of the chancel looked as insubstantial as gossamer. In this hushed miracle of stone, black-robed priests flitted about their business like ghosts.

He slipped into a side chapel and lit a candle for Amélie. He had never been a deeply religious man, that had been more in her nature, but when he knelt at the small altar, he felt strangely at peace. It had been the right thing to come.

His knees cracked as he got to his feet. A wretched business, this ageing: in a few years he might be dead. Would you forgive me, Amélie, he asked inwardly; would you understand if I took a wife?

*

210

He returned early to the Île de la Cité and, when he was satisfied there was only one entrance to the goldsmith's shop, stood out of sight on the opposite side of the street watching who came and went. The goldsmith's customers appeared to be respectable-looking members of the bourgeoisie, mixed with a few gallants in fashionable dress.

By the time the bells of Notre Dame tolled five, Lamotte's back ached and he was glad to see the goldsmith bow one last customer off the premises before pausing to glance up and down the street and pulling across his shutters. He had been back in the shop for no more than a few minutes when a man approached from the direction of the cathedral. Dressed in a black, fur-trimmed cloak and a black doublet and breeches made of expensive-looking silk, he went to the shop door and rang the bell. The door opened and after a brief exchange with the goldsmith, the man went in. Lamotte waited briefly then followed.

Riccardo Manfredi was as broad as he was tall with sharp, black eyes twinkling with bonhomie. His lips were fleshy and pink and his pudgy hands displayed an impressive collection of rings set with chunky gemstones. He held out a large paper cornet filled with cherries.

'Signor Lamotte! A pleasure to make your acquaintance! These are exquisite, would you like one? I was lucky to find them, most of the fruit sellers are complaining of the bad weather and the poor harvest.'

Lamotte took a cherry and smiled. 'Thank you.' The intense sweetness brought saliva into his mouth.

'Take another.' Manfredi held out the cherries. 'I am glad to see you haven't been infected with the English suspicion of fresh fruit. Most of them seem to live on meat and bread.' He patted his paunch. 'My dear wife, Anna Maria, is always telling me sweet things are not good for this. She complains that all the fruit I eat induces flatulence but when I am away from home, I can do as I please.' He pulled out a fine, white linen handkerchief and dabbed away the dribble of crimson juice on his chin. 'You are a married man, signor?'

Before Lamotte had time to answer, the goldsmith cleared his throat. Manfredi smiled. 'Our good friend rebukes me. Anna Maria always says I talk too much.'

'Shall I show you upstairs, gentlemen?' the goldsmith asked.

'By all means, signor.'

The room above the shop had windows looking onto the street. As the stairs creaked under the goldsmith's retreating footsteps, Manfredi went to survey the view.

'We are safe, I believe,' he remarked, looking out.

'How much does the goldsmith know?'

'Signor Albert? I told him we are arranging for the illegal import of some Venetian glass into England.' Manfredi sat down in a battered leather armchair. 'Well, Signor Lamotte, I believe our friend the Milord Walsingham thinks very highly of you.'

'And of you, Signor Manfredi.'

Manfredi smiled. 'I am flattered, although I understand you have served him many years longer.'

'Since I was a young man and he was the English ambassador in Paris.'

'And you are French?'

'Yes.'

'But you prefer to live in England?'

'My wife died and I had no family left here. Walsingham offered me work in England. My training and experience was of no use there but he helped me to fulfil a long-held desire to go into the theatre. In England, it is common for troupes of players to travel the country, with all the opportunities that affords to gather information.'

'Interesting,' Manfredi remarked. 'Now to business. You may tell our friend, Milord Walsingham, that Cadiz will not forget Drake's visit in a hurry.'

'That was the intention.'

'But what use was it? The Spanish are already building new ships to replace the ones that were lost. Drake took Cadiz by surprise but King Philip is determined such a thing will not happen again. Some of the ships weren't even Spanish. One was a Genoese, seven hundred tons of her, waiting in the harbour for the turn of the tide. She was bound for home laden with a fortune in cochineal, hides and wool.' He gave a rueful smile. 'I myself lost money there. Others were smaller merchant ships that Drake fired when he had the main prizes he wanted.' He shrugged. 'No doubt Queen Elizabeth will claim he acted against her orders but many do not believe it. Does she want the whole of Europe against her?'

A burr of impatience chafed Lamotte. Had he come all the way to Paris to be lectured? Manfredi had better have something more useful to divulge.

Manfredi lowered his voice. 'You frown, signor, but do not be afraid. Your journey will not be in vain. An old friend of mine has been appointed to a position in the household of the Marquis of Santa Cruz.'

Lamotte's ears pricked up. A man with inside knowledge of what went on in the house of the admiral of the Spanish fleet was almost as valuable as an informant in the Escorial itself, perhaps more so.

A shrewd twinkle came into Manfredi's eye. 'I think this is of interest to you?'

'Indeed it is.'

'My friend tells me the marquis is in a rage, not just at the destruction of the Cadiz fleet but also because, while Drake remains off Cape St Vincent, none of the Spanish fleet in the Mediterranean can reach Lisbon to join the rest of the Armada. Santa Cruz's main supply lines are cut off. He is short of guns and ammunition, even food for his crews. Meanwhile, Drake ravages the coast seizing any ships he happens to find. The fisherman cannot fish because they have no seaworthy boats left and coastal vessels are afraid to put to sea. Not long ago, Drake captured and burnt a cargo of

213

staves going down to Lisbon to make barrels for the Armada's food and water. They will have to be made of unseasoned wood now.'

The import was not lost on Lamotte: unseasoned wood meant leaky barrels, rotting food and bad water. Walsingham would rub his hands at the thought of Spanish crews too sick to fight.

The light caught Manfredi's rings as he flourished a plump hand. 'So, signor, I trust your time has not been entirely wasted. I expect more information from my friend very soon. When do you leave Paris?'

'When do you expect your information?'

Manfredi heaved himself out of the chair. 'It is hard to say. Shall we meet again in a week?'

Inwardly, Lamotte groaned. He must not refuse, but it meant being away from London for longer than he had planned. 'Very well,' he said reluctantly.

'I suggest you come to my lodgings. I never like to use the same place more than once.'

'I understand.'

'Rue des Vieux Marchands, number five.' He held out the cherries. 'Another?'

'Thank you, but no.'

Manfredi popped the last two in his mouth and ate them, spitting out the stones. He crumpled the paper cornet into a ball and threw it in the hearth. 'We must shake hands in the English way, signor. God be with you until we meet again.'

*

In the days that followed, boredom drew Lamotte back to the Parvis at Notre Dame. He studied the books and pamphlets at the bookstalls and bought a few. Many were so scurrilous in their abuse of the French king that if they had been written of Queen Elizabeth, those involved would very likely have lost their lives.

Then there were the same prophecies of doom that you could find on the stalls at Cheapside. He wondered, as he often had before, if they really were just old wives' tales. What did we truly know of the workings of the Almighty? Strange and terrible events were certainly not unknown. It must be seven years ago that the great tremor had rocked London. People said the earth had heaved like a stormy sea in other places too, bringing down church towers, chimney stacks and city walls. Some said they had seen darkness at noon and ghostly armies marching in the sky. Others spoke of a gigantic hunter crossing the heavens driving a pack of coal-black hounds.

Lamotte shivered. There was no use dwelling on such things. What would come to pass would come to pass.

One afternoon, he loitered on the edge of a crowd gathered around a preacher who had set up a makeshift pulpit near the cathedral. Murmurs of assent swelled as the man fulminated against all Protestants – especially Queen Elizabeth and her ministers – calling them necromancers and murdering heretics: tools of the Devil fit only to roast in the fires of Hell.

His words sent a chill through Lamotte. Fifteen years ago, in the name of religion, hatred like this had blazed through Paris. Human nature did not need much encouragement to turn to brutality. This man had his audience in the palm of his hand, blood lust gleaming in their eyes. As he reached the climax of his tirade, a flock of pigeons feeding nearby rose into the air in a flurry of beating wings. For a moment, imagining he heard the crackle of flames, Lamotte flinched. A sudden desire to be safe at home in England seized him. As soon as he had seen Manfredi again, he would be on his way.

*

That night, a storm rumbled for hours around the heights of Montmartre then broke over the city, flinging down sheets of

215

hail and rain that turned the cobbled streets to rivers and sent people scurrying to their homes. In his lodgings, Lamotte lay on his bed listening to the hammering of the rain on the roof. The idea of a farewell visit to the little grisette who had entertained him the night before had lost its appeal. Old age, he though with a sigh. It was a sorry state of affairs when the fear of a chill stifled a man's desire. In his youth, before he met Amélie, he would have braved a torrent to reach a pretty girl's bed. Gloomily, he turned over and closed his eyes. No doubt Amélie would have teased him for his old man's ways. Perhaps he was a fool to hope he would ever find someone to take her place.

He rose early the next morning and strolled in the streets. The storm had cleared the air and his spirits lifted. Paris was still the most beautiful city on earth and not all his memories were sad ones. He stowed what remained of Walsingham's money in a concealed pocket in his doublet and set out for the address Manfredi had given him, doubling back once or twice to make sure he was not being followed.

A bleary-eyed young woman answered the bell. 'Signor Manfredi? I haven't seen him this morning but after last night, I'm not surprised.'

Lamotte frowned.

'The storm,' she went on. 'If he was like me, he must hardly have slept a wink. It frightened the baby too. He made such a commotion with his squalling.' A thin wail came from behind her and she sighed. 'I must go and attend to him, monsieur. Will you find your own way up? It is the second floor, the door to the left of the stairs.'

'Of course, I'm sorry to have disturbed you, madame.'

'It's nothing.'

The stairs were steep and Lamotte's hamstrings grumbled by the time he reached the second floor. Wheezing a little, he knocked and waited. There was no answer. Strange; he was sure he had the right day. He knocked harder and a slit of daylight appeared between the door and its frame. It was not locked. Cautiously, he pushed it a little wider.

The room was plainly furnished with a table, two chairs and a cupboard against one wall. Dirty pewter plates and cups lay on the table with a dish of cherry pits, a half-empty carafe of wine, the remains of a piece of cheese and a few morsels of bread. The smell of cheese and stale wine lingered in the air. A metallic tapping made him jump but it was only the window banging. He went over and fastened the latch. Outside, a crazy patchwork of tiled and slate roofs glinted in the sun. At the sight of him, a black cat slunk away, swishing its tail.

The door to the next room was ajar but its shutters were closed. The stuffy air had a rank, meaty smell. It took a few seconds for his eyes to become accustomed to the dim light but then he made out a shape on the bed. He went to the window, undid the shutters and pushed them open. Then his gorge rose.

Manfredi lay on his back, his eyes wide open. His fleshy lips were no longer pink but stained crimson and between them was stuffed his severed tongue. Blood soaked the front of his cambric shirt and a swarm of bluebottles fed at the gash in his throat. More swarmed over his pudgy hands. They were covered with slashes, dark with dried blood. He must have fought for his life. A dark stain spread from his breeches to the sheets.

Bile rushed into Lamotte's mouth. He blundered back to the first room, drained the carafe of wine and wiped his lips. His legs shook. Had Manfredi been tricked? Had the contact he was expecting murdered him? All Lamotte's instincts told him to leave straight away but if there were any clues, he ought to look for them.

When he had steadied his nerves, he made a swift search of the lodgings but apart from a few clothes, he found nothing except bills from a tailor and a shoemaker in the city and a letter concerning the cargo of a merchant ship in which Manfredi appeared to have an interest.

217

Lamotte put the papers in the grate and reached in his pocket for his tinder box, but then he hesitated. Even though it was unlikely they were of any importance, Walsingham liked thoroughness and he should see them. He tucked them away then went downstairs and let himself out into the street.

Chapter 21

'Sluys has fallen,' said Walsingham.

Lamotte absorbed the news with dismay. Since Spain had seized the great port of Antwerp two years previously, the importance of Ostend and its neighbour, Sluys, the two remaining Flemish ports under Protestant control, had soared. Sluys's fall brought Spain within a hair's breadth of complete mastery of the Southern Netherlands.

'The Duke of Parma managed to smuggle his men across the marshes when the tide was low to take the island of Cadzand. That gave him the vantage point he needed to bring up his barges and blockade the deepwater channel leading to the city. Our forces tried to dislodge him before it was too late but they failed. After that, he was free to attack the city undisturbed.'

'What about our ships?'

'The Earl of Leicester was with the Dutch fleet off the coast but as has so frequently been the case, Parma outflanked him. Leicester launched a fire ship but he acted too late and Parma's men were ready for him. They simply uncoupled the barges in its path and let it through. If Leicester had been close behind it, he might have forced the channel, but he was not. Parma must have rejoiced when he saw the fire ship run aground on a sandbank and burn out harmlessly.'

Walsingham's low opinion of the military capabilities of the queen's favourite, Robert Dudley, Earl of Leicester, came as no surprise to Lamotte: many shared it. He was certainly no match for the Duke of Parma, who was universally hailed as the finest commander of his day.

'Our ships stayed off the coast for three more days,' Walsingham went on, 'after which Leicester abandoned hope of saving the city. Eight days later the garrison surrendered. Most of them paid with their lives for their defiance. It is a sorry tale. I hope you have better news for me.'

Lamotte braced himself. 'I'm afraid not. Manfredi's dead. After our first meeting, he asked me to wait a week then meet him at his lodgings. He told me he had an informer in the Marquis of Santa Cruz's household and was expecting news. I waited as he asked then set out to see him. When I arrived, I found him with his throat cut.'

Only a tiny tic at the corner of Walsingham's left eye betrayed his reaction to the news. 'Do you have any idea who killed him?'

'None. I had no reason to believe either of us was being followed and I didn't meet anyone connected with him except the goldsmith who arranged our first meeting. Manfredi told him we were discussing a contraband shipment of Venetian glass. He appeared satisfied with the explanation.'

'I'm sorry to lose Manfredi. He served me well and it will not be easy to replace him. You say you only had one meeting with him. Did you learn anything of substance?'

'The Spanish are already rebuilding their ships after Drake's attack on Cadiz, but Santa Cruz struggles to pay his sailors. He's also short of supplies. In particular, Drake seized and burnt large consignments of wooden barrel staves and Santa Cruz has been obliged to use unseasoned wood to replace them.'

Walsingham smiled. 'That was good work. The old pirate is no fool. Were you able to talk to Manfredi about the map?'

'I'm sorry. The time didn't seem right and then it was too late.'

'No matter. Are you sure no one saw you together apart from the goldsmith?'

'The girl at the house where he lodged saw me. She let me in and we spoke briefly.'

Walsingham picked up a quill and scratched a few notes. 'Did you find anything in his lodgings?' he asked when he had finished.

'Only these papers. They may be of no importance but I thought you might wish to see them.'

Walsingham took the sheaf of papers and glanced at them, then he smiled. 'I am glad you escaped unharmed, Alexandre. I can ill afford to lose another good man. Will you have a glass of wine with me before you go?'

Lamotte felt a surge of relief at such affability. It had not been beyond the bounds of possibility that Walsingham would blame him for the failure of the mission. Some of the credit for his escape should probably go to Drake's bonfires.

When a servant had poured the wine and withdrawn, Walsingham stared pensively into his glass. Still a little wary, Lamotte did not venture to disturb his train of thought.

'Do you believe in omens, Alexandre?' he asked at last.

'Omens? Why do you ask?'

'I dismissed them once but now I confess I am not sure I was right. No doubt some of the tales are exaggerated – apparitions, storms and floods of biblical proportions – but I cannot recall so terrible a summer. Perhaps we should heed the astrologers.'

'Certainly in Paris I found many pamphlets on sale predicting catastrophe.'

Walsingham's eyes narrowed. 'For England in particular, I suppose?'

'Yes,' Lamotte said quietly.

To his surprise, Walsingham's expression became animated. 'Omens may be of use. I believe there have already been many desertions from the Spanish fleet. If fear breeds with hardship, there will be more, for sailors are superstitious men. I intend to have pamphlets of my own printed and distributed among my agents abroad. They will circulate them where they are likely to do the most damage. But that is for another day. Let us drink a health to Her Majesty.'

Lamotte raised his glass. It was rare for Walsingham to be in an expansive mood. Perhaps it was an opportune moment to mention Tom again. He took a deep breath.

'I hope I do not speak out of turn, Sir Francis, but I wonder if you have had time to consider the case of my young friend, Tom Goodluck?'

'Tom Goodluck?'

'He was accused of the murder of a lawyer named Kemp.'

'Ah yes. I fear the press of business drove your request from my mind but now you have reminded me, I shall look into the matter.'

Concealing his disappointment, Lamotte smiled. 'Thank you.'

Chapter 22

London
September, 1587

Tom woke with a start to find the grey dawn light creeping through his cell's high window. He had slept fitfully. He doubted he would ever grow accustomed to the nightly cries and groans of the other prisoners. With a shudder, he realised that what had woken him was the tolling of a bell somewhere deep in the prison. Some forsaken soul would swing before the day was out. Fleetingly, despair engulfed him but he fought to suppress it. That path led to madness.

He relieved himself in the bucket in the corner. In the confined space, the smell of urine and stale faeces made him gag. He would have liked to pay Barwis for the bucket to be emptied and swilled out, but he didn't have much money left. If Lamotte did not return soon, he would need it for food. He frowned. It was easy to lose track of time in Newgate. How long was it since Lamotte had last come? He had promised to visit before he left for the West Country but suppose something had prevented him? Tom quelled a rising sensation of panic. If Lamotte had already gone, he might be away a long time. Travelling was certain to be slow. West Country roads were poor at the best of times.

He sat back on the bed and fell to thinking of Meg. Was she asleep now, her dark hair loose over her shoulders as he remembered? He pictured the swell of her breasts, the curve of her cheek and the glow of her soft skin and groaned, almost wishing he had not asked Lamotte to enquire about her. Did he really want to know if she was happy without him?

The gate at the end of the passageway clanged and footsteps shuffled along it. Barwis peered through the bars. 'Someone t'see you,' he said.

Tom's heart leapt. 'Who is it?'

'Keep your voice down,' Barwis hissed. 'It's your friend with the cash. I told him to come now while it's quiet but there's always ears flapping in this place.'

Lamotte stepped out of the shadows and dropped a few coins into Barwis's outstretched palm. The old turnkey examined them. 'Don't take too long,' he muttered then turned and shuffled away.

His joy at the sight of his friend brought tears to Tom's eyes. He wiped them away with the back of his hand. 'Forgive me,' he mumbled.

'I should be apologising to you. My errand took longer than I expected.' He lowered his voice to an undertone and crooked a finger for Tom to come close to the bars. 'Listen, I have news.'

Tom's heartbeat quickened. 'Of Meg?'

'No, I haven't been to Salisbury yet. I told you I would visit you again before I did. This is about you. Sir Francis has looked into your case. While you remain in Newgate, he cannot dismiss the charge against you – even he does not have the power to overrule the law.'

'So there's no remedy,' Tom said bitterly.

'Hear me out, there's more. He didn't say there is nothing he can do. Some prisoners are to be moved from Newgate to Wisbech, on the Isle of Ely. They are all Catholics imprisoned for their beliefs. You are to go with them. In effect, you will become a political prisoner under Walsingham's control.'

'How can that be?'

'One of the Catholics is a young man called Gilbert Rowley. He is already sick and likely to die. Walsingham's plan is for you to change places. Both of you will need to be moved to new parts of the prison of course, where the guards don't know you and won't ask questions. In your new cells,

224

"Tom Goodluck's" health will rapidly worsen. This won't surprise the gaolers. It's well known that gaol fever takes hold very quickly. Meanwhile, "Gilbert Rowley" will make a surprising recovery. It may be necessary to give you a draught that will make your illness more convincing until then, but don't be afraid. The effects will not last long.'

A thrill of hope went through Tom, swiftly replaced by doubt. 'Do you think it'll work?' he asked anxiously.

'Yes, as long as you play your part well. As far as Walsingham is aware, none of the men travelling with you know Rowley. Speak to them as little as possible on the journey. The fact you are recovering from a severe illness should be a good cloak for silence. If you have to answer questions, you are a London man, the youngest son of a Catholic family. The authorities have apprehended you on suspicion of treason.'

Tom raised an eyebrow. 'Have I committed treason?'

'Only through youthful indiscretion, but imprisonment has served to make you more fervent in your faith.'

'But when I reach Wisbech, surely my situation will be no better. Won't my chances of freedom be even more slender?'

Lamotte glanced over his shoulder. 'Barwis may come back soon. I don't want to have to speak of this in the yard where anyone might overhear us, so take heed. There is a price for Walsingham's help. You have to spend a few years at Wisbech but he promises me you will eventually be free.'

'A few years?' Tom felt a stab of alarm. 'What must I do?'

'Watch and listen. Gather information.'

'Walsingham wants me to spy for him?'

'Is that such a great burden in exchange for your life?'

Tom fell silent.

'It troubles you? Would you prefer to remain here? Your trial cannot be delayed for ever. Do you really think you are likely to be acquitted?'

Numbly, Tom shook his head.

225

Footsteps approached. 'That's Barwis,' Lamotte whispered. 'Tell me quickly. Will you do it?'

'Yes.'

'Good.' He reached through the bars and squeezed Tom's shoulder, 'I'll come to the yard tomorrow. Have courage.'

*

As he promised, Lamotte returned the following day but on his next visit, Tom was not in the yard. It seemed that the plan was on foot. He waited for two more days to pass then, at the appointed time, he joined the small group of men and women asking permission to visit the prison burial ground.

In the walled enclosure, he walked through the rows of graves to where there was a freshly covered plot. Standing over it, he removed his hat.

'Buried that one last night,' a voice behind him said. He turned to see a guard watching him. 'You a relative? A sovereign'll buy you a cross. Two if you want the name on it.'

'Tell me who's buried here first.'

'A fellow called Tom Goodluck. Odd, considering.' The guard guffawed.

Lamotte shook his head. 'The name means nothing. You won't get anything out of me today.'

'Who are you looking for then?' The guard loitered, not giving up hope of a tip.

'A man called Manfredi,' Lamotte answered quickly. It was the first name that came to mind.

'Never heard of him. Sure you've got the right one?'

'It's not important.'

Lamotte replaced his hat then walked back to the gate and out into the street. It was too early to be triumphant but at least the plan was underway. Tom, in the guise of Gilbert Rowley, would be on the way to Wisbech. There was

226

nothing to be done now except follow the company to the country and wait.

Chapter 23

October, 1587

A blustery wind filled the *Curlew's* sails as the small ship left the estuary and tacked northwards, hugging the coast. Below decks, Tom felt the buck and toss of the choppy waves. The hold stank of the fish that must have been the cargo on some previous voyage. The taste of bile rushed into his mouth and he retched.

'God help us if you're going to puke all the way to Wisbech,' the man beside him muttered, his voice thick with cold.

'Let him be, Hugh,' said a tall man with dark hair who sat on the other side of Tom.

The hold into which the guards had thrown the three of them was sweltering and cramped. Tom wiped his damp forehead. He had planned to use seasickness as an excuse to avoid saying too much on the journey but it seemed he would not need to dissemble very much.

'I'm sorry,' he gasped. 'Do you think they'll let us out of here? I might fare better on deck.'

The man called Hugh sneezed. 'We'd all fare better on deck,' he said morosely. 'But if it's like Newgate, every privilege will have to be paid for and the guards emptied my pockets before we left London. They said they needed what I had to pay for my food.'

'It was the same with me,' the tall man said.

They lapsed into silence for a time then there was a rattle of chains and the hatch opened. One of the guards peered in.

Shielding his eyes, Tom blinked.

'Let us up on deck, for pity's sake,' said Hugh.

The guard laughed. 'What's it worth?'

'You know I haven't any money. You made sure of that before we left London.'

The hatch slammed down and they heard the rattle of chains again. Hugh cursed.

'Try and sleep,' the tall man said. 'I slept a lot in Newgate, it passed the time.'

'You're very calm, Richard,' Hugh said wryly.

'What choice do I have? If it's God's will I am punished for my faith, I must accept it.'

'You may be resigned to rotting away in a damp hellhole, forgive me if I'm not.' Hugh squinted at Tom in the dim light that filtered through the salt-encrusted porthole. 'I don't know your face. Who are you?'

'Gilbert Rowley.'

'Gilbert Rowley? I heard you were sick - too sick to move. You don't look very sick to me apart from having the stomach of a green girl.'

'I told you to leave him alone, Hugh. It may be weeks before we reach Wisbech. However bad the journey may be, we should at least be civil among ourselves.'

With a grunt, Hugh used his hand to wipe away the mucus running from his sharp nose. 'I suppose you're right.'

Tom longed for sleep too, but the footsteps overhead and the creak of the ship's timbers as she rolled kept him awake. Hour after hour, he listened to Hugh's snores and coughs. At last the hatch opened once more and another guard's face appeared.

Disturbed by the light, Hugh woke. 'What do you want?' he wheezed.

'Captain says you're to come out and use the heads. He likes a clean ship.'

Hugh prodded Richard. 'Wake up! They're letting us out for a bit.'

Stiff and numb, the three of them clambered up the ladder and onto the deck where the guards waited for them, their muskets raised. Tom inhaled the salt-laden air and gazed around him. The coastline was so flat and marshy it seemed to bleed into the sea. Everything was as grey as a mouse's back but after the months inside Newgate's bleak walls, the scene had an eerie, shimmering beauty that fed his eyes.

'No dawdling.' One of the guards poked him with the barrel of his musket. Reluctantly, he shuffled along the deck to the heads and waited his turn. A dank smell rose from the stained planks. He lowered his eyes and tried to concentrate; after a while he managed to relieve himself. When everyone had finished, the elder of the two guards gave a surly nod.

'That'll do, down below with you.'

As they returned to the hatch, Tom drank in the view once more. It might be his only respite from the damp, fetid hold for a long time. At the ladder, his legs buckled as one of the guards kicked him.

'Get a move on,' the man growled. Stumbling, Tom realised he was weaker than he had thought.

'How many of them do you think there are?' Richard whispered when they were shut in again.

'I didn't see anyone except those two guards and the captain and his mate,' Hugh said. 'But four of them against us three, and us with no weapons but our bare hands?' He threw a scornful glance at Tom. 'And one of us as much use as a bucket of piss to a parched man. They might as well be a hundred.' He lay down on his side and wrapped his cloak around him. 'I'm going to sleep. It's all over with us.'

*

The monotonous days dragged by. Up on deck the weather was cold and windy, but the sticky heat in the pokey hold drained the little energy Tom had, although to his relief, his seasickness subsided. Once a day, a guard brought them salted herring that was tough as leather to chew. It gave Tom a raging thirst and, even though the small beer they were given was musty and full of chaff, he waited impatiently for his daily ration.

All of them slept a great deal and Richard also spent hours in prayer, his rosary beads clicking through his fingers. He seemed to Tom a gentle, devout person who was genuine in his insistence that all he sought was the freedom to follow his conscience. Hugh was a different matter, an angry man railing against his fate. He was the younger son of a Derbyshire family, arrested on suspicion of plotting against the queen.

'Ridding England of a heretic, more like,' he said bitterly. 'And what was the charge against you, Rowley? Come on, give an account of yourself.'

It was the question Tom had dreaded but to his relief, when he fleshed out the story Lamotte had given him, Hugh appeared to accept it.

'Richard is the saint among us,' he sneered. 'He trained for the priesthood.'

'That's not entirely true,' Richard objected, 'but when I was a young man, I hoped to. I even went to Rome and visited the English College but while I was there, I received the news of my father's death and came home.'

'Why didn't you go back when you'd settled his affairs?' Tom asked.

'My sister needed me to stay.'

'She had no husband to support her?'

Richard gave one of his rare smiles. 'My sister has a strong will. She was more than capable of running the estate without me but there were other problems. With the harsher anti-Catholic laws, if I had gone back to Rome, my family would have suffered crippling penalties on my account. I did not want that on my conscience.'

*

One day, the sea seemed calmer than usual. When they went on deck to use the heads, Tom understood why. Dense fog

231

swirled around the ship, obscuring everything that was more than a few yards in front of him. The sails were slack and, standing in the bow, the captain stared intently into the milky air. As they passed, he jerked his thumb at them.

'There's rocks hereabouts. Some of those prayers of yours wouldn't come amiss.'

Down below once more, it was hard to tell through the cloudy porthole whether the fog had dispersed but Tom guessed it was still there, for the ship's motion remained sluggish. Richard dozed fitfully or prayed but Hugh carped and fretted constantly. Much as he disliked him, Tom felt some pity for his sufferings.

'If we hit the rocks, it will be all over with us,' he moaned. 'Do you really think the guards will release us? Not them, why would they care?' He started as the timbers creaked. 'They'll leave the hatch chained. If the wood's sound, we'll have no chance of forcing it. We'll die like rats in a barrel.'

Richard's fingers paused on his rosary. 'If it is God's will we should live, He will keep us safe from harm.'

In the dim light, Tom saw Hugh's fists clench. As he lunged at Richard, Tom seized his arms and pinioned them behind his back. Hugh started to shout and struggle.

The noise must have alerted the guards for the hatch opened. 'That's enough down there,' a guard said roughly. He tapped his musket. 'Or you'll feel the butt of this.'

The hatch slammed down. Glowering, Hugh broke away and crouched in a corner. 'I won't forget that, Rowley.'

As night drew in, the others slept but Tom lay awake. Clearly, he had made an enemy of Hugh and the feeling was mutual. He would have few qualms about watching him at Wisbech, but Richard was different. He appeared to be a genuinely good man and his serene acceptance of his fate was remarkable. It seemed far more shameful to deceive him.

When at last a faint light glimmered in the porthole, Tom noticed the ship gather speed. He felt the tension leave his body; the immediate danger must be over. But what were they saved for? He fell to thinking of his last conversation with Lamotte. He had spoken of years, rather than months, before he won his freedom. Was he telling the truth or merely offering a crumb of comfort? Perhaps his imprisonment at Wisbech would last until he died. A chill came over him.

Richard stirred. 'Is it morning?'

Relieved to have his thoughts interrupted, Tom pushed them to the back of his mind. 'Yes, and I think the fog has lifted.'

'Our prayers were answered,' said Richard. 'God has kept us safe.'

*

'Storm's coming,' one of the guards said gruffly as they went up to use the heads later that morning. He pointed to the iron-grey clouds on the horizon. 'We'll need luck if we're to make landfall at King's Lynn before it reaches us. You'd best pray harder.'

With a sizzle like fat dropping on a hot skillet, the rain swept in just before dusk. Soon the scream of the wind in the rigging and the buffeting of the waves against the hull filled Tom's ears. He felt his nausea return as the ship pitched violently. Fear quelled even Hugh's belligerence. He crouched in a corner, rocking and mumbling a barely coherent string of prayers, but even in the terrible straits in which they found themselves, Richard's serenity did not desert him. As the storm's fury increased, Tom marvelled at his calmness.

Suddenly, a tremendous crash shook the hold. The ceiling splintered and part of it fell in. A wave of icy water gushed through the hole. Drenched, Tom leapt to his feet. 'We need to get out,' he yelled over the noise of the wind. Another wave crashed into the hold. As the spray cleared,

Tom saw water was seeping through the planking as well. The impact must have sprung its seams.

'You're the lightest of us, Rowley,' Richard shouted in his ear. 'I'll push you up. Try and undo the hatch from above.' He took a step towards Tom then stumbled backwards as the ship pitched violently. Another torrent of water gushed through the broken timbers.

Hugh's face was grey. He seemed unable to move. Steady on his feet again, Richard shook him. 'Don't be afraid. God is with us.' He held out his interlocked hands to Tom. 'Hurry!'

Tom clawed at the wet wood but it was too slippery. He felt a sharp pain as a splinter ripped into his palm. Blood oozed from the wound and he fell back.

'Try again,' Richard shouted.

His teeth clenched and every sinew straining, Tom jumped again. This time his grip held and he hauled himself through the hole.

The mainmast lay on the deck surrounded by mounds of canvas. He smelt sulphur.

'What's happening?' Over the wind, Richard's voice floated up from below.

'The mainmast's smashed. I can't see the crew or the guards.'

A wall of water towered over the ship and smashed on the deck almost knocking him into the sea. Tom grabbed the rail just in time. He clung to it, buffeted by the wind as the ship plunged. When it righted itself, he saw a body wedged against the starboard rail. He dropped to his hands and knees and crawled around the wreckage of the mainmast. The captain lay on his back, eyes wide open. His head lolled to one side. Blood seeped from a gash running from his temple to his jaw.

Another wave slewed across the deck and for a few moments, Tom could think of nothing but holding on. When the water subsided, he crawled back to the hole. 'The captain's dead,' he shouted. 'I can't see anyone else. They may have been washed overboard. I nearly was too.'

Richard cupped his hands to his mouth. 'Can you open the hatch?' he yelled. 'The water's already ankle deep.'

'I'll try.'

Battling the heavy chains took all his remaining strength but at last they yielded. He threw back the hatch. Hugh's terrified face stared up from below. Richard pushed him up the ladder and followed.

The ship pitched again, sending them slithering across the deck into the rail.

'We're lost,' Hugh bawled. 'The waves will smash us to pieces. I'm not staying here.'

Richard seized him. 'Don't be a fool. You'll never survive in this sea.'

Tom looked over the rail. In the dim light, the shore crouched like an animal at bay. It looked no more than half a mile away but it was half a mile of surging grey water. He fought down the fear that threatened to engulf him.

There was a clap of thunder and lightning flashed across the sky. Ahead, Tom saw the heaving sea changed to a maelstrom of white froth. Black teeth of half-submerged rocks bristled malevolently. His heartbeat raced. They were heading straight for them.

A few moments later, with a rasping growl, the ship reared out of the water. Tossed across the deck, Tom collided with the mainmast. He came to rest entangled in the streaming canvas around it. Richard lay dazed close by but Hugh tottered to his feet, swaying like a drunken man.

'I'll not stay here,' he repeated.

Before Tom had time to stop him, he hoisted himself over the rail. Ignoring Tom's shouts for him to come back, he started to clamber along the treacherous rocks. Tom watched in horror as he struggled, slipping into the crevices between the rocks and hauling himself out, until at last he disappeared into the white water, this time for good.

Numbly, Tom stared at the place where Hugh had been. The danger was not over. Hugh's fate might still be his own.

He stood on the deck, his wet clothes sticking to his shivering body. It was only when the wind calmed that he heard a groan and was reminded that Richard was with him. He knelt down beside him.

'Are you hurt?'

Cautiously, Richard sat up. 'I don't think so,' he said at last. He looked around. 'Where's Hugh?'

'I tried to stop him but it was no use. He fell in the water trying to reach the shore. I think he drowned.'

Richard staggered to his feet and almost fell. Tom seized his elbow. 'Don't move too quickly.'

With glazed eyes, Richard stared at the dark waters. 'Poor fellow,' he said sadly.

The sea made no more than a soft sucking sound now as it lapped at the base of the rocks. It was hard to believe that only a little while ago, it had raged so ferociously. The storm was over. Above them, the clouds were already parting to reveal a black, velvety sky pricked with hard, bright stars. Tom felt as if a great burden had been lifted from his shoulders. He lay on his back on the deck, staring up into the sky. Richard was speaking but he hardly heard him. His body felt weightless.

'Rowley!' A dash of salt water roused him. 'Get up,' Richard said. 'We have to get off the ship. If anyone sees the wreck, they'll be bound to come looking for plunder. We don't want them finding us.'

Tom struggled to his feet and strained his eyes to discern the dim outline of the shore.

'Can you swim?' Richard asked.

'Swim? Yes,' Tom said doubtfully. He had swum in the river in Salisbury many times but the sea was a different matter.

'The rocks are clear of the water now, we shouldn't slip but you need to be ready if you do.'

'Should we see if there are any pickings to be had before we go?'

Richard hesitated. 'I suppose money is no use to dead men,' he said reluctantly.

The captain's body was already stiffening and they had to drag his arms away from his sides to remove the knife and purse on his belt. In the cabin, they found more coins, a bottle of grog, some hard cheese and a small sack of biscuits.

'It might be the last meal we have for a while,' Tom said as they ate and drank hungrily. In spite of his sodden clothes and boots he felt the grog warm him. Richard had a faraway expression on his face.

'What is it?' Tom asked.

'I was wondering what we should do once we reach shore. We could be anywhere. If we try to get back to our families, we shall only put them in danger.'

'Let's worry about that when we're off this ship. It's time we were leaving.'

The wet rocks were smooth as glass under their feet. Frequently, Tom lost his footing and it was not long before he was a mass of bruises but, eventually, their painful progress brought them to the end of the outcrop. A narrow stretch of water separated them from the shore.

'We'd best take our boots off,' Richard said. 'They'll weigh us down. Just keep your shirt and breeches on, I'll tie the rest in my cloak and swim with it.'

When they were ready, he slid into the water and held out his arms. 'Give me the bundle and be quick about it. This water's freezing.'

Hesitantly, Tom threw it out to him then followed. He had been cold before but the sea knocked the breath from his body. For a moment, it closed over his head then he came up spluttering and managed to take his first stroke. Ahead of him, Richard ploughed determinedly towards the shore.

From the rocks, the distance had not seemed great but now Tom was in the water, it looked a very long way off. With alarm, he felt the current drag him in a direction where

237

he did not want to go. Suddenly, a tremendous pain gripped his legs making it impossible to kick with them. His mouth filled and his head went under. Dazed by panic, he tried to regain the surface but it eluded him. His lungs seemed on the point of bursting when strong arms pulled him upwards and he breathed air once more.

'Don't struggle,' Richard shouted. 'It's not much further. A few more yards and you should be able to stand.'

Spewing up water, Tom let himself be towed along until he felt Richard's grip relax. He put one foot down and felt shingle beneath it then stumbled upright to find the water came no further than his waist. A few moments later, he collapsed on the rocky beach.

'Thank you,' he panted.

'Thank God, not me,' Richard said gravely.

Tom succumbed to a fit of coughing. 'I think you are more worthy of thanks,' he said when he recovered his breath.

If Richard disapproved of such blasphemy, he did not show it.

They sat in silence for a while, Richard with his hands clasped in prayer and Tom thinking of the narrow escape he had had. Acutely aware of the cold, he wrapped his arms around himself and rubbed vigorously to try and keep warm.

At last Richard raised his head. 'I wonder where we are. I think we may have reached the coast of Norfolk by now, but I'm not sure.'

The darkness was fading and, on the horizon, streaks of crimson showed where the sun would rise.

Richard undid the bundle of clothes. 'I'm afraid they are not as dry as I hoped they would be. It was hard to keep them clear of the water. We'll just have to do our best to wring everything out.'

'We'll go west,' he said when they had re-dressed themselves. Perhaps we can find a road that will lead us to a town.'

Tom shivered in his damp clothes. 'What shall we do then?'

'Walsingham's men may think we have drowned with the others but staying in England is too much of a risk for the present. I shall find the nearest port where I can take ship for France and go to Paris. A friend I made in my time at the English College in Rome lives there. He's a priest now. I'm sure he will stand by me. I'd like to return to Rome but it is too late this year. By the time I reached the mountains, the passes would very likely be blocked with snow.' He smiled. 'If you wish to come with me, I'd be glad of your company.'

Tom shook his head. He felt a slight pang of guilt over concealing the truth from a man who had saved his life but he could not confide in him. 'Thank you,' he said, 'but there are matters I must settle in England first. I wish there was some way I could show my gratitude, though. I owe you my life.'

'I only did what any man would have done, but there is something you can do for me.'

'Yes?'

'I don't want my sister to grieve. Since the day the priest hunters came to our home, she must have suffered a great deal because of me. If I write a letter to her, will you make sure she gets it?'

'Of course, I'll deliver it myself. All you need to do is tell me how to find her.'

'That's very generous of you but you must not run into danger on my account. Take care you do not.'

'I will.'

'Our family home is a place called Lacey Hall in Devon. I'll explain to you how to find it.'

He stood up and wrung a few more droplets of water from his shirt tail. 'It may be some time before these clothes dry out properly, but at least we didn't lose them, and we have money to buy food.' He scanned the beach and pointed to a path. 'The way lies there,' he said.

With a last glance at the stricken ship, they set off.

239

*

They found a path that wound inland onto spongy moorland strewn with boulders encrusted with rust-coloured lichen. It was a raw, overcast day. Tom's damp boots chafed his feet and his stomach grumbled. Even salted herring would have been more welcome than an empty belly, but they did not pass as much as a hamlet where they might have been able to buy food.

They had left the rugged coastal land behind and reached softer uplands grazed by huge flocks of sheep when Tom heard a shout behind them. Balling his fists, he swung round but it was only a cart with an old brown nag ambling along in the shafts.

'Where are you going to?' Tom called out as the man passed.

'I'm taking this samphire to market at Norwich.'

'We'll give you a penny if you give us a lift.'

The carter studied them suspiciously. 'You're not from round here, are you?'

'We're merchants come from King's Lynn,' Tom replied.

'Funny road to take. Where's your horses?'

'We were set on in the night then we lost our way.'

The carter grunted. 'Tuppence. That's the best offer you'll get.'

Tom looked at Richard, who nodded.

'Very well.'

The carter climbed down and handed Tom the reins. 'Hold these and keep her steady.' Going to the back of the cart, he made some space then came back. 'There's the place ready for you. I'll have the money now.'

As he clambered on, Tom wrinkled his nose at the briny, cabbage smell coming from the dark-green bundles of samphire. He would have to put up with it, he reflected wryly. It was better than walking and at least they were sure they were going somewhere useful. He had heard there was a road from Norwich to London. With a jolt that threw him off balance, the cart moved off.

In the early evening, the carter stopped to rest the horse before the climb up to the city. Tom and Richard got down and stretched their legs. High above them, the cathedral spire soared into the sky. Before night fell, they rumbled through the gate. The next morning, they parted company and Tom set out on the road to London.

Chapter 24

London
October, 1587

'Will you come then?' Susan finished folding a shirt and put it on the pile. 'People round here will talk if I go on my own with Alfred. If you and William come, it'll be different.'

Meg hesitated. Sometimes she had noticed William looking at her in a way she didn't like, but it seemed unkind to refuse to help Susan.

Susan pouted. 'Peggoty hardly ever gives us time off. Don't you want to have some fun?'

'All right. I've never been to a London playhouse. At home we only had travelling players coming for Christmas and feast days.' She stopped, sadly contemplating the memory of her last May Day fair in Salisbury.

'I'll tell Alfred.' Susan beamed, seeming not to notice.

For once the weather was dry when they set off the following morning. It was warmer than usual and ribbons of cloud drifted across a pale blue sky. Arm in arm a little way ahead of William and Meg, Susan and Alfred were clearly engrossed in each other's company.

'They look very happy together,' Meg ventured.

'Alfred's a decent enough fellow. Apprenticed to a blacksmith. Wants to have a smithy of his own one day.'

'Yes, Susan told me.'

'She won't need to wash anyone's linen then. She'll have servants of her own.'

Susan turned, her chestnut hair shining in the sunshine and her eyes sparkling with mischief. 'And all the fine clothes I want,' she called out. She dug Alfred in the ribs, 'And a big four-poster bed for us to lie in.'

William guffawed. 'Better watch out, lad. She'll have the shirt off your back if you let her.'

'He wouldn't care if I did, would you, Alfred?' Susan giggled.

Flushing, he dropped a kiss on her cheek.

As she watched them, Meg felt a pang of sorrow. It was so hard to be without Tom.

'Penny for your thoughts?'

Meg shivered. 'They're not worth it.'

Beyond Holborn, they passed through the city gate and walked east along Cheapside and Poultry. Meg looked around her apprehensively. Even though there were thousands of people in the city it was difficult to dismiss the fear she might come across Ralph. She wished she was more like William. He seemed completely unconcerned.

Susan insisted on stopping to look in the windows of the grand shops in the Royal Exchange, exclaiming over the wares they displayed: fine fabrics, shoes fashioned from the softest leather, lavishly embroidered gloves and glittering jewellery. On the streets, dozens of vendors offered everything from oysters, pies and smoked fish to oranges, lemons and plums. The sweet and savoury aromas were tantalising. Alfred bought a bag of plums and they walked along eating them.

They came out of the city again through Bishopsgate and joined the crowds heading for the theatres in Shoreditch. Most of them were on foot but the better-off on horseback. In the distance, trumpets brayed.

'Come on, you two,' Susan shouted over her shoulder. 'They'll be starting any minute.' Dragging Alfred by the hand, she hurried on.

'Which theatre are we going to?' Meg asked as they caught up.

'The Curtain. I want to see Richard Tarlton. They say he has you in stitches just poking his head out of the wings. Alfred wants to see him too, don't you, Alfred?'

He nodded.

'That's right,' William chuckled. 'Learn to do as you're told.' He ducked as Alfred aimed a blow at his head.

They reached the gate, paid their pennies and went in. Meg had never been in a crowd like it before. She was glad the day was no hotter; as it was, the heat intensified every smell to an unpleasant degree. The play was a silly story involving two sets of twins and innumerable unlikely coincidences but Susan had been right about Tarlton, the crowd roared every time he appeared and Meg could not help joining in. There was no denying that being away from the steamy cottage and Peggoty's evil temper was a pleasant change.

'My sides ache,' Susan gasped as they trooped out afterwards. 'And I smell roast hog.' She tugged at Alfred's arm. 'Buy us all some, won't you?' she wheedled.

'Nothing to a rich fellow like you, eh?' William grinned.

'Well – oh, all right.'

As they waited their turn in the queue, Meg observed the scene. People were still pouring out of the theatre, laughing and chattering. Hawkers shouted out their wares and nearby, a man nailed up handbills for the next play. So this was the world Tom had wanted to be part of. How cruel fate was to stand in his way.

With a frown, she thought of the ring she had found and of the initials engraved on it – *WK*. How had it come into Ralph's possession? Did it mean he had something to do with William Kemp's death? If only there was someone she could take it to. Someone who would know how to use it to help Tom.

'Meg?' With a start, she realised Alfred was holding a piece of bread and meat out to her.

Susan squealed. 'Don't do that, Alfred! It's dripping. We'll need something to wrap it in. Meg and me don't want hog fat all down our dresses, do we, Meg?'

'No extra charge for you, my lovelies.' The stallholder grinned, producing two pieces of paper and passing them across the counter. Meg wrapped one of them around her bread and took a bite. The pork was moist and delicious.

'Bit different to the muck my sister serves up,' William mumbled through a mouthful. He wiped a speck of grease from Susan's cheek and returned Alfred's scowl with a chuckle. Susan pushed him away. 'Go and bother Meg,' she said.

'Shall I then? Yes, I think I will.' He grinned. 'Meg knows a good thing when she sees it, don't you, Meg?' He squeezed her by the waist and, instinctively, she tensed but he would not let go. His lips brushed her ear. 'I'll wager I could make you happy,' he whispered.

Meg wriggled away from him. She saw Susan give him a knowing wink then a man with a monkey on a chain diverted her attention. 'Ooh look,' she giggled. 'Perhaps he'll make it dance. Give him some money, Alfred.'

The little creature gibbered and cringed at the end of its chain as the man dragged it over to them. 'Only a penny to see it dance,' he said. 'All the way from Africa this monkey is. I can make it skip like it's on hot coals if you pay me.'

The monkey had such sad eyes, Meg pitied it. Susan nudged Alfred. 'I want to see that,' she said. 'Give him the penny, won't you?'

Reluctantly, Alfred fished out the penny and handed it to the man. With a barked instruction, he shook the chain and the monkey limped in a small circle.

William frowned. 'That's not worth a penny. Can't you make it do better than that?' The man shook the chain harder, jerking the monkey's neck from side to side.

Meg averted her eyes. She wished they could go home. She had finished her food but she still held the greasy paper in her hand. To avoid watching the monkey, she took a

245

closer look. It was part of a handbill for a play. A lot of the printing was too soiled with grease to be legible but some words were still clear. She read them and her heart lurched. The others were too busy laughing at the monkey to notice her run back to the hog roast stall.

'Where did you get this?' she asked the stallholder urgently.

'I pick 'em up when the plays are done. They come in handy. What's it to you?'

'Was it from one of the theatres here?'

He scratched his chin. 'Couldn't say for sure, let me have a look.' Coming round the side of the stall, he took the handbill from her and looked at it. Meg struggled to contain her impatience.

'It's from Master Lamotte's company. I got a stack of them a while back.' He glanced at a group approaching the stall. Meg seized his arm before he had the chance to leave her.

'Which theatre do they play at?'

'The Unicorn, down that way, but there's no one there now.'

Meg's heart sank. 'Have they closed?'

'No, just gone out of London for a while.'

'When will they be back?'

'A few weeks maybe. Now I haven't time for any more of your questions. I've got customers to serve.'

'Please, just give me another minute. Do you know a man called Tom Goodluck?'

'Tom Goodluck? I don't think so.'

Meg pointed to the handbill. 'His name's down here as one of the actors.'

The stallholder shrugged. 'That handbill's months old. People come and go all the time around these parts. I can't be remembering all of them.'

Tears welled up in Meg's eyes. 'Please, when Master Lamotte comes back will you tell him I'm trying to find

Tom? My name's Meg. I lodge at the laundress's cottage in Holborn.'

The stallholder gave a grudging nod. 'All right, now be off with you.'

*

Meg lifted a sodden sheet from the lye tub and twisted it into a rope to wring out the milky liquid. The foul smell of potash and urine still revolted her and her hands itched from the cheap black soap Peggoty used. It smelt of fish – and no wonder, for Susan said it was made with oil from the carcasses of whales. She noticed Susan was clever at keeping for herself the job of washing the fine linen their wealthier customers brought in. For that, Peggoty bought the best white soap, which contained imported olive oil and was smooth and soft.

She carried the sheet over to one of the lines and threw it across. Tangling instantly, it stuck to itself and she struggled to free it.

'Here, let me.'

Meg jumped. She hadn't noticed William come into the room behind her. She tensed as he reached above her to rearrange the sheet. When it hung smoothly, his hands dropped to her shoulders.

'Ooh, am I disturbing something?' Susan stood in the doorway with a bundle of sheets.

Furious, Meg ducked under William's arm.

He grinned at Susan, 'Jealous, are you?'

'Over you? My Alfred's ten times the man you are.'

Peggoty bustled in from the back yard. 'Get back to work, the lot of you,' she snapped. 'I don't pay you to lark about.'

'You don't pay me at all,' William muttered.

She put her hands on her hips. 'I give you bed and board, be thankful for it. Now go and finish those logs.'

With a scowl, William disappeared in the direction of the log pile.

'I wouldn't encourage him if I were you,' Susan remarked when Peggoty had gone. 'You wouldn't be the first girl he's got in trouble.'

'I don't encourage him.'

Susan laughed. 'With him it doesn't take much. You won't have to be so ladylike if you don't want him. I made sure he knew he was wasting his time when he tried it on with me.'

'I told you,' Meg said crossly, 'I don't encourage him.'

'Whatever you say.' Susan shrugged. 'If you've finished with the tub, I'll put these sheets in to soak then you can rinse them for me.'

*

That night, the questions going round in Meg's head tormented her. Bitterly, she thought of the time she had wasted going to Plymouth. If only she had come to London sooner, she might have found Tom and they would be together now. Why had he left The Unicorn? Was it because he knew he was charged with killing William Kemp and feared capture? Worse still, was it because he had actually been arrested? And if that were so, how would he defend himself? Who would speak up for him? She refused to contemplate the possibility he might be guilty but she had heard Edward and her father talk of such things often enough to realise that it was very hard for a poor man to prove his innocence.

As she often did, she wished she had someone to talk to. Susan knew a little about Tom but she was too preoccupied with her Alfred to be much interested and Peggoty's sour nature did not invite confidences.

It was almost dawn before Meg slept. In the morning, she was so tired that the basket of laundry she had to fetch from Lincoln's Inn seemed heavy as a millstone. Putting it

248

down for a rest, she stopped to watch the Trained Bands practising in the fields. Some shot arrows at targets; others fought with blunt, wooden swords or fired muskets. William, who liked to parade his knowledge of military matters, had once told her that musketeers should be able to load and fire two rounds in a minute. Archers should be strong and quick enough to shoot three arrows in the same space of time, but she didn't know whether to believe him or not.

Wearily, she lifted the basket onto her hip once more. She had better be getting back. Peggoty was in an even blacker mood than usual that morning.

'Alfred shoed a horse for a traveller come up from the country yesterday,' Susan was saying when Meg arrived at the laundry. 'He said there was a cow born with two heads at Canterbury and when he was coming over the Weald, it rained blood.' She shivered. 'Do you think it means the Spanish are coming?'

'Well, if they are,' said Peggoty, beating the dirt from a sheet with a paddle, 'I'll see them in Hell before I do their washing. They'll have to cut my throat first.'

'They might do that anyway,' William remarked, stacking logs by the fire. 'I wouldn't trust those fellows in the Trained Bands to save you. When the Spanish come, we'll need more than boys and granddads to send them back where they came from.'

'Then why don't you join up and show them how it's done?' Susan asked slyly but he ignored her.

Meg stayed quiet. She had seen enough of violence with Ralph and she remembered Edward and her father exchanging gruesome tales of how the Spanish dealt with their defeated enemies in the Low Countries. Her mind went back to Tom's play and the story he chose: the myth of how through his courage and guile, Perseus killed the snake-headed Gorgon when all others had failed. Who would be England's Perseus if Spain really did invade?

On his way out to collect more logs, William stopped and sneaked his arm around her waist. He glanced round to

249

be sure the others were not watching then squeezed her breast. 'Don't look so worried,' he murmured. 'If you're a good girl, I'll take care of you.'

The colour rushed into Meg's face as she saw Peggoty scowling at them. 'Get about your work.'

William sauntered out and Peggoty turned her scornful expression on Meg. 'As for you, there's a place for girls who let a man carry on like that and it's not in a God-fearing house. Keep that in mind.'

The unfairness of her remark took Meg's breath away but she knew that, with Peggoty, it was no use protesting. Silently, she unpacked her basket and got to work.

*

When she next had an afternoon off, Meg walked back to Shoreditch alone but The Unicorn was still closed. Feeling forlorn, she knocked on the big wooden doors, hoping against hope someone would answer but no one came. The hog roast seller was nowhere to be seen so she went round and spoke to the stallholders set up near the other theatres, but none of them seemed to know when The Unicorn was due to reopen.

She trudged despondently back to the city and by the time she reached the Royal Exchange, grey clouds filled the sky. A steady drizzle dampened her rough wool cloak and soaked her thin shoes. The grand shops Susan had been so excited about were shutting for the night. With dismay, she realised it was later than she had thought. Quickening her step, she arrived at Newgate as the daylight faded to find she had to fight her way through the carts and travellers wanting to come into London before the gate closed.

In Holborn, very few of the houses and cottages had lights in their windows. To save candles, most people went to bed at dusk and rose at dawn. Close to home, a black mongrel scavenging in the midden outside the alehouse lifted its head and growled at her as she passed. The door opened and a man rolled out into the street.

With a start, she saw it was William. Her face hidden by her hood, she hurried on but she had not gone far before he caught up with her. 'Where've you been, then?' he asked. 'It's a bit late for Peg's errands, isn't it?'

Meg walked faster. 'Just to look at the shops again,' she lied.

'What? On your own?'

He grabbed her by the waist and nuzzled her neck.

'If you make it worth my while, I'll buy you lots of pretty things when I get Peg's money out of her. The poisonous old witch can't go on forever.'

She wriggled free. 'Leave me alone, William.'

'You know you don't want me to,' he said hoarsely.

A gust of beery breath wafted in her direction as he made another lunge for her but, evading him, she picked up her skirts and ran the last of the way to the cottage. There were no lights in the windows and the front door was locked so she ran around to the back. The latch rattled under her shaking fingers. Inside the cottage, her heart still pounding, she ran upstairs. In the bedroom she shared with Susan, she stripped off her wet clothes and started to rub her hair dry with a piece of old linen. If only it was as easy to rub out the memory of William's groping hands.

Susan yawned. 'You look a sight,' she remarked.

'I went to Shoreditch. William saw me on the way home and I had to run away from him.'

'Did you now,' Susan chuckled.

'It's not funny. I just want him to leave me alone.'

'So did you go to look for that Tom you told me about?' Susan asked, ignoring her objection.

'Yes.'

'And did you find him?'

'No,' Meg sighed.

'Well if I were you, I'd forget him. You can't go mooning after a man forever. He's probably found someone else anyway.'

Meg's throat tightened. 'You don't understand. He wouldn't do that. He loves me.'

Susan shrugged. 'That's what they all say, but until you've been to church, you can't trust 'em. Even my Alfred needs watching.' She snuggled down under the covers. 'Blow the candle out, will you, before you get in?'

In bed, Meg lay awake listening to Susan's rhythmic breathing and the soft patter of rain on the roof. Peggoty's familiar snores reverberated through the thin wall dividing the two rooms. Miserably, Meg wondered whether Susan's way of looking at things was the right one. It would explain why there had been no message from Tom in all the months he had been gone. The blood ebbed from her heart. Perhaps he did not want to be found. She had never contemplated the possibility before but had she been a fool not to?

A wave of wretchedness broke over her; it was a while before her resolve returned. She must not give up hope. There was still this Master Lamotte to find. Perhaps he would know where Tom was. Whatever anyone said, until she heard it from his own lips, she would not believe he no longer loved her.

Chapter 25

London
Late October, 1587

The stallholders at Leadenhall Market were doing a brisk trade as Lamotte passed through on his way to Angel Lane. At a haberdasher's stall he bought scarlet and yellow ribbons for Bel and Janey then went into the cook shop next door to get sweets for Jack and Hal.

'Master Lamotte!' Janey met him at the top of the lane, Hal on her hip and a basket of bread over her arm.

'How are you, Janey?'

'Not so bad.'

'Forgive me for not coming sooner. We've not long been back from the West Country.' He took Hal's plump hand. 'And what about this little fellow?'

'Poor little mite's got a tooth coming. Bel's tried giving him a rag soaked in the brandy you brought us but he still has us all awake in the night.'

'I'm sorry to hear it. Is Jack at home?'

'He and Bel went to the river to catch eels. They won't be back before dark, but will you come in?'

'Only for a moment, then I need to go to the theatre. I just wanted to be sure the four of you were all right.'

Inside, Janey set down her basket on the table. Hal wriggled out of her arms and crawled towards the hearth. 'Likes to play with the poker, he does,' Janey sighed. 'If I've told him off once, I've told him off a hundred times.'

Lamotte fished out the packages, unwrapped one and broke off a piece of marzipan. 'Have this instead, Hal.' He

253

put the packages on the table. 'The rest of the sweets are for Jack and the ribbons are for you and Bel.'

'You're very good to us.' Janey smiled.

'It gives me pleasure.'

Contentedly sucking his sweet, Hal sat on the clean, rush-strewn floor. Lamotte ruffled his fair curls.

'Are you all right for money, Janey?'

'Yes. Bel helps me with the sewing, and sometimes Jack gets work holding the horses outside The Curtain and running errands.'

'I hope we won't lose him for good.'

Janey shook her head. 'No chance of that.'

'Then tell him we open in a few days.'

Her expression was troubled. 'Master Lamotte, Jack went to the prison a few days ago to see Tom and there was no sign of him. The warders wouldn't tell Jack anything. Tom's not ill, is he?'

'No, he's not ill. He's been moved to another prison. But you mustn't worry, it may be all to the good – although that's not for anyone else's ears but your own.'

Janey's face lit up. 'Do you mean they'll let him go?'

'It may not be as simple as that.' He saw her face fall again. 'But he may be safer than he was in Newgate.'

'I don't understand.'

'As soon as I can tell you more, I promise I will.' He stood up. 'Now I must go. Don't forget to tell Jack.'

'Master Lamotte, nothing bad's going to happen to Tom, is it?'

'Not if I can help it.'

As he walked up to Shoreditch, though, Lamotte could not banish a feeling of unease. How easy would it really be to rescue Tom? Walsingham always played a close game. Was the scheme simply his way of disposing of an inconvenient problem? Perhaps in Wisbech Tom would be no better off.

In Shoreditch, laughter and clapping drifted from The Curtain. They were lucky to have Tarlton to help fill the house. If only there were more like him to go round.

Up at The Unicorn, he went in and surveyed the place, seeing it with a more critical eye after the weeks away. The scarlet and yellow paint peeled from the stage columns and there was plenty of dirt and bird lime needing to be scrubbed off everything. Dust and mouse droppings lay under the benches and the galleries had a musty odour. The theatre needed a new cat. Much of the wood the carpenters had used last year had warped and shrunk already, that would need attending to as well. He grimaced. Baltic timber: it was no substitute for good English oak. Still it was better the oak went to build Her Majesty's ships than to support wealthy burghers' backsides.

He sighed. In past years, the prospect of the new season had always excited him. What was different about this one? Had the dismal summer oppressed his spirits, or was it the fear of old age with all its indignities?

Backstage, he unlocked the store where the props were kept: tin crowns, swords, daggers, breastplates and plumed helmets; a ship six feet long made of wood and paper; animal costumes and a bear's skull. At least they were all serviceable. Tomorrow, he would hire a few men to spruce the place up and call in the players to make a start on rehearsals.

He locked up and left the theatre. Outside, food sellers waited at their stalls for The Curtain's performance to end, but there were fewer of them than usual. Lamotte strolled over to a pie man he knew and greeted him.

'A good house in there today,' the man remarked. 'But business could be better. Some fellows have gone south of the river to try their luck at The Rose.'

'We open next week,' Lamotte said through a mouthful of pie. 'Things will look up then.'

At home, he ate a cold capon for his supper and drank a bottle of claret then settled down in his chair by the fireside to go over his plans. The familiar aromas of old leather and tobacco soothed him. Drowsy with wine and the warmth of the fire, he let the papers in his lap slide to the floor and closed his eyes.

When he woke, the candle's charred wick floated in a pool of wax and daylight lit the room. All that remained of the fire was a heap of ash and he was stiff and cold. Testily, he wondered why no one had roused him and helped him to bed but perhaps he should not complain. The servants were too much accustomed to his bachelor habits.

He stood up and rang the bell. 'Get my breakfast and relight this fire,' he said when his servant, James, appeared.

'Yes, master.' He looked slightly sheepish.

After he had gone, Lamotte scooped his papers from the floor, dumped them on his desk and sat down. Only old men fell asleep in their chairs, he thought gloomily. They did not notice if their shirts were stained with grease either, or if yesterday's egg yolk streaked their beards.

He sighed. Where had he got to? He sifted through the papers. Yes, there it was: *The Siege of Troy*. The parts for that needed copying in good time. Most of the players wouldn't know it, but the old faithfuls alone would not be sufficient for the theatre to pack the audiences in and hold its own.

He dipped a quill in his inkwell and wrote a note, but the quill needed sharpening and the ink smudged. With a snort, he blotted the paper.

There was a knock at the door and James came in with logs for the fire. 'Cook's making your breakfast straight away, master.' He put the logs down in the hearth. 'And Brocket told me to give you this message. It came early this morning.'

Lamotte felt a jolt of apprehension. It might be something about the theatre but it could also be from Walsingham. If so, was it good or bad news?

Slitting the seal with his knife, he ran his eye over the words with mounting astonishment. They were brief. Tom was free and near London. He was waiting at a tavern in Leyton and he needed help.

*

As he squeezed Tom's shoulder, tears welled up in Lamotte's eyes. Quickly, he dashed them away. 'I could hardly believe it when I read your message. How did you escape? When did you get to London?'

'There was a storm. The ship was wrecked. The captain and one of my fellow prisoners died. The other one, a man called Richard Lacey, reached shore with me. As for the rest, there was no sign of them, and in such heavy seas, it would be a miracle if they lived.'

'Where is this man Lacey now?'

'He planned to leave England and go to Paris. Eventually, he intends to go to Rome.'

'He's a Catholic?' Lamotte's voice was sharp.

'Yes.'

'Did you tell him the story that we agreed?'

'I did.'

'Do you think he suspected anything?'

'I've no reason to think so, but in any case, I believe he's a decent, compassionate man. He would not seek to harm me, or England.'

Lamotte raised an eyebrow. 'He's still a Catholic, but if he helped you, I shall forget what you've told me. As far as I'm concerned, Richard Lacey lies at the bottom of the sea. Now we have more pressing matters to discuss. We have to decide where you will go.'

Suddenly, Tom felt downcast. He had been so intent on reaching London that he had not given any consideration to his future after that.

'I suppose it's impossible to go back to my old life?' he asked miserably.

'That much is certain. Walsingham's protection always has a price. He won't be so willing to extend it if you

257

haven't performed the services he expects of you. In case you're recognised, it would be best for you not to come to London for a while.'

Tom sighed. 'I suppose you're right. In any case, I promised Richard Lacey I'd go to his home and give his sister a letter from him.'

'Where does she live?'

'At a place called Lacey Hall in Devon.'

'Very well, but make sure you trust no one and be brief. After you leave Devon, come back as far as Winchester. I know an inn there where I've often stayed on my journeys to and from the West Country. The landlord is a good man. I'll give you a letter for him and he'll see to it you're well looked after. Send me a message to let me know you have arrived safely. Meanwhile, I'll do my best to think of a plan.'

'Thank you, I owe you more than I can ever repay.' Tom hesitated.

'Is there something else?'

'You said that when you were in Salisbury, you would see what you could find out about Meg.'

'I'm afraid I haven't any news of her. I was late joining my men and by the time I caught up with them, they had already moved on from Salisbury.'

Lamotte scrutinised Tom's disappointed face. It was understandable that his thoughts had returned to this girl. Time dragged in prison with little to occupy a man. But he wished now that he had never promised Tom he would seek news of her. It had been a mistake to encourage him in this hankering after the unattainable. He frowned. 'Take my advice, Tom, forget her. Nothing but trouble can come of it. And promise me you won't go to Salisbury yourself. It's far too dangerous.'

Lowering his eyes, Tom was silent for a few moments.

'Come, Tom, give me your word.'

Tom looked up. 'Very well, I promise.'

Chapter 26

November, 1587

As Tom rode out of London and set his course for Devon, niggling doubts entered his mind and grew there. Master Lamotte had been so good to him; was it right to continue to accept his help? I shall be a burden at best, Tom thought. At worst, I may cause him to lose Walsingham's favour and endanger his own life. As for Meg, Tom knew in his heart that Lamotte was right. He should forget her. She was lost to him and nothing could change that. A leaden weight lodged in his chest, but there was no use grieving. He must concentrate on what he would do after he had visited Lacey Hall.

He remembered a map he had seen in William Kemp's office, which showed the places of note in the West Country: Salisbury, Exeter and Plymouth among them. He might have more luck in Plymouth than anywhere else. It was where the English fleet was berthed and he had heard that men were being recruited in readiness to resist the Spanish if they tried to invade. He was no sailor but he could fight. A ship would be as good a place as any to hide and earn his livelihood. The further he travelled, the more resolved he became that this was what he would do.

When he reached King's Barton, he put up at a small tavern and made enquiries in order to reassure himself he had the right directions to Lacey Hall. The landlord's surly response unsettled him. It seemed to indicate the Lacey family were not well regarded in the district. The story of Richard's arrest had probably spread.

Early the next morning, he covered the last few miles to the Hall, arriving to find the windows dark with no sign of life in them. He wondered if the place was deserted and he had wasted his journey, but nevertheless, he dismounted, went to the front door and knocked.

A biting wind whistled around the corner of the house as he waited. He stamped his feet and blew on his cold hands to warm them then knocked again but still no one came. He stood back and scanned the windows. To his relief, a faint light flickered in an upstairs room. So there was someone there. At last, the door opened a crack and a man peered out. Over his shoulder, Tom saw a lofty hall with an oak staircase leading out of it. Richard Lacey had a fine house. It was sad to think he might never see it again.

'What do you want?' the man asked.

'I'd like to see Mistress Lacey.'

'She's not here.'

'Do you know when she'll be back?'

'Who wants to know?'

Tom hesitated, unsure what name to give. 'A friend,' he answered at last. 'I have a letter for her. Will you make sure she gets it? I've travelled a long way to give it to her.'

A look of grudging acquiescence came over the man's face. 'I'm her steward,' he said. 'Give it to me and I'll see she does.'

Tom handed over the letter and the man took a step backwards. He seemed uninterested in asking any questions and closed the door, leaving Tom standing on the step. Perhaps his hostile manner was unsurprising. This household probably had reason to mistrust strangers.

He left the Hall and, muffled in the warm cloak he had bought in Norwich, rode all day. The sun emerged fitfully from the leaden clouds, casting a coppery glow over bare, undulating fields edged with leafless trees and hedgerows. He passed through a few poor hamlets and farms and just before sunset stopped at one where, in exchange for a few pence, the farmer gave him food and a bed for the night.

The following morning he left early to continue his journey. The sky was overcast but the air was warmer than it had been the previous day. The road climbed slowly up onto moorland covered with rough turf and scrubby gorse. He slackened the reins and let his horse amble along while he tried to empty his mind of his troubles. The hardest task of all was forgetting Meg, but he was sure now that it was the right thing to do. She had her life to lead and he must take no part in it. He had nothing to offer her except danger and disgrace. What true lover wanted that for his beloved?

The present returned with a jolt when his horse lurched forward. He grasped its mane and narrowly avoided a fall. When he regained his seat, he looked around him. A faint, winding track had replaced the road. The rock upon which his horse had stumbled was part of a long, low outcrop of granite rising to one side of it out of a carpet of emerald moss.

The sun was behind the clouds, making it difficult to get his bearings. The map he pictured in his mind placed Plymouth to the south west of Lacey Hall, but did the track lead that way? It was hard to be sure but it was the only one visible. He guided his horse back to the centre of it, cursing himself for paying so little attention. What if he didn't find shelter before nightfall? This moor was a lonely place and he had no idea how long it would be before he reached the other side. With a shudder, he recalled stories of evil spirits and the lights of the wandering dead that lured unwary travellers to their deaths.

Only the jangle of the horse's bit and the creak of the saddle broke the eerie silence. Soon, curls of mist loomed ahead. Tom pulled up his horse, wondering whether to turn back but when he looked over his shoulder, he realised the mist had crept in from behind too. There was nothing for it but to go on. Cautiously, he rode forward. Around him, the moor glistened like a huge ice field. It was not long before his horse baulked at some unseen terror and refused to move. Tom dug his heels in to urge it on but it was no use.

A sulphurous smell of decay assailed his nostrils. He understood why when he slid from the saddle and felt the ground quiver beneath his feet. His mouth went dry. In the mist, they must have wandered off the path again, this time onto boggy ground. It plucked at his feet as he took his first tentative steps. His horse whinnied and shied.

'Steady,' Tom gasped, struggling to control it and keep the fear out of his voice. 'We'll try another way.'

With the next direction he explored, he felt firmer earth beneath his feet and, if he strained his eyes, he could just see the path's route for several paces ahead. His palms clammy, he leant against the horse's neck and drew air into his lungs. 'Safe now,' he murmured. 'Here's the track again. All we have to do is stay on it.'

Chapter 27

Lamotte walked through Bankside under a heavy, grey sky. There was the threat of snow about it. Passing the Clink gaol, he heard a groan. Almost level with the fetid, rubbish-choked gutter, a bony hand clawed at the iron grille. Grimly, Lamotte hurried on, his thoughts turning to Tom. There had been no message from him since he left London for Devon. It worried Lamotte. Sometimes he feared Tom had gone to Salisbury, but then, he reminded himself, he had given his word not to. His other fear was that Tom had been recaptured. No, if that was the case, Walsingham would have mentioned it.

The conversation he had had with Walsingham after the loss of the *Curlew* had been a very difficult one. Lamotte had been forced to dissemble many times. The old spymaster's displeasure at the possible escape of the *Curlew's* Catholic cargo as well as at the failure of his plan to infiltrate Tom into the prison at Wisbech had been withering. In fact, in general, his usual steely reserve was ruffled by ill temper and impatience. It did not surprise Lamotte. The situation abroad was far from propitious. Reports that a Huguenot army under Prince Henry of Navarre had defeated the much larger one of the Catholic Holy League had been hotly followed by the news that another Huguenot army marching from the east towards Paris had been routed at the city gates.

The Catholic leader, the Duke of Guise, had claimed the credit for saving the city and the Parisians hailed him as their saviour. It was common knowledge that they felt nothing but scorn for their king. It was his fate to be caught between the warring factions, unable to please anyone, certainly not the Parisians. People said they had rearranged the letters of his name to insult him and the chant of *Vilain Herodias* rang out in the streets. If he failed to keep control and the Duke of Guise usurped his power, France would be nothing more than Spain's puppet. England would be hemmed in from the south as well as by the Duke of Parma's forces in the east.

The houses in the narrow alleys of Bankside were built so close together that even on sunny days they were dank and gloomy. From the open door of a brothel, a painted woman with carroty hair flashed Lamotte a gap-toothed smile and pulled down the neckline of her dress. 'Why the hurry?' she cajoled, but he shook his head. The Bankside stews were notorious for the pox.

He came out of the alleys close by The Rose. If he had not been so preoccupied with getting his own autumn season off to a good start, he would have visited the recently built theatre sooner. He wanted to see what the owner, Philip Henslowe, had made of it. It was a new idea to build south of the river. Presumably Henslowe hoped to draw custom away from the older-established houses in Shoreditch.

Sat in the gallery, Lamotte smelt the stench of unwashed bodies from the pit where the groundlings stood. It was not improved, he reflected, by the bilge water smell of the winkles and clams most of them scoffed.

The play that afternoon was Marlowe's brutal tale, *Tamburlaine*. The groundlings lapped it up with the same glee as the spectators at the bear pit did the real blood spilt for their amusement. For Lamotte, it was the vivid, powerful language that gripped him. He saw its influence in Tom's new play. The memory of that made him sad.

Marlowe's final scene drew to a close and the crowd jostled into the streets. Mulling over what he had seen, Lamotte was carried along on the tide. The house had been fuller than most of the Shoreditch theatres ever were. A change was in the air.

Outside The Rose, the smell of wood smoke and hot pies reminded him he was hungry. He noticed a familiar face at one of the stalls and went over.

'I see you've got a new pitch – and no roast hog.'

'Not enough money in it. I'm doing better with the pies, although the old lady complains about the extra work.' The stallholder gestured to where a small boy played in the dust. 'I brought this one out with me today to give her some peace.'

'What have you got?'

'Mutton or eel.'

Lamotte fished in his pocket. 'I'll take mutton.'

'Have you left Shoreditch for good?' he asked after he had swallowed the first bite.

'The old lady likes it better down here.' The stallholder raised his eyebrows. 'Wants to be near her ma. Business all right up there, is it?'

'Not bad. Folk like to take their mind off their troubles.'

'Plenty of those about.'

Lamotte brushed pastry crumbs from his lips and nodded. 'You're right about that.'

'Oh, I almost forgot.' The stallholder grinned. 'Last time I was up your way a girl was asking for you - shapely lass, dark hair and a pretty face.'

'Did she have a name?'

The stallholder scratched his chin. 'Let me see, it might have been Meg. Yes that was it – Meg. She said she lodged at the laundress's down Holborn way. Very upset she looked, as if she was in some sort of trouble.'

Lamotte started. 'Did she say anything else?'

'Not that I remember.'

As he walked away, Lamotte's brain was in a fever. Was this Tom's girl, come just as Tom had promised to forget her? But what would she be doing in Holborn when she had a rich husband in Salisbury to keep her? No, the name must be a simple coincidence. He was worrying about nothing.

The stallholder had said this Meg seemed very upset. Lamotte remembered a carpenter he had let go in the spring for bad workmanship. Briefly, he considered the possibility it was a wife or daughter coming with some hard-luck tale, hoping to get the job back. It had been tried before, but it would do no good this time. More than ever, he needed men who pulled their weight.

A tug at his cloak made him turn. The stallholder's boy looked up at him with round eyes.

'What is it?' Lamotte asked.

'Tom,' the boy said shyly.

Lamotte frowned. 'Is that your name?'

The boy shook his head and scampered back to his father.

'What does he want?' Lamotte asked following him.

The stallholder cuffed the boy around the head. 'Shallow in his wits he is – can't remember a message from one minute to the next. I told him to tell you I remembered the other thing she asked. She wanted to know if I'd seen a fellow called Tom something about, seemed to think you might know him.'

Lamotte felt a jolt go through him. 'Where did you say this girl lived?'

'Holborn, at the laundry. Is something wrong?'

'Nothing at all,' Lamotte said briskly. He touched the brim of his hat. 'Well, I must be off, thank you.'

The sun was setting as he crossed London Bridge. It was too late to go to Holborn tonight. By the time he reached the western gate it would be shut. Tom's Meg, if it was she, would have to wait until morning.

Chapter 28

Peggoty's smile was ingratiating. 'Can I help you, sir? If it's washing you want doing, you won't find better rates than ours in the whole of London.'

'I've not come for that. I'm looking for a girl called Meg. I believe she lodges here.'

A surly expression replaced the smile. 'She's not in some sort of trouble, is she?'

'No, I just want to talk to her.'

'She's not here.'

'When will she be back?'

Peggoty was already closing the door but he wedged his foot in it.

'I don't want anyone wasting her time,' she said with a scowl.

Lamotte produced a shilling and held it out. 'I promise to be brief.'

'She's gone to Lincoln's Inn with some washing, but there's plenty more work to do when she comes back.' She snatched the coin. 'Now get your foot out of my door.'

Taken aback by the ferocity of her tone, Lamotte removed his foot just in time as the door slammed in his face. This Meg was to be pitied, he thought ruefully.

He hadn't gone far when a girl carrying a basket of laundry caught his eye. He stopped. The hair slipping from her white cap was dark and luxuriant. Her expressive eyes were of such a dark blue that they were almost black. As she went up to the door that had just been slammed on him, he called out to her. 'Meg?'

Frowning, she turned and stared at him. 'Yes. Why do you ask?'

'My name is Alexandre Lamotte. I heard you were looking for me.'

She turned pale. 'Master Lamotte! Please tell me quickly. Do you know Tom Goodluck? Does he work for you?'

'He did.'

'But do you know where he is now? Is he safe and well?'

'I believe he is, although I can't be sure.'

She swayed and he caught her elbow to steady her. 'Forgive me,' she gasped.

'I'm the one who should be sorry,' Lamotte said with consternation. 'I shouldn't have frightened you like that. Let's find you somewhere to sit down then we can talk.'

He led her to a wooden bench under an elm tree nearby. Taking out a handkerchief, he dusted down the seat before motioning her to sit. She gave a shaky laugh. 'I'm a poor washerwoman now, Master Lamotte. I have no airs and graces.'

Lamotte frowned. 'How has this come about?'

'I ran away from my home and my husband. At first I tried to find Tom but it was hopeless. Misfortune brought me to London then, by chance, I saw a playbill with Tom's name on it. The man who gave you my message told me you owned the theatre.'

When he set out that morning, Lamotte had intended to do his best to put this girl off in any way he could, but now she was before him, so clearly distressed, he found he was unable to dissemble. When he told her of Tom's capture and imprisonment, Meg trembled. 'I was afraid of that. Is he still there?'

'No, he was moved to another prison away from London.'

'Is it far away?'

'Yes, but he escaped on the journey.'

268

'Oh if only I could find him!'

'It may be possible. He promised to deliver a letter to the family of another prisoner who escaped with him.'

Meg rallied. 'So perhaps they will have some news of him?'

'They might. I had thought of going to see them myself. They live at a place called Lacey Hall near Exeter.'

The colour drained from Meg's face once more. 'Lacey Hall? What was the name of the prisoner who escaped with Tom?'

'Richard Lacey.'

'It can't be,' she whispered.

'Why do you doubt it?'

'I know the Laceys. They helped me after I ran away from my husband.' Her voice shook. 'Did Tom tell you how Richard was captured?'

'No, do you know anything of it?'

Meg felt a terrible sense of foreboding come over her. 'I was there when the priest hunters came to the house. We knew they were close by, but they struck so swiftly, Richard only just managed to hide before they broke in.'

Her fingers twisted in her lap. 'I knew their leader, a man called Ralph Fiddler. He once worked with Tom in Salisbury.' She broke off. 'You've heard his name before?'

'Yes. When Tom was arrested for William Kemp's murder, I asked him if there was anyone who might wish him ill. He said the only man he could think of was Ralph Fiddler.'

'Ralph offered me a chance to save Richard, at least I believed he did, but now you've told me Richard was captured, I fear he lied to me. He said that if I went away with him, he would give up the search for Richard and leave the house for good.' A sob caught in her throat. 'I agreed. He made me promise not to explain my actions to Richard's sister Beatrice – they lived at Lacey Hall together. Of course she was horrified and angry that I seemed happy to take up with a man who was our enemy. It broke my heart to leave,

269

knowing what she thought of me.' She bowed her head. 'So Ralph arrested Richard after all, how Beatrice must hate me.'

'Where is Fiddler now?'

'I don't know. He had me taken to his house in London. Later on, he followed me there, but not long afterwards, he disappeared. While he was gone, I ran away and that's how I came to be at Peggoty's.'

'You must put it all behind you,' Lamotte said firmly. 'There's no use distressing yourself over what's past. I'll take you to Lacey Hall and hope there's news of Tom there.'

A look of alarm crossed Meg's face. 'Beatrice! Must I face her?'

'When she hears what you have told me, I'm sure she will forget her anger. Now we have plans to make. Will it be too arduous a ride for you?'

'No.'

'Then tomorrow I'll buy a well-broken mare and, if you will permit me, suitable clothes for you to travel in.'

She smiled. 'You're very generous, Master Lamotte. I don't know what I've done to deserve such kindness.'

'Reuniting you with Tom will be ample reward.'

'What shall I say to Peggoty?'

'The harridan I met when I came to find you? Don't worry, I'll deal with her.'

'Master Lamotte?'

'Yes?'

'It may be of no importance but before I escaped from Ralph Fiddler, I found a gold ring inscribed with the letters *WK* at his house.'

'And you thought the initials were William Kemp's?'

'I wondered if they might be,' she faltered.

Lamotte pondered for a few moments. 'Even if you're right, I doubt that alone would be sufficient proof that Fiddler is the murderer,' he said at last. 'He could simply have stolen the ring after, or even before, Kemp died. But we should certainly not dismiss the possibility that there is more to it than that. Do you still have it?'

270

Meg nodded.

'Then with your permission, I shall take it with me. There's someone I'd like to show it to.'

Chapter 29

Lacey Hall
December, 1587

'I hoped we wouldn't meet again,' Beatrice said coldly when she had dismissed the manservant who answered the door to Meg and Lamotte.

Meg's palms were clammy. Her legs felt as if they would give way beneath her.

'I suppose Ralph Fiddler has left you,' Beatrice went on. 'I hope you don't expect pity. You don't deserve it when we never showed you anything but kindness.'

A few paces away, Lamotte watched them, uncertain whether to intervene, then seeing that Meg was close to tears, he put aside caution and stepped forward.

Beatrice gave him a wintry glance.

'Who is this?'

'My name is Alexandre Lamotte, madam. May we have your permission to come in? We've had a long ride from London.'

'Not of my requesting, sir.'

Lamotte checked a sharp reply. 'Madam, you are angry but if you will hear us out, I think your anger may be assuaged.'

Beatrice's eyes narrowed.

'I believe you already know your brother is in France,' he persisted, 'but there are other matters that need explanation.'

She frowned. 'Who told you where Richard is?'

'Please, let us in and we'll tell you everything.'

After Meg finished her tale, Beatrice was silent for a while then she went to Meg and took her in her arms. 'Can you forgive me for doubting you?'

Meg's voice trembled. 'Of course I can. I understand how it must have seemed to you. I was a fool to trust Ralph.'

'Do you know where he is now? I often fear he'll come back. Agnes still wakes crying at night. None of us sleep easy in our beds.'

Meg shook her head. 'I've heard nothing since the night he left me in London.'

'I hope bad fortune has befallen him,' Beatrice snapped.

A look of sympathy came into her eyes. 'I expect you were hoping to find your Tom here. If only we had known who he was. I was away from home when he came. We had all been in such low spirits, I decided to take Sarah's children to the Advent market at Exeter. Bess and Alice accompanied us, so only Steward John, was here to speak to Tom. When we returned, I chided him for asking no questions of a man who had brought us such good news. Anything more he could have told me of Richard would have been so welcome. I had no idea how unfortunate John's omission was in other ways. I'm so sorry I can't help you but you will find him, I'm sure you will. You mustn't give up hope.'

Watching them, Lamotte wished he felt as confident. He and Meg had stopped at the inn in Winchester on the way to Devon but the landlord had not seen Tom. Now there was no news at Lacey Hall of his whereabouts.

But he must keep Meg's spirits up. 'Mistress Lacey is right, Meg,' he said.

With a start, as if she had only just remembered his presence, Beatrice acknowledged him. 'Sir, please forgive me for offering you such an uncivil reception.'

'There is no need to apologise, madam. These are unusual circumstances.'

Beatrice smiled and the warmth of her smile banished the memory of the inauspicious start. 'Thank you for your generosity, sir.'

Lamotte glanced at Meg's dejected face, knowing that she was very little reassured. It was possible something had delayed Tom on the road, but if he had headed for Winchester after he left Lacey Hall, it was odd they had not found him there a few days ago.

'What should we do, Master Lamotte?' Meg asked. 'Should we go back to Winchester?' She turned to Beatrice. 'Tom was to go there when he had seen you. Perhaps he's there by now.'

'I think I should go alone,' Lamotte said, silencing her protests with a frown. 'The journey here was wearying enough for you and the weather is becoming more treacherous with every day that passes.'

'I agree,' Beatrice broke in. 'I won't hear of you going. You must stay with us. As soon as he finds Tom, Master Lamotte will bring him back to you.'

The memory of Amélie's brisk voice flashed across Lamotte's mind and he smiled. 'It's good advice, Meg. You must take it.'

Chapter 30

London
March, 1588

Where it slowed to pass through the arches of London Bridge, the river still froze. Often, Lamotte stopped to watch groups of boys playing boisterous games on its glassy, perilous surface. In those dying days of winter, when the sun was rarely seen, he frequently filled his spare hours with solitary walks. Some of the time he went to visit the family in Angel Lane, but often he simply felt the need to be alone with his thoughts.

Tom had never arrived at the inn in Winchester and January and February went by without any message from him. Meg was still at Lacey Hall and it grieved Lamotte that he had no good news to send her in response to her anxious enquiries.

Often, he was tempted to go and visit her. It would be an opportunity to become better acquainted with Beatrice Lacey. But always, at the last moment, he held back, telling himself that the roads would be seas of mud or it was a bad time to leave the theatre. The latter was certainly true. London was an uneasy city and apprehension increased the price of daily necessities. The theatre was a luxury and The Unicorn's takings were down.

As he had agreed with Meg, on his return to London, he had taken the ring she had given him to Walsingham. The spymaster had been distracted, almost brusque, but a flicker of interest crossed his face as he listened to the story of where the ring had been found. He had asked to keep it, but that was more than two months and Lamotte had abandoned any serious hope of the subject being raised again. No doubt Walsingham was far too preoccupied with the threat from Spain to have time for the petitions of ordinary mortals. The start of the month had brought alarming news from merchants coming to London from Lisbon. The mouth of the Tagus was black from bank to bank with fighting ships. Crews to man them were being pressed into service from every available source.

April arrived but brought no better weather with it. The sunless streets remained dingy and the days were cold. On one of his walks along the river, Lamotte watched a sharp wind whip the grey water into choppy wavelets. On the ferries and barges, people huddled in thick woollens as if winter had never left.

The clock of a nearby church tolled twelve and, wrapping his cloak around him more tightly, he started for home. In Lombard Street, a gang of apprentices loitered, hooting at passers-by. Lamotte ducked into an alley, relieved he had noticed them in time. In spite of all the years he had lived in London, he found his swarthy looks still marked him out as a man who was not a native by birth, and, as the Spanish threat grew, it was easier to find a flock of white crows than an Englishman who loved a foreigner.

'Is the fire lit in my study?' he asked his servant, James, as he took off his cloak in the hall at Throgmorton Street.

'Yes, master.'

'Then bring me a bottle of claret there and tell Cook I'll eat as soon as the meal is ready.'

'Yes, master. Master, there is a message for you. I left it on your desk.'

Lamotte groaned. It would be theatre business, no doubt. He hoped it didn't mean he needed to go out again, just when he was looking forward to a warm fire and some good claret.

In his study, he picked up the message with distaste then stopped. The hand was a familiar one. He steeled himself. What did Walsingham want this time? As usual, the note

276

was short and there was no indication that he needed to attend as a matter of urgency, but in spite of the cold, he decided to go that afternoon. He would only waste the time in speculation otherwise.

He sighed. The last thing he desired was to be sent on another mission. He hoped that was not the reason he was summoned.

'Tell Cook I'm not ready to eat yet after all,' he said when James returned with the claret. 'And fetch my hat and cloak.'

Ten minutes later, with a fortifying glass of claret warming his blood, he was on the way to Seething Lane.

*

Walsingham looked up from the papers he was studying. 'Good of you to come so promptly, Alexandre. You are in tolerable health, I hope, in spite of the weather?'

'Thank you, yes. I hope your lordship can say the same?'

Walsingham nodded and Lamotte tried to contain his impatience. Surely Walsingham had not summoned him to discuss his health or the weather? He wished this polite preamble was over.

'Please, sit down.'

Gingerly, Lamotte took a seat. Walsingham leant back in his chair and steepled his hands. 'You are to be congratulated, Alexandre.'

'I am?'

'Indeed. Thanks to you, your friend Tom Goodluck is no longer charged with the murder of William Kemp.'

Lamotte was dumbfounded.

'Let me explain. Do you recall the papers you found in Manfredi's lodgings?'

'I do.'

'As a matter of routine, I gave them to my decipherer to read. I was surprised when he came to see me. He believed one of them contained a code he recognised. I told him to

277

study the matter further and eventually, he unravelled a story that carried us along some very profitable paths. One of them led to the man Ralph Fiddler who you mentioned to me a few months ago in connection with the ring you gave me.'

Lamotte stiffened - all attention now.

'My men had for some time been watching a Salisbury lawyer named William Kemp. We suspected he was a Catholic and his work as a lawyer made him privy to a great deal of information about the affairs of the wealthy men in his locality. We believed he was passing some of this information to a Spanish agent in London, to be used if the invasion succeeded. At some point Manfredi became involved. It appears he was working for both sides and eventually paid for it with his life.'

Walsingham paused. Trying to hide his impatience, Lamotte waited for him to continue.

'We were close to arresting Kemp when he was murdered. He was already dead when Ralph Fiddler came to my attention in London. I noticed him because the speed of his promotion to pursuivant was unusual.' Lamotte remembered that Walsingham preferred to use the formal term for a priest hunter.

'I was not involved in the matter,' Walsingham went on. 'A watch is being kept on the men who were. As I'm sure you appreciate, the role of a pursuivant provides excellent opportunities for amassing information about the men who hunt down Catholic traitors. Such information is of great interest to Spain. If she conquered England, those men would be among the first to be seized.'

'You thought Fiddler was working for Spain?'

'We strongly suspected it. I set one of my agents to find out his history and it came to light that he had been employed by William Kemp. The question that arose then was whether Fiddler knew of Kemp's secret life. Were they in league? When you brought me the ring, it interested me. If it had belonged to Kemp, why would it be in Fiddler's possession? One possibility was that Kemp had given it to him, but he might also have stolen it.'

Lamotte strove to take in the labyrinthine web of plots and counter-plots that were second nature to Walsingham.

'In any case,' Walsingham continued. 'I decided it was time to apprehend Fiddler. He must have sensed he was being watched for he had left his house in London. My men eventually arrested him at Dover, trying to flee to France.' He smiled grimly. 'We did not need to interrogate him for long before he admitted he had found out about Kemp's activities. He claimed he would never have sought to profit from them personally – something I strongly doubt in view of his subsequent career. His story was that he was waiting until he had enough information to report Kemp. But then matters took a different turn. Late one night after a May Day celebration, Fiddler returned to his lodgings at Kemp's house. He admitted he had drunk a good deal and was in a resentful mood with Kemp because the old man had denied him wages on some trivial pretext. He challenged Kemp and there was an argument. During the course of it, Fiddler struck Kemp hard and he fell.'

Walsingham stopped and cleared his throat. 'When Fiddler realised his master was dead, he became desperate. Then he remembered he had seen Kemp's groom very drunk at the celebrations. The groom had let slip that your friend Tom Goodluck had promised to help him home. If by chance Tom had been weary enough to snatch some sleep at Kemp's stables rather than return to his own lodgings, there might be a way of putting the blame on him. To cut the story short, the plan worked. Later Fiddler used the money and information he found among Kemp's possessions to obtain favours and further his ambitions in London.'

Lamotte felt a surge of relief. 'So Tom really is cleared of the charge of murder?'

'Indeed he is.' Walsingham's shrewd eyes studied Lamotte. 'I never found out for sure if he went down with

279

the *Curlew*. Your demeanour suggests otherwise, but you do not need to tell me anything more.'

'Thank you,' Lamotte stammered.

Outside, he gave way to jubilation. Tom was a free man. At last there was good news to take to Lacey Hall.

Chapter 31

Plymouth
April, 1588

The creamy-white sails of dozens of fishing boats flecked the grey waters of the Sound. Wood smoke curled from the chimneys of the squat, mud-walled cottages huddled around the harbour. On the quayside, gulls skirmished over discarded fish heads and guts. The air smelt of brine and bilge water.

The day was little different from all the others since Tom had joined up, using the name Tom Black for safety's sake. Over the winter, all the ships of the Western Squadron had been careened on the beach for their hulls to be painted with tallow and their fouled ballast shovelled out and replaced. The work was hard, but in a strange way, he was glad of it. Hard work made it easier to forget.

As he had anticipated when he chose to come to Plymouth, the town was bursting with soldiers and sailors, both old hands and raw recruits. Almost outnumbering the local population, they thronged the streets, spending their pay – when they were lucky enough to receive it – in the taverns and brothels. Sometimes he visited the brothels too, but the perfunctory tumbles always left him hollow with longing for Meg.

Rum was a better friend. It helped deaden the monotony of waiting for something to happen and, until its effects wore off, made the world a happier place. Happiness was a rare thing, for when he had a sober moment to reflect, he found nothing to be glad of.

He had resolved to keep his whereabouts secret from Lamotte. It had been a painful decision after all his friend's kindness, but he was sure it was the right one. If he survived the war with Spain, he would start a new life. He might even go to the New World. He had spent many an hour listening to the stories of the sailors who had sailed across the ocean with Drake and Hawkins. Perhaps there would be a place for him in those far-off lands.

All winter, the inhabitants of Plymouth had lived on a diet of rumours. By spring, some of them were claiming that the Armada had left Lisbon and had already been sighted off the Lizard; others said storms had driven it back to port. A third story was that it had been wrecked on the murderous coastline of the Scillies.

The news brought by merchants and privateers returning from the south was probably more reliable. Many of them reported that even though Philip of Spain was impatient to begin the enterprise of England, his admiral, the Marquis of Santa Cruz, was determined to wait for better weather.

'The old fox is ailing and not the force he was, but he will be hard to budge,' said a Flemish merchant who was drinking in a tavern frequented by Tom and some of his shipmates. The merchant claimed to travel extensively in Spain, trading broadcloth for olive oil and the wines of Jerez. He obviously liked to pass as something of an expert on Spanish affairs.

'The king sits up in his palace at the Escorial,' he went on, 'convincing himself he does God's bidding and a miracle will do the work, but I doubt Santa Cruz believes in miracles.'

A few of his listeners grunted their agreement.

'Half the crews are too sick to work,' he continued. 'Santa Cruz's recruiting officers are emptying the prisons to make up the numbers, but even thieves and murderers aren't keen to oblige. Philip insists his ships be ready at all times to sail, so there's no shore leave.'

After weeks in the company of sailors, Tom appreciated how unpopular that would be.

'They say the ships stink like sewers,' the merchant added. 'And the men get little except rotten rations and foul water to live on.'

It was no wonder they fell ill, Tom thought. With all its hardships, life sounded better in Plymouth than in Lisbon.

The news that the Marquis of Santa Cruz's illness had finally carried him off was greeted with rejoicing by the English sailors. For Spain, the death of the Armada's supreme commander would be a serious blow. Over his long years of service, he had richly earned the soubriquets 'the invincible' and 'the thunderbolt in war.' To replace him, King Philip had appointed his cousin, the Duke of Medina Sidonia. In Plymouth, sailors who had taken part in the attack on Cadiz the previous spring remembered that name. Medina Sidonia was a fine soldier, they said. If he had not been so quick to bring up his troops to defend the city, Cadiz would have fallen to the English for sure. But he was no sailor.

'Though anyone who expects that to save us is a fool,' one of the old hands remarked. 'There's plenty of captains who know what they're about in the Armada and he'll have the sense to give 'em their heads, just like Howard does with Drake.'

A rumble of approval went round his listeners at the mention of Drake's name. Tom had seen him several times in Plymouth. His short, stocky figure and florid, irascible face were unmistakable, as was the admiration, bordering on awe, he inspired in the sailors. Who else would have ventured on so great an enterprise as sailing around the whole world? Who else would have come home triumphant?

The days lengthened and a fever of anticipation gripped the town. On the headlands, the beacons were made ready with piles of brushwood and barrels of pitch. The look-outs were under orders to light three flames in turn: the first to warn that the Armada had been sighted; the second to

283

summon the militias and the third, most dreaded of all, the signal that the Spanish had landed.

The arrival from Chatham of the queen's galleons screwed the tension to a higher pitch. Gaily painted in her colours of green and white, they rode at anchor among the ships of the Western Squadron. Soon, private ships that had been requisitioned followed, until the harbour bristled with masts.

In the taverns, the ancient rivalry between soldiers and sailors flared. The sailors boasted this would be a new kind of war, decided by seamanship and gunnery, not grappling and hand-to-hand fighting. The soldiers claimed they would be the ones who would defeat the Spanish. For the first time, Tom realised this was not a game. It might be a month, it might be two, but the Armada would come, and his mettle would be tested. He would have to prove himself, or die.

Chapter 32

Lacey Hall
May, 1588

As soon as he had arranged his affairs at the theatre, Lamotte left London and rode to Devon with his news. He wished he was also able to tell Meg that he had heard from Tom but he had still not done so. He would just have to do his best to comfort her with assurances that one day there would be word - even if he found it hard to believe himself.

The journey was very different from the one he had undertaken in December. Instead of bare fields and foul weather, the countryside looked freshly painted with green. Lamotte told himself it was the fine weather that raised his spirits but, in truth, he knew it was also the prospect of seeing Beatrice again. He often thought about the short time he had spent in her company.

He intended to stay no more than a few days but he was made so welcome that he remained a week. The only thing that marred his pleasure was Meg. At first she had been joyful at the news, but soon her excitement waned and it was clear she was pretending to a cheerfulness she did not feel.

'It grieves me to see her in low spirits,' said Lamotte as he walked with Beatrice by the lake. A pair of swans foraged in the weed growing at its margin. Clouds like puffs of down floated in a sky as blue as a starling's egg.

'I share your feelings,' Beatrice said sadly. 'Your news has given her considerable comfort, but I fear she will never be truly happy unless she has Tom by her side.'

'She mustn't give up hope.'

'After all this time, it's hard not to,' Beatrice said quietly.

'It must be difficult for you too without your brother.' He looked at her sideways, watching the play of emotions on her face. 'I'm sorry,' he said gently, 'I didn't mean to pry.'

Beatrice shook her head. 'There's nothing to be sorry for. Yes, I do miss Richard a great deal.' She gestured to the lake and the fields beyond. 'He loved all this. He used to walk for miles with Hector.' She glanced at the wolfhound, who was warily stalking the swans. 'Foolish creature, they will attack if he comes too close and he'll get the worst of it. Hector! Come here!'

The dog ignored her and remained by the lake, wagging his tail uncertainly as the cob hissed and swayed his head to and fro.

'Don't worry, I'll fetch him,' Lamotte said, surprised by his own confidence. In London he usually avoided dogs.

'I think the swan would have had the better of a fight,' he remarked, as he brought Hector back. He scratched the wolfhound behind the ears and it leant into him, a low rumble rising from its throat.

'He likes you. But push him away if he's a nuisance.'

'I don't mind.'

A companionable silence fell as they contemplated the view. It was Lamotte who broke it first. 'Such peace,' he said. 'I have lived in cities all my life - first Paris, now London - but I begin to understand there is another way of life that can bring contentment.' He smiled. 'Provided one has someone to share it with.'

She didn't reply and he hesitated. Had he misread her? It was hard to tell, but he couldn't resist the urge to go on. 'Business obliges me to return to London tomorrow, but if I may, I would like to visit you again soon.'

'I'd like. . . I mean we'd all be delighted to see you whenever you wish to come.'

Ah, perhaps he was not wrong. 'Thank you,' he said softly.

286

She sighed. 'In truth, sometimes I am afraid when I consider the future. What do you think will happen to us all?'

'You mean the Spanish threat?'

She nodded.

'Why, we shall fight them and we shall triumph.'

'You make it sound easy,' she said, laughing.

'Why do you doubt my words?'

'Because I believe you are only saying them to comfort me.'

'Is there anything wrong with that?' he asked with a grin.

'Nothing at all.'

Chapter 33

Plymouth
July, 1588

By the middle of the month, news reached Plymouth that storms in the Atlantic had forced the Spanish fleet to turn back from their progress towards the Narrow Sea and seek shelter at Corunna. It seemed increasingly unlikely they would attack in the near future.

Lord Howard, the admiral of the English fleet, immediately gave permission for Drake and some of the other captains to take a force of ninety ships to harry the Spanish galleons in harbour. Sir John Hawkins's ship, *Victory,* to which Tom had been assigned, was among them.

Hawkins was a quieter man than the flamboyant Drake, but he was a fine sailor and greatly respected by officers and men alike. Even though he lacked the Devonian's piratical boldness, Tom learnt that many people thought his contribution to England's chances of success was even greater than Drake's. The new ships Hawkins had designed for the English navy were faster and more seaworthy than those of any other country, and quicker to ready for action. The Spanish galleons, with their towering fore and stern castles, were well suited to the calm waters of the Mediterranean but severely hampered in the Atlantic's heavy seas where their gigantic height and size made them unstable and hard to manoeuvre.

A week after they set out, however, the ninety ships sailed back into harbour, battered by heavy seas and with the plan in disarray. They had never reached Corunna, for violent storms had forced them to turn for home. Their provisions were sorely depleted. The rations of four men had already been stretched to six and now some of the ships had no food at all. There was sickness on board too. Lord Howard ordered that those too ill to fight should be removed and he sent requests to the justices of the peace in Devon and the surrounding counties for new recruits.

Ships' carpenters set to, repairing masts and spars, while sail makers mended ripped canvas. There was no time to careen the ships and rummage them thoroughly but the decks were scoured with sharp sand and the filthy water was pumped from the bilges.

Like the rest of the crews who had no skilled tasks to perform, Tom spent his time hauling supplies of gunpowder, shot, water and food onto the ships. As he worked, he looked forward with relief to having something to fill his belly in the coming weeks.

July drew to its end and the warning beacons on the headlands remained unlit. On clear days, distant fields of corn gleamed in the sunshine and the thoughts of many of the local men pressed into service turned to the harvest. They talked quietly among themselves of jumping ship.

Then late one Friday afternoon, a privateer dropped anchor in Plymouth harbour and its captain, Thomas Fleming, raced ashore. The chandlers and roperies were preparing to close for the night and the taverns and whorehouses were deserted, for most of the crews were on board their ships, but the captain's arrival had been observed. Soon, news jumped from ship to ship and cottage to cottage like a plague of fleas. At dawn that morning, from his perch high in the mainmast, the lookout on the *Golden Hind* had sighted a huge flotilla of ships off the Scillies.

'Drake's up on the Hoe at his game of bowls,' one of Tom's shipmates grinned. 'Says there's time to finish it and beat the Spanish too.' A bubble of laughter went round the other men.

'It's more than a jest,' a grizzled Cornishman growled when the laughter subsided. 'With this southerly wind and the neap tide running, no ship'll get out of harbour till it turns.'

Tom had little appetite for his rations that evening. It seemed the other men on the *Victory* felt the same for the usual noisy banter was absent. At ten o'clock, with the turn of the tide, the fleet began to sail out into the open sea, heading to anchor at Dodman Point.

Early next morning, Tom went to his station on the gun deck and spent the day carrying shot to the gun lockers and rolling and filling paper cartridges with powder. The gun deck ran the whole length of the ship, its low ceiling spanned by gnarled oak beams as thick as a bull's neck. It was divided by the great trunks of the masts and every surface was black with the soot of gun smoke and spent powder. Small pools of light glowed by the open gun ports, augmented by single lanterns hanging at each end of the deck. The heat was already tremendous. Sweating profusely as he worked, Tom wondered how he would bear it when the battle commenced.

The following dawn revealed an empty sea. After rations, the sails were hoisted and anchors weighed but a morning of sailing furnished no sign of the Armada. In the daylight, Tom's fears receded and he went about his duties feeling calmer than he had expected.

It was early afternoon when a squall swept in from the west. The rain hammered down and the wind set the gun ports rattling like dice in a shaker. Suddenly, there were shouts from above. The men nearest the hatches raced up the ladders and Tom followed. On deck, the crowd was so large it seemed every member of the crew had left his work to stare into the rain. In the distance there was a broad, dark shape like a giant anvil. As the minutes went by, it separated into the outlines of a multitude of ghostly sails.

The teeming rain soaked into the men's rough woollen clothing but not one of them moved. At length, the howl of the wind in the rigging faded as the squall moved eastwards. In the clearer air, Tom saw a crescent of ships so vast that the sea seemed to groan under the weight of it. Hundreds of flags fluttered from the mastheads; they bore the scarlet cross of Spain. The blood roared in Tom's ears. The torment of waiting was nearly over, but now he wished fervently that it was not.

The Armada anchored out of range of the English guns. On board the *Victory*, the crew spent the hours of darkness preparing for battle. Soldiers cleaned their weapons and checked their powder and shot; gunners inspected their ammunition lockers and made sure the guns were firmly lashed in place. Hogsheads of water were made fast on each deck and old blankets and rags placed by them in readiness to put out fires. Tom shuddered to see the sawdust strewn on the decks, knowing it was there to mop up the blood that would be shed on the morrow.

When his duties were done, he wrote letters for some of the men. The messages of farewell to their loved ones and the scrupulous disposition of their few possessions wrung his heart, yet he envied them – at least there was some chance of their wives and sweethearts reading their messages. If only he had some way of telling Meg how much he loved her.

The watches of the night crawled by and he smelt the fear around him but there was courage too in the grim set of weather-beaten faces and the clench of calloused fists. No Englishmen needed to be reminded of what would happen to their homes and families if the Armada was victorious. The sea would be clear for the Duke of Parma and his army to cross the narrows from the Spanish-held Low Countries and invade.

At first light, a signal pennant flew from the mizzen mast of the flagship, the *Ark Royal*. With a noise like thunder, the gun ports that had been closed for the night were hauled up and the guns run out. The decks shook as the *Victory's* guns roared. It was the loudest sound Tom had ever heard. Answering volleys came from the other English ships then the noise ceased.

'It's a brave show,' one of the men muttered, 'but it'll be no more than a pinprick on an ox's hide to them.'

A master gunner near them scowled. 'That's enough. Keep to your battle stations.'

The din and chaos of the battle was beyond anything Tom had imagined. As the guns were fired, hauled in, swabbed and reloaded over and over again, sweat drenched every inch of him. What had once been air was a lung-searing inferno of soot and smoke. His tongue stuck to the roof of his mouth and every muscle in his body ached. The faces of the other men were tar black and glistening; their eyes glowed like the coals of Hell. Tom knew his must look the same.

When at last the firing stopped, the deck was strewn with spilt powder and spent cartridges. The silence was eerie. Only when Tom saw other men's lips move did he realise the noise of battle had deafened him. It was some time before a faint humming replaced the silence.

The worst of the filthy smoke slowly settled although the glowing guns still steamed. Tom joined the working parties sweeping spent cartridges into the sea through the open gun ports and mopping up spilt gunpowder. A tall man walked among them, pausing to speak with each one. As he did so, they pulled off their caps. He came nearer and Tom saw it was the captain, John Hawkins.

He stood to attention as Hawkins reached him. The captain studied Tom with a grave, pensive air. 'Your name, sailor?'

'Tom Black, sir.'

'You gave a good account of yourself today, Tom. All of the men did. I fear there is more to come but two of the Spanish ships are in no condition to fight again, and our casualties are less than I feared.' With a nod, he moved on to speak to one of the gunners, leaving Tom staring at his retreating figure.

*

292

With first blood drawn, the guns remained silent. In the days that followed, the English fleet dogged the Armada's ponderous progress eastwards up the Narrow Sea. It seemed to Tom that time crawled. At night, the crew slept restlessly, tormented by the slow drip of fear. When Tom had cause to go on deck, he saw the Armada's gigantic ships riding the grey sea, the bloody cross of Spain still starkly visible on their bellying sails.

The two fleets passed Start Point and joined battle again west of Portland Bill. Once more, the guns roared and cannonballs whistled above the decks, shredding sails and tangling rigging before they crashed down into the chaos below. Planking shattered, barrels burst and men shrieked under the impact of shot. Dagger-sharp splinters sliced through the air, increasing the carnage.

To Tom, as he stuck grimly to his work, cannon fire and the screams of lacerated men ringing in his ears, it seemed the world was set to end. He could not have said whether the battle lasted for hours or days but when at last it was over, he was too exhausted to lift his head. He was grateful for the deafness that once more afflicted him. It dulled the cries of the wounded.

As the men who were still able-bodied were ordered on deck to help the wounded and make what repairs they could to the ship, the mood on the *Victory* was sombre. The English had fought hard, with great expense of life and shot, but in spite of that, victory still eluded them. The prospect of swiftly despatching the Armada was fading as fast as the shore lights of Weymouth Bay.

'They know how to fight, I'll give them that,' a Dorset man said, wiping smears of soot and blood from his haggard face. 'Even Drake and Cap'n Hawkins will have their work cut out to get the better of them.'

There was a rumble of reluctant assent from the men in earshot.

'None of that talk unless you want a flogging,' a passing lieutenant barked. 'Get on with your work.'

The Dorset man spat at the lieutenant's retreating back. 'Here,' he muttered to Tom, 'help me get this one below.' Together they lifted a sailor whose shoulder was a shattered mess of exposed bone and torn flesh. The man groaned in a rum-soaked stupor as they jolted him down the gangway to the surgeon's quarters. Tom's pity for him was tempered by fear for his own skin. It might be his turn next.

The fact was, despite the damage the English gunners had managed to inflict on the Armada, only two Spanish ships were too badly hit to be out of the battle and it seemed neither of them had been crippled by English fire. One, the *Rosario*, had lost her bowsprit in a collision with another of the Armada's ships. The other, the *San Salvador*, was a smoking hulk after an explosion, but none of the English ships claimed a direct hit on her and the sailors on the *Victory* suspected a careless spark in her gunpowder hold had done the damage.

Two more days passed, and twice the English fleet beat off the Armada's galleons at the approaches to the Solent. Tom's duties brought him on deck more often, for ammunition was running short and the intrepid small boats darting to and from shore with fresh supplies needed unloading. Alarmingly, few of the cargoes contained the cannonballs for which the gunners clamoured. Tom helped to haul the motley collections of scrap iron and ploughshares on board, fearing they would not be much use against Spanish shot.

But by the time the two fleets reached Calais Roads, it was clear from the slowing of their rate of fire that the Spanish ships were running short of ammunition too. They anchored in the harbour beneath the walls of Calais Castle, leaving the English fleet standing out at sea. On the *Victory*, the men's weariness and dejection turned to angry frustration. Some said the Armada should never have been allowed to come so far up the Narrow Sea. They questioned Admiral Lord Howard's decision to stand off from the Spanish ships rather than challenge them head on.

Sunday morning came and after he had said prayers on deck, Captain Hawkins ordered four of the crew to row him out to the flagship, the *Ark Royal*. Soon Tom noticed small boats setting out from other ships in the same direction. On Hawkins's return, he called the crew together once more. Tom listened as he told them the Armada was to be attacked with fire ships.

A frenzy of activity followed. Hawkins had offered one of his own vessels and a group of men were detailed to tow it into line and rope it together with the other seven destined to burn. With another small group, Tom found himself in a longboat, rowing between the doomed ships and the rest of the fleet. Every muscle and sinew in his body ached by the time the stores and fittings to be taken off were removed. The mainmasts, spars and sails were left in place, for the ships would go into Calais under full sail. The guns also remained on board, double shotted with their muzzles crammed with any pieces of metal that could be found.

In the rigging of each ship, sailors clambered about daubing a mixture of pitch and resin on the masts and sails while down below, others coated the decks with the same foul-smelling mess. Small crews were chosen to sail each ship on her final mission. Tom was glad he did not have the skill to be among them. They would have only a few seconds to make their escape after their ships were alight. When everything was ready, the long wait for darkness and the turn of the tide commenced.

Night fell and below the castle walls, the Armada's lights bobbed like giant glow-worms on the dark sea. The early watches passed quietly on the *Victory*. It was a calm night and the flags on the mainmast drooped. Midnight approached when, feeling a breath on his cheek, Tom looked up and saw them flutter into life. The wind was rising; the crew's spirits lifted.

At the stroke of twelve, the fire ships broke loose from the fleet, sailing one behind the other. The tide was at the flood, running towards the land, and the wind was astern. It did not take them long to reach the mouth of the harbour where a defending screen of Spanish pinnaces and ships' longboats awaited them. Tom saw two fire ships swing out of the line. The Spanish crews must have managed to fling grappling hooks aboard them and pull them aside, but the rest forged on.

Suddenly, deafening roars split the night as their guns exploded and tongues of flame leapt into the sky. Quickly, the flames spread, racing up the masts and engulfing the sails until each fire ship was a floating inferno. A pall of smoke crept across the water. Surely, Tom thought, there would be nothing the Spanish could do to stop the remaining fire ships now.

The English were too far away to see clearly what was happening, but as Tom stared into the semi-darkness with the rest of the *Victory*'s crew, he could not suppress a pang of pity for any victim of such a fearful conflagration. When the fires dimmed to a glow, however, many on the *Victory* shook their heads. It was too soon, they said. If the fire ships had succeeded in setting any of the Armada's ships alight, the blaze in the harbour would have lasted much longer. Perhaps more than two of the fire ships had been diverted and the sacrifice was in vain.

It was only when the sun rose that a roar went up from the decks of the English ships. All that remained of the fire ships were blackened skeletons but they had done their work after all. The Armada had been forced to escape from the harbour into the open water. It was no longer in its impregnable crescent formation and, less manoeuvrable than the English ships, some of the great galleons were already foundering in the heavy seas, vulnerable as sheep to circling wolves.

Officers barked orders and the crew scrambled to hoist the sails and haul up the anchors. In a whirl of flapping canvas, the English ships set off after their quarry. Drake led the charge, but soon, in the confusion and smoke, it was hard to tell what was happening. When Tom did catch a glimpse of another ship, it was impossible to be sure whether it belonged to England or Spain.

It was late afternoon before the fury abated. When the smoke of the guns cleared, a scene of terrible devastation was revealed. Frantic horses and desperate men thrashed in the churning grey water. The lucky ones clung to shards of smashed masts and hulls as they waited for help. Tom did not want to think of the men who had already sunk into the grim depths.

Many of the Spanish galleons were crippled, their decks a shambles and their guns silent. When they listed, something too dark for water poured from their scuppers. Several were low in the water and before Tom's eyes one slowly sank beneath the waves. The rest were being driven northwards by a westerly wind towards the treacherous rocks and shallows of the approach to the North Sea.

Like most of the crew of the *Victory*, Tom was too exhausted to feel jubilant. All he wanted was to sleep, but there was work to be done. The day would not belong to England until the last of the Armada's ships was broken and defeated.

A thin rain fell and there were patches of fog on the debris-strewn water. Cold to his bones, Tom went about his business, obeying orders to clean the bloodied sawdust and spent powder from the gun decks. He shuddered at the cries of wounded men coming from the surgeon's quarters. They mingled with the creak of the ship and the jangle of the rigging as the crew turned the *Victory* to run before the wind, following the stricken Spanish ships.

*

The westerly wind held and at first it seemed that it, and the Gravelines sandbanks off the Flanders coast, would do

England's work for her. The sea off Gravelines was treacherous even for sailors who knew it well and the Dutch rebel pilots had long ago removed the markers indicating the safest channels. The Armada seemed to be drifting and in danger of running out of deep water. The wiser course would be to anchor and wait for high tide but there were rumours that in their haste to escape at Calais many of the Spanish crews had cut their anchor chains, leaving the anchors on the seabed.

There was little doubt in anyone's mind that if any Spanish ships grounded in the shallows, the Dutch rebels would be swift to exact vengeance for the years of cruelty they had suffered at the hands of the Duke of Parma's forces. What might be left after they had plundered the ships and killed their crews would soon be smashed to matchwood in the next storm.

Tom's heart lifted. Soon all this might be over and they would be able to return to a safe port. But the old hands around him sniffed the wind like dogs.

'I don't like it,' one muttered. 'There's a squall coming. If the wind changes, we might still lose 'em.'

Just as the sailor predicted, the squall descended – out of nowhere, as it seemed to Tom – and hid the Armada behind an impenetrable curtain of rain. The crew on the *Victory* raced to trim the sails and for a time, all else was forgotten in the struggle to hold the ship steady. But when the squall roared away to the south, to everyone's dismay, the Spanish had made good use of the wind to evade the shallows. Stood off to the north, the remnants of the Armada had resumed their crescent formation ready for battle.

Along with the rest of the English fleet, the *Victory* kept her distance. Her ammunition lockers were bare and in spite of the damage the Spanish had suffered, they were still a formidable foe. Did they have the stomach for a fight? It was impossible to say, but Tom saw the exhaustion on the faces of his fellows and doubted many Englishmen did.

Ten days of brutal battle had left a terrible mark. Rations had almost run out and there was little to assuage the men's hunger and thirst. Dirty, bloodied bandages covered festering wounds; salt-blistered skin was crusted with grime and pocked with powder burns. Most of the men's clothes were filthy and scorched. Tom's own hung from him in tatters. When he lay down to sleep, it was on bedding damp with mildew and blackened with soot. The *Victory* herself had suffered. Her sails were patched where shot had ripped them apart and her rigging was scorched and frayed. The stench of blood and brimstone oozed from her very timbers.

Another day came and went. The Armada sailed on northwards before a strengthening wind and the English followed. Then at dawn the next day, they saw the Armada once more in danger of grounding, this time on the Zeeland Banks, but yet again the wind changed– a Catholic wind, the sailors said sourly – and the Armada escaped.

A rumour ran around the *Victory* that if the Armada passed the Firth of Forth, the Lord Admiral would order his ships to turn back and leave the Spanish to the mercy of the sea. Tom prayed fervently it would come to pass. All he wanted was to be on dry land. After that, he gave no thought to the future.

Chapter 34

Lamotte tested the edge of his sword with his thumb. It was not sharp enough yet to slice a Spanish throat. He struck the blade on the whetstone once more and saw the sparks fly. That was better.

The Trained Bands, swelled to ten thousand men, assembled daily in the fields outside the walls and he had joined the company raised by his own ward. He hoped that when the time came he would acquit himself honourably. The thought it might not be long before he found out chilled his blood. The last report had been that the two fleets were in the North Sea but whether Spain or England had the upper hand, no one knew.

Out in the streets that morning he had watched men bring out whatever weapons they could unearth, some of them so rusty they had probably not seen service since the days of the wars of the houses of Lancaster and York. His back ached from working on the neighbouring stretch of the city wall. So much of it had been allowed to fall down in the years of peace. Few of the fallen stones remained and their place had to be filled with anything that came to hand: old timbers, carts, even hides and carcasses from the shambles. The chains that had barred the streets against Wyatt's rebels fifty years ago had been lugged out from the Tower and stretched across the main roads into the city.

Often his thoughts strayed to the family at Lacey Hall. It was hard to ignore the fact that his life and Beatrice Lacey's were very different. If she cared enough for him to have him,

300

there was a great deal he would be obliged to hide from her. Was it right then to speak of his feelings? Lamotte was unable to decide. In any case, the lives of everyone in England might soon be turned upside down.

Hurrying footsteps approached and his stomach lurched. If it was news, it was unlikely to be good, but when Jack burst in, his face glowed with excitement. He doubled over gasping as his words tumbled out.

'Calm down, lad. I can't understand you. Is there news of the Spanish?'

Jack took a deep breath. 'I ran all the way, Master Lamotte. It's the queen. She's going to Tilbury. She's going to fight them!'

Lamotte could not suppress a chuckle. 'What? All alone? Well, we'd better go and see for ourselves, hadn't we?'

By the time they reached the river, Lamotte's shoulders ached from the effort of pushing through the hordes waiting to see the queen's barge sail by. A boatload of trumpeters heralded her arrival with stirring music. They were followed by the yeomen of the guard in a fleet of gaily painted boats, their armour glinting in the sunshine.

The queen herself was resplendent in a gown of pure white velvet, its bodice covered by a silver cuirass. In her right hand she carried a silver sceptre chased with gold; jewels glittered in her auburn hair.

She bears herself like an empress, Lamotte thought admiringly. Who would not fight for such a woman? All around him, men were calling out to her and throwing their hats in the air. More leant from the high windows of the houses on London Bridge, adding their cheers to the clamour. Impulsively, Lamotte grabbed Jack and, forcing his way down to the riverbank, seized a place on one of the small boats setting off to follow the procession.

At Tilbury, the shout that greeted the queen's arrival rolled down the river like a great wave. Lamotte struggled to look over the jostling heads and shoulders, just catching a glimpse of her as she disembarked at the marshes. A stocky white horse was brought up for her to mount. She bestrode it with her back as straight as an arrow and her head held high, then she set off down the causeway towards her troops.

The thunder of cannon greeting her arrival at the camp seemed to make the earth shake. Lamotte and Jack had come as close as they could but they were still too far away to see more than a small figure passing slowly between the ranks of armoured men. Eventually she stopped. It was clear she was addressing the assembled company. It saddened Lamotte that he was not near enough to hear the speech, but the roars of approval told him it was a magnificent one. He felt his heart lighten. Let the Spanish come. England would fight and prevail.

*

A few days later, the first of the queen's galleons docked at Chatham. They brought news that the English fleet had left off pursuing the tattered remnants of the Armada and were returning to their home ports. More good news came from the Low Countries. The Duke of Parma had withdrawn his forces from the coast.

A riot of celebration swept London. Taverns and theatres strained at the seams. His days crammed with work, Lamotte snatched a few hours' rest when he could but he was becoming weary. I am an ungrateful cur to wish it otherwise, he thought, but I shan't be entirely sorry when London settles back into her old ways.

As he left the theatre late one evening, a figure moved in the shadows. Lamotte reached for his sword, then a voice spoke his name. He rubbed his eyes. It was not possible. Or was it?

'Tom? Is that you?'

'Thank Heaven I've found you,' Lamotte said when he let Tom go. 'Where have you been? No, tell me when we are back at home. You must eat, you look exhausted and there's not an ounce of flesh on you. Come on.'

At Throgmorton Street, Tom fell on the cold fowl Lamotte's cook hastily provided.

'I've found your Meg,' Lamotte said. 'Or rather she found me.'

Tom dropped the wing he was eating. A fierce shaking overwhelmed him and tears sprang to his eyes.

'I'm sorry I shocked you,' Lamotte said gently. 'She fled from her husband and ran away from Salisbury, but she is safe and well.'

'Where is she? Can I go to her?'

'She's at Lacey Hall.'

'What! But why is she there?'

'So I almost found her,' he said bitterly when Lamotte had explained.

'There's no point dwelling on that.'

'Do you think Edward Stuckton is looking for her?'

'I doubt it. According to Meg, he found out about the two of you from Ralph Fiddler. Stuckton put it about that Meg suffered a miscarriage and lost her mind through grief. She became a danger to herself and had to be committed to an asylum.'

Tom's fists clenched. 'How dared he—'

Lamotte raised a hand. 'I understand your anger but let me finish. When I went down to Lacey Hall to tell Meg the news that the charges against you had been dropped, I stayed a few days in Salisbury on my return and made a few enquiries in case more information might be useful one day. I discovered Stuckton has taken up with another woman. It seems he went further in the end and claimed Meg's illness worsened and she took her own life.'

He looked at Tom intently, unsure how he would react to this further slur on Meg's name.

Tom was silent for a moment. 'In truth, it is better for us,' he said at last. 'Does Meg know?'

'I haven't told her. The whole subject of her past life is distressing for her and I preferred not to remind her of it.

Perhaps you should be the one to mention it when you judge the time is right.'

'Thank you.'

'There's more I need to tell you, concerning Ralph Fiddler in particular.'

By the time he had heard Lamotte out, Tom's head reeled.

'So, you know the whole story now,' Lamotte ended. 'The next thing you must do is sleep. Tomorrow we'll make plans for your journey to Lacey Hall. Meg will be anxious to see you. I'll provide you with a horse and some money. You can leave in the morning.'

All at once, Tom felt his courage fail him. 'So much has changed since we last met. It's as if I am a different person. Suppose she doesn't want me any longer?'

Lamotte raised an eyebrow. 'Love does not die so easily. Do you still love her?'

'Of course I do.'

'Then go to her and find out, or you will regret it for the rest of your life.'

*

Lacey Hall glowed in the warm evening light. Late musk roses bloomed around the stone-mullioned windows and the breeze was perfumed with lavender. Tom brought his horse up short at the edge of the lawn and caught his breath. A figure in a kingfisher-blue dress walked along the broad, stone path skirting the front of the house. He would have known her anywhere.

Fear overwhelmed him. It was no use; he should go back to London. He would never be able to offer her a life like this. Then Lamotte's parting words sounded in his head. He swung out of the saddle. A few moments later, Meg was in his arms.

Chapter 35

London
October, 1588

The crisp autumn afternoon drew to an end and the first performance of Tom's new play was almost over. After a great deal of discussion, he had entitled it *The Island*. It had been a success, Lamotte thought, even though it was very different from the kind of drama audiences were used to. Tom had every right to be proud.

He glanced over to where he sat with Meg, her arm in his and their heads so close they almost touched. She whispered something in his ear and he smiled. It warmed Lamotte's heart to see them so happy together.

Beyond them sat Jack and Bel with a wide-eyed Hal squirming in Bel's lap. Even Janey had made the journey from Angel Lane; Lamotte had hired a carriage to bring her. 'I feel like a queen,' she said when he handed her down from it.

On stage, the chief player was coming to the end of his final speech. Lamotte let his attention wander. The speech was a good one, but he knew how it went. Would Tom stay in London and write more plays, he mused. Sometimes he talked of going to the New World but there was a great deal to be considered first. The journey was still a dangerous one and even if it was safely accomplished, life there was beset with uncertainty.

Lamotte suspected Meg would have strong views of her own too. Her friends were happy at Lacey Hall and her maid, Bess, had found a sweetheart at the farm there. Even with Tom at her side, it would be a radical step to leave all of them and her homeland. For his own sake, Lamotte hoped the idea was no more than a passing fancy.

He fell to contemplating his own future. Was it time to make some changes? He was still Walsingham's man but perhaps not for much longer. The end of the Spanish threat seemed to have quenched the fire in the old spymaster's belly. Perhaps he felt his work was accomplished. It was all too apparent his health was declining. England will be the poorer for Walsingham's death, Lamotte thought, but it will set me free.

The prospect sent a frisson of anticipation through him. Freedom – what would he do with it? His life had been circumscribed for so long. What changes should he make? Was it time to let a younger man take charge at the theatre? Tom, if he wanted to? And then?

In his mind's eye, he saw Beatrice's dark eyes and warm smile. Suddenly he knew for sure that when the time came, if she would let him, he wanted to be with her and make her happy.

As the theatre emptied, a young man dressed in black with receding hair and a high forehead approached Tom and Meg. Tom recognised the playwright Lamotte had once pointed out and praised. It seemed like a lifetime ago.

The young man bowed. 'May I congratulate you on your play? It is an excellent piece. Your idea of the castaway is a very interesting one and I was beguiled by your magical island.' He smiled. 'If you have no objection, one day I'd like to explore the theme in a play of my own.'

'I… I'd be honoured.'

'No, the honour is mine. Perhaps we will talk again?'

'Of course.'

The young man bowed to Meg and kissed her hand. 'Forgive the interruption, madam. I shall take my leave.'

'Who was that?' Meg frowned as he walked away.

'His name is Choxper - William Choxper of Stratford.'

'I think he's most impudent to try and steal your ideas,' she sniffed.

He squeezed her arm. 'It's the way of the world, my love: ideas are free. In any case, he may steal what he likes, as long as I have you.'

Printed in Great Britain
by Amazon